A TIME TO BURNISH

A TIME TO BURNISH

RADHIKA NATHAN

First published in India in 2016 by Kiwi Books

ISBN 978–93–85523–91–5

Typesetting and cover design: Kiwi Books

Cover image artwork: Kunal Kundu

Kiwi Books
an imprint of Dogears Print Media Pvt. Ltd.
Plot No 16, Housing Board Colony
Gogol, Margao
Goa 403601 India
www.cinnamonteal.in

RP & SR:

I owe you the plot

Author's Note

I wrote this book in the harsh summer of 2015, months before the tragic rains in Chennai. I hope that the little homeless girl who Josh encountered on the street found someplace safe.

I would like to thank my family and friends for their unfailing support of whatever I do, and early readers for their valuable critique. Specifically, Akshata, Ananya, Devin, Gayatri, Mithun, Prathiba, Ranjani, Rishi, Sairam, Sanjay, Srikant, and Shreya. And my friend Ashok, who had he been alive, would have as always had words of encouragement.

Chapter 1

"Come on, man! It's not like there's a dead body!" Josh Winslow grumbled.

Tom's response was a solid grunt. It came in loud and clear over his headset from the other end of the telephone line, managing to convey impatience and scorn.

Josh stared morosely at the London sky through the bay windows of Heathrow Airport. The clouds loomed low and grey, matching his mood. It was just after 11 a.m. on a cool, wet Tuesday in the first week of June. Josh had been up since four. A lightly buttered toast washed down with a glass of orange juice was all he'd had for breakfast. He was hungry, tired, and irritated.

Terminal 5 was moderately busy and unexciting. Passengers either stood lazily gawking at the watery tarmac, shuffled aimlessly killing time, or scrambled toward their gates. Retail stores, gleaming under bright, artificial light, displaying chocolates and perfumes and jewelry, were mostly deserted. Travelers clearly had the more mundane on their minds that morning and were patronizing the coffee shops and the newsstands instead. The general hum of ambient noises was broken from time to time by announcements of imminent departures and final calls for boarding.

"No dead body, not even a smoking gun," Josh persisted, knowing full well it would exasperate Tom.

"Not literally, no. But white-collar crimes are not victimless, as you imply. That's such a commonplace and inaccurate view."

Knowing Tom, that statement was a precursor to a stinging sermon on the complex implications of art theft. Tom, as it was, enjoyed lecturing Josh, and he likely thought it was justified, even more so than usual under the circumstances.

The clock said it was late morning, but to Josh, it didn't feel like it. Since his arrival in London five days ago, he had spent all his time cooped up indoors, sleep deprived, facing the constant glare of his laptop, straining his already jet-lagged system. He was perpetually yawning, and his body felt as though it was on the last bar of battery life and desperately needed recharging. This trip farther away from home was hardly going to help.

He was dressed in a hoodie over a grey T-shirt, dark blue jeans, and sneakers and carried a coffee cup in one hand and his carry-on in the other. With cables dangling from his ears and a backpack, he must have looked like a young Silicon Valley professional, perhaps on a business trip. He was a techie all right, but as for the purpose of the trip, well, only Tom seemed to think there was a purpose, he thought sarcastically.

He ran his hands through his hair.

"Honestly, Tom, we aren't even sure a crime has been committed, white collar or not. And here I am on a wild goose chase to some hellhole halfway across the world."

Josh had had absolutely no plans to visit India four weeks ago. He didn't think he would ever voluntarily make any such plans. Granted, he had been finishing up his workload at his office in Seattle to embark on his yearly vacation. But that was to the UK to visit his older brother Tom. A vaguely pleasant anticipation had filled him then, unlike the sharp sense of annoyance he was feeling now.

With a sigh of edgy inevitability, he trudged past the sleek array of display screens announcing, in quick changing words, flights to every corner of the globe—Aberdeen, Amsterdam, Austin...

He stepped onto an escalator and refusing to be hurried by the other passengers climbing briskly past him, he stood grudgingly listening to Tom.

"Don't be flippant," Tom reproved. "We are confronted with the probability of a major antiquities theft here. A distinct possibility of it, I should say. Illicit trading of cultural artifacts is the third worst of the trafficking crimes tracked by Interpol. Did you know that?"

"Third! That changes everything," Josh mocked, rolling his eyes.

"After drugs and arms!"

"Seriously? Those are your top three? Drugs, arms, and art? I thought human trafficking would be up there."

A short silence greeted those words, and Josh smiled to himself.

Knowing Tom, he was likely taken aback at the legitimacy of the comment, however frivolously it had been made, and was weighing it against whatever journals and scholarly accounts on international crimes he had read. Josh could bet his life Tom would cross verify all the references as soon as he hung up.

There was a faint creaking sound on the line, breaking the silence. Tom must be turning his wheelchair sharply about.

Tom had suffered a major lower spine injury that had consigned him to a life on wheelchair at the age of twenty-one. Years of treatment barely got him to walk a few feet without tiring himself out. Despite that, his approach to life was filled with goodwill and cheer, spirited yet thoughtful. Tom was, in short, the most over achieving, know-it-all, pain-in-the-ass brother that anyone could possibly have the misfortune to have.

Stepping off the escalator, Josh paused for a moment, checking the direction to his gate.

"Third or not on the list, you ought to consider it with seriousness."

"Give me a break! I am sorely tempted to turn around and walk out of the airport. Or maybe catch the next flight back home."

"So why don't you? Maybe you have some latent interests in history and art after all?"

"God, No! I'd rather admit to a misplaced sense of brotherly love and loyalty." Josh took a large swig of his now-tepid black coffee and dumped the empty cup with needless force into the trash can. "You got some old thing through some uncertain means. So what? There are no victims. Just buy the damn thing and enjoy your spoils. I bet, you'd take better care of it than those guys anyway."

"Firstly, it isn't an 'old thing.' It is an antique idol."

"Tom, don't push me!"

"Secondly," Tom continued, relentless, "the means of acquisition does matter, and people do get hurt. In fact, many artifacts were stolen and moved during times of war. Blood art, like blood diamonds. Iraq, Cambodian antiquities—"

"Man, you take great pleasure, don't you, in riling me up with your ... your—"

"Scholarliness?"

"Bullshit." He shook his head, reminding himself it was a useless exercise. Tom wasn't going to budge. Josh was twenty-nine, but Tom, just five years his senior, still treated him as though he was in high school.

"It may be my blood and my dead body by the end of the week you know," he grumbled.

"Oh, come now."

There was a heavy, unexpected silence that followed, and as though a sliver of doubt had just entered his mind, Tom stammered in a voice that was halting and doubtful.

"You... um ... you don't think it's dangerous, do you, Josh? It's not like there are Kalashnikov-toting crooks in every corner of India."

"Are you reassuring me or yourself?" asked Josh dryly and then continued in the same vein. "I had malaria in my mind though."

He reached the gate and could not help but groan at the sight of the seating area. Every seat was occupied, and the spill overs stood leaning on the windows, squatted on their luggage, or were, unbelievably, already queuing up. Carry-on baggage choked up the pathways, and young children ran about.

Josh, after one look, determinedly walked past, toward a quieter area two gates away. Dumping his backpack nearby, he sprawled on a corner seat. He pushed his carry-on in front of the seat and propped his feet on it.

"Are you checked in yet?" asked Tom.

"Yeah, yeah! I'm checked in and waiting to board unfortunately," he said and, unable to resist, mimicked Tom's earlier words in a chirpy tour guide tone, "to Chennai, erstwhile Madras renamed to Chennai in the nineties to unshackle it from the legacy of its colonial past."

"So, you were paying attention! What's more, it all seems to have registered, too, in some corner of your jet-lagged brain." The perpetual cheer that characteristically laced Tom's voice was back, which Josh supposed was a good sign.

"Don't get your hopes up. I have no idea what I'm saying."

Every year for the last six years, around Memorial Day, Josh packed his bags and left home to spend a couple of weeks with Tom. They usually met twice a year, briefly during Thanksgiving and for a longer spell during the summer.

Right from when they were young, Tom somehow always managed to bend people to his will. With charm oozing out of every pore of his body, he was absolutely charismatic. He could sell tanning lotion to Indians. Usually, he used his skill for something innocuous. The previous year, he had made Josh buy a painting that was a mess of colors, guaranteeing the artist would shoot from obscurity to stardom in a year. The year before, he had made Josh give up red meat and donate a hefty sum to Doctors Without Borders. Josh had been prepared to give up white meat this year. Heck, he smiled grimly to himself, he would have happily become vegan compared to what Tom had in store for him instead.

Tom asked, his voice laden with worry and concern, "Josh, you won't ... uh ...do anything too dangerous, right?"

"Weren't you the one who insisted on this trip? What was that you said, 'Whatever it takes, Josh'?"

"Yeah, well ... I may have ... been a tad more forceful than necessary." Tom cleared his throat.

"What happened to the 'my reputation, and by extension my life, is at stake'?"

Josh got up and stretched.

Tom had a doctorate in history and was the assistant curator at the most prestigious museum in London, much respected by his peers. He routinely wrote scholarly articles with hard words and harder themes, ran some exhibition or the other, and acquired artifacts for the museum's collections. He was the kind of man who would relish a complicated, obscure paper on the Ottoman Empire for breakfast.

Josh, on the other hand, could as well use it as a tranquilizer. For the life of him, he could not understand Tom's fascination with history. While Josh's classmates at MIT were coding software that heralded the social media world, he had dabbled in the networking and security aspect of it, managing to carve a successful and highly lucrative career out of it. Josh viewed himself as a modern man of this wonderfully net worked, digitally enhanced, high fidelity times. On good days, he thought of Tom's vocation with tolerant amusement or baffled indulgence.

This was not a particularly good day.

Tom, after a pregnant pause, added in a very quiet voice, "Josh, you know it'd be hard for me to travel to India by myself, and I wouldn't ask if it wasn't the last resort. In my selfishness, I am putting you in harm's way, aren't I?"

"Stop laying a guilt trip on, would you?"

As soon as the words were out, Josh mentally kicked himself for his thoughtless, crass, and thoroughly unfair response. Tom was fiercely proud, and this was an uncharacteristic display of vulnerability. Josh knew how much it was costing Tom to acknowledge his limitation and seek his help.

He quickly added, with deliberate lightness, "Yep, definitely harm's way. I might get bitten by a mosquito and die."

The travel advisory website he had glanced through had listed a litany of shots that he needed to take and had urged him to visit his GP at least four weeks before travel. It had warned him of dire consequences in the form of hepatitis, dysentery, and even brain fever if he chose to ignore the recommendation.

"Or get a bad case of Gandhi's revenge just by drinking the water and die of that," Josh continued. "And get this, my favorite, food poisoning by eating those chilled monkey brains for dessert."

He got his reward in Tom's light chuckle, and, of course, Tom had gotten the movie reference immediately.

"*Temple of Doom*? Really?" he asked with mock indignation and then added for good measure, "Identifying with Indiana Jones, are we?"

Josh smiled.

"You know I meant getting arrested by the Indian authorities or hurt by the underworld, don't you?" Tom asked, sounding troubled, despite the casual words.

"It's still not too late. I could come back, and we could do this my way," Josh responded, half-hoping Tom might miraculously agree.

No such luck, of course. Tom's tone immediately became brisk. "No, no, Josh, going there is our best option."

Josh cursed forcefully. Out of the corner of his eye, he could see the gate was open and they were beginning to board. Dark clouds beyond provided an ominous backdrop.

"You owe me big for this. Hey, did you hear anything else from the PI?"

"No, nothing. Just be careful, will you? I called to tell you I've mailed you the hotel booking details. There will be pickup at the airport, and I will ask Vidya to meet you in the morning."

"Vidya who?" Josh queried.

Tom exhaled audibly. "You weren't listening completely after all."

"I was," said Josh, indignant. "Chennai, a thriving metropolis by the sea, in the south of India, population—"

"Josh!"

Hearing the note of annoyance in Tom's voice, he stopped. "Umm... yeah, Vidya, your girl Friday in India."

"Vidya, my friend," said Tom in a pained voice. "My best friend really. I have spoken to you many, many times about her."

"Best friend? How old are you, thirteen?" Josh vaguely recalled Tom mentioning this girl. "Is she hot?"

Tom's exasperated sigh was predictable.

"I will ask her to come meet you tomorrow morning at the hotel at 9. That should give you ample time to rest and get ready. She could help you there on the ground."

"Listen, I am not too thrilled about you inviting everyone to this party. It's a bad idea. I'd like to keep things under the radar as much as possible."

"Under the radar! Ha! Even I know our conversation is being tapped by the powers that be."

"Yeah, yeah! Listen, the NSA is the least of my concerns. I am worried about a lawsuit. Who knows, all this could end up in court one day."

"So you agree there is cause for concern about the idol." Tom pounced at the first opportunity.

"No, Tom, I meant all this could end up in court because I am going to kill you when I come back," he declared.

Tom groaned in exasperation. "I see no reason to be secretive."

"I am sure you don't. Have you ever? This female, what does she know?"

"It just so happens, *this female* doesn't know much. She was busy with her cousin's wedding when I first came across the idol, and then she had the flu, and then with all the complications... We never really got around to talking about it. She does know that I am in the middle of an acquisition for the museum, but nothing about the object."

"Keep it that way, Tom. I don't really need to meet her. I don't need her help."

"Yes, you do."

"No, I don't."

"Yes, you do. And that is that."

"I can only hope she'd have better things to do and decline to meet me."

"For me, she would postpone her other engagements."

Josh let out a frustrated sigh as he gathered his belongings.

"You are such a bully, you know that? At least make up an excuse for my visit. No need to be generous with the details. I will call you after reaching Chennai."

Tom, as expected, did not immediately say yes to Josh's suggestion. He demurred, claiming it was in their best interest to let her know, bemoaned Josh's suspicious nature, but finally agreed.

"As much as I'd like to not do this, they are about to finish boarding now, so let me go."

"Okay, Josh, take care. You do remember we have only a couple of days, don't you?"

"You've said that about a thousand times already," Josh breathed deeply. "You have the money from the donor, and it comes with some complicated clauses. You also have a press release going out on Friday with glossy pictures and grand words about the idol. Not to mention, you have to pay the quote unquote owner of the idol soon."

That gave Josh roughly two to three days to fix the mess, with one day lost in travel. He had worked against deadlines before, but this was a whole new ball game.

They finished the conversation, and Tom ended the call with a worried sounding goodbye.

Josh yanked out his headphones abruptly and tapped off the player that restarted after the call. He slid the phone back into his pocket and stretched again. His growling stomach made him wish he had stopped to get a bagel.

Josh stared blankly at the high arches of the steel and glass roof, and then at the gate where the line had dwindled to the last couple of passengers. He tried to shrug off his reluctance and frustration and summon a modicum of energy, if not enthusiasm. He stood wearily massaging his temple until the very last moment and then slowly walked over to board.

Chapter 2

A few days earlier, when Josh had arrived in London from Seattle, Tom had come to pick him up at the airport. Josh had not been surprised. Tom enjoyed driving his new wheelchair-accessible car, a Christmas present from Josh, whenever he could. Besides, they liked to start their brotherly bickering early on.

Tom had looked serious and sophisticated, dressed in blue jeans and a blazer with a striped cotton scarf loosely knotted around his neck. He appeared to have had been to work that morning before heading out to the airport. He had also seemed preoccupied, asking mundane questions and answering Josh's queries in monosyllables.

It had been a pleasant afternoon with white cotton clouds, smudged with grey, floating gently over swatches of brilliant blue. The traffic toward Kensington had been smooth, and the car smelled clean and fresh after the long flight and lost hours. Josh had felt good about getting together with Tom.

He and Tom had gotten into the rhythm of meeting twice a year, specifically after their parents' death. It was more so because of Tom's efforts, Josh had acknowledged that to himself many times.

During the summer, they usually spent one week somewhere in the countryside and one week in London in what Tom called the "Culturization of Josh." Essentially, it meant opera, museum circuits, fine dining, and visits to art galleries. Josh rather enjoyed Tom's authoritative commentary, though he never let on. He sometimes played the philistine to Tom's cultured elitist so well it caused Tom considerable annoyance.

The first indication that something was off was when Tom had no jibes on Josh fiddling with the radio to play the music he liked. Josh had initially thought it might have something to do with Tom's ex, whom

Josh did not particularly like. There was only one word—regrettable—to describe their heated interaction the previous winter around the time of Tom's breakup. Josh had said some unfortunate things about Tom's naiveté, and Tom had said some equally unfortunate things about Josh's insensitivity. Josh had made up his mind not to revive that topic at any cost.

Instead, he had pretty much stuck to enthusing about a few exciting developments in the world of technology. Tom, his brows furrowed, had only been half listening. At one point, he had cryptically announced that he was in a terrible predicament, though he had not shed any further light on his dilemma during the entire afternoon.

Later that evening, they had gone to the New Age sushi place that Tom liked, and Josh had just been curious, not necessarily concerned, about Tom's odd inattentive air. They had been sitting at a corner table to accommodate the wheelchair, away from the gleaming glass bar counter upon which the *itamae* placed artfully designed dishes. Tom had stared unseeingly at the black and white tile work on the wall for quite some time. He had extended a simple smile to the waiter with no discussion on the merits of Koshu wine over sake. Shockingly, he had also accepted, without a word, the sea bass and tuna recommendation for their order.

Josh let him be for a few minutes, but finally, somewhat irritated by Tom's obvious distress yet lack of communication, he snapped, "What's going on, Tom?"

Tom drummed his hands on the table and breathed deeply as though he was bracing himself for something painful. His next question had been unexpected.

"What is my area of expertise, Josh?"

Recognizing the question for what it was—an opener—Josh bit back a groan. Tom reminded him of an old modem in a slow network; the connection light had to get steady before the data light started blinking in a measured pace.

He replied, "You know I can answer that question in my sleep! Growing up, it was all that residue hippie stuff, all that ghastly sitar music, thanks to Mom and Dad. Then you had to go pick India as your area of interest."

There was no answering smile on Tom's face, just an abrupt headshake of a refusal to rise to the bait.

"What specifically in India?"

"South India."

"Your brilliant grasp of the specifics never ceases to amaze me," Tom said with the same maddened note that crept into his voice when dealing with Josh's indifference toward his profession.

He poured out the warm saké from the flask and took a delicate sip from the cup.

"For the zillionth time, my area of specialization is the Chola Empire, covering roughly the ninth to the thirteenth century."

"I know," acknowledged Josh, sensing this was not the time to say "whatever." He made an effort instead. "The rise and fall of the Cholas, with special focus on that dude who was a great warrior and visionary—Maharajah Chola."

"You mean Rajaraja Chola."

"Yes, of course, what was that paper you wrote? 'The social order under Rajaraja and the later Cholas'," Josh said with pretentious nonchalance. Tom produced many such papers and was either a member or a fellow or some such on various societies.

Tom laughed for the first time that evening. "There may be some hope for you after all."

Josh grinned.

Tom rubbed his eyes slightly and then, leaning forward, started talking about the Cholas with the passion and intensity that usually marked him.

"At its peak, the Chola Empire covered the bulk of South India, parts of Sri Lanka, touched Maldives, and even Malacca. The medieval Chola kings were great patrons of art and literature, they made major strides in governance and foreign relations, and they were builders of magnificent architecture... Let's just say, the height of the Chola Empire, especially the time of Rajaraja, can be thought of as a golden age. Think Italy during the Renaissance."

"Must I?" Josh muttered, fidgeting a little. Tom ignored it.

"You know, as part of my job, I work on acquisitions of relics of rare value?"

"Yes," Josh nodded. What was it that Tom had acquired the previous summer? Wasn't it a manuscript of some sort? He wished he could surreptitiously pull his iPad out and do a quick search on his email.

He needn't have troubled himself. Tom continued, almost ignoring his answer, his brows furrowed.

"My limited budget hardly allows for anything major. A piece of an intricately carved wooden door, an old silk sari, a palm leaf book, those are the kind of things I usually go for. A Chola bronze icon is in a whole different league. You could even say it's the top artifact of the period. These bronzes are typically delicate, sensual icons of the gods and the saints or occasionally royals. They still make bronze icons in south India, but the Chola bronzes are antiques—they could be millions of dollars' worth." Tom paused for a moment, his face troubled, full of worry.

Josh raised his brows and whistled lightly. "Millions, huh?"

"Yes, millions. Josh, in my enthusiasm, I have made a grave mistake. You have got to help me. I have no one else to turn to." Tom's voice took on a strained, and nervous quality.

Josh raised a hand.

"Hang on! What are you talking about?"

Tom sat back, grimaced, and then enunciated slowly. "I need you to help me track a Chola bronze."

"What do you mean track?"

"Find all the information there is about a particular Chola bronze. I believe I have in my possession an antique bronze that has come into the UK likely through illicit art trafficking. My gut says there has been a major art theft, and if I don't act now, I am going to be an accessory."

***

The air hostess greeted Josh cheerfully as he walked into the narrow confines, smelling the nauseous combination of exhaust fumes and disinfectants, ruing the long flight. He nodded and smiled at her in an abstract fashion and, after depositing his baggage in the overhead compartment, settled down in his comfortable business class seat.

He looked away from the window as they prepared for takeoff. The captain's voice sounded reassuringly competent, and the hostess seemed anxious to please. She hovered about, helping with his bag, offering a glass of wine, and presenting an artfully placed selection of newspapers for his reading pleasure. Josh took the solicitous service in his stride with the unabashed confidence of a young, handsome, rich, self-made man, comfortable in claiming it as rightful.

It started to drizzle, a fine spray, as the plane taxied noisily. He stretched his legs and yawned hugely.

Soon the plane leveled, and Josh took out his iPad and skimmed through the unread mails.

Tom had attached some pictures of the hotel, as though that'd entice him. No major security threats had broken out in the software world between the time he had stepped into the shower and boarded the plane. The same couldn't be said about the real world though.

Dropping his tablet into the sleeve in front of the seat, he connected it and his phone to power. He briefly toyed with the idea of pulling his Kindle out to read one more book on Chola history, but then deciding he knew enough, he simply reclined.

He wished Tom had believed in his ability to solve the problem while staying in London instead of insisting on the trip.

"I don't really need to go there, Tom," he had tried to explain. "See this funny looking device? It's called a smart phone. It's a modern day magic carpet that you can surf the world with."

But Tom would have none of that. "You need to go there, that's the only way we can resolve this," he had insisted.

Tom was not necessarily a Luddite, he enjoyed and used technology as much as the average Joe, but he did not grasp its enormous power to transcend human limitations. He sighed, poor Tom was old fashioned.

He shrugged off his disgruntlement. He had a game plan of sorts. Everything got recorded somewhere or the other, and the Web knew and the Web remembered. And Josh was the expert who could find those pesky little bits of data wherever they were.

He sincerely hoped that Tom's friend, whose name he just couldn't recall, would not be a hindrance. He sure didn't need her help.

Chapter 3

Vidya Thyagarajan was desperate for filter coffee and set about to make herself a cup. It was a sunny day, as it almost always was in Chennai, with the mercury showing no immediate signs of sliding down. The late afternoon remained hot with a mere hope of the onset of the sea breeze to make the evening tolerable. She'd normally be at the multi-national bank she worked for at this time of the day, talking her business customers into investing in one or the other of their products. The start of a headache manifesting as a dull pressure above her brows, threatening to grow in intensity, had brought her home early.

She had intended to get home before the commuter traffic picked up but, as a result, had had to suffer the scorching outdoors for the better part of half an hour on her Scooty Zest. She could even now feel her hair plastered on her damp neck and sweat rolling down her front.

She heard her phone ring. The special ringtone of a Skype call, insistent over the inherent melody, beckoned her. Only Tom called her through Skype. She glanced at the wall clock and saw that it was half past three. Too early for Tom to expect her home though, she thought frowning.

She dabbed her handkerchief on her forehead, grabbed a bottle of cold water from the fridge, and rushed to the living room to fish out her phone from her handbag and answered the ring that had started again with a happy greeting. She missed talking to him.

"Tom! Long time, no hear," she gushed. He had not called, not even texted her, for the last four days.

"Hey, Vidya, I am so sorry to bother you at this time. Can you talk for a few minutes?"

"Of course, I can!"

It was always a pleasure to talk to Tom. He was a charmer. He was cultured, erudite, a delight to talk to.

"Are you all set for your vacation?" she asked, leaning on the window sill. She took quick gulps of the ice-cold water from the bottle.

"Well, there's been a change of plan," he said after a moment's pause. Vidya picked up something in his tone she couldn't quite place.

"Oh? I thought you called to tell me that you and Josh are on your way to Cambria."

She knew of Tom's brother. Tom often talked very proudly of Josh's accomplishments—he'd built his first computer when he was twelve, he'd been paid to write software when he was fourteen, he'd gone to MIT on a scholarship, he routinely spoke at prestigious conferences— the brag list was endless. On occasion, he would even share some of the more colorful exploits that were bordering on, if not downright, illegal. "We never paid for cable or AOL. Josh hooked us up somehow and pocketed the subscription money from our parents," she remembered Tom regaling her.

Tom had told her in one of their earlier conversations that Josh would be visiting. They were going to Wales; the Cambrian trails were calling, Tom had said. He had even promised to paint her a watercolor of the mountains.

"It didn't quite work out the way I thought it would. The trip isn't happening."

Vidya realized what it was that had bothered her earlier; Tom's voice was usually full of mirth and amusement, but just then, his voice sounded tired and disappointed.

"Oh! Umm ... I am sorry to hear that," she said, feeling bad for Tom. "I know you were looking forward to the time off."

"I am sure I will get to go there some other time."

Vidya made a concurring, sympathetic noise. She knew Tom didn't usually like to dwell on such disappointments and so remained silent, allowing him room to change the subject.

"Vidya, listen, I called to ask you a favor."

"Anything, Tom." She switched on the ceiling fan and pulled at her *kurti* that was feeling sticky.

"Josh, believe it or not, is coming to India."

"India!"

"Yeah, he has, um, he is on his way to Singapore, on a business trip. He is stopping over at Chennai for a few days en route, just sightseeing—

that sort of thing. Umm ... just ... a couple of days really."

"Wow! When is he coming? Where is he staying?" She fired the questions in enthusiastic staccato.

"Slow down, slow down." Tom laughed, sounding his usual self for the first time that afternoon. "He is uh ... coming tonight," he said.

"Tonight?"

"Yes, tonight, no I should say tomorrow morning. Will you be able to meet him tomorrow and.... perhaps show him around?" he asked.

He sounded so terribly uncomfortable, stuttering uncharacteristically, asking her for the small favor that she hastened to reassure him. "Of course, Tom, I'd love to. I wish you'd come too."

"I wish I could too, kiddo," he said wistfully. Tom, almost nine years her senior, addressed her as "kid" or "kiddo" usually in jest, and occasionally in friendly endearment. Today, it sounded affectionate, almost poignant.

"I am sure you will, some other time," she said, hopeful and earnest. Tom didn't travel much, she had gathered, and on the rare occasion he did, the place was chosen after meticulous consideration to its wheelchair friendliness. Not happy about having brought an implicit focus to Tom's handicap, she said in a teasing voice, "That your big favor?"

"Yes, well, you don't know Josh." He sighed dramatically, and they both laughed.

She felt the mood lighten, and they continued the conversation discussing the trip, her job, and the weather.

"Hey, Tom, I almost forgot. The answer is 'The Muses,' right?" she asked.

It was a game between them, almost habitual, Tom questioning her, posing riddles and her finding answers to the clues. The questions and the clues were starting points to conversations that often meandered into untrodden territories and sometimes new discoveries, both general and personal. Tom had briefly talked of another exciting addition to the museum collection and had challenged her to find out what it was.

She now answered with a triumphant note, "It was a tough one. You said 'Nemo Nine,' and I'll admit I got sidetracked at first, but then soon I realized it is 'Mnemo' with an M! It's the Nine Muses, the children of Mnemosyne and Zeus, right?"

"Very good!" The appreciation came quickly, almost reflexively, but beyond that, instead of the words of wisdom she had expected, Tom fell oddly silent.

"Umm … Terpsichore, that's your next clue," he said after a pause, without elaboration, sounding unusually reluctant.

Perhaps he was just distracted.

Vidya vaguely remembered the name. Was it one of the muses? She'd have to look it up later.

She asked him about the weather in London and the latest in politics, but he didn't engage as easily as he normally did. A certain elusive heaviness came back into the conversation. He rang off soon after, with a promise to talk the next day, leaving her feeling bereft.

***

"Vidya, can you get me some coffee?" asked her father as he emerged from his bedroom, wiping his freshly washed face with a white hand towel. A tall man of medium build, he was attired in his usual white *vetti* and white collarless T-shirt. With brown eyes that usually held a thoughtful, slightly distracted expression, strong jaw and a head full of greying hair, R.S. Thyagarajan had the look of a scholar about him.

Lately retired and recovering from heart surgery, he usually dozed off after lunch and surfaced around four o'clock in the afternoon. Soon he would be out for his evening walk, leaving her with the chore of making dinner for them. Finding her home that afternoon, he was quickly passing on the responsibility of making coffee to her as well. Despite his otherwise very modern and forward thinking, he ventured into the kitchen only under the direst of needs and thought of it as her realm. Surely some residual effects of her late mother's excellent cooking and housekeeping skills, she thought with a sardonic smile.

Their modest living room was lit by sunbeams slanting from the two west-facing windows. The bamboo and cane furniture upholstered in vibrant jamakallam fabric was arranged for conversation. Her prized Marudu print of a prancing horse in red and golden hues hung on the main wall, facing a Picasso print of a factory in cubist lines, together presenting an eclectic style. Beyond the living room was the small dining area, a bookshelf fully covering one wall, and an opening on another out to a small patio. Usually, later in the day, she'd sit there and exchange messages with Tom.

"Now that you have finished consorting with the imperialist, can you get me something to eat too?" he added as he sat down, draping the hand towel on one shoulder, to get his afternoon dose of TV news. They typically conversed in Tamil, though he was wont to pepper his sentences occasionally with English phrases. He had clearly listened to some part of the conversation, enough to discern that she had been talking to Tom.

"Tom just lives in the UK, RST." She used his initials that the rest of the world referred to him by. "He and his brother are Americans, so they are not really imperialists. Besides, *appa*, is consort the word you want to use in the context of your daughter?"

"Consort is also used in another context, as in 'consorted with criminals,' when you use it to refer to association with seedy characters." His brown eyes sparkled with amusement. He wiped the residual water off the back of his neck and motioned to her to speed up the fan.

RST was a true blood socialist who still harbored hopes for a world envisioned by Marx and Engels. A relentless activist, albeit less fiery now than in his early years, he was extremely skeptical about the new wave of American influence in Indian youth. The Americans in particular and the capitalist West in general were often the butt of his jokes.

Brandishing the remote, he said, "All right then, let me rephrase my question more appropriately. Can I get coffee now that you have finished consorting with the capitalist?"

"One of the capitalists is coming here tomorrow," she responded and, seeing his surprise, added with a smile, "Here as in Chennai, not our home. I know we don't invite capitalists home."

All the same, she would have loved for Tom to visit India and, despite the joke, stay with them.

RST gave her a quick smile and asked with passing interest, "What is he here for?"

"Sightseeing. He is a tourist, appa. Why else is he going to come here?"

"Who knows? Maybe to open one of those fast food chains? There are a billion people here to make obese."

"No, he is into computers," she responded mildly, despite her usual irritation with what she thought of as her father's negativity to all things western.

"Mystery solved. He is here to set up an outsourcing center then."

"That'd be terribly disappointing."

"Yes, the digital bourgeois generally is." He flicked the remote, switching between the news channels.

"You know, your sons are into software as well," she parried.

"Ergo, the conclusion," he returned and turned his attention to the latest news, signaling the end of the conversation.

Vidya returned to the kitchen with an exasperated smile on her face. Both her brothers held cushy jobs abroad in Fortune 500 companies. RST never missed an opportunity to jibe at his sons' lifestyle, albeit very subtly, on generic terms.

She bustled about their small kitchen, fetching the cups and plates as the water boiled. After spooning a generous amount of ground coffee into the top tier of the old-fashioned filter, she poured the hot water into it. They both liked their coffee strong. While she waited for the coffee to percolate down, she reflected on her conversation with Tom.

Along with the minor excitement, there was also something baffling about the phone call. Tom was always involved in the conversation, never as reserved, restrained almost, as he had sounded just then. She felt he had grown distant of late. The visit felt too rushed, too unexpected, and a little weird. One didn't plan an international trip so easily, did one? Didn't travelers need visas?

She shook her head to clear her thoughts. She supposed Josh's business trip must have come up all of a sudden.

The sun beat down on her face through the window as she stood watching the milk simmer. She drew the back of her hand, wiping the beads of sweat from her forehead and knotted her hair into a high bun.

After setting the cups, she placed some *murukku* on the plates. She poured the hot milk over the brewed decoction, and added a spoon of sugar, making filter coffee just the way they liked. Wanting to escape the heat of the kitchen, she hurried over to the living room and handed the cup to her father, who was busy reading some fliers. He would read labels off of matchboxes.

Josh, her best friend's brother, was coming to visit. She smiled to herself at the thought. Whatever was bothering him temporarily, she knew Tom would bounce back and she would get to talk to him about Josh and the trip later. Catching her humming a tune, RST cast a sidelong glance at her.

"You seem quite enthusiastic about this meeting," he mumbled now with raised brows. He looked up with a smile that for all it calmness and gentle humor she didn't particularly like.

"Not more than usual," she responded evasively, annoyed with him for having put the thought in her head that she was perhaps unduly eager.

She knew sometimes she was quick to read censure in his comments when perhaps there wasn't any and that it was more to do with her own vague and confused sense of inadequacy than anything he expressed.

She thought of her mother and how she'd always maintained her composure. Without any further comment, she walked over to the shady patio with the remnants of a frown still on her face.

A lone *magilam* tree that miraculously managed to keep its spot in the corner of their patio, stood motionless. Their small two-bedroom house, in one of the oldest neighborhoods in Chennai filled the corner lot of a by-lane allowing for the tree to branch into the street and survive. There was just enough space for a few herb plants apart from the tree. They had a street view from most of the rooms, and they enjoyed the good light that came with it.

The house was in the middle of the city, something they couldn't imagine buying in this day and age. If not for her mother's management of finances, they couldn't have bought it years ago either. RST, from what she knew, squandered all his earnings on mostly undeserving elements. Her mother had been a banker as well, a senior manager in a nationalized bank, when she had died of cancer.

Vidya stood outside, enjoying her coffee, listening to music from her phone. Sweat trickled down her spine. Still, the hot coffee was soothing, and she felt the headache ebb away.

She would make sure Josh had a good time in India. She owed it to Tom. Perhaps she could show him around Chennai herself. He could then maybe go for a trip to the cape, visit some beaches in Kerala, and definitely a few temples. Vidya was warming up to the idea of helping Josh with his travel plans, despite her minor misgivings.

"*Mana, mana, mana mental manadhil,*" crooned A.R Rahman cheerily on the headset, uplifting her mood.

A gentle, long awaited breeze brought along with it the elusive perfume of *magilam* flowers. RST left for his walk, and she got up to get back to her chores, wondering where Josh was at that precise moment.

Chapter 4

Josh stared at the cirrus clouds below the window. The airplane was cruising at around 35,000 feet. He wasn't in the mood to listen to music and had his noise-cancelling headphones on.

Josh had done enough time zone hopping to know not to drink too much or to take a sleeping tablet unless he wanted to suffer severe jet lag. But he was too wired to even hope to unwind. He wished he could power up his laptop and get to work instead of sitting cooped up with no connectivity. It was as though the world was moving on, and he was adrift, away from civilization. Which century were they in with no Wi-Fi inflight?

He sighed and leaned back. He reflected on the last three days, willing his tired brain to follow every thread to make sure he hadn't missed anything.

At the sushi dinner, once the initial words were out, Tom had elaborated on the story.

"Three months ago, I came across a Chola bronze idol for sale." Tom paused for a second, inhaled deeply, and repeated the words signifying how momentous that was. "A Chola bronze, Josh!"

Josh strove to look impressed. He didn't want Tom to digress into a lecture about his lack of finer sensibilities.

"It is a stunning, one-of-a-kind idol, not just any icon. An idol, you ignoramus, is a bronze of a god or a goddess."

Josh took a sip of his sake, and nodded, keeping his impatience in check, letting Tom tell the story.

Tom leaned forward and continued, "It is extremely rare to find a Chola bronze idol in the market. The few outside India are already in the hands of private collectors or major museums, and the ones in India stay there. I was thrilled, ecstatic really. I lobbied for money, and got lucky with some hefty grants—an expat Indian industrialist donated a large sum. With a heady rush, I confirmed the sale. It cost me eight million dollars."

"You?"

Tom winced. "I mean, it cost the museum. Clearly, this has become too personal to me. The museum," he continued, the emphasis underscoring the ownership, "has signed an agreement to buy the idol. It is there now, in storage of course, not yet displayed. We are working on a broader exhibition on South Indian iconography, anchored by the idol, in the next couple of months."

Tom paused as the waiter arrived with their sushi. His expression unusually remote, he answered the waiter's solicitous questions in monosyllables and brief smiles. He resumed only after the man placed their order and left.

"Josh, how can I make you understand that the minute I set sight on that idol, I fell in love with it; I fell in love with him—Nataraja! Oh those eyes, so alive!"

"What? Who?"

"The idol is that of Nataraja. It's a form of Shiva, the Hindu god. Nataraja, literally meaning king of dance, is another name for Him." He paused, grimaced at Josh's blank expression, and then continued. "Never mind all that now. Just take it from me that the idol is a magnificent piece of art. This particular one, I believe, could be from the tenth century, made during or even before the ascension of Rajaraja."

There was a brief silence. Josh looked straight into Tom's face. He may not know about the Hindu gods, but he had enough brains to guess the direction the narrative was heading toward. He queried, his voice soft. "Tom, whom did you buy it from?"

Tom's smile was half appreciative, half sardonic. He dipped his nigiri in soy sauce, popped it into his mouth, chewed, and swallowed it with no apparent enjoyment. It must be a first for Tom, thought Josh, and waited for him to continue.

"From a German named Reinhold Eichendorf," he said at length. Then his voice and expression turned earnest, almost pleading to make sure Josh understood what he was about to say. "There is a solid proof of provenance. One of Eichendorf's ancestors was part of a mission; he was an assistant to a priest who travelled all over India in the eighteenth century. He wrote a journal of his wanderings in southern India."

"And the journal confirms possession of this idol?"

"Yes, he mentions a Nataraja idol that he brought home in 1768. He doesn't quite state the place he got it from though."

"Got it how?"

"Through some underhanded means I suspect, but naturally he doesn't admit to that in his journal. It can be inferred from what he says that he acquired it from an abandoned temple site in modern day Tamil Nadu, somewhere between Madurai and Thanjavur. Apparently, it was easy in those days, or so he claims. Josh, I was so damn excited even to hear about it! And when I saw the idol ... " Tom sat back, and inhaled deeply, seemingly to get a grip on himself.

Josh shook his head slowly, in dismay, putting two and two together.

"You have now found out that the journal is a fake, I take it?" He felt a rush of sympathy but was also irritated that Tom had not been thorough and had let his trusting nature get the better of him.

Tom's next words surprised him.

"No! Give me some credit! The original journal is in a *museum* in Amsterdam. It was published in the mid-nineteenth century. Our museum has a copy of the printed work, and it matches the original word for word. I read it myself—the descriptions, the words are all authentic."

"Huh!"

"Also Eichendorf's great-grandfather presented a paper on Indian artifacts in the late nineteenth century, and he, too, talks of a Nataraja idol in his possession."

"Okay?"

Tom continued, his voice measured, the excitement still palpable. "It was a major coup. A Nataraja of that size ... Josh! The bronzes are usually, say three feet. This one is seven feet high. I am including the base; still, it's quite tall and weighs just under a ton. There are clear pointers for its antiquity, mostly visual of course. But I also got a compositional analysis done from a micro drilling—copper percentage in the alloy is close to 95, lead and tin contents are low, all consistent with the earlier bronzes. A neutron analysis is a much better non-invasive way, but the waiting time—"

"Earth to Tom." Josh raised a hand, interrupting the flow.

Tom blinked. "Yes?"

"So you have some journals, you did an analysis, all good. What's the problem? What went wrong?"

Tom rubbed his eyes and looked gloomily at Josh.

"I felt driven until I closed the deal. The specter of private collectors swooping down and driving up the price gave me quite a lot of sleepless nights. Once the initial euphoria settled ... after we signed off ... I don't know, I had a nasty feeling, as though I was making a mistake."

Josh raised his brows disbelievingly. "Seriously? You have been acting up the whole day because you just happen to have a nasty feeling?"

Tom raised his hands in a hear-me-out gesture. Then he leaned forward, his fingers steepled under his chin.

"Herr Eichendorf had indicated that he had lost his job and was going to sell his ancestral home. He claimed to have found the idol while clearing out the attic."

Tom's face across the table held a muddled expression. Josh nodded, encouraging him to go on.

"I gathered later he had never held a steady job and had been pretty much raiding his inheritance for the last twenty years. Josh, how could he have not sold the idol for this long? The question has been haunting me for the last three weeks. How could he have not known about it?"

"Maybe it was in a really dark corner, maybe Eichendorf didn't understand the significance of it until now. You've got to admit not everyone can spot a dancing Hindu god right away for what it's worth."

Tom gripped the glass and looked away at the other diners, his body language suggesting frustration at what he probably thought of as Josh's lack of seriousness. "I seriously doubt it. Once I started down that path, I couldn't help but notice other worrisome inconsistencies. The journal doesn't really describe any unique markers of the idol, nothing about the height, or say about the difficulties of transporting such a heavy piece."

"You said the ancestor could have gotten it through some shady deal. Maybe he didn't want to leave an easy trace to its origins."

"Yes, possible, but still, what if?"

Savoring the pungent taste of the pickled ginger, Josh frowned. "What if ... what?"

Tom took a sip of the saké instead of answering, as though he did not want to articulate his worst fears.

"Are you saying what if the Nataraja idol you have is not the same as what Eichendorf is supposed to have? What if the idol is not the one that is mentioned in the journal?"

"I don't want to think that."

Josh brushed off Tom's despair. "Well then, if they're different, where did this seven-foot idol come from?"

"That is the eight million dollar question, isn't it?"

Josh finally fully understood Tom's dilemma. He leaned back, a hand over the back of the chair, intrigued, but in a detached, academic capacity.

The brief silence that followed amplified the hum of cheerful voices and laughter from the now full restaurant.

Tom looked away for a moment, a haggard expression in his face. "Listen, all I am saying is something is wrong. I feel it in my bones."

Josh knew what Tom was talking about. To be perfectly honest, it wasn't unlike the kind of hunch he himself had about a potential software breach. Besides, in a given situation, Tom was likely to err on the side of gullibility than on suspicion that there must be something to this newfound distrust. Josh made a grunt of sorts that was neutral and possibly encouraging.

They ate quietly for a few moments while Josh tried to process Tom's words, his quick mind assessing possibilities.

At length, Tom resumed, "Well, the upshot of all that is I engaged a PI to investigate Eichendorf."

Josh raised a surprised brow. Tom must have clearly felt serious apprehension to have taken the step. "And?"

"The man is your average alcoholic, living on his ancestors' money, nothing particularly surprising or unexpected. Except for one thing."

"Yes?"

"Eichendorf has been flush with money of late, and I haven't paid him anything yet."

Josh slowly finished the last roll and thought through the story that Tom was presenting. The turn of events seemed logically explicable to him. It was possible the German got a loan or perhaps he sold something else he found along with the idol. Tom strove for perfection as it is and with this idol, he was clearly emotionally involved. The right thing to do was to gently explain his reasoning without belittling Tom's fears.

Tom, however neither welcomed his explanations nor was convinced in the least.

"Take my advice, Tom, don't sweat over it. Just enjoy the success of the acquisition."

"I should." Tom rolled his eyes. "This could be a classic chance find by someone who didn't know its value, who might have sold it in a yard sale for a few thousand dollars, but, by a miraculous chance, has come to me instead."

"Yeah, why can't you accept that? It is innocent until proven guilty after all," said Josh dryly. "Besides, does it matter? You are buying it for a museum, not for a private collection. You are going to make it available for many other bozos like you," Josh continued with a teasing smile, "isn't that a big deal?"

"It's not that simple. I want to be ethically accountable, set an example. There are too many instances of such unscrupulous behavior. I refuse to be one of those guys! Because, if it is not the Eichendorf Nataraja, where, by heavens, did the idol come from? What is its true provenance, what story does it conceal? I must know the answer. Help me out Josh."

Josh drummed his fingers and blew out a breath. He caught Tom looking at him, with a hint of panic and entreaty.

"I'll see what I can do." He sighed.

He would do some quick poking around and find enough evidence to convince Tom to go forward, he decided. There must be something in the PI's report or even on the Web that he could use. If he could unravel it in the next two days, the trip would be much more peaceful and enjoyable after all.

Tom looked relieved.

"You reeled me in, didn't you?" Josh was partly irritated with Tom for co-opting him and partly annoyed with himself for agreeing to it.

"I am just glad, Josh, that you got my back," said Tom in all sincerity.

They left the restaurant, Josh feeling unsettled, Tom, maneuvering his wheelchair and keeping up a steady stream of conversation. Tom made an effort to talk about their upcoming vacation, his hopes for the weather to hold up, not that he was outdoorsy he joked, and optimistically even listed the obscure books he was planning to read. They hailed a cab, and Josh helped Tom settle onto the seat, folded and put away the wheelchair with a practiced hand, and slid in beside him.

Josh had noticed how tired Tom looked and wondered how often his brother went out. He had, in a moment of sympathy-induced sentiment, thought that he would do everything in his power to sort the problem out for Tom. He hadn't necessarily thought going to India would come under the gamut of everything.

Chapter 5

Josh had felt the first stirrings of unease a day later.

They were back in Tom's apartment, on the top floor of a three-story building overlooking Kensington Street. Tom's apartment was what anyone who knew him would expect, a reflection of his warm personality. There were neat rows of hardbound books on shelves, their monotony broken by lush green ferns and small objects of art, and original acrylics and museum prints on the wall. A wrought iron shelf with LP records and a player stood in a corner. Above that hung an antique map of India with brown and pink and green lines running skewed all over. There were clusters of family pictures on the mantel. The modern furniture upholstered in blue had a simple elegance to it but was also minimalistic. There was plenty of room to enable Tom easy access, which exuded a feeling of open airiness.

Tom's rooted quality was quite in contrast to his own foot-loose and fancy-free attitude, Josh mused. He had moved to at least four cities in the last eight years, to wherever work beckoned him. He usually moved into a fully furnished apartment that he felt no compulsion to personalize.

Josh appropriated Tom's desk, a sleek contemporary thing in glass and wood with fancy metal insets, and settled for some quick hunting. He went about methodically trawling the Web for information about Eichendorf. He searched for and sifted information, storing and analysing every reference carefully.

Tom went to bed, but Josh stayed awake, partly fuelled by his jet lag, partly by the intrigue. He spent the late hours learning what he needed to about the idols and the dark underworld of art trafficking.

Later, after a few hours of restless sleep, he woke up to bright blue skies and a sunny summer day outside. The sunshine remained largely ignored and wasted but not regretted as the research absorbed him completely.

Tom stepped out briefly to go to the museum, after which he remained at home. He hovered about, a mass of nervous energy. The moment Josh looked up for something, Tom turned and raised his brows. Josh shook his head, half amused, half resigned.

"Give me some news, Josh, or else I will become a nervous wreck."

"Eichendorf does not seem to have much of a presence or a personality."

"That I know already."

Josh smiled. "I meant digitally. Not much of a social media presence, no siblings, divorced, no children, few friends, and no steady job."

"Okay, what next?"

"I have a phishing ruse in play."

Tom shook his head impatiently. "The one you told me not to fall for? Fake emails that lure you into typing your password so the hackers can get to it? I don't count much on that ploy," he declared. He also urged Josh to use his brain to come up with something more intelligent.

Josh rubbed his forehead as he went back to his research. Tom was going to drive him crazy in the next few days.

As less information there was about the man, there were masses of documents about his ancestors—many in German—journals, scholarly articles, and the like that Josh began gathering.

Despite Tom's dire prognosis, much to his relief and triumph, Josh soon got an alert that told him Eichendorf had fallen for the carefully constructed bait.

He ran a program to look for references to Chola bronzes in the data that he had been collecting, to come back to later. The email access was more promising.

He painstakingly rifled through the man's email, forming a mental picture, building a timeline. There were some uninteresting personal mails, marginally useful summary statements from his bank, and a treasure trove of credit card bills. The man sure liked his sports clubs, automobiles, and porn sites. There was clear indication of increased spending of late, confirming what the PI had reported. Then there was an entry for ten thousand Euros, certainly not chump change, incoming through a wire transfer around the same time as Tom's initial meeting with Eichendorf. Tracking it to an account in Cayman Islands was interesting but not immediately useful.

He continued his detection with no further results.

Sometime late in the night, Josh fell asleep, exhausted, on the couch that had been, like the previous day, neatly made up with clean sheets and soft pillows.

He woke up to cloudy skies and the smell of coffee, for a moment unsure if it was morning or evening. Tom was seated by the window quietly working on his laptop.

"I have coffee brewing and breakfast ready," he said with a smile after wishing Josh a good morning. He did not say anything else. His empathy levels were always high, especially when it came to Josh before his morning coffee.

A large coffee and a hot shower later, Josh went back to his task, deciding to change tacks. He went through the mails one by one, going backward from the date of the incoming money transfer, looking for any atypical behaviour.

In the mail trail was a ticket for a day trip to Zurich, four months earlier, a month before the money transfer. Right then, Josh knew instinctively he was on the brink of a breakthrough.

"What business did you have in Zurich?" he mumbled to himself and promptly shut up at Tom's all curious, "What?"

He drummed his fingers as he contemplated on what else he could do to track the details of the trip. He did love a good chase.

Credit card bills, he thought. A quick review showed him a purchase at a store in Ramistrasse the afternoon of the day trip. After mulling over it for a few seconds, he ran a search for any Indian reference within a mile of the store.

He hit pay dirt.

Gallerie de Kohinoor, selling high-end Indian artifacts, was in the same block. Josh surmised from the slick marketing on Facebook and the fancy website that business must be good. The owner, an Englishman named Nigel Banner, looked suave in the publicity pictures and spouted deep philosophy and admiration for India on his blogs. They had a bronze idol in their catalogue but nothing like the one in Tom's possession.

Josh pushed back on the chair and ran his hands through his hair.

He stared at the ceiling. His instincts screamed a connection to the idol and the art gallery.

"What is it, Josh?"

Tom moved his wheelchair closer, sensing something. He could always read Josh well. Josh gave him a tight smile, tilted the screen for Tom, and pointed to the website.

"Your man Eichendorf likely visited this Indian art store a few months ago."

"And sold something like you said?" Excitement mingled with relief lit up Tom's face.

Josh hesitated. This was his opportunity. He could easily fake a transaction confirming that, and Tom might let it all go. But he couldn't do that to Tom. Damn, he couldn't let it go himself. He sighed. "I don't think so. There is no communication between the gallery and him. No enquiries, no quotes, no invoices, nothing. Nothing at all! It isn't the 1980s. There would have been something electronic!"

"The gallery is involved," pronounced Tom in gloomy tones.

"I'd safely say so."

They stared at each other for a few seconds, and then in an unspoken agreement, Tom called the PI and gave him a new target to investigate.

Over breakfast, Josh discovered that the gallery website was on a shared CMS system maintained by a third party. It wasn't likely going to yield any more secrets.

They spent all of Sunday morning indoors.

Later, Josh went for a run around the park and got some take-out. Tom played some shrill opera and hung about with a mournful expression. They chatted a bit about friends and co-workers over a leisurely late lunch, keeping up a steady stream of banalities while their attention was consumed by the possible next steps.

If the unprecedented state of his usually well-organized and clean desk was any indication of his current woes, Tom was in an extreme state of agitation. His laptop was sharing space with printouts, half-eaten bowls of cereal, and little cartons with leftover Chinese. Coffee mugs with dry brown stains in the bottom lay carelessly abandoned in a corner.

They pored over every detail about the gallery, the reports from the PI, and data from art crimes websites, speculating on different scenarios.

Sunday evening, Tom had suggested, for the first time, with a near bland expression, "Perhaps we should consider ... I think you might have to go to India."

"Sure, sure." Josh had guffawed, truly reading it as a joke. He hadn't realized Tom had made the next connection in his head already.

By late evening, the PI reported that the gallery routinely got shipments from Mumbai, and they sold all over Europe. The PI also shared that Mr. Banner did not have a good reputation amongst the local law enforcement, but so far, there was nothing they could charge him with.

Tom had put him on the speaker, and Josh was listening in on the conversation. They stared at each other in frustration at the information than neither debunked nor upheld any of their theories. Josh had independently arrived at similar conclusions based on his research.

The PI concluded, "I don't know if this is of interest to you. A few months ago, the gallery got a shipment from Chennai. They usually get their shipments from Mumbai."

Tom visibly paled, and Josh sat up straight.

"From where specifically, do you know?"

"No, I don't. I wiggled this information out from a beautiful Fräulein who works there. I met her at a bar this evening."

"It's extremely important we find all about the shipment, its contents and its exact origin," Tom said grimly.

The PI had hung up soon after that. That was when Tom's India trip idea progressed from being suggestive to determined to downright adamant.

"Okay, Josh, there are two possible scenarios here. First is, Eichendorf owns the Nataraja, provenance is real, and he just happened to coincidentally take a trip to a gallery in Zurich. We have nothing to categorically rule out that the incoming money transfer was not legitimate."

"And the second?"

Tom took a deep breath. "Eichendorf is a pawn to help fabricate the provenance. It is after all well documented that his ancestors had a Nataraja idol. Eichendorf visited the gallery to get familiarized with the idol and got paid for his part. The idol was in the shipment from Chennai. It is a Chola antique that has been illegally trafficked out of India."

"Why illegally?"

"Because Indian law says you cannot legally export an antique bronze even if you, by a miracle owned one. Even within India, the antique bronzes are typically in temples or museums."

There was a heavy silence. Josh saw the logic in Tom's words, and truth be told, he suspected the same as well.

"Why don't you simply pull out of the acquisition? You haven't paid him after all."

"What?" Tom's cry was soulful. He then recovered enough to try to sound academic. "Of course I could, but on what grounds? There is no mention of any such stolen Nataraja idol in art crimes websites, news sites ... you checked all that. From where on earth did this idol materialize, then?"

Josh let out an exasperated laugh. "Are you kidding me? It was you who started down this path of inquiry suspecting something."

Tom moved his wheelchair back and forth like a caged animal. He sighed deeply.

"Don't I know that? I want it to be scenario one, and I am afraid it is scenario two," he said in a voice that spelt doom.

"Look, even if it is scenario two, you still have—what do they call it—plausible deniability. If, and it's a big if, it does turn out to be a stolen idol, the case would go on for years. Who cares?"

"I care. I really care. It's extremely irresponsible, let alone a legal quagmire to proceed with the acquisition. But beyond the legality of it, I am consumed by the question of its origins. We have to find out what was in that shipment and ultimately where it came from. I have to know. The answer is in India."

"No, it's in Zurich. It's Sunday today and tomorrow I'll make some calls and—"

"The PI will find the source in India, you don't waste your time on that. We have to get ahead of the curve, to track beyond." Tom stopped moving about and looked at Josh.

Josh groaned at the impassioned entreaty. "Even if I were to agree with you, you can't possibly believe I have to physically go there? What am I going to do, knock on every Hindu church and ask them, 'Have you, by any chance, lost an idol lately, about yea high?' I am no Indologist like you."

"That is abundantly clear. You'd knock on every 'temple', not Hindu church," Tom said, rolling his eyes. "And, technically, I am a Dravidologist."

"See I don't even know what that means."

"My friend Vidya, the one I have told you about, she can—"

Josh tried hard to be patient. "I work better in the digital dimension, Tom. There are laws, many of which I might end up breaking. I'd rather do it from here than there. God knows what kinds of torture Indians specialize in, some ancient voodoo stuff likely."

Tom ignored his sulky tones.

"I need you, someone I trust completely, someone who thinks logically. I know ... I know we won't be able to resolve this sitting here. You heard how the PI was able to get his information by taking a girl out for a drink."

"Yeah, well, he gets to take hot girls out for a drink while I get to go to the boondocks?"

"Josh, we are both treasure hunters at heart, and I know you are curious too. You have always been good at solving puzzles. You are a security expert, for God's sake."

"A software security expert, Tom!" Josh interjected with considerable annoyance. "I do my work in a room in front of a computer. There is absolutely no need to run off to the exotic East at the first excuse. I absolutely, positively, refuse to go."

He had really told his brother off.

Chapter 6

Josh removed his headphones and stood up from his seat as the hum of the plane grew louder. Most passengers had settled to watch a movie or were fast asleep. He walked up and down the aisles, stretched as much as the narrow confines would allow, and struck up a conversation with the hostess. Some other time, he would have gotten her number.

He polished off the lunch, too hungry to bother with the taste. He also drank wine and copious amounts of coffee, knowing full well it was going to wreak havoc to his system.

He was too restless to doze off and too distracted to watch a movie, as his busy mind kept jumping from one thought to another. The next few hours passed in a haze. Sunlight wore off, and it quickly became dark outside as they raced away from the sun.

Finally, in the flight information channel, the little cartoon plane looked as if its nose was about to touch Chennai. The lights came on in the airplane, and Josh straightened, rubbing his eyes. The airhostess announced they were approaching Chennai airport.

Josh took a peek at the darkness outside as the plane lost attitude. The city came into his view in pinpoints of lights forming lines and polygons in a plane, bright white and muted yellow, steady and shimmering and twinkling, slowly resolving into a highway, a stadium, until, with a thud, they were on the ground racing toward the neon glare of the gate.

The airport was well lit but also quiet, and he followed the crowd to the immigration line. He cleared immigration, wondering if the purpose of his visit could really be construed as tourism as he claimed. The unsmiling officer seemed to believe what he said on the form and waved him off without a word. He walked through the green channel out into the city.

He emerged out of the airport to a crowd mostly of men standing and jostling about behind makeshift dividers, almost forming a gauntlet, bringing him up short. He blinked. Noticing the placards with names, mercifully all in English, he realized they were waiting to receive the passengers.

The night was warm and muggy, a huge contrast to the London weather. There was a light breeze that didn't help, and Josh promptly removed the hoodie he had worn almost out of habit just before disembarking. The smells of cigarette smoke and exhaust fumes scorched his nose. As he inhaled, he could almost taste the dirt and the gasoline in the back of his throat. The din of people speaking in an alien tongue filled his ears. From the airport, he suddenly seemed to have emerged into a different world.

He remembered Tom telling him someone from the hotel would be there to pick him up. He looked around and spotted his name on a board, held up by a man dressed like a chauffeur.

He walked over and introduced himself, and before he knew it, the man had grabbed his luggage and had started walking briskly away. Josh attempted to follow him, but he asked him to stay put, pointing to the curb a few feet away.

A full two minutes passed. Josh texted, *Namaste, the eagle has landed,* to Tom and then stood watching men and women get into cars, loading large pieces of luggage, talking cheerfully. He wondered if he had managed to get robbed within minutes of landing in India. That was not the case, as he saw a car of Japanese make, with the name of the hotel painted on its side, stop right by him. The driver waved him in.

He boarded the cab, vaguely embarrassed by the hat and the uniform of the driver. They went through mostly deserted roads with everything quiet and closed, no doubt due to the ungodly hour.

His phone beeped; Tom was clearly not yet asleep and had acknowledged his text.

Josh noted with budding happiness the data plan of the SIM card he had bought at Heathrow was working. It was going to cost him an obscene amount though. Still, best to use that than his regular phone.

As always, the power of the digital network thrilled him. Here he was, halfway across the world yet connected to Tom, hopping over cell towers and satellites. All was well with the world.

His distracted mind registered various glimpses from time to time—a

BMW showroom, its insignia unmistakable, a building that looked like a palace from Arabian Nights, left side driving, a gas station, and then an unexpected view of a full moon aglow on the sky.

They pulled up at the hotel after about a half-hour. Not having had the foresight to exchange currency in the airport, Josh attempted to pay the driver in dollars.

The man shook his head as he unloaded the bag.

"I don't have Indian money. Can you wait? I'll check at the reception."

"Okay sir," the driver said, but again shook his head.

Thoroughly confused, Josh explained once more slowly.

"Okay, okay. Hotel will pay," the cabbie answered slowly as though he was exasperated with Josh.

A bellhop took charge of his luggage, putting it through security screening, and ushered him toward the reception. The hotel was posh, and the receptionists looked bright, even for that time of the night. The man was in a suit, and the woman had a sari on. Josh was fascinated by the red dot on her forehead that was the exact shade of her lipstick.

He felt high, as though he was stoned, and tried hard not to stare.

She checked Josh in with efficiency and a brilliant smile and signaled to the bellhop. They rode up the elevator in silence. Josh soon found himself in a wood-paneled room decorated in understated elegance, with curtains drawn, and a large bed already turned down. He breathed a sigh of relief.

After the bellhop accepted his dollars and left, Josh pulled out his phone and tried the Wi-Fi password. Hallelujah, there was good Wi-Fi connectivity. He checked his mail, dropped a note to Tom, and pulled out his multi-country plug adapters and figured out enough outlets to at least charge his phones and laptop. Ignoring the fruit basket, he took the sealed cold water bottle from the small bar and drank lustily.

He stumbled to the well-appointed bathroom and stared at his reflection. Two days' worth of stubble, bleary eyes, mussed-up hair, crumpled shirt, disheveled appearance ... All in all, he looked like hell and absolutely unfit to follow the trail of the mighty Indian god Shiva, albeit in the form of a bronze idol. He needed to have his wits sharp. He needed a good night's sleep. He needed to kill Tom.

He crashed onto the bed.

***

London, some hours earlier ...

In the cold, poorly lit storage room in the basement of the museum, the assistant curator specializing in ancient Rome and Greece paused for a moment by the Nataraja. He had come down to check on a Corinthian amphora he was planning to put up for display and was hurrying past, but the idol drew him, made him pause in front of it with a magnetic pull.

He knew all there was to know of the cool, white marble Greek and Roman sculptures that occupied the wide expanse of the museum's first floor. He specialized in Greek antiquities, but as a historian, he had the natural curiosity and appreciation for any such relics. He had read the memo; they had talked of it during a team meeting. It was the idol of Shiva as Nataraja, the dancer. He knew about bronzes, there were enough in the Greco-Roman world, but did not know enough of Hindu symbolism to appreciate with discernment the particular idol. Yet it drew him.

The metal shimmered in the dull light, its dark even patina adding to its majesty, and likely to its value as well. He stared fascinated at the smiling face of the Hindu god projecting a sense of mystery in the shadows. Was it his imagination or was there an extra sheen on the face?

The idol towered over him. Tom Winslow had said, in understated excitement, that it might be the only antique idol of that size outside of India. The Nataraja's left foot was stamping a half-human creature, which he had heard was the demon of ignorance and the right foot was upraised, crossing over the left. His hands, four of them, one holding a tongue of flame, one a drum, were frozen in gestures that he could only presume to be rich in meaning. Dreadlocks fanned either side of his face. A cobra writhed around his hand raising its hood, ready to strike. The slender figure, encompassed in an oval halo, was graceful yet commanding.

"Powerfully gentle, with tranquil joy." Tom had paraphrased Auguste Rodin's words for another such Nataraja idol, as he had finished his presentation, the screen freezing with a picture of this idol. "Shiva Nataraja, ladies and gentlemen, dancing in grand bliss."

He appreciated the acquisition. He even liked young Tom. He had always known Tom would get ahead of him. There was talk of grants being cut, of downsizing in the museum. Tom was much favored, but as an American, he was still the outsider, whereas he himself was a native and a long-timer. He had hoped they wouldn't lay him off when push came to shove. But with this brilliant acquisition, and an exhibition that'd surely follow, he wasn't hopeful anymore.

He wished hard, as he stared at it, that something would happen and the idol would not belong to the museum anymore.

He then sighed and walked away. Perhaps he could move to a smaller museum up north and become the chief curator there. Perhaps there wouldn't be a layoff. He worried as he awaited the elevator.

Chapter 7

The morning had dawned with the usual warmth and noises, as well as a promise of an exciting day. The sun was already gliding high up the sky, and dust motes danced in the summer light beams brightening their small kitchen.

Vidya had started her day a tad earlier and was well on her way to finishing her chores. She went about tidying up the kitchen; she put away the breakfast things and wiped down the counter. The maid had already swept and mopped the floors and had washed up the dishes.

She had emailed her manager that she would be taking the day off and had rescheduled her meetings. There was one client who was bringing in a considerable amount of forex. She'd have to check in on the exchange rates with treasury a little later, she reminded herself.

An alapana in Thodi filled the air, managing to match her sense of anticipation and impatience. Having finished the cooking with considerable haste, she swiftly put out her father's lunch dishes on the table—millet, radish sambhar rich on dal, string beans diced to bits and steamed, a large bowl of salad, all mildly spiced and less on salt. She had particularly labored over the salad, which was a colorful mix of cucumbers and tomatoes and peanuts, but she knew RST wouldn't even notice, let alone appreciate. Food was food for him, and he would eat the simplest dish and the most elaborate and delicious dish with the same indifferent and inattentive air.

She had once asked her mother, who cooked heavenly fare, how she dealt with his apathy. "Perhaps I write a diary, full of desperate poetry," she had answered with a twinkle. Sometimes, she thought, it was a response in jest, telling her not to take herself too seriously, and sometimes she wondered if she would find such a book, after all, amidst her mother's things.

Her uncertainty over the impact of such differences in her parents' marriage definitely colored her own views of matrimony, and she thought the process of finding a suitable partner was to be executed with infinite caution and calm reflection.

Dismissing her wayward thoughts, she rushed to her bedroom to get ready. She imagined Josh up and about, waiting impatiently in the lobby, all set to enjoy the sights and sounds of Chennai.

A few minutes later, she emerged from her room and surveyed the living room and the dining area, mentally checking to see if she had forgotten anything. She made sure her father's medicines were on the table. He was prone to miss his tablets, not to mention sneaking a smoke from time to time.

She caught her reflection in the large mirror she had strategically placed on one wall of their small dining room. The delicately embroidered olive green cotton kurti, and the pencil-leg jeans looked good on her. She examined her reflection critically; hair well brushed framing her face with the longer strands reaching mid-back, a light dash of lipstick, black eyeliner highlighting her dark eyes, matching earrings ...

Admit it, she told herself, *you want to make a good impression.*

Josh was her best friend's brother. She supposed it was only natural that she wanted him to take back good things about her to Tom, about her looks, her intelligence, and character.

"Good thing you have taken after your mother," said her father.

She turned. RST liked to spend his mornings sitting down on his recliner by the large windows for his post-breakfast ritual of immersing himself in the papers and weeklies. He now studied her from behind a half-folded newspaper with a slight smile. Vidya bit her lips, slightly abashed. He rarely noticed her appearance, let alone commented. He must have caught her staring at her reflection.

She smiled at him. He was a handsome man himself, but her mother had been a dazzling beauty with the classical loveliness that, even when she was older, people routinely commented on.

The story was that RST had been on the verge of resigning his job, determined to sacrifice his life for the party, when his mother had nagged him into "seeing" this girl she had arranged for him. One look and a month later they had been married. RST never talked about it; neither did her mother.

"Yes, well, thanks to genes and the big bad cosmetic industry," she quipped.

RST routinely wrote pamphlets on various topics that the party published in dull newsprint and gave away in some conference or the other. He had, some years ago, written an elaborately scathing account on the very subject that she was sure no one read. Poor RST, outnumbered in his own family and the world, she thought, a relic of a dying species.

Vidya was surprised he had no response to her comment. There was a moment of unguarded wistfulness in his eyes right before he buried himself in the next news item.

Was he thinking of her mother or was he regretting the influence of the capitalists? Surely he missed her, he grieved her?

She let the moment pass.

She bid him farewell with her usual instructions for the day and grabbed her purse. He waved her away, as always distracted by current affairs.

She walked out to a warm sunny morning, the sun's rays feeling sharp and prickly on her skin. The little area in front of the house, washed out every morning, was already fully dry. The white powdery lines of the decorative *kolam* drawn upon the wet ground that morning were, by then, broken by tire marks and were fading into the dirt.

There was shade thanks to the rare leafy street. A few old trees had miraculously survived the onslaught of new multi-storied apartment buildings replacing the small houses in a hurry.

She dabbed at the sheen of sweat already forming on the back of her neck with her handkerchief. It was the end of May and the *kathiri veyyil* heat wave was supposed to have finished, but it didn't feel like it. The weather reports were already talking of delayed or weak monsoons, raising the specter of the heat continuing into June, and of subpar agricultural yields. It affected the market too. She wondered where the Sensex would be by September.

She walked over to where her two-wheeler was parked, feeling conscious of her appearance and slightly ridiculous about her excitement.

The stray brown mongrel reclining in the corner of the lane, stole a sleepy glance at her and tapped its tail perfunctorily. The traffic noises from the main road sounded muted and distant. The trees were still, and with the departure of the office-goers and the school children, the morning was winding down.

She stood hesitating for a few moments before deciding to take her car instead. It was a small car that she rarely drove. She didn't think Josh would be adventurous enough to pillion ride on her Scooty.

She typed a note to Tom, though he was likely still asleep. *Morning. On the way to meet Josh.*

She walked into the posh, five-star hotel a few minutes later and requested the receptionist to put a call through to Mr. Josh Winslow. After a few moments, the receptionist gave her a helpless smile; the phone was obviously still ringing unanswered. Perhaps Mr. Winslow was having breakfast, she suggested.

Vidya looked around unsure of what to do, and then decided to wait for a few minutes. She sat down, caught up on her mail, talked to the client about incoming funds, and checked the market.

Fifteen minutes later, she presented herself again before the receptionist who tried calling the room again. He finally seemed to have picked up the phone.

"Mr. Winslow will be right down," the lady said with a relieved smile.

Vidya thanked her and walked back to the seating area. She stared at the marble flooring, the metal chandelier, stood gravely inspecting the large still water urn filled with rose petals, and then, having nothing else to do, sat on a low sofa and caught up on a few more calls she had to make.

"Is there someone waiting for me?" she finally heard a voice querying the receptionist after a good fifteen minutes.

Vidya looked up from her low seating to find a young man turn toward her. It struck Vidya how she had never imagined Josh would stand tall at about six feet. She had seen pictures of Tom in his wheelchair and had video chatted with him online. Naturally, Tom's height had never been part of any conversation.

She stood up hastily and, in her flustered mind, somewhat clumsily.

Josh had the fit and well-toned look of someone who was not a stranger to regular workouts. He was dressed in a blue gingham shirt tucked in with sleeves rolled up to just below the elbow and dark blue jeans and wore a backpack.

His hair, freshly washed, wasn't fully dry yet, and he seemed to have hastily run a brush through it. He had likely relinquished shaving in the interest of time or was growing a beard. The latter, she thought, was a bad idea.

She could see the resemblance to Tom's good looks in his thick brows, his tired yet lucid eyes, and his straight nose. But in the tilt of his head, in the way he strode, in his stance, he also had an air of brashness. Tom exuded confidence, but Josh seemed to lean toward arrogance, which she found off-putting.

She then mentally chided herself for being so quick to judge before the poor man had even opened his mouth.

He had come to stand nearby while she was busy scrutinizing him.

"Mr. Winslow? Very nice to meet you," she said, extending a hand.

"Sorry I kept you waiting. Good to meet you." They shook hands, and he hesitated, causing Vidya to suspect he didn't know her name.

"Please call me Josh," he said.

"Vidya," she offered.

"Vidya," he repeated, slightly mispronouncing her name. "Um ... Have you had breakfast?"

"Yes," she responded, surprised. It was nine forty.

"I am starving. Do you mind if I grab something first?"

"Not at all, would you like to go out somewhere?"

"No, the restaurant here is fine." He moved aside slightly, allowing her to join him.

The receptionist directed Josh where to go, and they walked toward the elevator in silence. He swiped his room keycard and pushed the button to the access controlled top floor.

Vidya expressed her delight and surprise about his trip.

He grunted in response.

The restaurant serving a breakfast buffet was bright and welcoming, with light streaming in from the large bay windows.

As they waited to be seated, Vidya commented that it must feel quite hot, enquired if the hotel was to his liking, and asked if his journey had been comfortable.

He shrugged, nodded, and made a neutral noise respectively in response.

They sat down by the windows. Gleaming silverware, sparkling clean ceramic plates, and glasses were set on pristine white tablecloth. Sprigs of orchids in fluted vases completed the setting. There was only one other man finishing his breakfast, and the restaurant was quiet.

"Would you care to have something?" Josh asked, putting together a full sentence for a change.

Vidya opted for a coffee, already feeling oddly let down. He headed out to the buffet after ordering a coffee for her and a black coffee for himself.

She had concluded the previous evening, after some deliberation, that it must have been disappointment that he couldn't himself travel that had weighed down Tom. She now wondered if perhaps there was a different reason for Tom's distraction. She felt a sense of discomposure again.

She took a sip of water and a deep breath.

Chapter 8

He had to get rid of her, Josh thought, as he stepped away from the table, massaging his forehead.

He felt sluggish, like an overloaded system. After tossing and turning until about four a.m. he had given up on sleep and had gotten lost in Techmeme and Hacker News. Finally, when it was almost dawn, he had fallen into a fitful sleep.

Later, he had rushed through his shower and had gotten ready fast, managing to take only a cursory look at his mail. Tom had sent him a curious mail that he couldn't make head or tail of about some work Josh was supposed to have in Singapore.

He was thoroughly irritated with Tom for foisting her on him. He now vaguely recalled Tom talking about this woman quite a bit during their phone calls around Christmas. She probably wants to be a hospitable host, he thought sullenly. It might have worked, too, if only she didn't speak with the speed and rhythm of a firing machine gun.

He was not being completely fair, he drew in a breath; she had actually sounded quite cultured, and her voice had a honeyed quality to it.

He surveyed the buffet setup, feeling ravenous and brightened at the familiar items and the signs, thankfully in English.

The white marble counter top looked opulent with an array of gleaming silverware full of continental selections. He piled up his plate with warm croissants, toasts, and sausage, skipping the cheese and fruit platters. Jars of juices, in green and purple and orange, arranged on bowls of melting ice cubes added splashes of color. He eyed them suspiciously and, after some hesitation, took a glass of the orange juice. The steaming Indian selections were set up on large sunken bowls on another island, which he ignored.

He went back to the table and began to resolutely polish off his large breakfast. She asked him if he would like to try the Indian dishes and suggested a couple, going on to spout short descriptions that sounded as if they were from a cookbook; he declined firmly.

No wonder Tom likes her, he thought morosely. As though she knew what he was thinking, she talked about Tom, gushing about his intelligence and erudition.

"Yeah, he is an unending fountain of wisdom," he acknowledged.

She went silent, looking taken aback. Josh reined in his resentment and regretted his sarcasm. Her reaction also made him take a more measured look at her.

She had lustrous dark hair, eyes the color of a rich whisky, and smooth caramel skin. He had believed she would be closer to Tom's age and, for some odd reason, hadn't expected her to be this attractive. *Smoking hot, really,* he thought. With her seemingly accurate reading of his derision, he now upgraded his impression unhappily to include *potentially bright.* Taken all together, the exotic meter was on alluring levels.

She asked with a curious glance, "So, Josh, did you have any thoughts on what you want to see? Would you like me to suggest a few things to do?"

"No. No, that's fine," he said hastily, sounding more alarmed than he would have liked. He cursed Tom mentally again when she looked away, hiding a quick frown.

He took a sip of the juice, buying time to gather his wits; he needed to give minimal, plausible explanations without giving away the true purpose.

"I am on a business trip, just stopping over. So want to be very selective in how I spend the time," he hedged.

She smiled which indicated he had redeemed himself, but a head bobble that accompanied it was confusing. He got reminded of the cabbie from the previous night and realized the gesture probably meant affirmation.

"Yes, Tom said you were on your way to Singapore and were only stopping here for a short visit."

Ah, so that was the meaning of Tom's message. He nodded with a straight face.

As a dutiful lieutenant to Tom, unaware of his rather violent feelings on the matter, she proceeded to list some tourist sites they could visit.

He took a deep breath. If he didn't nip it in the bud, before he knew it, he would be held in some museum and be made to hear a lecture on Indian history.

The waiter, clad in a dark suit, brought their coffee.

"Is everything to your liking, sir?" he asked in good English.

Josh nodded.

"Would you like to try some dosa or aapam from our live counter?"

Josh shook his head.

"More toast perhaps? Or some eggs?"

"No, thank you."

"Enjoy your meal, sir," the man said and, finally taking a hint, left them alone.

Josh noticed she was looking at him expectantly, waiting to know what he wanted to do during the day. He was stuck with her, whether he liked it or not, at least for the next few hours. Perhaps he ought to use it to his advantage.

"What I would really like to do is shopping," he declared with what he hoped was an innocent smile.

"Are you getting married?"

"What the—What?"

She chuckled merrily. "I was joking. Those who come to Chennai for shopping usually do so for wedding silks and jewelry."

He tried not to grit his teeth and forced a good-natured laugh in return.

"Let me share a secret. I plan to buy a gift for Tom's birthday, something fancy and Indian like a ... uh ... bronze idol. It wasn't much of an inconvenience to fly into Chennai, buy it, and then proceed on my way to uh ... Singapore. So here I am!"

Josh had decided he might as well make himself useful and do some groundwork until the PI discovered the name of the source. He suspected, like in many cases of art-trafficking, an art store was likely involved in India as well. He had made a plan of sorts to visit various stores to gauge their capacity to pull off such an operation, and to do some reconnaissance on their billing systems. Following the money trail was the best bet.

He should also check on the status of the exploits he had run earlier to track the path of the cargo, he recalled with a frown.

"I see," she said, snagging his attention. The pleasant expression remained on her face, but he could sense she was troubled and bewildered. He cautioned himself to tread with care.

"You could help me with the bargaining. I am sure they'd try to outwit the white guy," he joked.

Vidya didn't join him in his mirth. At best, her smile could be called strained.

"Tom's birthday is four months away," she said unexpectedly. The tone betrayed a faint disbelief.

Josh was taken aback. How was he supposed to know they were on birthday sharing terms? Especially when he had specifically told Tom what a security risk that was. What else did she know, their mother's maiden name?

"Yeah, well, my trip to India is now," he recovered and then offered a more logical reason. "It'd have to be shipped from here, and that would take time."

From the head bobble, he couldn't tell for sure, but it seemed like she believed what he was saying, even like she was mustering some enthusiasm for the endeavor.

"Yes, I could help with that. I know a few places I could take you to," she replied and rattled off various names.

Over the weekend, he had come up with a list of potential stores to visit. Pulling out his phone, he noted with mounting hope that some of those names appeared in his list as well. Provided he had heard those tongue twister names right, that is.

"Great, let's do it then."

He drained his coffee and signaled the waiter before things became worse. It was going to be a long day.

Chapter 9

They left the restaurant and rode down the elevator wordlessly. Josh was vaguely conscious of the need to make small talk, but his mind was busy coming up with paths for himself or the PI to explore, that as he followed her out, he was still silent. An attendant in a suit, whose only job seemed to be to mind the corridor, wished them good morning.

As they headed out, Josh wondered about transportation.

"Do we get a cab?"

"I have a car," she replied.

That brought on a memory, and excusing himself, he went back to the reception and exchanged some dollars, sure he was being ripped off. After being told the pickup was part of the hotel package, he left a tip for the cabbie from the previous night. He checked the ride-sharing apps and the taxi rental apps that he had had the forethought to download and noted happily he had multiple options for a cab for later. Hail to the mobile revolution.

She waited patiently as he walked toward her. The doorman, looking tall and grand with a curling moustache and a maharajah turban, dressed in white except for a red sash for a belt, smartly wished him good morning and held the glass door ajar. She remained quiet as they walked out, and he felt a momentary prick about his uncharitable thoughts earlier.

As soon as he stepped out, heat washed over him, sharp and stinging in his forehead and in his lower arms. The sky, a pale blue haze of vigor, was a complete contrast to the gray sullenness of London. Squinting against the blinding sun, he realized he had forgotten to get his sunglasses. He didn't feel like making her wait again while he went back for them.

She headed toward a small maize-yellow car that resembled a mouse. Staring dubiously at it, he bumped into her as he headed to the passenger side. With a brief smile, she motioned him to the other side. He was almost disappointed she didn't elaborate on the fact that they drove on the left side of the road.

After tossing his bag on the back seat, he somehow managed to stuff his six-foot frame inside. He would have to rent a bigger car for the next day.

Vidya, whatever her last name was, backed the car out and started driving. She paused by the exit gate of the hotel for what seemed like half a moment and swept a full right turn without a care into heavy incoming traffic on the narrow road and merged in by a hairline.

Josh convulsed. The previous evening, he had arrived late to empty streets. Now the road was teeming with two-wheelers and little yellow tuk-tuks along with cars and buses jostling for space, literally bumper to bumper. The noise of honking, impatient and irritable filled the air. The smell of gas assaulted his nostrils. Sunlight bounced off of car trunks, handlebars, and even the mirror work on a young woman's dress, hurting his eyes. A woman rode pillion, holding a little baby precariously on her lap. In a surrealistic scene, he caught a vendor hand pushing a cart full of green bananas, weaving it across the congested intersection with gay abandon.

It hit him. He was in India!

Josh sat immobile, clenching his fists, an earlier exchange with Tom coming to his mind.

The evening before the flight, throwing his clothes messily back into his bag, he had grumbled on about the trip.

After listening to him for some time, Tom had said, "All things set aside, this trip will do you good. You are sorely lacking on the spiritual side."

That had set Josh off. "Oh jeez, what are we in now? Eat, Pray, Love?"

Tom rolled his eyes but stood by his words. "You know what I mean. Travel broadens the mind and all that." He also added somewhat inexplicably, "It's good to allow your system to get exposed from time to time to a new experience, a new element."

"What am I? A metaphor for a prejudiced white man? Come on, Tom, that is so passé. I have even had an Asian girlfriend."

Tom laughed. "I remember Anita. Yeah, right, if she is Asian, then I am Indian. And oh you dated her for 2 long months, didn't you?"

"I do know Apu, Asok, and Rajesh Koothrapalli very well."

It took a couple of seconds for Tom, but he made the connection. He put up his hands in an exaggerated gesture. "Whoa, you are all set then. You have acquired a profound understanding of India."

"The point I am making, Tom, is this is not one of those bigot spends time with natives and redeems himself stories."

"I never said you were a racist."

"Oh, thank you. I am touched."

"You've just been in your yuppie bubble for too long," Tom had finished doggedly.

"Give it a rest! I am going, aren't I?" he had exclaimed in irritation.

Please, can I have my yuppie bubble back with its wide-open roads where drivers follow rules? Josh texted to Tom.

Vidya maneuvered her little car while Josh sat tense. She drove like a maniac; though, to be fair, everyone drove like a maniac. The only method to the madness seemed to be to occupy any unoccupied space irrespective of the side and that the bigger vehicle had the right of way.

A woman darted in front of the car and crossed the road. Two trucks ran a red light. After what seemed like an eternity, while Josh sat, fists clenched, thinking he really should have read up on traffic rules in Chennai instead of on Chola bronzes, they finally arrived at a store.

She made some complex maneuvers and parked the car between two bikes that were barely apart. Josh inched out through the door that he could only open halfway and stretched, ready to kneel down and give thanks for his safe arrival.

No wonder people find spirituality here, he texted Tom.

He looked dubiously at the street.

The store was in a broad street that had become very narrow thanks to a row of parked cars and bikes along with a row of street vendors and a truck that was idling in the middle of the road with no care for the cars backing up. Alleys crammed with small shops branched off. Men and women walked about carrying big bags of sundry stuff. Bicycle bells rang, a loud unintelligible conversation was on between two men, a horn tooted continuously though he couldn't discern any reason for it. They liked making noises, he concluded. It stank of spices and dirt when it didn't of exhaust fumes. The heat burnt his skin and he felt sweat break out within moments.

'Puhar Traders' proclaimed a small board in front of the unassuming three-story store.

A fawn-colored cow stood between him and the storefront, staring at him with soulful eyes.

Josh was stunned.

"Are you kidding me?" he muttered to himself. What the heck had he gotten himself into, a cow for God's sake, in the middle of the road in a city!

He stared, and the cow stared back. Then it calmly lifted its tail, relieved itself, and shit on the street. Having imparted its opinion of Josh, it moseyed out of his way.

Josh looked at the shit and the little puddle in front of him and then followed behind Vidya as she deftly stepped over and led him into the dingy interiors of the windowless store.

He did take a moment to message Tom a picture, saying he was done with all the bullshit.

Chapter 10

Vidya felt inconsiderate that Josh might have found her small car uncomfortable. He hadn't complained, but she noticed he was stretching when he got out. He had hardly said anything; she had posed him open ended questions, which Tom would have loved to answer exhaustively, but Josh had stuck to monosyllables as responses.

She was now almost getting used to his reticence. He glowered at everything around him with a pronounced hunted look as though he would give an arm and a leg to catch the next plane and leave Chennai. His act was beginning to grate on her nerves.

"Relax, we are not going to eat you alive," she said.

He looked momentarily startled and then, for the first time that morning, grinned, albeit sheepishly. His tired eyes took on a gleam of amusement.

"Well, only about a quarter of you are vegetarian after all."

She had by then concluded he was sort of an unpleasant man, incapable of convivial conversation let alone mild humor, so the repartee and the manner in which he took her veiled criticism in his stride, was thoroughly unexpected and welcome.

With a slight smile, she waved toward the rickety wooden stairs and started climbing up to the second floor where the bronzes were kept. He followed her with a thoughtful look on his face, seemingly more interested in the lady at the billing counter.

The hall was medium-sized, replete with gleaming metal artifacts. Tables and shelves were filled with rows of brass lamps of sharp edges and rounded stems, copper plates with etchings, and temple bells with carved handles, all shining under the tube light.

Vidya attempted a commentary about the objects and their significance in Hindu rituals but trailed off, perceiving a certain preoccupation in him. Instead, she silently led the way toward the bronze idols in the back, placed unpretentiously on wooden slabs covered in dull white sheets.

After a few moments of silent scrutiny, reminding herself this was a present for Tom after all, she pointed out a few beautiful idols of Vishnu and Lakshmi and one of a happy, chubby Ganesha. She resisted the temptation to explain the gods and refrained from adding any further comments.

"I am interested in a Nataraja," Josh said.

Vidya stopped short. Had he just said Nataraja, let alone pronounced it correctly? Then she noticed him unerringly walk toward a Nataraja idol displayed prominently in the center of the set of bronze idols.

Granted, the Nataraja idol was the most iconic of the bronzes, the most recognized anthropomorphic depiction of god Shiva as the cosmic dancer. Yet, it felt odd and unexpected that he knew of it. As she walked over to stand by his side, something niggled at the back of her mind, something that she felt she was forgetting.

The bronze was no match for the old idols in the temples but exhibited respectable workmanship that grasped the essential nature of the great dance.

"You like the Nataraja?" she asked with the beginnings of grudging respect.

He paused for a moment considering his answer.

"It's what Tom would like. I'd prefer it to be taller," he said, spoiling any good opinion that she might have allowed to form. At about three feet, Vidya thought the idol was quite tall.

"You know of the iconography?" she persisted with suppressed curiosity.

"Uh-huh, *News week* did a cover piece with Obama in this pose."

Whatever little bonhomie and semblance of respect that had begun to sprout inside her died a quick, violent death. She was disappointed, perhaps more deeply than she ought to have been.

Her mother's voice chanting the *Thiruvasagam* came to her.

She felt the need to defend the treasure trove of symbolism that the idol depicted, to say something clever and compelling about how scholars and scientists and philosophers have interpreted the Nataraja for ages. But her own knowledge of all that the idol represented was limited and superficial. She was fair-minded enough to acknowledge the irony of that, yet felt thoroughly justified in her outrage at his callous and flippant dismissal of something so iconic.

"Nataraja represents some profound, core tenets of Hinduism," she said, bristling with righteous indignation.

"Uh-huh."

"Your father, I understand, had studied the *Upanishads*?" The question was innocent enough, but the mild disbelief and censure in her voice couldn't have escaped him.

His eyes met hers in a silent duel. "I have no idea, though it sounds like something he would have read," he responded, unmoved, regarding her as though she was a petulant child.

She averted her glance to hide her irritation.

An old man inspecting a brass lamp nearby, met her eyes, and muttered in a low voice in Tamil. "Can the donkey know the perfume of the incense?"

It was an old proverb about refined sensibilities, apt for the situation; she bit back her laughter.

Feeling Josh's intense gaze, she turned. His eyes bored into hers, making her suspect he knew the comment was about him.

"Is there a salesman around?" he asked, his voice impatient, even harsh.

She hailed a salesman, identifiable as much by his seasoned air as by a name tag tucked into the front pocket of his shirt. He greeted her with a polite, "Tell me, madam."

"Do you ship abroad?" Josh wanted to know.

"Where to, sir?"

"Zurich," he responded at the same time she said, "London."

"Zurich," Josh corrected firmly. "I will get it sent from there on Tom's birthday."

The salesman confirmed with an artless pride that they routinely dispatched items to cities all over Europe and that many foreigners bought their goods.

As soon as she finished translating his words, Josh fired the next question. "How long would it take?"

"What are you interested in, sir?" The salesman looked expectantly, so did Vidya.

"That Nataraja and maybe a few other items."

"By ship, it should reach you within a month."

"You'd take care of it through and through?"

"Yes, sir, we have agents to take care of all the formalities."

Josh stood staring blankly at the idol, seemingly processing what the salesman had said.

The salesman pointed out the idol's workmanship and emphasized it was a particularly good buy.

Josh nodded absent-mindedly, but continued to stand there without any further questions.

Vidya and the salesman exchanged remarks about the weather.

After a polite interval, the salesman asked if Josh would like to buy the idol.

"Do you have anything taller?" he asked.

"No, sir," the salesman shook his head. "You would have to commission one, it won't be available ready-made. If you are interested, we could check with our suppliers in Swamimalai and get back to you about the cost and the time."

"Yes, please do. Cost is not a problem," Josh declared.

He then proceeded to take down the man's phone number, promising to call him later in the afternoon. Vidya felt a sense of discord.

After the conversation, he looked at her and gently tilted his head toward the steps as though he was done.

As they walked down toward the exit, Vidya followed Josh's gaze and noticed the object of his curiosity was once more the billing counter where a different man sat now.

It was nothing but a couple of desks forming an enclosure. A picture of Ganesha was on the wall, and below that a bunch of half-burnt incense sticks exuded smoky straight lines heading toward the ceiling. The man in the counter sat behind a computer and was billing the purchases of a middle-aged woman, talking to her animatedly about them.

"Anything the matter?"

"Um ... no, I was just ... curious about the billing system."

They trooped silently out of the store to where she had parked her car.

"Do you know where I can get a bottle of water?" he asked apologetically. "I am parched."

He accepted her suggestion that he wait inside the car with an insulting alacrity. Leaving him to his devices, Vidya walked over to a small shop nearby to buy a couple of bottles of water.

"Next store?" she asked simply once she got back, and he nodded, after thanking her for the water that he proceeded to gulp down thirstily.

This time as they drove, he toyed with his phone, and Vidya noticed with surprise he was looking at a map app, seemingly tracking their route. He asked her a few questions about other stores, mangling their names beyond recognition, about how big they were, were they well reputed, and had they been around for long.

After the quiz, he remained mostly silent except for a stray remark or two on the lack of road signs and the traffic, steering clear of any other topic.

The same story continued in Mint Street. Vidya grew progressively silent as he got more adept at understanding the gestures of the Indian salesmen. The store had two large Nataraja idols right in the front yard, yet they did not satisfy his height fixation.

He simply repeated his interest in spending a lot of money to buy a spectacular bronze idol for his brother and took down more numbers, promising to call back.

As they headed out, they crossed the counter. "Hand-written receipts?" he exclaimed with incredulity. There was a moment of silence, and then meeting her eyes, he said with an ironic smile, "Just ... curious."

The smile muted the obnoxious derisiveness of his earlier comment and confused her. Vidya decided she would not mention the rotating power cuts that they endured, which would only reinforce an opinion that they belonged in the Dark Ages.

Back in the car, they didn't talk much. She rolled up the windows, got the air-conditioning on, and wordlessly offered him another bottle of water, afraid he'd keel over due to dehydration. At the rate he was sweating and the color of his skin, it seemed like a distinct possibility. She also handed him a box of tissue as he dabbed at his forehead with his sleeve. She concentrated on carefully negotiating her little car around potholes and speed bumps, lest he hit his head on the low top and faint.

It was for Tom's sake she must endure this, she carefully reminded herself, though that shouldn't prevent her from hastening things a bit.

The fifth store was government run. One look at the staid premises and he bolted right out. After that, Vidya decided with grim determination that she would take him to the most pretentious shop in town, one that would totally rip him off. She took the shortest route through small by-lanes, and they arrived in record time at Sarathy's.

The metal board displaying the name was understated but elegant. The large display window showcased a single stone sculpture of Krishna, playing his flute, a smile of mystery and charm adorning his handsome face. They walked into a cool, well-lit hall with a high ceiling. The subtle smell of a lavender air freshener permeated the space. There was faint sitar music that set the mood yet was not intrusive. The few bronzes were placed in a section of their own, in neat rows, under lamps that strategically highlighted the craftsmanship.

The salesmen wore ties and spoke English slowly, clearly trained to deal with foreigners. Josh perked up visibly and carried on a conversation with the salesman, pretty much ignoring her. He was a consummate rich American ready to pay the big bucks for a seven-foot bronze idol of the Nataraja.

The salesman signaled to someone, and an unopened, chilled can of Coke was soon presented to Josh. Proceeding to open it, the salesman poured it onto a glass, and offered it to Josh with deference. As he sipped it delicately, the salesman spoke at length, assuring Josh of their exceptional service.

"Please have a look here, sir." He pointed to a four-foot Nataraja. Vidya looked at the discreet label surreptitiously, and her brows went up at the fifteen thousand dollars price tag. Granted, it seemed to fit his requirements better than most, but it wasn't in any way better than the ones she had shown him earlier.

Josh still prevaricated. She had absolutely expected him to flip his credit card. But, instead, he dithered and continued to ask his usual set of questions to the salesman—would they ship abroad, when would it reach Zurich, what would the approximate price be, did they have branches or tie-ups in Europe, and lastly, would he be able to get a bigger Nataraja?

He then casually yet clearly moved away toward the exit, and the salesman and Vidya trudged behind. The salesman offered to check back with the suppliers in Swamimalai when he realized Josh was set on acquiring a taller Nataraja and nothing else. Josh took his card as well and promised to call back later in the evening.

They walked out empty-handed again.

She grudgingly admitted to herself he was being thorough. He now had answers to the same questions from at least six different stores and would likely get the best deal. But the methodical approach, she thought, stripped off any element of love from the process of buying a gift.

Josh then made her wait while he fiddled with his tablet, standing right in front of the store. Something urgent he had to take care of, he mumbled distractedly. He gazed intently at his tablet and typed furiously, not budging from the spot.

What could possibly be so important that he had to stand in the hot sun with fat beads of sweat forming on his forehead and running to his brows? He looked up after a full three minutes and had the grace to mumble an apology, but to Vidya, it was woefully vague and inadequate.

She began to think of engineering a polite way to part. As they headed out, her mind was already at work, on the potential clients she could still visit that afternoon.

Chapter 11

Josh dropped his tablet back into his bag. Sensing his movement, she turned toward him and he nodded that he was ready. She led the way back to her car that was parked just a few feet away.

The afternoon sun was beginning its descent but was still blazing hot. He was fully drenched with sweat within the few minutes of standing outdoors. Heat had built up inside the car, and Vidya unrolled the windows to let in some air circulation. She also switched on the AC. Josh wiped the sweat off his brows and neck, grateful for the rush of cool air.

Traffic was light; buses, the color of sand and muddy brown, ran half empty. A metro corridor seemed to snake through most of the roads he had visited, but he didn't actually spot anything running on it.

Thanks to the sweltering heat haze, he felt drained. How on earth did she manage to look bright after the blitz of the energy sucking sun?

It was half past one, and as if on cue, she asked what his lunch plans were. His body seemed to be finally reconciling to the fact that it was afternoon. Josh was glad to feel hungry again, but didn't want to take his chance with hot Indian food right then.

"Is there a KFC or a McDonald's type fast food joint anywhere around here?" he asked hopefully. He just wanted something familiar, however unhealthy it might be. Besides it had the added advantage of annoying Tom who was bound to hear about it.

She paused and thought for a while. "McDonald's is a little far. There are some pizza chains nearby," she suggested instead.

Josh said that would do.

As she drove through the streets, Josh stared outside at the sights, too tired to follow up on the routes in his phone.

The city was dusty and was built of unimaginative low-rise buildings.

The roads and lanes were winding, uneven, and occasionally leafy. There were many bicycles and motorcycles on the road and many more parked by the roadside. He could spot no parks or squares or wide-open spaces.

Colorful posters covered the walls, billboards loomed high, announcing movies, greeting politicians, newlyweds, religious leaders, and a few in black and white mourning someone's death, words both in English and in the pretzel letters of the local language. In one stretch of the road, large billboards recurred every few feet with an image of the same lady, the honorable chief minister, he read. He figured outdoor advertising must be a profitable business in Chennai.

In fascination, he watched the little tuk-tuks, Vidya had called them auto-rickshaws, with their bright yellow bodies weaving in and out with much dexterity.

And there were people, men and women and children, walking briskly, standing expectantly, talking on the phone, and in one case squatting on the pavement ...

His phone beeped, and he saw an incoming text from Tom. *Can you talk now?* It was early for Tom and the message was abrupt.

No, I am with your friend. What is it? He responded and awaited Tom's next words, hoping it would contain an update from the investigator.

They finally arrived at a pizza place, which was mostly empty except for a couple of working professionals. The restaurant, part of a US chain, looked brighter than it did in Seattle. A television was playing some news channel that didn't feel any different from the American news channels. At least three lines of text in English with breaking news, stock market tickers, and tweets scrolled on the bottom of the screen.

Vidya sat tight-lipped, with no remnants of a smile. Josh realized his actions perhaps came across as ill-bred. *I am single-minded, so sue me,* he thought.

With a simple excuse, she turned slightly away to make a telephone call. Though she spoke in soft tones, since it was in English, he could mostly follow. It was about some compliance related paperwork that she was going to send for someone's signature. It sounded important but also reinforced the lack of reliance on electronic data. He wondered what she did for a living.

His phone beeped again, indicating the arrival of Tom's response.

The PI tracked a garage attendant who recalled a delivery to the art gallery in our time window. Guess why? Because it was an 8X7X3 feet box and weighed a ton. He remembered the name of the trucking company.

Josh felt the words hit him like the first nail in a coffin, supplying an unwelcome strength to their fragile suppositions.

A young waiter brought them the menu. Josh studied it, his mind on the problem at hand. This was still not conclusive proof, he told himself, massaging his temples.

He felt gloomy; he was not familiar with the feeling of being ineffectual, almost helpless. Most people spoke English, but their accent was thick, and he had to make an effort to understand them, let alone pick up any nuance or grasp a hint that could provide a clue. Technology wasn't as pervasive as he had thought it would be. The sights, the smell, the noises, the weather, everything was so alien that he felt disconcerted and disoriented.

Even the sun shone different.

This was as he had thought, a futile, mad, mad trip. He felt the now recurrent impatience wash over him.

Tom must be anxious to talk, he realized, but he didn't want to call Tom in front of her. He wondered if she sensed something was amiss. For now, though, she was simply treating him to a chilling courtesy.

"What would you like?" she asked, breaking the silence.

"Hmm ... no pepperoni ... " He stared at the menu. "Chicken?"

She suggested he get a medium pizza for himself, politely explaining she was vegetarian and ordered some pasta for herself.

The jet lag was playing havoc with his system. His eyes felt gritty, his brows heavy, and his body was stiff. He hoped he wouldn't get an upset stomach as well. He had been careful to not eat anything spicy, but he had already gulped down a mouthful of water from the tap that morning before his sleepy brain had registered that he was in India. The litany of diseases he could get scrolled up in his mental screen.

"Tom says he likes Indian food. He is very enthusiastic about trying new cuisines," she said. And then, as an afterthought, she smiled in an effort to take the edge off her voice.

He nodded, played with the cutlery, looked around.

She stared at the television screen, checked her phone, and texted someone.

We could very well be a long-married couple, he thought wryly.

"So you are into computers? What exactly do you do?" she asked, clearly wanting to break the silence that was beginning to get uncomfortable.

"I am primarily a network security expert, but of late, I am doing more of general digital forensics."

"Sounds glamorous," she said. "Or do you just dust fingerprints off of computers?"

"Something like that." He smiled at her attempt at humor.

He commented on the weather for his turn, but it sounded trite even to his own ears. It seemed a strain to think of anything interesting to say. He didn't know what to do with her; that was to say, under the circumstance.

"You and Tom are very different, aren't you?" she asked.

Josh was irked, interpreting disapproval in the seemingly innocent question.

"Yes, we are," he said tersely and drummed his fingers on the table impatiently. He did not like people who were judgmental like her, besides it was her dear Tom who had gotten him into this mess in the first place.

Evidently, she didn't understand his irritation or perhaps wanted to goad him. She blithely continued in the same vein, talking of Tom again, of the scholar that he was, of his adventurous spirit.

She thankfully grew silent after a few moments, catching on to his disinterest. She stared outside, her face betraying a certain disappointment, even mild anger.

He intently stared at the TV screen. The panel discussion, he could tell from the ticker, was about some sort of an anniversary of the present government. There was a weather report, and Josh saw that the mercury was still soaring across the sub-continent with deaths being reported due to the heat wave. It was not just the temperature; it was also the prickliness of the heat. He grabbed a couple of tissues and wiped his face and neck, thankful about the coolness of the room.

"Are there any other major stores?" he asked after the silence stretched for a minute. It was not her fault really, and he ought to mind his manners.

"Not really. If these stores don't have it, it's highly unlikely you'd get it in any other. Maybe you could revisit them and try commissioning one," she said.

"You," not "we," he noted. She had given up on the idea of accompanying him. Josh couldn't really blame her. She was quite a nice girl and had been quite patient so far.

She read an incoming text and suppressed a smile. Josh had a feeling she was texting her friends about him. He could only hope she wasn't tweeting. Hashtag MoronAtLunch.

This beautiful young woman likely thought he was a brute. *Thank you, Tom, I owe you.*

The food arrived, providing a much-needed break from having to stare at the TV screen intently. She seemed equally happy about it.

"You seem to know Tom really well," he said as a truce offering as they started eating.

"Yes, for quite some time now. He is so knowledgeable, not just about India, in general of culture and history and politics, he is amazing ... "

"Hmm." *Alright, alright, enough with the gushing.*

"He is quite the charmer, a true renaissance man, a free thinker—"

"You seem to be completely in love with him." He had intended for the comment to be playful, but it came out offensive, rude.

She stiffened. "And it matters to you how?" It was not a question, but a challenge, bringing the simmering antagonism out into the open.

"Tom is gay," he snapped and immediately regretted his nasty voice. The right response would have been a gentle shrug, a big smile and a light, "Everyone loves Tom."

Whatever had possessed him to react so badly?

She quickly turned away, but not before he got a look of loathing and disgust. Josh was horrified by the sudden realization that she might not have known Tom's sexual orientation before. He mentally cursed. He had messed up badly.

They finished the rest of the meal in haste with hardly any conversation. She was completely withdrawn, her mouth clamped shut, frown lines between her brows. A comment about the spiciness of the pizza and the weather earned a monosyllabic response from her.

After lunch, she said she was really sorry she had to cut the day short, but she had to go back to her work.

"Unavoidable," she said with cold civility. She would be happy to drop him back at the hotel though.

Josh made concurring sounds, said he completely understood, that he would follow up with the stores later. He was deeply troubled as to whether it was his disclosure about Tom that made her want to leave.

They went back to the hotel, the long drive made bearable by the official sounding calls she had had to take allowing him to remain lost in thought. She parked the car in front of the gate, clearly intending to leave without getting out. A bright thank you from him elicited a nod and a wish for a happy stay.

He walked back into the hotel slowly, reflecting on his next steps. He had taken out his helplessness and tiredness on her. He was uncomfortable about it, but he didn't dwell on it either. He had bigger problems. He needed a new guide, and he better get back to the approach he had put in the back burner to track the source; otherwise they'd run out of time.

Chapter 12

Josh rode the elevator and walked through the silent corridor toward his room. A male housekeeper hurrying with a set of towels paused to wish him a good afternoon. Josh returned the greeting absent-mindedly, swiped his key card, and stepped into his room.

The room was cool and quiet, and the sheer cotton curtains were drawn to cut out the full glare of the tropical sun. Josh pushed the screen aside and stared at the late afternoon, pale blue sky outside the window. The scenery outside, a concrete jungle of low-rise buildings with few trees, was drab.

He fished out his phone and dialed Tom's number.

Tom answered the phone on the first ring. Tom always claimed to be in the middle of something, and it would be the fourth ring before he would get to the phone; obviously, he had been waiting for Josh's call that day. It was mid-morning in London. Josh could hear ambient cafe noises in the background. He guessed Tom must have stepped out for a brunch, possibly having skipped breakfast in his anxiety.

"Saw my note?"

"No preamble, huh?" Josh grimaced.

"Did you?"

"Yes, I did. It doesn't prove anything."

"Right!" Tom snorted. "The box has the dimensions to fit the unusually large idol in my possession, and it doesn't prove anything."

"Tom, listen ... "

"No, let's not get into that yet. First tell me, where are you now? How was your day?"

Josh stared outside, wondering if Tom was regretting his decision to track the idol. A cat lazily roamed the roof of a neighboring building, and cumulus clouds very few and far between drifted lethargically across the dull blue expanse. He turned away.

"My day was mostly wasted. I am back in the hotel after the roundup. Let's see, I can confirm an idol of that size is unusual and rarely ready-made even today. As for the stores, a couple of them are candidates but nothing conclusive."

There was a short silence, punctured by the sound from some cutlery. "I was really hoping you'd have better news. The acquisition has been formally reviewed by the registrar and the recommendation fully approved by the director. We are cleared to pay a portion of the money right away, and the copy for the press is ready."

"I am going to advise you to—"

"I know what your advice is. I have duly noted it."

"And?"

"Is there anything else you can do to track?"

Josh sighed. "All right, Tom, I'll see what I can do. The name of the trucking company would definitely help."

"Thanks, I will send it to you. I have told the PI to continue looking for the source."

He still had to break the news about Vidya. Josh rubbed his eyes, so not wanting to explain. He recognized, uncomfortably, that he might have underestimated their closeness and if Vidya grew distant now, it'd break Tom's heart.

"Tom?" he said, his voice sounding weary and subdued to his own ears.

"Yes?"

"I need a new guide."

"What did you do?" Tom tone was full of reproach and irritation now.

"What do you mean what did I do?" Josh asked indignantly. He sat on the bed and kicked off his shoes.

"Remember the Asia map incident?"

"I was ten, and it was an accident, for God's sake. Besides, I confessed within five minutes after you came in," Josh responded, falling on his back onto the bed.

"Yeah right! Accident! Anyway, when you finally came out from under the bed, the first thing you said was 'Tom' in that same tone."

Josh groaned. "Like hell I did."

"What happened? Vidya is smart and sensible—"

"And I'm not?" Josh interrupted, spoiling for a fight.

"Josh." Tom's voice held a warning note. Josh took a deep breath and tried not to aggravate the situation further.

He knew he was stalling. Having to tell Tom what he had done was painful.

"God! She kept talking about you. You are the sun and the moon, and she looked at me like I am some moron and—"

"What. Happened."

"Well, I snapped at her and said that she shouldn't fall in love with you because you were gay." Josh tensed as soon as the words were out.

"Tom?" There was a small silence. "I shouldn't have revealed that, man. I am so very sorry." Josh apologized awkwardly, sincerely.

"Why? I have been out for years." Tom's voice was calm, impatient, but calm.

"Well, she is Indian, and I don't know what impact this information will have on your relationship. I had no right. I may have jeopardized your friendship. I feel terrible."

"Ah!" said Tom after a few moments. "As much as I am tempted to milk this, in the interest of time, let me put your troubled mind at rest. She knows."

"She knows?" Josh hadn't expected that. "I didn't realize you were that close."

"You chose not to," said Tom. His voice taking on stern undertones, he added, "But you snapping at her is unforgivable."

While he was annoyed with her—couldn't she have told him that she knew, before storming off in righteous indignation?—Josh was relieved her disgust had been for his own uncouth behavior, and not for Tom.

At his silence, Tom continued, "No response? Do I take it you agree that your behavior was unforgivable?"

"Oh, I was responding alright. I was extending my middle finger."

"I should've known." There was faint amusement in Tom's voice.

"Okay, let's talk about options. I am gonna get a cab—"

Tom interrupted right off the bat. He wanted to disclose everything to Vidya. They went back and forth, arguing the pros and cons of involving her, all pros naturally listed by Tom. The only con he would allow was that it was potentially dangerous.

"Face it, Tom. If we don't get conclusive evidence that it is stolen, if on the chance you do decide to proceed with the sale, she would always have a hold on you. You trust her that much?" Josh asked, already aware the answer was likely going to be a yes. What was impressive was the swiftness with which it was delivered.

"Yes, I do," said Tom right away. "She is my friend, Josh. Last winter when uh ... Jason moved out, she was a pillar of support. You—you were practically gloating."

Josh winced a little. He didn't think her helping Tom through a breakup meant much under the circumstance but decided it was prudent to remain silent.

"Before you left, you told me she was just a face on the screen and questioned the prudence of entrusting oneself based on a single dimensional relationship. You have looked at her now. What do you think?"

Josh dithered. "Umm ... she has a nice rack, long legs, tight ass—"

"Must you resort to crude levity, Josh Winslow?" Tom interrupted in a scathing voice.

Josh smiled despite himself; he could easily push Tom's buttons. Tom was too serious. He mimicked, "Must you resort to haughty gravity, Tom Winslow?"

"Does she seem trustworthy or not?" Tom asked, enunciating the words one by one.

"I suppose so," he admitted grudgingly. "But that could be a moot point, I doubt she'd come back, even under the onslaught of your full on charm."

Tom laughed. "I'll talk to her."

"Sure."

"Only I don't know her phone number, and she is not online." Tom sounded worried. "We have Skyped and chatted every day, but I never knew her cell number. Can you find it please?"

It was likely easier to find her phone number than dissuading Tom. "Hmm ... Okay."

"Just so you know, her last name is Thyagarajan, not very unique, and sometimes she goes by T. Vidya, as most people in Tamil Nadu," Tom fretted.

Josh painstakingly took down the spelling, before ending the conversation.

He stood up and stretched.

Reaching for his bag, he pulled out and powered up his laptop. A quick check confirmed there were no directories or white pages he could refer. Rubbing his palms in anticipation, he plugged in some music.

He could find her workplace and call there with some story and try to get her personal number. He wasn't sure if his accent would be of help or a hindrance.

Deciding to try a simpler approach first, he looked up the cell number series for the Chennai zone operators and picked the first four digit combinations for the top providers. Four down, still lot of digits to go. He quickly modified his custom search engine crawler with seed sites relating to social media and India. He customized the algorithm further by using a distance ranking so it would prioritize webpages where her name and the phone number appeared closer together. He also added words like phone, mobile, call, and number into the mix.

He ran his program and, while it searched, walked up to the mini bar and got himself an Indian beer and opened a can of Pringles. He plopped down on the chair and wondered whether, even if he found the number, she would listen to Tom.

He smiled in memory of Tom's indignation at his comment about her looks. He wondered if she was single; there hadn't been a wedding ring, but she might be in a committed relationship.

"Woke up in London yesterday!" he sang along with One Republic, "This is gonna be a good life!"

Running quickly through the result index that his program was spitting out, he found the name Vidya and fully formed phone numbers in quite a few websites. He could spot about ten distinct phone numbers right away. Of course hers might still not be any of those, but he was an optimist.

He looked up more details on each of the numbers. Four of the Vidyas turned out to be advertising some product or other. The fifth was a Mrs. Vidya, who seemed unaware of privacy settings in Facebook and posted gazillion pictures of her baby. Next was a doctor's number from a hospital's appointment system. He dialed the sixth number, listed in some company website, and the voice that answered wasn't remotely close. The seventh had a photo of a woman who was older by a few decades.

The eighth was from a mailing list archive. There was a mail to the group from Vidya, listing her cell number, seeking blood donors for her father's surgery. It was signed off just as Vidya but the "From" field was Vidya Thyagarajan.

The Web knows all, and the Web remembers all, he smiled.

He toyed for a moment with the idea of calling the number to check but decided against it. Some instinct told him it was her. He called Tom instead.

"Did her father undergo a heart surgery recently?" he asked Tom.

"Yes." The surprise in Tom's voice was perceptible.

"Okay then, here you go. I got you her phone number." He rattled off the number and then read the email.

There was a beat of silence on the line.

"You can say it, Tom. I am a genius."

"Yeah, yeah, okay," said Tom, with equal measures of humor and exasperation.

After hanging up, through Tom's account, he looked up her Facebook posts. Tom's password was easy to break. Pictures of cute babies, dogs, rain, trees, flowers, and inspirational quotes abounded. She and Tom always liked each other's posts. It almost seemed like a requirement. There wasn't any sign of a boyfriend. She had not chosen to update her relationship status in Facebook. He spent some time on her book reviews in Goodreads.

He then got to her LinkedIn profile and gathered she worked for a major multinational bank as a customer relationship manager, whatever that was. Her two brothers lived in Europe and Australia.

She had said the hospital was in an area called Mylapore in the email. After some hops, he found an obituary item in a local newspaper announcing the death of her mother a few years earlier. The voters list for that area got him her home address and her exact age. She must have been in college when her mother died.

Deciding that was enough of stalking for the day, he stopped.

Feeling good about himself, he got up and stretched again. He saw the time, noticed the evening was still young, and, deciding it was better to tire his body out, went looking for the pool.

Josh walked through the well-lit lobby littered with fashionably dressed people. A young man in a suit was playing the piano, his fingers gliding on the keys, producing a jazzy tune filling the air. The restaurant was open, though empty. He walked past, following directions to the pool.

The outdoor pool side with trees lining the area was pleasant. The trees rustled, the gentle breeze made quiet ripples on the water surface, and a stray leaf danced softly down. The air was heavy with the scent of unknown tropical flowers.

Josh felt his tension ebbing away as he plunged into the warm water. After a vigorous thirty laps, he came up and reclined on a chaise.

The sun was well on its way to set. There were a few other Caucasians, who nodded to him. A woman lounged nearby, possibly American. A waiter came by to get his order.

Over the glass of the champagne that was soon delivered, he debated whether he should introduce himself to the woman or not. Deciding this was not the moment, he just leaned back instead, with his music on.

The branches swayed, and Josh could feel the welcome breeze presumably from the Bay of Bengal.

Soon it was twilight, and he sat staring at the darkening sky.

A memory of his dad cycling with the two of them to the open fields for star gazing popped into his mind. He remembered the moment from years ago with a clarity that was startling, from Tom's big-for-his-age philosophical questions, to the rough grounds, to the dark bejeweled sky, down to the cool air against their skin as they raced their bikes.

He tried to work out the constellations. Unable to do it on his own, he took out his phone from the pouch and downloaded a sky map app.

Cosmology had held tremendous fascination for his father, a physicist and a philosopher. On an impulse, he logged into the cloud account where he kept his father's papers and searched for any reference to Nataraja. He was astounded to find one.

His father had written a lengthy paper on particle physics, and quoting Bohr and Capra had interpreted quantum inter connectedness and bosons in the context of ancient philosophies. Captivated, Josh read that paper, as well as excerpts from Capra. "For the modern physicists, then, Shiva's dance is the dance of subatomic matter."

He had written almost a page about the Nataraja idol, going into raptures about his handsome face and wild hair and how his dance represented the cosmic dance of particles, of energy, of continuous destruction and creation.

As he read through his father's well-researched, well-written paper, he regretted that his father hadn't lived to hear about the discovery of Higgs-boson. Or for that matter, hadn't had an opportunity to see the Nataraja idol that was in Tom's possession.

He then wondered if his father ever really saw an idol.

He recalled Vidya's barely concealed outrage earlier in the store at his indifference. Perhaps it was justified. He recognized for the first time, with newfound respect, the importance of such an antique idol and with unease, the gravity of his mission.

After a while, he got up and headed to his room. Tom's incoming text was terse. *Vidya will see you tomorrow.*

The young woman had caught up with a group of her friends, and they were talking about their work. Josh could make out they were part of the software industry and were there for a conference.

Whether it was the laps in the pool or the useful minutes on his computer, he didn't know, but he felt much better. He could even see the humor in the situation.

He ordered in a light dinner, a chicken kheema pav and a pint of beer. He would have liked to order a salad but wasn't feeling courageous enough to try uncooked food.

He settled in with his laptop, and looked up the information about the trucking company. He was able to break in very quickly into their systems, thanks to a basic SQL injection vulnerability. By the time he got to the small lava cake on the house, he had not only broken in but was rifling through their data.

He found some interesting contracts that opened up other avenues for exploration. Though he was able to access active data, the details corresponding to their shipment had already been archived, which posed a temporary setback.

It had been a long day, and Josh found himself feeling drowsy. He decided to take a break and pick things up in the morning, the sooner his body got into the rhythm of day and night, the better.

His phone beeped. *No further insights from the PI*, said the text from Tom.

It beeped again. *Don't muck it up this time with Vidya,* Tom added helpfully.

He rolled his eyes and put away the laptop and phone to charge.

Yawning hugely, he settled on the comfortable bed and fell quickly and deeply asleep.

Chapter 13

Vidya stared blankly at the patch of sky through the silhouette of the branches and leaves. Sprawled on the comfortable cane chair, her foot up on the low table, her hair behind the backrest, she sat still, too perplexed to get on with her chores. Even Amit Trivedi's alluring "Sham bhi koi," flowing over the headset did nothing to calm her.

The sun had set, painting the late evening sky a dark grey. The lights were beginning to come on in the neighboring houses and the mosquito army was swelling in numbers; she really ought to get up, switch on their porch light and get inside.

She had reached home by about half past five after squeezing in an hour at work. Seeing her arrive, the neighborhood kids had enticed her to a game of street cricket. Now that school had reopened, they had complained they didn't have too much time to play. The spirited game with its noisy exuberance had helped her get over her earlier disappointment.

The day had not been a complete waste after all.

It was past six by the time she had quit the game. RST, clad in his white vetti and white shirt, was back from his evening walk with observations on the protracted heat and the lack of breeze.

He raised his brows as they crossed the threshold together. "I thought you were going to be late what with all the association with the capitalist? Here you are playing cricket."

"I brought the association to a quick end," she responded, shaking her head.

"That is good news but rather unexpected," said her father dryly.

He sat on the sofa, beckoned her to sit as well and gently prodded the story out of her. The ceiling fan droned on as they talked. She recounted

Josh's behavior at the hotel and in the stores with quick clarity and a good dose of sarcastic humor.

"All in all, he mostly spoke in monosyllables, and when he put a few sentences together, I wished he had stuck to the monosyllables," she finished.

RST's mouth creased into an indulgent smile. Still, he reasoned, "Perhaps you had great expectations; perhaps you thought Josh would be another Tom. That wouldn't have been fair to the man."

That comment pricked her enough to protest. Josh's lack of even minimal touristy interest in anything other than the idol and his overall reticence was annoying enough for anyone. For Tom's brother, it was a crime!

"He has had a long journey, must have been jet-lagged. Besides, he certainly is not the first person to use money as a means of showing love, let it go," RST shrugged with a smile.

It must have been the overall disappointment that made her snap at him in response. "Oh, since when are you so forgiving in your judgement? When it comes to your own children, to our so-called materialistic behavior, you are usually full of disdain and contempt."

RST's smile faltered and he shot her a telling look.

He had then paused for a moment, a frown on his face, and had stood up. "Clearly you have had a disappointing day. Relax for a while."

His parting shot had been, "Look at the bright side—he is not an idol smuggler."

***

The empty coffee cup near her brought back the memory of the large cup of black coffee Josh had drunk that morning. She supposed India could be a bit of an overload on the senses for someone unfamiliar with the scene. Even accounting for all that, there had been something off about the whole day.

Gathering her cup, she headed to the kitchen to prepare dinner. She busied herself with cooking, her mind still inevitably mulling over the events. On a normal day, she would be exchanging messages or even talking to Tom by then, about her dinner plans, his morning and a variety of topics. She would not go online yet, she decided. She needed to think about her responses to questions Tom was sure to ask.

Josh had been inconsiderate and ignorant of her cultural sensibilities. Many of the idols from the Chola period were being worshipped in grand old temples across South India. They were sacred, part of a living, breathing, unbroken tradition of over a thousand years. Tom would have been more respectful.

Her thoughts wandered to the conversation with RST. Her words to him had been neither wise, nor fully just. He never criticized them personally, his comments were usually detached and few and far between, nothing to warrant her phrasing. He was the most selfless man she ever knew with very meager possessions and she was cognizant of her own insecurity about his approval.

She chopped cabbage into small shreds for a lightly salted and mildly spiced vegetable while the tomato rasam boiled. The pressure cooker hissed, announcing the millet was well cooked, and she felt herself calm down at the familiar noise and chores.

Then, with a sudden, shocking clarity, RST's words about idol smugglers came back to her and she realized what had bothered her all day. She paused chopping the vegetables mid-way, her hand holding the knife still.

Abandoning her task, she rushed to pull out her phone from the charger. She opened a browser, and quickly searched for Terpsichore. Wikipedia said Terpsichore was the muse for dancing.

Nataraja was the god of dance.

Tom had been distracted and the clue was for her to identify an acquisition.

Her thoughts raced through impossible scenarios as she slowly walked back and finished the cooking, almost in reflex.

What was Tom up to?

She had known him for over a year now. On behalf of her neighbor, a seventy-year-old retired history professor, Vidya had emailed a query to the museum. It had landed in Tom's inbox and he had responded. They had continued to write back and forth and had become friends, best friends really.

But ultimately, he was a face on the screen, a voice over ether, she thought. Was she being naïve and gullible and a pawn in some elaborate underworld machinations?

Her phone rang.

The caller ID showed a 44 country code. She stared at it for a few seconds and let it ring and stop. The ringing from the same number started again, insistent, as though the caller knew she was having second thoughts. She picked up the call with a tentative hello.

"Hey, Vidya, so what are you cooking today?" said a familiar voice.

"Tom?" she enquired, disbelieving. Then she laughed at the opening line. "My God! Tom!"

"Yes, hey, I am sorry to bother you. Can you talk for a few minutes?" he asked, his baritone voice close and clear without the disturbances of a Skype call on Wi-Fi.

This was Tom, Tom her friend. Surely, no one could consistently fake a personality over a period of one year. Despite the barrier of the online relation, or perhaps fueled by it, they had shared their inner dilemmas, their hopes and aspirations freely. She knew him. She felt a reassurance and a little discomfiture for her earlier, albeit momentary, doubt about Tom.

"Yes, sure. How did you get my number?" she asked.

"Never mind that. Tell me about your day, kiddo. I understand it didn't go well?"

Vidya paused for a second, warmth spreading at the familiar endearment.

"Vidya?" he queried, reminding her of his question. There was a trace of laughter.

"I'd say that's an understatement," she said slowly.

"Yeah, Josh said you wouldn't go anywhere near him again even if your life depended on it."

Vidya paused for a beat. "He said that?"

"Yes."

He realized that? Vidya was surprised. She had thought he hadn't been aware of her ire, that he did not demonstrate an ounce of empathy or insight. At best, she had expected him to tell Tom she wasn't of any help.

"Tom, what's going on? Your acquisition, is it somehow connected to a Chola bronze, a Nataraja?"

Tom became silent for a moment and then added in his usual forthright manner, "I told him there was no need to hide things from you. You're right. It has to do with a Chola bronze. I have acquired one, only I don't know where it came from."

"How could you not know?"

"I wish I could see your face. It's hard to explain on the phone. There are too many little details and I have a meeting now that I must attend. It'll be late for you by the time we finish. The bottom-line is, I have in my possession an antique bronze—"

"You already do?"

"Yes, but I don't know its origins. Can you meet Josh once more tomorrow? I'll ask him to tell you everything. And then you can decide what to do next. Please."

Tom's voice was beseeching and serious. Vidya felt a strange foreboding, but she couldn't bring herself to say no.

"All right, I will," she said.

"Thanks, Vidya, I owe you." The relief in Tom's voice was apparent. "Let us talk tomorrow again, okay?"

"Okay."

"And, hey, you know what?"

"What?"

"Give him a chance. I know you'll love him."

Vidya waited a beat and then said dryly, "I'll settle for tolerate."

He laughed, but rang off in a hurry.

Tom was in some kind of trouble, and she would do everything she could to help him. She put the phone down, bursting with curiosity, excitement even.

***

A little later, she set the table and beckoned RST to dinner. There was a curious tension about him that she realized came from her earlier comment that hung in the air, unexplained. The topic was not revived by either of them.

He remarked something about the condition of the migrant laborers working on a high-rise building coming up a couple of kilometers away. He would later note down points in his thick diary to be presented forcefully in some conference full of sundry union members, bent upon blocking development, she thought with mild exasperation.

They also caught up on neighborhood news and family gossip as they slowly finished their dinner.

Vidya cleared up, mixed up the leftover, and went out to dump it in the bowl for the street dog. As if on cue, it came wagging its tail, sniffed approval, and lapped the food up. The kitchen was spic and span, and she drew a small pattern of kolam on the granite top. The interleaving pattern in white powder against the black stone looked neat and pleasing. Her mother had done it for religious reasons, and she had picked up the habit after her mother's death for sentimental reasons. She stared at it absently for a few moments, feeling a lump in her throat.

RST came in to get his bottle of water after having finished watching the news. He must have caught her staring at the kolam, but he didn't comment on it.

He must have seen her mother draw the kolam hundreds of times. Did he ever bother to admire it? Arranged marriages usually brought together a man and a woman of similar background, with similar expectations from life. Her parents' marriage was that of opposites. As always she wondered, how her mother had survived it. His participations in agitations, his giving away all his earnings, year on year, how did she?

Vidya acknowledged the need for companionship, but not enough to just settle on someone, or to endure such major differences.

Unaware of her thoughts, RST wished her good night and went to bed with the latest Sahitya Akademi prize-winning novel, clutched in his hand.

She closed up and retired to bed.

Vidya had braced herself for a fitful night that she'd spend wondering what Tom was up to, but surprisingly, she soon drifted off to a peaceful sleep. The only thing that remained was a feeling of curiosity about Josh and what kind of a person he really was.

***

Zurich, five months earlier ...

The delivery man carefully maneuvered the heavy crate off the truck onto the motorized dolly. The basement parking lot was cold and dark, not much different from the gloomy winter day outside. He set the dolly on its way, steering it up to the first floor of the gallery, humming to himself.

He saw her immediately, a very beautiful girl, sitting behind her desk, busy clicking the mouse, staring at the computer screen. She must be an office manager or a receptionist. She turned and smiled. She even seemed excited to see him.

"Mr. Banner has been personally enquiring about this shipment," she said instead of a greeting, dampening his spirit a little.

He guessed Mr. Banner must be someone important, perhaps the owner of the gallery. He looked down casually examining the bill of lading. It had been shipped from a place called Chennai. He saw it written on the box, though he couldn't quite pronounce or make out all the words in the address. He himself was of West African descent and knew oftentimes beautiful sounds from native languages lost their color when written in English.

She signed for the box and acknowledged his predictable comment about the snow with a smile. Chantal, he read her name to himself. She even shared with him her plans for going skiing that weekend. Then she promptly dismissed him with a friendly nod and moved behind the desk to dial a number. As he walked out, he could hear her voice, "Mr. Banner, the shipment has arrived from Chennai."

He hadn't been inside an Indian gallery before, but he liked what he saw on the front. There was a dark wooden elephant about two feet high, with its trunk up, ears flared, its white tusk sharp and curved, that stood behind the fancy display window. Someday, he would like to have a small version of it. He had seen an elephant once in a zoo when he was a little boy, an African elephant, wilder and more majestic than the Indian one. Had they gone for a ride on it? It was a faint memory, almost like a dream. His mom had died a few days after that in an accident.

He tapped the crate gently as he walked out. He wished desperately he could have a family of his own, a child he could take to the zoo someday.

Chapter 14

The thin strip of bright light attempting to storm in through the edges of the curtains told Josh it was morning. He woke up to the clock on the nightstand displaying 6:00 a.m. full of energy, his wits sharp. It must have been the overload to his senses combined with the physical exercise that had exhausted him. A deep and dreamless sleep had finally gotten him rebooted and reloaded.

He opened the thick screens, and sunlight surged into the room with little warmth. The air-conditioner was still laboring hard to keep the room temperature at the 18 degrees Celsius he had set it to.

He brewed himself a tall cup of black coffee in the machine and watched the evening news from the US.

After he'd had the caffeine shot, his sense of adventure came back to him, and deciding to venture out of the hotel, he quickly got ready in shorts and T-shirt, got his music on, and left his room. He had no company in the elevator, and the corridor was deserted of guests. A different doorman greeted him and held the door open with the same flourish. A curly moustache covering the cheeks must surely be a job requirement.

He got out and, after a moment's hesitation, turned right. He couldn't spot any street signs right away, and when he did, he wasn't sure he would remember the mile length name with multiple initials. But he soon got the hang of noticing markers—a building, an overpass, a billboard, or a statue. He could always look up the map app, but for some reason, it didn't seem sporting.

The winding road was not walker friendly, and where there were sidewalks, sometimes slabs were broken in between, and he gingerly walked right on the road the way others did. The lethargic morning traffic simply flowed around him. He noticed stores with shutters down, many boasting popular US brands. Electric cables strung between poles ran low, sometimes precariously over tree tops, sometimes dangerously dangling at eye level.

He crossed men and women casting curious, unsmiling glances at him. A few stared unashamedly, but he didn't sense any hostility. Josh hadn't really visited any country where he felt so out of place, where his alienness was so obvious. It was a strange, unfamiliar feeling of isolation.

Soon he came upon a street market full of hawkers, squatting behind wares spread atop bright yellow tarp sheets on the dusty pavement, or standing behind their carts, selling vegetables and fruits—tomatoes and deep purple eggplants and heaps of potatoes, and mounds of bananas, a rainbow of produce. His Instagram was going to rock.

Josh was fascinated. There was something curiously alive about them. It was early enough in the morning, but they were out and about, and a general din and clamor of voices talking, laughing, haggling—there was not a price tag in sight—filled the air. They looked as though they were fully ready to tackle the day.

The sun was up, bright rays already beating down from under a cloudless sky, beginning to hint at its upcoming might. He could feel the heat and the sweat. And a stinging mosquito bite, he added to himself, as he swatted the bug.

After walking for another twenty minutes, he came upon a small building with a colorful, wedge-like roof. It dawned on him, it was likely a temple. The structure did not resemble that of a church, and he wondered how he knew it was a place of worship. Was it the vendors in their carts selling incense and garlands of tropical flowers, whose perfume was beyond his reach? Or was it from a long-forgotten memory in the dregs of his mind, perhaps a picture in a book that had been tucked away on his father's shelf?

It hit him again. He was in India; the words ricocheted about in his head, over and over.

His parents and Tom would have so much loved to trade places with him right then. He thought of his parents and desperately wished they were alive and that he could call them. It had been six years since they had both passed away, and Josh felt he had never missed them as much as he did in that moment.

His dad's cotton tunic and his mom's bead necklaces came to his mind. He could hear the forgotten strains of the sitar and even a chant. All the resentment and irritation left him, and Josh unexpectedly found a film of tears in his eyes.

Eat, pray, love, he thought with a rueful smile.

The traffic noises were now picking up and so was the smell of the gasoline. He turned away.

By the time he found his way back, he was sweating profusely and his T-shirt was clinging to his body. The sun was on his face, and he felt warm and damp and sticky, yet totally invigorated.

He found a newspaper tucked inside a burlap bag outside his room that he took in for later reading.

After a quick divinely cool shower, settling in front of his laptop, an email check later, he picked up from where he had left off. He pulled up information dealing with intercontinental shipping, mapping shipping lines and port data. He let run a few of his exploits on one particular shipping line that he had narrowed.

Realizing it was quarter past eight, he decided to pause. He had to meet Vidya after all. He packed his bag and, after finishing his breakfast, was in the lobby ten minutes early. After texting Tom that he was ready for the day and that he would try not to muck it up, he wandered around.

She walked in almost on the dot at 9. He noticed afresh how gorgeous she looked. She was wearing a plain purple tunic and jeans. Her hair was tied back into a ponytail, and her face was devoid of any expression, altogether projecting an image of grim determination. He wasn't sure if he should be amused or deterred by it.

Josh stepped out from a corner into her line of sight. He noticed the momentary hesitation as she saw him, and then there was a brief curve of her lips and a nod.

He walked up to her.

"Good morning, thanks for coming. I thought it was a fifty-fifty chance," he said.

"You are an optimist," she replied with a ghost of a smile.

Josh grinned, liking her sparkling repartee. This was definitely a better day. "If only you knew how well liked I am," he returned.

Her smile widened. There was still some uncertainty in her expression but some humor nevertheless.

"How could I not come? Tom messaged you were as contrite as you were when you spilled ink on his map."

"Accidentally. That's the operative word. Accidentally spilled ink. So shall we sit over there?" He pointed toward a quiet nook he had noticed earlier that was sparsely occupied.

The ceiling was six floors high with a chandelier almost half the length, its many crystals sparkling in sunlight. Beyond the French window, there was little greenery and a narrow view of the chaotic morning traffic. A television, on mute, was on a news channel, and there was faint pop music flowing from somewhere. They sat on the two tall-backed chairs upholstered in deep red.

After ordering a cappuccino for her and an espresso for himself from an attendant who greeted them, Josh braced for the conversation. He stretched his legs and settled comfortably.

She had nothing to say and sat legs crossed, arms folded, with a watchful, speculative glance.

Truth was he was still not completely onboard with the idea of revealing everything to her, but he knew there was no way to get out of it, now that Tom had given her the outline.

"I am not here for sightseeing."

"You are here about a Nataraja."

He nodded. "You don't need a lecture on that dude Maharajah Chola, do you?"

That brought on a brief smile. "You mean Rajaraja."

"Right." He took a deep breath and quickly recounted what he knew about the idol in Tom's possession. He related the circumstance around Tom's acquisition, faithful in the details, taking care to explain about the journal, making sure she knew Tom had good cause. He stressed on how the provenance had initially seemed solid. She unfolded her arms and sat back a little.

The waiter brought their coffee, and there was a small lull in the conversation. They both took sips of their coffee, and Josh waited for a few moments to see if she had any questions.

He then moved on to the next part of the story and explained Eichendorf's connection to the gallery, and the large shipment they had received from Chennai, glossing over the detail of how they had found it. She likely inferred they got the information from the PI.

She scowled as she stirred her coffee over and over. Josh waited as she worked out the conclusion.

"So you suspect Tom's Nataraja was smuggled out of India and Eichendorf is the front man because he could provide a convincing provenance?" she asked cutting to the chase, quickly connecting all the dots, earning his respect.

"Yep, that's the possibility Tom wants to make sure isn't true."

She stared absent-mindedly at the bulbous jar on the side table with two bright red flowers. There were faint frown lines between her brows, and a piqued expression.

They finished their coffee in silence.

"Tom didn't breathe a word," she said after some time.

"I guess he didn't know what to do," he replied, his voice placating. If they were such good friends, it was hurtful, he supposed that Tom had kept it all a secret.

She looked up, met his eyes, and smiled. "It's fine. I am sure Tom had his reasons."

Josh truly understood the depth of her friendship with Tom for the first time.

"So Tom has sent you on this mission to track the origins of the bronze?"

"Yep, you said it. Mission it is!"

"Only Tom and you know about this?"

"Until this moment. Now you know what we both know."

Josh sat back and waited in silence for her move as she studied the empty cups with a thoughtful expression on her face.

He wanted to know what she was thinking, curiously as much for the sake of getting on with the next steps as for the sake of getting to know her better.

Chapter 15

Vidya leaned back, twirling a strand of loose hair, and stared at the television screen. The breaking news about a political war of words was benign compared to an announcement of a stolen seven-foot Chola bronze.

She instinctively checked the ticker to see if the market was holding steady. Her boss had sounded irritated at her unplanned leave, and her father had been puzzled at her second meeting with the capitalist. But she knew she had to get to the bottom of it after Tom's cryptic call.

When Tom had said the idol was in his possession and that he wanted to track it, she had vaguely assumed it had to do with an event from the distant past. She now sat, rather stunned at the possibility of an antique idol being smuggled out of the country in this day and age. Where did it really come from? Was it ever in a temple? Had it been worshipped? The questions echoed in her head.

She turned to catch Josh's eyes on her. He sat with an arm resting across the back of the chair, with his long jeans-clad legs stretched comfortably, a watchful, expectant expression on his face. The grey polo t-shirt looked good on him, she noticed.

She asked, intrigued, "What exactly were you trying to do yesterday though?"

"Preparing, laying the groundwork." He shrugged. "I suspect the PI would come back with the name of an art store as the source. I thought to study the stores, their systems, and their setup in general. Maybe I'll have to take a peek in later."

The words puzzled her until she made the connection to his profession. He meant to hack into their systems.

"That's why you complained about the cash transactions yesterday!" she exclaimed with sudden insight.

A gleam of amusement lit up his blue eyes and she had a glimpse of the man Tom often described.

She studied him with much curiosity. Could he really pull off the "peeking into"? What were his motives anyway? Did he really want to get to the bottom of it?

"That's all the ideas you've got? Then I'd have to either suspect your detective powers or your intent," she said with a twinkle, framing her question intentionally provocative.

He gave her a look in response to the jibe.

"Come on, even if I were making a halfhearted attempt, you should appreciate that I am making the effort. It is for a museum, and honestly, in my opinion, the provenance was good enough until Tom decided to mess around," he admitted with a frankness that surprised her a little.

"I am glad you said 'was'. From what we know now, it is clearly ill-gotten."

"We ... ll," he drawled making a face, "It is not so clear-cut. There is no recent report of any stolen idol. We don't know what was in the box."

Catching her disbelieving look, he raised his hands in a gesture of surrender. "I'm just saying is all."

She made a mental note to review all the Tamil papers and magazines for any reports of odd incidents connected to old temples. Only a grand temple could boast of an idol of such large proportions surely—a holy site like Chidambaram or Madurai or Tirunelveli. It would be impossible, she reassured herself, to smuggle an idol from those temples.

Even contemplating art trafficking seemed fantastical. Hers was a world of middle class safety, the world of regular jobs and conventional neighbors. The underworld stayed away in movies and media reports, except for an occasional glimpse through her father's activism.

"This could get dangerous," she remarked.

"I know. Art trafficking, that too at the international level. I told Tom not to involve you. It isn't too late, you could—"

"Excuse me?"

He stopped at her sharp interruption.

She was annoyed as much with the implication that she was incapable of handling the risks as the idea of him, a foreigner, deciding if she should or shouldn't be involved in the matter.

Her feelings must have shown on her face. He paused and then again lifted his hand in a gesture of submission. "I get it. I neither have the right nor the power to keep you out," he said.

His quick reading of her and his matter of fact reaction calmed her down.

"No, it's fine. You were being considerate of my safety." He deserved that acknowledgement.

Their eyes met and they smiled slowly at each other. There might be something tolerable about the guy after all. She had a feeling he was thinking the same thing about her.

She returned her attention to the problem. "So what next?"

"I have a lead."

He pulled out his laptop and switched it on, placing it on the table in between. He clicked and typed busily and then leaning forward, tilted it so she could see. He had a spreadsheet with a timeline of sorts, with what seemed to be information on shipping lines.

"The trucking company, I found out from a contract, is the preferred partner for Starline Shipping."

"How did you get that contract?"

"It's best you don't ask me such questions."

His eyes twinkled and she found the self-assurance with which he said it appropriate and attractive unlike the previous day.

"Isn't that a big assumption that the idol was shipped through Starline?"

"I cross verified it." He smiled as though he appreciated her doubt. "There are many shipping lines operating in this area, Maersk, Cosco ... quite a few. I did a search for all the ships that had docked in Europe arriving from India within a month of the delivery to the gallery. Guess what?"

"There was one from Starline?"

"Yeah."

"How many total?"

There was another approving smile.

"Total seven, one Starline. But ... it was the only one that also docked in Chennai in late November last year, within our time window. The port is busy but not as busy when it comes to direct lines to Europe. I see this as the swiftest and most economical route to Zurich."

"What does all that mean?"

"It means the conclusion is not fool proof—I optimized it for Genoa, not Gersheim, as the port of discharge, my time window could be off and all that. But if we had one shot at finding the source, I would bet on this ship. In retrospect, the fact that they shipped from Chennai is our biggest break." He shrugged. "Or our biggest drain of time depending on the outcome."

"I see. So the only way for us to get the source is from this shipping line."

"Not the only way, the Indian Ports Association would also have the details, it is export across international borders, you see."

"Are you going to hack into their systems too?" she asked, shocked at the possibility.

"Are you asking me to?" his lips curved into a lopsided smile that was full of mischief.

She was a sucker for such a smile. Shaking her head to clear her thoughts, she straightened. "God, no! Let's not do anything illegal, at least, not yet."

She felt a sudden energy as a thought occurred to her. "So we have the name of the ship, the date, the 'to' address, and we need a 'from' address, right?"

"Yep."

"You know, I think my cousin's uncle-in-law works for the port authority. If we ask the right question, we might have a shot at it."

"You know a guy who knows a guy. Seriously? No wonder Tom nagged me to get in touch with you." His smile expanded into a grin.

"More like I have a cousin who has a cousin. We have lived here forever, and I have enough cousins and uncles and aunts to have connections everywhere."

Vidya spent the next few minutes calling, finally getting through to her cousin, who confirmed his uncle-in-law indeed worked for the IPA. He gave her his number and promised to message him an intro.

Vidya relayed the message to Josh who was watching her closely, trying to follow the conversation.

"Okay, so I have to ask who shipped something last November to The Kohinoor?" she queried, making sure she got it right before calling the man.

"Yeah, that's a good question to ask."

Josh crossed his fingers in an exaggerated gesture and sat intently staring at her face as she spoke in Tamil.

She introduced herself, and the officer took his time to enquire after her—what did she do, weren't her brothers abroad, had he met her during her cousin's wedding, and so on. She answered the questions without showing the impatience she was feeling until finally she got to the point.

Vidya wondered if Josh got the drift of the conversation by the English words popping from time to time—confirm, shipment, Zurich ... She spun some story about a friend in Europe wanting to know where his suppliers were getting their products from.

Her contact dithered, understandably reluctant to respond to the unusual request. "It's not easy to find the information, and even if I did, I cannot just give it, I am sure you understand," he explained. She reached over and drew the laptop closer. Peering at the screen where he had already pulled up the details, she pressed on with all that she knew.

"We have the shipment detail, when, to where, all that. I just need to know who shipped it, it'd have been written on the box, no?" she asked playing down the notion of confidentiality.

The man thawed a bit.

"Can you give me an idea of the from address? As a favor, I can confirm if it is right or not," he said, implicitly agreeing to help.

Vidya hesitated, biting her lips.

Josh raised a brow. "Just a second," she said and putting the phone on mute, she quickly recapped what the officer had told her.

"I did some research. The stores we visited first and last are the ones most equipped to ship abroad. My bet's on the first," he said.

"My bet is Sarathy's, the one we visited last."

"Really?" he responded with a look of surprise.

"Yes, really. The first store has a solid reputation, been in business for generations."

She clutched the phone and gave the officer the two names, saying she suspected it was Sarathy's.

"I will call you back in a few minutes," he assured her.

After ending the call, she sat back. "Well, we will see how that goes."

Josh snapped his laptop shut and leaned back as well.

"What do we do now? Wait here?"

"We could visit a few more stores," she said halfheartedly. She doubted anything worthwhile would come of it, but she didn't see any point in sitting idle.

"Yeah, anywhere outside is fine. Let's get out of here," he said, echoing her need to do something, go somewhere. He quickly checked something on his computer, signaled the waiter for the check, and packed up his stuff.

They stepped outside the hotel into the sunny morning and Josh, clearly better prepared than the previous day to handle the morning glare, donned his sunglasses. They walked toward her car and he instinctively moved toward the driver side again.

She smiled. "Sorry, I don't have the guts to let you drive here."

"Apparently I do," he shot back.

"Oh come now, I am such a good, safe driver," she declared and laughed, catching his mock horror.

As they got into the car, she caught him shift a little and asked almost apologetically, "Is it very uncomfortable? I didn't think we were going to go out today. We could hire a cab, but I don't want the driver to overhear us."

He smiled, removing his glasses. "Relax, its fine."

Vidya took a quick sidelong glance at him as she deftly steered the little car into the afternoon traffic. A big bus bore down on her, and she got out of its way, getting reminded of his earlier comment about her driving.

The sky was a pale blue, and the road shimmered with the heat of the scorching day.

They spent the next hour and a half exhausting many more unimportant stores, now tired of the commonplace Nataraja idols that they all invariably put up in the front. As they walked out of the last store, and truth be told, they were all beginning to blend together, she called the uncle-in-law again for the third time. He did not answer.

"Maybe your contact changed his mind. Perhaps I should take your advice and hack into—"

"Let's give it a few more minutes."

She called her cousin and asked him to check in with the officer.

Josh raised his shoulders in a gesture of resignation. "Okay, should we head back to the hotel in the meanwhile?"

Vidya stared at him, thinking of Tom and of the plans she had made to take Josh around and the one place she had not thought of for a long time. "I don't want this trip of yours to be a complete waste."

He raised his brows at her. "You want to take me sightseeing?"

"Just for an hour? Who knows, you might never get that opportunity if you get caught hacking into government servers."

"Where do you want to go?" he asked with a faint smile.

"You will see."

He shrugged his shoulders, his palms facing outward in a "whatever" gesture.

She smiled at the somewhat boyish gesture, glad that his earlier statement about being well liked might not have been an empty boast after all. It'd have been tragic if Tom had a boor for a brother.

Chapter 16

"Of course! A museum!" Josh half laughed and half groaned when he realized she had brought him to the government museum.

He had been working on his laptop, checking the status of his exploits only to note that he was still unsuccessful in breaking into Starline shipping data, when she had brought the car to a halt in front of the museum.

It was a modest two-story brown brick building with a colonial facade of arches and pillars. The parking lot was the gravelly, unpaved grounds by the side, and there was little greenery amidst the predominantly brown and ochre scenery. Overhead, the sky was a washed-out blue-white, and he had a distinct feeling of being gently roasted.

She parked her car under a lone tree offering some shade, and Josh, now adept at unfolding himself from the small vehicle, got out. A dirt path led to multiple annexes.

There was a small booth for tickets right by the entrance that was manned by a distracted employee flirting with a young woman leaning by the door. There was hardly any queue. The atmosphere was one of relaxation and peace. He firmly stopped Vidya from paying for the ticket, though it seemed ridiculously low priced.

"My dad and I used to come to that library very often, the one over there. It's like a hundred years old or something. I was wondering how I could show you an antique idol when I remembered this museum and the bronze gallery."

"Aren't there any temples nearby?"

"Not the kind where you'd find such antique idols; besides, the really old temples are unlikely to allow you inside the sanctum." She sounded defensive, which amused Josh.

He pulled up his phone and swept it around to record the ambience.

They walked past cannons that he presumed were from famous battles toward the right, following the signboard to the bronze exhibits. He took a passing notice of the stone sculptures, busts and faces, and full-length figures displayed outside carelessly on cement bases. They walked on the winding path toward a small building. A stray dog lounging by the shade got up with alacrity and followed him throughout, wagging its tail.

"Worried about rabies?" Vidya asked with a twinkle.

Josh tried to smile in return, but his anxiety must have shown on his face because she chuckled. She shooed the dog away and, much to his embarrassment, declared herself to be his knight in shining armor.

"Oh, it was harmless. I like dogs." He sounded lame to his own ears.

It was blazing hot, but the place looked like a small haven with the old trees providing shade, away from all the traffic and noise.

A couple of policemen sat on plastic chairs beneath the arched entrance. They paid only cursory attention toward her, but they surveyed him for a few seconds longer, which appeared to be more due to their casual curiosity about a white man. A newspaper lay on another chair, and he guessed they were discussing some headline.

A man took a look at their tickets and then ushered them inside.

Josh's eyes slowly adjusted to the dim lighting inside. A carpet of Indian red ran through the middle of the long, rectangular hall that had no pretensions of splendor, housing bronzes inside glass boxes along its walls. There were some simple signboards that stated the provenance of each item.

This was no large hallowed hall with high ceilings, and there were no bright yet understated pedestals or lights. There were hardly any glitzy placards or brochures.

Museums suffering poor funding appeared universal, he thought drily.

He soon noted the exhibits spoke for themselves, even in that mediocre setting. Dozens of idols glimmered behind their glass cases with a glint on a sharp nose here, a sheen on the curve of a breast there. Josh sorely missed Tom.

He felt mesmerized staring at each of the figures, varying in age, and pose, mostly under four feet and somewhat off proportion. The idols felt more expressive, even alive, than in the pictures. Josh could tell the sculptors knew what they were doing, their knowledge of human anatomy was obvious in what they had chosen to embellish. The male forms were deliberately a tad more broad-shouldered, projecting an aura of power, and the female forms exuded a heightened sensuality. The goddesses were scandalously near nude.

"So, I see that the idols' lower bodies are cast as though they are clothed, but not the upper bodies. Is that consistent with historical attires?" he asked, fully aware of the indelicate nature of the question.

"I doubt the women went topless. Besides, in our temples, these idols are adorned with real clothes and ornaments." He could sense she strove to keep her tone matter of-fact. He bit back a smile.

They walked from one idol to another, and she described them a little, the different gods and the goddesses, thankfully not going overboard.

Josh found it a mind-boggling concept. He vaguely remembered his father had written a paper on polytheistic religions. He must have looked perplexed.

She explained, smiling, "It must be hard for a non-believer to grasp. My mom used to say, as you go deeper, it becomes complex, and if you dare go further, it becomes simple."

He smiled in return. "That sounds awfully like what my father would say."

They walked until he came to an idol that was clearly half male and half female. The "Ardhanareeswara" reminded him of the "Sleeping Hermaphroditus" marble. That museum tour couple of years ago had been part of Tom's relentless "HelpJosh" campaign.

He recalled that his father's papers had notes on the symbolism around this god as well. What he had thought of as a teenager as some weird pictures that his father inexplicably liked, shifted to a representation of collision, or rather the connectedness, of physics and philosophy and spirituality.

He turned to see her waiting for him. They exited and walked up the poorly lit stairs to the second floor. The stairs were narrow, and walking together brought them close enough to bump into each other. She seemed conscious of it and hastened one step ahead, yielding him a delectable view of her backside.

The second floor was specially focused on Nataraja idols, almost thirty or so in various sizes, all smaller than the one in Tom's possession. Josh realized anew how spectacular an idol of seven feet would be. Tom had given him a crash course on how there were various pointers to figure out the period the idols belonged to, but Josh didn't analyze anything. Did it really matter whether the arc of flame was oval or circular, or how ornate the headdress was, to admire the exquisite workmanship?

"Obama pose," Vidya quipped.

"Ah yes. Feel compelled to lecture the dumb American?"

"I didn't peg you as an ignorant American," she said. And after a beat added, "I know you got Google."

He read the small board that talked about the "Natesa" idols, which Vidya informed him was a different, purer version of the word "Nataraja".

One more floor and they went around, this time seeing the Vishnu bronzes. Josh wasn't sure when he stopped recording, when he stopped paying attention to the exhibits. There was a glut of bronzes for one thing and he was getting captivated by her for another. He was focusing more and more on how she twirled the little strands of hair that hung loose, and how she chewed her lips, than on the bronzes.

After a full circuit, they went down the stairs.

"You know I have argued with Tom many times about the relevance of museums at the face of digitization," he said to her.

"I can tell which side Tom's on."

He chuckled. "He never bought my argument that you could get even more up close with technology."

"But?" she queried shrewdly, sensing he was rethinking his position.

"There is something to seeing the idols like this, with sunshine and sweat and … ," he trailed there without adding the 'you' that hovered on his lips. He was neither clear as to how she would take it, nor sure of how it did matter to his experience of the museum. "Anyway, not that Tom would agree to that idea either! It'd mean he would have to repatriate the idols in his museum after all."

Tom believed art was universal. He often argued in favor of the major museums' ability to preserve the artifacts, provide contexts and availability to millions of people.

He repeated that to her, and she smiled. "Yes, Tom would also argue we need them there for those who cannot make it here. Like Tom himself."

"I guess so!" Josh was startled and chagrined. Somehow he had failed to grasp the personal, emotional angle to what museums meant for Tom and had taken the intellectual arguments at face value. His attachment to the idol took on a more poignant hue.

It was noon when they came out, and the sun was overhead, way up, farther in the sky than Josh had ever seen. He was in the tropics. The canopy of leaves muted the powerful sun's rays that still filtered through, making a pretty pattern of light and shadow on the dusty walls and the stone pathways. The policeman sitting outside in a shady spot by the entrance was using the newspaper as a fan. He stroked his moustache as he gave a momentary glance in Josh's direction and went back to his fanning, lost in some thought.

"Is it me or is the security really lax here?"

"I am sure there are appropriate alarm systems. This is government run, and there are policemen on duty. It would be much easier to steal something from a temple, sadly."

They walked out and Josh could feel the heat beginning to drill through his skin and the top of his head.

He noticed a small bookstore of sorts, just a few glass-doored shelves really upon which dust had settled like a fine powder, with scholarly books on bronzes and other artifacts. He bought a book that had the longest and most complicated title and a few postcards for Tom. Placing them on the dusty wall and borrowing a pen from her, he wrote, "It should have been you here."

It was a silly old-fashioned gesture, there wasn't even a mailbox in sight, and he could have simply sent a picture on his phone. But he had done it and Vidya gravely took it from him with a promise to post it.

They walked back toward the entrance on the same path they had come in, but it was now hotter and noisier. He wiped the sweat off his brow. His throat felt parched and he could feel his shirt plastered to his back.

A set of school children had arrived for a field trip, and they were all playing boisterously. The teachers, already tired, sat on the steps, shouting instructions to them from time to time in the local language.

Josh watched their rambunctious enthusiasm and energy with much curiosity. The sun seemed to energize and not drain them. This was a young country he realized. He noticed a remarkable number of young people compared to when he traveled to towns in Europe.

Sunlight played through the leaves of the tree. Someone talked loudly somewhere. The afternoon wore on. He felt he needed to capture this moment, something for himself. The bronzes were not his thing; neither was India. But that place, that moment, would have meant everything for those he had ever felt closest to.

As if she knew it, she asked, "Would you like to pose for a picture?"

Josh nodded and handed her his phone, and she clicked a few. There was something pensive about him standing alone by himself beneath the green canopy with the rust colored building in the background. It was a vivid and beautiful picture, but somehow he didn't like the lonely feeling it evoked.

He asked if they could take a picture together. Josh clicked a selfie, which had them both grinning into the camera with distorted coverage of the background. She made a passerby click a proper picture of them standing next to each other in front of a pillar, he casually leaning back, hands thrust deep into his pockets, she slightly turned toward him, smiling into the camera.

"That's much better," she said handing the phone back.

"Yes," he agreed.

He said a simple thank you, and she graciously tilted her head with a mega-watt smile.

Chapter 17

Josh waited by the car as Vidya excused herself to make some phone calls. She sounded apologetic, and the way her eyes crinkled in request was beautiful.

She paced a little as she spoke, one arm folded and the other clutching the phone. It was fascinating to see her go on to a business mode and talk with utter focus, almost ignoring him. Her tunic did full justice to her graceful figure, and taking advantage of her distraction, he continued to watch her unhurriedly.

The first set of her calls seemed to be related to work.

"The spot is jumping to 64—"

"Now, the twenty to thirty paise gain you get with this—"

"We expect the situation in Greece to deteriorate early next week—"

She mouthed, "two minutes," when she felt his eyes on her as she switched to another call.

The next one was clearly to a friend. She spoke in the local tongue and laughed as the other person said something. She turned her body slightly away and tucked a loose strand of hair back. She was likely talking about him. He smiled. Then occurred the sobering thought that she could be talking to her boyfriend for all he knew.

After she finished her calls, as they got back into the car, her phone rang.

"It's the officer." She turned her face up at him with wide-eyed excitement.

She answered the call, with a tense voice. As she listened, a triumphant smile lit up her eyes and she gave him a thumbs-up sign. Profusely thanking the man, she finished the call.

"It is Sarathy's." She grinned.

They gave each other an exuberant fist bump. After the initial moments of euphoria, they sat in the parked car in silence as the news set in.

"Did he say anything else?"

"Yes well, he advised me to mind my own business and not get into trouble trying to help others. In a needlessly ominous voice, I should add," she grumbled. Josh smiled at her piqued expression.

It was stuffy and hot. She started the engine and let some air circulate. "So, what next? Do we go to Sarathy's?"

He rubbed his eyes and dodged the question for the moment. "Lady, be a hospitable host, I need food."

She smiled. "I was just asking my friend for directions to McDonald's."

Josh was touched she had taken the pains and was even more thrilled that the call had not been to her boyfriend. "Thank you. I actually feel like Indian food today. My constitution is faring better than I thought. But slave master Tom would want results, so I guess fast food and then Sarathy's?"

She nodded, but he noticed a smile that was lurking. When he raised a brow in question, she said with a sheepish, apologetic smile, "I thought you were a complete—I mean I thought it odd that you ate only Western food the whole of yesterday."

"Yeah, say it why don't you. You thought I was a complete jackass."

"Yeah!" she exclaimed in a teasing voice. "You are Tom's brother for Gods' sake, I so wanted to explain the subtleties of Indian food and there you were shoving croissants and pizza in your face."

He shook his head feigning deep hurt.

She chuckled and then added in a serious tone, "I am sorry. I shouldn't have been so judgmental." She was obviously a straight shooter and he liked that about her.

"So does this mean I am no longer considered a jerk?"

"Well, let's see, to borrow an American expression, 'the jury is still out on that."

Their laughter rang out as she backed the car and headed for the restaurant. Josh watched as she chewed her lips and stared blankly ahead, lost in thought as they waited for the light to turn green. He noticed she was consumed by the problem enough to not notice him. It was an unusual experience, and he was marginally nettled by it, but also liked her for it. He presumed she was thinking about the idol. He, on the other hand, for the first time in days, surprisingly, did not have the bronze at the top of his mind.

Soon she came out of her reverie, and they made small talk. He asked her about her job, and she explained what she did, they talked a bit about where he lived, and she gave brief descriptions of the sights.

As they laughed together yet again, Josh admitted to himself that he was attracted to her. Nothing would come out of it, of course, but he was enjoying himself better than he'd thought he would.

They soon stopped at a McDonald's.

Once he stepped out of the air-conditioned car, even walking for a couple of minutes from the parking spot to the restaurant had him dabbing at his forehead. Coming in from outside the bright sunlight, everything except the over lit menu boards felt dark at first until his eyes slowly adjusted. The familiarity of the menu and the seating was comforting yet disappointing. He noticed the lack of hamburgers, guessed it must be a nod to the local sentiments.

They ate their burgers and fries quickly, easy with the small talk.

"What do we do when we get to Sarathy's?" she asked at one point.

"Let's first check the place out a bit more carefully," he responded, a little hesitant to show all his cards.

"I will see if I can get some reference for local detectives," she offered.

Josh still harbored a hope that they would ultimately be able to go ahead with the acquisition and was not comfortable with bringing in more people in the know unless they had to.

"I don't think we need to," he said.

She must have heard the reluctance in his voice.

"Are you sure you want to find the truth?" she asked perceptively.

"I am here, aren't I?" He grumbled.

"Easy ... I get that," she conceded.

He felt a twinge of guilt, realizing how his reluctance must read to her. She probably thought there wasn't any other option.

They finished their lunch and headed out. Josh crinkled his eyes against the bright sunlight outside and put on his glasses noticing most people did not wear any glasses, including her. They were bare-headed too and fully clothed.

"Sarathy's seemed to be fully digitized," he ventured tentatively as they got into the car and drove on, trying to gauge her reaction.

"Did you not say you could take a peek into their records?" she asked, not sounding particularly horrified at the idea. "How difficult would that be? How long would it take?"

He made a decision.

He answered, "About two minutes and twenty seconds."

She took a quick, surprised look at him at the precise answer.

"You already did? That's fantastic!" Her eyes, back on the road as she negotiated a right turn, were round, and her mouth agape. "That's what you were doing making me wait in the sun yesterday, weren't you?"

"And when you went to get that bottle of water at Puhar Traders."

He didn't hide his triumphant grin, truth was he was aching to show off. And her brief display of awe and admiration was quite intoxicating. "Just preliminary stuff, mind you. If nothing's changed since yesterday, I could try and get something useful now."

"I can't wait to get there," she declared, swinging a rash left at the next intersection.

Josh winced. "Me too, but preferably in one piece."

***

The salesman recognized them as they wandered back into the showroom. Vidya waxed something eloquently at her mile-a-minute speed. Only he wasn't entirely sure what she was saying about him.

"Hey, you just called me an idiot with money, didn't you?" Josh whispered when the salesman trotted away toward the counter. "Like that old man yesterday?"

"How did you know?" she asked shifting uncomfortably.

He narrowed his eyes in dramatic anger. "He did, huh? I thought so, from the way you vigorously nodded at his comment."

"No, no ... I didn't ... "

She looked thoroughly mortified that he had to smile. "Your expressions are so easy to read," he added, surprising her, as well as himself, with that unnecessary explanation.

111

"So where have you sent the guy?" he asked quickly changing the subject, pointing to the salesman.

"I asked him to find out how we can commission an idol, thought that might give us some insight into their operations," she answered.

"That's good."

She looked at him expectantly and feeling an impulse to tease her, he walked around innocently examining the wares. He could feel her impatient eyes on him as she followed him.

The salesman returned to inform that the manager had stepped out, and asked if they could wait. Josh seized the opportunity to say they'd come back later. She looked at him with an uncertain expression, and as they headed out, leaned closer to whisper furiously, "Josh, what about the hacking?"

"It's not telepathic," he smiled and then catching her doing what he presumed was the Indian equivalent of the eye-roll, he added, "Let's step out now that we have established we were here for a legitimate reason."

She had got a prime parking spot right in front of the building and Sarathy's Wi-Fi signal was powerful enough to reach where the car was. They got into the car, and Vidya unwound the windows and switched on the AC.

The parking attendant came by, seemingly to help them back out into the traffic. Josh wanted to remain in the car for a few more minutes. Her eyes widened as she realized what he was about to do.

"I am going to go get you a bottle of water. I can't be a witness to a crime in progress, can I?" She grinned.

He smiled a little as she got down and engaged the attendant in an easy conversation, and they both walked away. He was feeling eternally thirsty, the water bottle was a good idea anyway.

Josh pulled out his laptop. Cursing the heat, he wiped his brow. He had cracked their Wi-Fi WEP password the previous day. Thankfully nothing had changed overnight; he got in and from there it was a matter of breaching a service and getting to the data. He transferred as much of it as he could, storing things away for later.

The attendant was back to sitting on a small bench in a little shaded area and did not seem interested in him. Josh worked in the unobtrusive low hum of the afternoon traffic and the air conditioner, tilting the screen for privacy and freedom from glare. He poked around a bit more but did not find anything useful right away.

Vidya came back, handed him a cool can of Coke along with the water, and raised her brows in question, looking all agog.

"I have downloaded all the information. I do have to convert the format for some data to make it understandable. But for now we are good to go," he said, closing his laptop.

She drove out quickly as though someone was about to chase them.

After a few minutes she stopped over at a gas station. Attendants moved busily around, filling gas, collecting payments, checking tire pressure and directing vehicles in the small space.

"This could all be so easily managed as self-service, would be faster and less expensive in the long run," he remarked.

"It'd eliminate jobs though."

Before Josh could respond to that, she shook her head. "God! I can't believe I sounded just like my dad!" she exclaimed.

The rueful expression in her face was almost comical and he couldn't help but look at her, begging the question.

"My father is a dyed in the wool socialist. He is forever making such statements," she said pursing her lips. He gathered she didn't approve.

He wanted to know more about her, but wary of the strong pull of attraction that was fueling the interest, he kept quiet.

A call came in for her as they drove out and she answered with a frown.

"I have to go to work. Something urgent has come up," she relayed with a sigh after finishing the call. Josh felt a sharp stab of disappointment.

"Oh! I could catch a cab back," he offered.

"No, no! I will drop you back at the hotel, but too bad I can't stay," she said, sounding obviously and thoroughly let down.

"I know! It's hard to leave my company," he sighed dramatically.

She met his eyes, her lips twitched and then she burst out laughing. She was still smiling when they stopped at a light a minute later. She had undone her ponytail somewhere in between, which she now gathered and tied again. She exuded a certain Tin vibrancy, and there was an optimistic enthusiasm about her that he liked. She had a habit of biting her lips from time to time, he noticed.

"Hey, have been meaning to ask you, how the heck did you get my phone number? What sort of a hack was that?"

"Number, ha! I know a lot more about you," he said and rattled off her brothers' occupation—he couldn't recall their names—her birthday, and the place she worked, and that her father had undergone surgery recently.

"Tom, I suppose?" She wrinkled her brows.

"Why don't I throw this in then? Your father's blood type is A+."

She turned toward him, speechless. He grinned.

"Oh my God! How on earth did you get my father's medical records? Don't tell me you are working for the NSA or something? Are they interested in everyone on the planet?"

He laughed. "Don't let your imagination run riot. I am not connected to NSA, though they may very well be interested in everyone on or outside the planet. In some mailing list, one of your old emails is archived, and it's on the web. You had mailed a blood donation request with your phone number."

"Wow!"

"Welcome to the new world. Privacy is dead."

"Well, privacy was never alive in India," she replied in a resigned tone. "What else did you find out about me?"

"You are twenty-five, you majored in economics, you live in a place called Mylapore, and you are single—"

"What do you mean I am single?" she interjected.

"You don't have a ring, and you don't ... " He hesitated for a second. "I don't think you have a boyfriend."

There was a brief silence, and then he asked, "Do you?"

"Rings are not always symbols of matrimony in India," she said but didn't venture any more information.

"Are you married?" he croaked out after a beat.

"No." There was a hint of a smile before she added, "But I do have a boyfriend."

He couldn't bring himself to continue that topic, feeling an unexpectedly huge disappointment and dampening of spirit.

The traffic moved slowly, and there was a brief silence. "You know so much about me. You have to share something in return," she said, pouting adorably.

He didn't have a lot of information about himself on the Net. He knew how to keep his private data private, but he found himself talking a lot about himself. She was easy to talk to, a good listener.

"I started off by writing a software program that was used in grid computing. And then I became a network expert. Protecting networks was interesting but somewhat boring. So I moved on to being a white hat."

"What's that?"

"It's like someone you would employ to try breaking your door lock to make sure it is not breakable." That was when he'd made his first million, by spotting a major vulnerability in a new OS version. He had subsequently held a high paying job as an intrusion detection expert, dabbled in payment security, and was, of late, consulting for a government agency about a financial fraud spanning multiple countries.

He didn't like talking about his net worth, but he did end up bragging a little about his professional achievements. By the time they reached the hotel, Josh felt, as a security expert, he should have been appalled at his own runaway tongue. But really, he could have talked for longer.

It was early evening by the time they got back.

"Will you call me as soon as you find something? You know my number," she said.

He nodded and got out of the car to still lean over and say goodbye one more time. They engaged in further small talk, something silly about her rash driving and his feeble heart.

She, too, seemed reluctant to leave but managed to do so at the exact point when it was becoming obvious. Josh stood watching until her car was out of the exit gate. He would have liked her to stay for longer, maybe have a drink with him, maybe walk up to his room ... yeah, that'd have gone down big with her.

He smiled to himself as he walked in. He rejected with derision, the idea of love at first sight but acknowledged to himself there was something brewing. He must check up with Tom on the boyfriend.

Chapter 18

Josh decided he wouldn't start his research right away. He needed to clear his head a bit before he embarked on processing all the information he had in hand.

After a quick change, he went to the pool and swam some swift underwater laps. The sun-warmed water surrounded him, drowning out any other noise, internal and external, as he pounded stroke after intense stroke.

After the workout, he headed out to the in-pool bar, spotting the American from the previous day sitting there nursing a drink.

Marie was a UI architect, a total tech-chick working out of San Jose. They traded latest gossip from ValleyWag, speculated on acquisitions and valuations, and discussed the newest episode of *Silicon Valley*. He had to lie through his teeth, making up a plausible work reason for his trip; he thought it would seem odd that he was vacationing in India.

She accepted his reason of advising a stealth mode startup, even commenting on the amount of startup money flowing in. She shared her views on the vibrancy of the scene in Bangalore. Chennai, she sighed, was comparatively dull. She asked if he had any plans for the weekend. He dodged the question with some vague answer about doing something with his colleagues, surprisingly without any regret.

He texted Vidya about the meeting as he rode up to the room.

Ooh a hot date! She texted back.

So hot I am literally heading straight for a cold shower. He typed.

Between getting back to his room, the shower, and changing, he had exchanged a couple of more messages in the same vein. He caught himself smiling as he called Tom to brief him about the day. The number was busy.

He opened a can of Coke, switched on the TV and surfed the Indian news channels while he waited. There was news of the intense heat wave again and a possible delay in the monsoon that could cause severe draught. The previous year didn't seem to have been any better, as some data on farmer suicides ran on the screen.

Tom called him back.

"IS has captured Palmyra, and there is speculation they have bulldozed the ancient ruins," sighed Tom as way of beginning. He then exhaled as though it was pointless to dwell on it. "So, how was the day, and what do you think of Vidya now?"

"The day was good, and Vidya is hot!"

"What?" Tom's startled echo made Josh realize he wasn't expecting that. "I thought you would say the day was hot, and Vidya is good." Tom laughed.

Josh chuckled as well.

"I just chatted with Vidya. Looks like you have made some progress."

"Tom, you are creating an unnecessary trail of our investigation," chided Josh. He switched off the TV and walked over to stand by the window, pulling open the sheer curtains.

"Firstly, I called her. I meant chat in the original sense. Secondly, I meant the personal impression you made on her."

"Oh! Um ... what did she say?"

"Curious, are we?"

"You are going to exasperate me now, aren't you?"

"Naturally. I didn't think your thoughts would turn carnal so soon!"

"Soon? It's been two whole days! Did she say anything about how handsome and charming and smart I was?"

"How old are you? Thirteen? Shall we talk about my problem please?" Laughter bubbled through Tom's voice.

"How self-centered can you be, Tom? Is your job and reputation more important than a girl's impression of me?"

"Not to mention the possibility of going to prison."

Josh laughed, but a part of him was really curious about Vidya's opinion of him and wished he could pressure Tom into revealing it as well as her relationship status.

He took a peek outside the window. The light outside was fading, the evening hues pleasant after the harsh light of the day. Passing clouds floated on the grey expanse, and the moon, a huge silver disc rose from the eastern skies. It was a scene that had not one tenth of the high-fidelity or even the beauty of his screen savers, so why on earth was the word romantic popping into his head.

He took a large swig of the Coke, more so to stop himself from saying something stupid. He supposed Tom was right. He was acting like a thirteen-year-old. He shook his head to clear his thoughts. He turned away and started briefing Tom about the day's events.

Tom being Tom, the breakthrough about the source paled in comparison with the museum visit. He certainly wanted Josh to poke through the material he had downloaded from Sarathy's, but that was conveyed in a mere matter-of-fact tone. His cross-examination of Josh about the museum visit and his impressions was much more animated, the excitement palpable in his voice. Josh felt sympathy welling inside him.

After quizzing him for a full five minutes, Tom ended the topic, sighing in satisfaction. "A museum stands for continuity, for eternal learning. Was it not great to feel the exhibits with all your senses?"

Josh listened indulgently but couldn't resist saying, "Ha! Like they allowed me to touch the million dollars' worth of idols. Now, a VR system—"

"Okay, okay!" Tom laughed. "You've got me there! But at least admit," he paused and quoted dramatically, "'There are more things in heaven and earth Horatio, than are dreamt of in your philosophy.' Maybe I should say technology. Do you know who says that?"

"Horatio's smartass brother?"

"Yeah, right. Josh, national boundaries melt in the face of art that is true and pure. Only humanity remains. We need museums to show us, to remind us of our diversity yet underlying unity. And to experience it in isolation beats the whole purpose."

A vision of Vidya and himself walking about the hall rose in Josh's head.

He decided it was time to change the subject. "Listen, Hamlet, all that is good, but tell me what progress you made on the quest."

"Wow! Quest, huh?"

Josh groaned, regretting his choice of word.

"Nothing much. I reviewed the papers with a lawyer and made sure the provenance part is ironclad. I haven't heard anything from the PI. I am still holding on to the press release and the payment."

"Okay, so the only lead now is the store then."

"Right, let's pursue that some more. We don't know yet what was in the box after all."

"Okay." He wondered again if Tom was having a change of heart. On both days, he had seemed less and less inclined to talk about what they had found and had done nothing to put a stop to the acquisition. Josh decided he would tread carefully and act indifferent. If he encouraged that strain of thought, then just for that, Tom would go back to being mulish.

"We don't have much time. So call me with frequent updates."

"Aye-aye, Captain, will do," said Josh, saluting with the Coke can. "I'm going to go over the records now. If I find anything, I'll give you a call."

The room was cool and getting dark, the air conditioner's hum barely discernable. He stretched. Pulling out his laptop, he sank into the chair by the window and stretched his legs on the table.

As he clicked on his playlist, and settled to "Cry Me a River" by Sinatra Jr. he noticed anew the screen's comforting familiarity. His laptop, his phones, his tablets were all heavily and minutely personalized. His eBooks were tagged to his liking, so were his photos and music. He even had specific tastes in his background pictures. He wasn't as foot-loose as he had thought, he was simply creating roots in a digital home, he realized with sudden insight.

Tom was wrong. Art wasn't the great leveler; it was digitization. The same information about Chola bronzes and monsoon was available wherever you were, whoever you were. And a clever VR system could indeed easily get him to virtually touch that million-dollar idol and feel the smooth, coolness of the metal.

With a gentle sigh, he got on with his sleuthing. Better part of a half hour spent poking through the financial data got him nothing; it was a dead end. There was no reference to the gallery in Zurich. Perhaps that was good news.

He stood up, cracked his knuckles and stretched. Walking over, he examined the contents of the mini-bar, and opened a small can of nuts.

Popping some into his mouth, he stood pondering.

An unrelated thought occurred. He had run a search earlier in London, looking for Eichendorf references in the large corpus of documents he had collected. There hadn't been anything attention-grabbing in the results at the time. On an impulse, he leaned in and with a shrug modified his search to look for the word "Natesa" instead of Nataraja, recalling the purer word from the gallery visit, keeping all other parameters the same.

Within a few moments, a result popped up. Josh paused, his insides tightening at the solitary reference.

With a deep frown, he clicked open the document. It was a journal by a German lady written at the turn of the previous century. He could surmise she had written about a dinner party at the Eichendorf home. He read a translation—

Frau Eichendorf boasted of her Chola bronze and bored us to death. When she finally allowed me to see it, I thought the idol of the god Natesa looked commonplace on the side table, barely taller than a foolscap paper. On closer inspection, though, the features had a mysterious aura about them, and the dancing form seemed hideous and alluring at the same time. We all stared down at it for a few minutes dutifully and wished she would just stop droning on.

Josh sat slowly down, the words ringing over and over in his head. It was done.

"Barely taller than a foolscap paper." There it was. Not seven feet of towering majesty, proving beyond any doubt that the Eichendorf Nataraja was not the same as the one in the museum vaults.

Truth be told, Josh had, in his heart been hoping for an impasse, not a resolution, and absolutely not such a resolution. He cursed volubly. The blow, though not completely unexpected, still fell hard. He stood up and paced.

Tom was thawing, in the absence of conclusive proof, he could be persuaded to proceed with the transaction, Josh was sure of it. Vidya would have been a problem, but again, without concrete evidence, she might not have stopped the acquisition. It'd have made more sense for the museum to have the idol than a private collector.

After a couple of minutes, he slowly pulled himself together. The journal had been digitized recently, Banner, the gallery owner, was probably not aware of it. Bots might not create strong connections any time soon, thanks to the 'Natesa' reference. Even on the remotest chance someone spotted it in some distant future, would they make the connection to the idol in the museum? Besides, how many people other than Tom would be interested in researching the idol anyway?

Tom deserved a good break in his life. He need not, must not break this to Tom. On the other hand, Tom would never forgive him, if he found out. Was he willing to risk Tom's eternal condemnation? More importantly, was it the right thing to do?

Josh closed his laptop in despair. The night was young. He needed to assess his next move. He needed to step away. Most importantly, he needed to get a large drink.

Chapter 19

Josh headed downstairs dressed in his jeans and T-shirt.

Two young women, fashionably dressed, were glitzy beacons to the swanky bar that he had noticed the previous day. Trailing them, he looked dubiously at his attire, but the bouncer in a dark suit guarding the door waved him in.

He was usually a beer kind of guy, but today he needed something stronger. Ignoring the deep leather couch seating, he headed to the counter and perched himself on the bar stool.

Josh finished his first drink, a vodka martini, real quick, and was popping the olive into his mouth even before a bowl of chips had been placed in front of him.

The crowd was sparse, perhaps because it was a weekday.

The lighting was mellow, sparkling on the crystals and the mirrors, the music wasn't too loud, and Flo Rida, unlike him, was having a "good feeling." Stairs vanished down to a cavernous dance floor that was empty.

He rubbed his eyes and reviewed the menu as he tried to collect his thoughts. Deciding to try an Indian cocktail, he signaled to the bartender and ordered a different Vodka cocktail from the menu next.

He sat sipping the next round a little more slowly, enjoying the kick from the spices, occasionally watching the other patrons but mostly staring blankly into his drink, hoping for something that'd save him from having to make a decision.

He should have tried harder to convince Tom to just go ahead, back in London, when he had had the chance. He was a damn fool, he sat berating himself, to have let it come this far. He, who knew how much the idol mattered to Tom, and how difficult Tom's life had been, should have protected him from the heartbreak that was sure to follow.

The crowd picked up slightly as the minutes passed. Young men and women in Western clothes with Western mannerisms sat drinking and talking and laughing. Josh pecked on some sort of a savory Indian mix that had been served with his second drink and then ordered another martini.

A young Indian, obviously a regular, strode in with an entourage and they all sat noisily not too far from Josh. His clothes and glasses and watch were all from top European designers.

From his vantage point, he could observe the group easily. Was the color of their skin enough to claim ownership rights and a closer affinity to the idol? Why should he believe they cared more about the bronzes than he himself did?

The bartender set his next drink in front of him and asked if he was enjoying himself. Josh smiled mirthlessly. A bowl of roasted nuts appeared this time alongside the drink.

Josh knew Tom wouldn't take such a crude position about the ownership. His stance about art and cultural artifacts outside of their origin spot was more nuanced. But Josh was too far gone in his vodka induced resentment to bother with subtle arguments. In his mind, Tom, who appreciated, adored, and respected Chola art, deserved to get the idol.

He finished another round as he watched them and ordered one more.

The young Indian told the bartender something, and within a few minutes, another barman came in to their loud cheers and whooping. He greeted them and started mixing their drinks of shooters and daiquiris and then flipped and tossed the empty bottles to their cries of admiration. Finally, he finished with an elaborate act of juggling fire-lit bottles.

Heck, Tom's more Indian than these guys, Josh told himself with a hot belligerence that was courtesy of the alcohol. Tom deserved the career growth that'd come with the acquisition. He would be the best curator, best authority on the Cholas, any museum could hope to have.

The young Indian signed the receipt, threw a fat wad of bills for the barman, and left with his entourage. Now there was only music and distant voices and clatter.

Life was so bloody unfair, he thought, graduating to a deep, hazy sorrow as he finished another drink. He shared that thought with the barman, who nodded sympathetically.

The barman placed a fresh glass of water in front of him and asked if he had tried the Indian restaurant in the hotel.

Josh shook his head.

"That's more Tom's style you know, he loves India. First he lost his legs and then last year that bastard boyfriend of his, after four years ... no, actually that was good riddance. But I wasn't really ... I mean I could have been more sympathetic, you know."

The bartender said he completely understood.

"I'm not gonna tell him," Josh declared.

After a while, having a vague feeling of having spent a lot of time in the bar by himself, he headed to his room. A hefty looking attendant standing in the corridor hastened to help him with the elevator buttons. Josh thought he ought to stop being so deferential and reminded the man about living in a democracy, not a colony.

"Of course, sir!" the man agreed and used his card to get the elevator going.

Josh walked toward his room, peering at the numbers on the doors. The light was really low, and the corridor was very quiet. As he struggled with the keycard, he felt his decision was all wrong. He needed to tell Tom right away. He had to get it over with, just tell the man. He pulled out his phone as he fiddled with the door to his room and put the call through. He needed to first apologize and then break it gently.

The sadness was immense, shattering.

"I am so sorry, Tom, I am so sorry," he slurred weepily as soon as he heard Tom's voice. "I am here, and you are there. You are the man, the hero ... I am sorry the frau didn't like the idol, the Nata—Nataresa ... You are there in a wheelchair, and I am here, and they all wear designer clothes and ... and designer shoes. I am sorry you didn't get to do that. I am really sorry about that."

He finally got in, stumbled onto the bed, and fell asleep, only half hearing Tom's alarmed voice.

Chapter 20

The urgent summons that had got Vidya to her office had only allowed for a brief catch up with Tom who had been thrilled about their visit to the museum. Despite the rushed nature of the conversation, Tom had particularly asked her, with mild anxiety, if she had revised her opinion of Josh.

She had more than revised her opinion, she thought uncomfortably. They had progressed from hostility to polite friendliness to comfortable teasing in an alarmingly short span. Flirting felt like the inevitable next step.

By the time she got back home, it was already seven. Cars and two-wheelers were back, parked on the street by the compound walls and under the trees; the members of the neighborhood cricket club had dispersed to do their homework, and the mongrel had returned from its evening foraging. She could hear the sundry noises from the televisions blaring in their neighbors' houses.

After a quick, cool shower, she heated up the leftover sambhar, made fresh vegetables—beetroots that stained her fingers red—and cooked some rice. She cut up some guavas and bananas for dessert. Her mother had instilled a healthy eating regimen in her, so much so that she felt terribly guilty and even physically sick if she didn't have a balanced diet. She wondered, as always, how her mother managed to keep the house spic and span, cook great food, and have a career as well.

She set up the table and reminded RST, who was busy writing something in his notebook, that it was time for dinner. She had got a desktop set up for him in his bedroom, but he preferred to write long form on a notebook using an old-fashioned ink pen that he maintained with meticulous care. He put away his books and notebooks neatly, and then arrived for dinner after washing up.

"How is your American friend?" he asked as he pulled out a chair to sit for dinner.

"He is quite a character, smart, not at all egotistical, even funny. I was wrong about him yesterday. And—" She stopped mid-stream at the look of surprise on RST's face. Vidya found herself tongue-tied for a moment, realizing how out of place the exuberance in her voice must have sounded to him. She could feel discomfort wash over her face.

RST was sure to have picked up on the extent of the change in her perception as well as the sparkle in her demeanor. He would see through any further clumsy attempts at explanations.

"What did you do all day?"

She tried to respond with a pretense of calmness and went on to talk at length about the museum visit.

"Appa, the idols were stunning. How come we never went there?"

He took a few moments as he poured the sambhar on his rice. "We used to go there often when you were little. We would go to the library and sometimes to the museum too, during the summer holidays. Don't you remember? We'd finish the day sitting on the steps eating slices of raw mangoes and pineapples. You'd insist on the spicy masala to be sprinkled on the fruits and then would run around claiming it was too hot."

She was astonished at his air of indulgence and his recollection of the details of what was clearly a fond memory. "I vaguely remember the library visit but not the museum. I thought you'd have summarily dismissed the idols as religious residue or bourgeois decadence," she said, her brows raised.

"And advocate their destruction?" he asked with faint mockery.

"Well ... maybe not that far."

"Chola bronzes do not bear the identity of the person who made it, or for that matter, who commissioned it. There must have been an intent to evoke a feeling of community ownership. I must admit defining what we mean by community here is problematic, but still, I find it fascinating. Some twenty years ago I wrote an article on the commoditization of temples, and religious art, in which I took a stronger position against them, but over the years ... " His eyes took on a contemplative expression. "Let's just say my views on aesthetics and religious art have evolved." He then went on to quote Engels and naturally, a quote from Marx followed.

Vidya was unsettled, even distressed that she neither remembered the visits, nor understood what he was trying to say despite having heard him speak of such things for so long.

He looked at her and raised his brows in question.

"I don't think I fully understand you as a person, appa," she admitted. He looked taken aback but waved his hand in dismissal.

"Anyway, all that is old doesn't deserve to be revered. And I think it's a pity such deep knowledge of metallurgy didn't manifest elsewhere so vividly beyond religious works. But, tell me, did the man get his wish? Did he get to buy an idol after all?"

Vidya hesitated for a moment trying to make her answer innocuous. "Not yet, but he is close to getting one made for order."

"Your opinion of him is clearly much improved." After a small pause, he added, "He must have redeemed himself spectacularly."

"Well, I may have misjudged him, as you said," she mumbled.

"Hmm ... " Her father gave her a thoughtful look and then, after a pause, changed the subject. He talked of an article he had written for the newspaper about the farm bill.

Vidya calmed down as her father's familiar voice soothed her. As always, he talked of big subjects in a voice, full of quiet strength and conviction.

Of late, she had grown to feel sorry for him, that he had wasted his life for causes and people that didn't give anything in return. She thought it must pain him terribly to see his life's beliefs lay defeated all around him. She had always wondered how her mother endured his single-mindedness. Now, for the first time, she wondered how he did.

After they cleared up the table and the kitchen, he went on to watch prime time debates on the TV, and she retired to her bedroom, her mind going back over her day with Josh as she remembered conversations and recalled incidents. She smiled about this and pondered over that.

She wondered what had prompted her to tell Josh she had a boyfriend. It had partly been to make a point that he couldn't have found out everything about her, but she suspected it was also a wall she'd erected.

Switching on the AC and reclining on her bed, she powered up her laptop, a hand-me-down from her second brother that served her well. Like most houses, they too only had their bedrooms air-conditioned.

She chose Nostalgia by Thaikkudam Bridge to keep her company.

Before she could start her exploration, a call from her cousin, who had helped her with the introduction to the officer, interrupted her. They exchanged pleasantries and she thanked him for his help.

"Listen, I was at work this morning, so couldn't talk to you for long. Uncle was concerned about your inquiry."

"Was he?" she asked, keeping her voice cautiously neutral.

"He was troubled, extremely anxious actually."

"Why?"

"Because the owner of the store that you were enquiring about is apparently a big shot, with very powerful friends."

"Oh, I hope you reassured him I'd never reveal his name."

"No, Vidya, you don't understand—he was worried about you."

Vidya swallowed, unsettled by his grave tone. She tried to ease his concerns but knew her faltering explanations were inadequate.

He sighed. "You know we all look out for you. It's dangerous to cross paths with these type of people, Vidya," he said, the advice generic but serious, even severe. "They will stop at nothing."

He listed worriedly the man's political connections and the businesses he owned, reiterating she should not get involved even if it was for a trivial matter.

She would stop, she reassured him. After a while the call ended, and Vidya sat wondering what to make of the grave warning, feeling uneasy, a little frightened. Why had the officer felt compelled to give her cousin the details? She recalled he had tried to warn her off as well.

She texted Josh about it. There wasn't any reply; he had stopped texting some time ago. Perhaps he didn't want to overdo it. Or maybe he was in the middle of that hot date, she thought, unreasonably disappointed. Unlike him, she wasn't going to fritter away valuable time, she told herself crossly as she started on her research.

A beep from her phone told her there was an incoming text. She grabbed it expecting it to be from Josh.

Is everything all right? said the message from Tom.

What do you mean? she responded.

He asked if he could call and, after she agreed, did so.

"Josh called me, and he sounded like ... like he was quite drunk and quite troubled. I haven't seen, or heard, him plastered like this ever before."

Vidya frowned. "When I left him, he was fine," she said.

"Never mind, he must have gotten bored and headed for the bar." Tom tried to laugh it off, but his worry was palpable.

"Do you want me to do something about it?"

"Of course not! I just wanted to talk. What's keeping you up anyway?"

"Had to go back to work for some time, and then dinner got late. You know how it is, one thing pushing another."

His voice softened. "Hey, Vidya, I am so grateful for your support, such unconditional friendship is a rare gift." There was a catch in his voice.

"Shut up, Tom."

"Okay."

"You know, Tom, I was proud and ashamed at the same time, seeing all those bronzes in the museum. I mean I have never bothered to really learn about them."

"Yes, what's within easy reach is what we ignore."

And how unfair it was that she and Josh got to spend the time in the museum and not Tom. She then realized the same thought might have occurred to Josh as well, resulting in the inebriation.

Since they were really talking about it for the first time, Tom talked to her about the idol in his possession and then the topic meandered to the museum visit.

"The museum didn't seem to have particularly high security."

"Chola bronzes are solid, not hollow, they weigh a lot. Getaway won't be easy. Secondly, they are all well fingerprinted."

"What do you mean? Fingerprinted?"

"There are a set of descriptors for each idol, like high quality digital pictures, chemical composition details, even pores—the bubbles that get trapped when the metal gets solidified—all that can be detected by radiography ... You get the picture. All the descriptors taken together form a fingerprint, uniquely identifying the idol. You can't sell it to any reputed collector. If caught, it's very easy to repatriate."

"Tom?"

"Yes?" Tom chuckled as though he anticipated her next question.

"Did you um ... compare our idol with ... ?"

"Yes I did, and, no, it doesn't match any known idols. The height itself is quite unique." He then paused for a beat and continued in a soft voice, "Mind you, the idols currently being worshipped in the temples haven't been formally fingerprinted."

So potentially their idol could have been stolen from a temple. The possibility shook her to the core bringing forth the gravity of the matter.

Tom was a good storyteller and for that night, Tom regaled her with stories about two famous idol-heists, both from places at just a distance of an overnight journey from where she lived. The first involved swapping an antique in a temple with a modern replica and smuggling the original. The second, a little more complicated, involved the idol being found when someone dug up a well. Instead of reporting the find, the man had sold it illegally and the idol had ultimately been moved out of the country.

"Could ours have been buried?" She realized her unconscious use of the word "ours" was telling. She had meant it somehow to include Tom and herself, as though the idol was theirs.

"Possible, but the corrosion on the idol doesn't quite fit in with something that was buried in the soil. The patina is more consistent with a stable, indoor exposure over many years."

"What's a patina?"

"It's um ... have you heard the word tarnish?"

"Yeah."

"It's similar, like a layer of corrosion, a discoloration of the surface as the metals, predominantly copper, react with their atmosphere. Over years, some idols get this beautiful, well-settled patina on their surface. Have you seen pictures of the statue of Liberty? Her green coloring is a patina. Some statues aren't so lucky. Ugly streaks and deeper flaws develop."

She listened to Tom's voice, quietly passionate and wise and friendly.

"Bronze is the earliest alloy. Not all copper alloys are the same though. Greek bronzes have different constituents compared to the Chola bronzes. But essentially, you take copper and add other chosen metals like tin and lead, in the right dozes, and the resultant bronze gets characteristics that are even more desirable than that of the parent metals. There's a philosophical message about it, don't you think?"

"I suppose so," she smiled. As always, Vidya listened indulgently as Tom talked about art and history, of wars over temple riches, of religion, but soon, it was time to say goodbye.

After hanging up, too wired to go to sleep, Vidya decided to do more homework. What was the history of the idol? Who made it? Had it really been shipped out just months ago? The questions overwhelmed her.

She continued to scour the Tamil newspapers as well as the English newspapers and other websites for anything about bronze idols published in sync with the time line Josh had plotted.

The countryside was littered with temples, many centuries old, thriving with a continuous line of worship. All the reports she read, talked of colorful festivals and special prayers and miracles and renovations, nothing that she deemed unusual, certainly nothing as dramatic as burglary.

She saw one scholarly article on antique idols and their patinas that was intriguing, so she printed it out. She was not sure of the significance of it, but her instincts told her she was onto something that needed to be verified. She also found some interesting facts about antique art law and rules for shipping Indian artifacts abroad. She realized there was a way they could find the contents of the box and made a mental note to talk to Josh about it the next day.

After a while she closed her laptop and prepared for bed.

As she lay down, she wondered what Josh was up to. She quickly shook off a vision of Josh passionately kissing a faceless woman and forced herself to think of other things. Still, it was quite some time before she drifted to sleep.

***

Six months ago

For an observer from an airplane, Starline's cargo ship The Copper Princess *might have looked as though it was moving in a stately pace across the Red Sea. In reality, the freighter was riding the waters at breakneck speed. After a month on the Indian Ocean from the South China Sea, making a port call at Chennai, they were now on their northward path toward Genoa.*

A deckhand, having finished his day's work, leaned over to watch the frothy waves, as always, enjoying the fresh air. He liked being out at this time, seeing the evening sky with the familiar constellations coming slowly on, inspiring awe. His work for that day, scraping rust off of a wall and painting it, was done, and he could soon retire to his little cubbyhole.

The little cabin boasted more space than what he had shared with his three brothers back home in his little village in the south of Vietnam. He thought of the girl he had loved and lost long ago and wondered if she was happy.

He liked working on the freighter. There were less than a dozen in the crew. They were polite to each other, went about their work in a quiet pace, and the days stretched in peace. There had been a storm once, and they had, at one point, learned of a pirate incident, but mostly their 30,000-ton beauty of a ship had done the east and westbound- runs without any incident. He had lost count of the number of ports he had visited, the number of times he had watched the sunset. Later, he would write one more poem in his little book.

He walked around, staring at the containers, all of the same breadth and height and length. They felt like different shades of grey now, but in the daylight, they would shine red and blue and dull grey and cream. The uniform size made them all easy to load and unload and stack when they docked in the ports.

For a moment, he wished they were all irregularly shaped, giving away clues as to what was inside them. They came under the general category, so perhaps there were cars, plush furniture, maybe even smuggled weapons hidden inside the cushions, he thought idly. He'd always had a vivid imagination.

He looked up at the vast sky, his hand resting on the side of a container.

Someday, he wished, he could go home, build a small house, and grow pepper or rice in the fields. And tell stories of the faraway ports he had visited, from Lisbon to Singapore to Adelaide to San Francisco, publish his poems, maybe teach.

He sighed wistfully and went back to his cabin.

Chapter 21

On Friday morning, despite the late night, Vidya woke up as usual at six to the faint sounds of the birds and the sunlight streaming through the ground glass windows.

The milk packets, delivered at dawn, lay on the basket at the threshold, minute drops of water condensing on their surface. She put them away in the refrigerator and changed into track pants and a t-shirt; her neighborhood was not ready for her in shorts and tank top, which would have been more suitable for the weather. She was soon out for her morning run on Boat Club Road.

On weekends, she'd usually drive to the beach and run the long stretch from the lighthouse all the way to the Triumph of Labor statue and back. She loved to be there at daybreak, amidst all the serious athletes and the sleepy tramps, before the road became choked with traffic. The statues of poets and statesmen lining the breathtaking promenade enforced a sense of timelessness, of majesty and history. The crashing waves and the acres of powdery sand, the blue sky merging with the dark blue seas and the orange ball of fiery flame climbing quickly into the sky energized her.

On weekdays, like today, she settled for Boat Club Road, with its wide, clean, tree-lined avenue, with all the multi-millionaires' mansions, much closer to her house. The road was busy with all the other walkers and the morning was already bright and warm, but there was also a pleasant southwesterly wind that gently rustled the trees.

By the time she came back, she was hot and sticky and fully ready to handle the day. She made coffee for RST and herself, and they sat on the patio enjoying their morning cup, reading the newspapers, and discussing the headlines.

Bubbling with suppressed excitement, she quickly finished her cooking. The noises of bicycle bells and the last-minute rush to hand over forgotten lunch boxes told her the neighborhood kids were leaving home for school.

Getting ready for breakfast, she played the *Thevaram* with its beautiful lyrics describing the dancing god—"Those thick brows, that mischievous smile, that luxuriant hair ... "

As they sat eating their *upma and chutney*, she thought of the various articles she had read and her conversation with Tom from the previous night. Based on a quirky law in an Indian court, the god Nataraja himself could be the plaintiff seeking his own repatriation. It could end up being God Nataraja versus Thomas Winslow, she thought wryly.

After getting through her chores, she put on a rough cotton kurti of mossy green with hand-painted white creepers that she thought was particularly flattering, brushed her hair until it shone with russet highlights and stared at her features on the mirror. Satisfied, she got to the living room, gathered her purse, and bid RST goodbye.

"Skipping work again?" he asked. She could hear a light censure and a good deal of concern in his voice.

RST rarely intruded, her safety mattered to him but beyond that he hardly questioned about her friends or her activities. She knew he was often criticized by their relatives, well-meaning or otherwise, for his lack of interest in changing her matrimonial status in particular, and for his permissive behavior in general, but he remained stoic, unperturbed.

The stern, upturned face waiting for a response just then was unusual.

"I ... um ... promised Josh that, um ... I'd help him," she said, trying to sound casual.

"I see. I thought he already ordered his present." Vidya sensed an edge, a vaguely accusatory note in his tone.

She chewed her lips. "I am going to show him around a little."

There was a beat of silence as he stared at the wall, clearly unconvinced, as though he was trying to carefully form his words. Then he turned and looked at her face searchingly.

"Tell me you are not doing anything stupid."

"Define stupid," she joked.

His gaze was direct and unyielding. "Not the answer I was hoping for. Vidya, you know I believe in respecting your space. But ... "

She stared back at him, irritated about his questioning. It was not like she was particularly rebellious; she hardly did anything seriously objectionable.

"Have I ever caused you worry?"

"That answer is not helpful right now." His frown grew deep.

His newfound interest in her activities was both inconvenient and annoying.

"I am just having fun showing around a friend. What's wrong with that?"

He paused, seemingly to think over her answer. "I didn't realize he had become 'a friend.' Fine, just ... I am feeling uncomfortable about this. I wish your mother was alive. She always knew ... never mind." He shook his head and sighed.

She clenched her jaw in an inability to handle the remark, and it was not just because he was treating her like a child. Vidya had often been bothered, even hurt about the fact that RST never reminisced about her mother—her habits, her demeanor, and that he never mused over fond memories of their life together. She felt a surge of anger that the first time he had chosen to share the pain of her absence had been in that context.

"You miss amma for her ability to ask me such questions?" The resentment in her tone would have been hard to miss. RST gave her a look, paused, and then his face a mask of stone, he bid her a brisk goodbye and hid behind his newspaper.

She turned away in an angry move and stepped out of the house, banging the door shut behind her.

She stood for a moment squinting against the sunlight that scorched bright and white now, having shed its morning yellow wash, and took a deep breath.

Her neighbor, standing by the vegetable cart, busy haggling with the vendor, paused in the middle of gathering a basket full of the choicest lady's fingers.

"Hey, someone looks extra beautiful today," she called out.

"Thanks, Aunty." She forced a smile in response. She answered her question about what she had cooked for the day, almost mechanically.

"You know, Vidya, you are growing up to be so like your mother."

Her anger dissipated as her breath caught in her throat in a stupidly mawkish moment. Managing to wave a goodbye she walked toward her car. The mongrel got up, followed her all the way and stood by the side until she started the car, as though it sensed her disturbance.

An open altercation with RST was very rare in their house and she was tempted to turn back, but refrained from doing so. How could she possibly explain the situation anyway? He would likely see it as the evils of free market economy and wouldn't care a bit about the nuanced position that Tom was in.

By the time she reached the hotel though, with her mood much improved, feeling a compelling need to patch up with him, she picked up the phone and called.

"What's the matter?" he asked, devoid of any particular inflection.

"Appa, about this morning ... " She paused and then smiled. "Don't worry. I am not planning to elope with Josh."

There was a short silence, and then with a discernable humor, he said, "I know I have brought you up well. I know you wouldn't elope—"

"—with capitalists or imperialists," they finished in unison.

"Unfortunate state of the world. That doesn't leave you with much choice," he teased.

They both laughed, and she could feel the relief restoring her spirits. She apologized for her outburst that he promptly brushed off and she bid him goodbye and disconnected. After circling around a few times, thanks to no parking spots available inside the hotel, she finally found one on the street. She checked her face in the rearview mirror and, with a smile, ran up the stairs of the hotel.

Stepping into the now very familiar hotel lobby she stopped short. The lobby was crowded with men, women, and children, standing in clusters, in a variety of fine clothing. A handful of men in dark suits, a few more in kurtas in heavy brocades, and several in pristine white shirts and vetti with a hint of zari. Women in saris, the color of mango and copper sulfate and parrot green, with changing widths of intricate zari works, some stiff, some shimmering and slithering, with varying degrees of skin exposure in the back. The rubies and pearls and diamonds around their necks and on their ears pushed the understated elegance of the lobby atmosphere to glittering, gleaming opulence. Happy chatter in Tamil and English and boisterous laughter filled the air.

She spotted Josh already in the lounge, sitting in a corner reading a newspaper. He lowered the paper as though he knew she had come in, and smiled rather tiredly at the sight of her. Wishing him a good morning, she sat on the adjacent sofa he gestured at.

"Quite busy; wedding party!" she said, tilting her head toward the crowd.

"India is a poor country?" He waved his hand with a mildly incredulous look on his face.

If there had been a hint of sarcasm, she would have had several comebacks. But there was something genuinely perplexing in the way he asked the question, almost to himself than to her, that she let it go with a noncommittal shrug.

She noticed his eyes were bloodshot and he generally looked worse for wear. There was something different, almost disquieting, about him up close. It was in the tightness of his jaw, and in the pensive crinkling of his eyes.

She settled in and made some generic remarks about the weather and the wedding party. He acknowledged her comments with short and equally commonplace observations. She hesitated perceiving some reticence in him, but unable to curtail her enthusiasm any longer, she pulled out the notebook in which she had meticulously jotted down various points.

"You've got to hear this. I did some research yesterday and found some really interesting things."

Josh shifted his gaze from the ceiling down to her.

"Yeah?" he asked, seemingly more out of politeness than out of any curiosity.

She frowned in confusion for a moment, before plunging into her explanation. "During the seventies, the Indian government passed laws relating to antiquities, essentially to make sure they stayed in the country. For example, as per this law, even if I legally inherited an artifact, I should register it, and while I can sell it, I cannot do so to someone outside the country."

"Yeah, I know." His response was weary. He bent forward, and with his elbows resting on his knees, he massaged his forehead.

She paused for a moment at his obvious fatigue and then continued undeterred, "To tighten illegal exports the law also says, when one ships anything that could potentially be an item of heritage, they have to get an NOC, a 'no objection certificate', from the Archaeological Survey of India saying the ASI agrees it is a modern piece and not an antique."

"A specific form of export clearance, yes, I read about it somewhere," he agreed straightening, still not demonstrating any interest.

She waited. Someone from the party laughed aloud, a new arrival was greeted noisily, and a mother cautioned her child not to run. Since he didn't speak, she did. "So, Sarathy's should have got a certificate from ASI."

"I suppose so. How could someone from the ASI have cleared a Chola bronze?"

"I don't know, negligence, bribe ... "

"Yeah, maybe, what does it matter?"

Vidya looked searchingly at his face, surprised he had not caught on to the significance of what she was saying. Whatever had he been drinking on that hot date?

"Josh, you are missing my point. The certificate, if it exists, is like a manifest, we'd know for sure what was inside the box."

"Vidya," he interrupted in a peculiar tone. He ran his hands through his hair. "Listen, I ... I don't know. Maybe I already said this to Tom—and whether I should—oh fuck." He stopped talking, crossed his arms and slid down farther in the sofa like a sulky kid.

"What is it?" she asked, alarmed at the unexpected expletive. "Josh, what's wrong?"

"There's been a development," he almost mumbled, his voice drowned out amidst the noise.

"What kind of development?"

He sat there for a few seconds, immobile, staring at the colorful blur of the wedding party, seemingly wrestling with an inner dilemma, and then he sighed. He leaned over, and pulled out his laptop from his bag.

As she watched puzzled, he opened his laptop and clicked rapidly. He then turned the screen toward her and wordlessly pointed toward it. "You should read this."

Vidya leaned forward to get a clear view of the screen. There was a document open on it, with a portion highlighted. It was a journal entry about the Eichendorf idol, she realized as she quickly read through the paragraph.

Noise welled and echoed around them as more guests arrived and were shepherded toward the wedding hall. In their corner, there was acute silence.

Chapter 22

Over the course of the last twenty-four hours, Vidya had not had a lot of time to deliberate over the origins of the idol. She had, nevertheless, harbored some vague hopes of matters resolving in a manner that was victorious all around, that so stark a confirmation took her breath away.

"Foolscap paper," she repeated under her breath, stunned.

"Yeah."

She looked up. He was blankly staring at the ceiling.

"This proves beyond any doubt that Tom's idol is of unknown provenance."

"Yes."

He reached up and shut the laptop screen down in an angry gesture.

"Then the shipment from Sarathy's did—"

"Yes, yes, yes." He leaned forward again, holding his head between his hands.

She eyed him sympathetically. "That's what got you drunk?"

He grunted.

"Did you think of hiding this from me?" she asked. "From Tom?"

He groaned, in a gesture that implied awareness of the futility of that thought. He sat back and crossed his arms again.

"Tom would disown you."

"I know, very tempting," he responded with a ghost of a smile.

She returned it briefly.

His gaze, filled with frustration, rested on her. "He sent me a few hundred messages last night asking if I was all right. I replied this morning saying I was fine and I will talk to him around eightish, his time. I don't know, maybe I already told him about this. I don't quite recall what I said."

Vidya waited a beat. "No, you haven't told him anything yet. He spoke to me last night."

"Any chance you'd cry on my shoulder and beg me not to break it to your friend?"

"None."

"On both counts?"

She smiled.

"Didn't think so," he grumbled.

"I won't insult Tom or his resilience by doing that," she said gently.

Beyond a derisive noise, he ventured no other opinion.

"Are you just going to sit there?" she asked after a few moments of silence.

"What else is there to do?"

"Eichendorf's Nataraja is not the one Tom has. That's all that has been established. Shouldn't we be figuring out the origins of this one?"

"My main motivation is gone."

"How so? Tom would still want you to follow this."

"I don't care about what Tom wants. I just wanted to go on the goddamn vacation. That ain't gonna happen now. He can go to the cops, do whatever he wants, I couldn't care less."

He swung his hands over the back rest of the sofa and observed the dwindling crowd of guests, presumably heading toward the wedding hall, with a studied indifference, even a touch of stubbornness that was oddly not off-putting.

She waited for a few moments, surveying him in silence.

"What?" he asked with irritation, without meeting her eyes.

"Listen, I know you are feeling bad, but are you going to stop sulking any time today?"

As soon as she said it, she bit her lips in consternation. Her close friendship with Tom or even her lighter tone did not justify what was ultimately a rebuke.

He turned to meet her eyes for a few still seconds, and then straightened slowly. He drummed his fingers on his laptop and then muttered under his breath, "Sorry. You're right. Shame on me. As the great Yogi said, 'It ain't over 'til it's over.'"

"Who?"

"Never mind!" He leaned forward. "Let's talk about that ASI certificate that got you very excited."

In that moment, as he raked his fingers over his hair and breathed deeply, she realized that she liked him, really liked him. His motivations, his actions, his remorse, his recovery all resonated with her, and to put it mildly made a positive impression on her.

He looked at her face and raised a brow. "What?"

"Nothing," she mumbled as unwelcome heat washed over her face.

"If you say so." A smile lurked in the corners of his mouth and his eyes twinkled. The smile, full of boyish charm had her heart somersaulting.

He moved, making room on the sofa, and beckoned her to sit next to him, which she did.

"Listen, I really appreciate your faith in Tom. I still wish ... Anyway," he started, opening his laptop again. "I looked over at least a year's worth of Sarathy's sales data yesterday. I didn't hit anything useful."

"Look for images. The ASI certificate could be a scanned copy."

His fingers flew on the keyboard, and after about a couple of minutes, he looked up and nodded solemnly. On the screen lay a scanned version of an official looking form, the ASI clearance, listing just three items as the contents of a shipment to Zurich. Two tall brass lamps and a seven-foot Nataraja idol made by artisans working for Sarathy's with an address in Swamimalai, along with the one in Chennai.

Vidya wondered if the officer from the port authority saw the clearance when he was checking up on the address for her. The mere mention of an exported *Panchalohah* Nataraja idol, modern or not, was enough to get anyone seriously anxious and would explain the jitters.

She bit her lips in worry. Would he have talked to someone else?

Josh rubbed his eyes and massaged his temples. "They got the export clearance by claiming the idol is a modern replica. Apparently, it's a classic technique, essentially passing off an antique as new to get it out of the country."

She shouldn't have been surprised, but the rapid unraveling left her reeling, and she could infer, by the bemused look on his face, that Josh felt the same.

Tom's Nataraja had recently been smuggled out of India through Sarathy's to Gallerie de Kohinoor in Zurich. It was as clear as the bright tropical daylight.

She sat flipping the pages of the notebook in her hand, contemplating the origins of the idol. Then a thought stuck her from the previous evening.

"Josh."

He looked at her, and caught something in her tone, "What?"

"Josh, I told you I wanted to share two things."

"Go on."

"Last night I read up a lot, newspapers, articles, websites, the lot. Search facility is not that great, I had to skim through many Tamil newspapers. I covered a period of three months around your timeline for any reference to Chola idols."

"That is a lot to review."

"Yes, well, I sped through most of it, to tell you the truth."

"And you found something."

She hesitated, biting her lips. "I don't know ... it may be nothing ... maybe it is relevant. I mean I may be jumping to conclusions when ... "

"Are you going to share it with me anytime today?" he asked with a wry smile, clearly noticing her obvious self-doubt, mimicking her own words.

She grimaced and pulled out the sheet of paper she had printed out the previous evening. "Around six months ago, right around the time the Nataraja was shipped, this man, K.Ramanathan, wrote an article in a Tamil newspaper. He is an amateur historian. The byline calls him out as an executive in a public sector insurance company."

He took the paper from her hand. It was a clipping from a local newspaper with the article written in Tamil, along with a grainy black and white photo of a Chola bronze. Josh couldn't read it, and nothing about the bronze itself was eye-catching, but he stared at it intently.

"It's a different idol, must be a stock photo."

"After reading the article, I messaged Tom and asked him if he had heard of the author. Tom says he is not an expert and is a bit of an egotist but generally reliable because his papers are simply rehashes of conventional wisdom."

"Okay, what about the article?" he asked, fingering the paper abstractedly. "What does it say?"

Vidya exhaled. "It is an article that talks about a process, or say a technique, to distress, to give a bronze an even patina of green or dark brown, like an antique finish."

"Huh?"

Josh looked up with surprise. Vidya nodded, seeing the significance of it dawn on his face. He stared at the printout, his lips pursed, a frown appearing on his forehead, looking disconcerted.

"Why did this catch your interest? Just the timing?"

"Not just that. Tom coincidentally talked about patina yesterday and then ... listen to this sentence in the article. 'Whether it is of seven towering feet or a humble foot, a Nataraja that looks antique evokes a stronger presence of divinity than one that looks glossy and new.'"

They stared at each other. The wedding guests had been shepherded into the hall, and the silence in the lobby was deafening.

"I bet he has seen the idol."

She lowered her voice. "Scholarly articles about Chola bronzes don't get published in newspapers every day. In fact, this is the only one published in the last year, apart from news items. And look at the date. It's roughly a week after the idol was shipped."

"So what are you saying? That we are chasing conmen and not smugglers? That the idol is actually modern?"

Vidya faltered as she heard what she suspected articulated abruptly and clearly by Josh. He cut to the chase for sure. "I ... I am not sure."

His jaws clenched in deep thought, he stared at her. His voice carried with it the weight of a new twist, as he said, "This is totally out of the left field!"

"I know! If the expression means what I think it means. I don't know how Tom could mistake a modern piece for an antique. Don't they do carbon dating or some such thing?"

"For carbon dating, you need some organic material. The idol is metallic. Often the methods of dating a bronze are indirect, like the workmanship and the patina."

"It's about six in London. Shall we call Tom? He would know more about this, right?"

Josh tapped his fists on his chin, absent-mindedly. "No, hang on. Why would someone go through such an elaborate con?"

"For money?"

"I suppose. But why would they show the idol to this guy, what's his name?"

"Ramanathan."

He stared at her, mulling over the latest developments as his frown dug deeper and his jaw hardened. After a few moments, he asked, struggling manfully over the name, "Let's see if we can find out more. Where does this Rama-Na-than ... live?"

"The article is in the metro section. There is a good chance he lives in the city."

"If Tom has heard of him, the guy might have an Internet presence," he said getting to work with renewed vigor.

Vidya sat back a little more comfortably, moving slightly away, leaning against the hand rest, watching him type and click with a ferocious intensity that was fascinating. He gave her a running commentary of sorts, mumbling now and then, talking through the steps he was taking as he found Ramanthan's Facebook page and drilled into his posts.

"Thank God for geotags," he soon declared triumphantly. Vidya leaned in to see a picture of what looked like someone getting felicitated. A taller, thin man was draping a shawl on a shorter, stocky man while a cluster of people looked on, frozen in the act of applauding. She was not sure which one was Ramanathan. She saw Josh hop to a maps app to figure out the location of the office. It was the office of a public sector insurance company not too far from where they were.

Ramanathan did indeed live in the city.

"We have to engineer a way to meet him,"

"Right."

"I want to understand his connection to the idol. Why did he get to see it? What part did Sarathy's play? I would rather have as much information as possible before we wake up Tom."

"Yes," she agreed, chewing her lips. "The office is about an hour away. Why don't we get started? In the meanwhile, I will try to find a mutual acquaintance."

"Through a cousin who has a cousin." He smiled. "Yes, let's do that."

He packed his laptop, picked up the newspaper, and stood up, stretching. They left the hotel lobby, heading toward her car parked on the street, walking under the bright sunlight. She watched, with amusement, Josh hastening to don his sunglasses. She noted with surprise he was comfortable walking on the street.

"So what news story kept you captivated? I saw that you were reading the paper quite intently when I came in," she said, pointing to the newspaper rolled up like a baton in his hands.

"Oh! Was reading about the heat wave, a hundred people died apparently?"

Vidya sighed. "Yeah."

"That's terrible."

They continued walking on the road, sometimes together, sometimes one behind the other, adjusting their strides to the traffic whizzing past. She noticed with growing enchantment, he moved to the outer edge every time they walked together, putting himself between her and the traffic.

He continued, "I haven't read a physical copy of a newspaper in a long time. I read articles on specific topics of interest but pretty much digital editions. It was odd actually holding a large newspaper in my hands."

Vidya waited since he looked as though he wanted to say something more. There was a nostalgic note in his voice that intrigued her.

"Growing up, we had this wooden table with mismatched chairs in the kitchen where we would have all our meals. Our house was full of cheap knickknacks, but it was warm and cozy. On Sundays, my dad cooked breakfast, and my parents would have the newspapers, Sunday editions that were thick, spread out on the table, and discuss passionately about art and politics and science."

A reminiscent smile lit up his face, and Vidya was loath to see the train of conversation break as they reached the car.

They settled in, and as she drove on, Vidya called her brother's sister-in-law who worked for the same insurance company and relayed her interest in meeting Ramanathan. An American she knew would like to get Mr. Ramanathan's advice on buying a bronze idol, she explained. Could she manage an introduction?

The call done, they resumed their conversation. He asked with much curiosity, "So the delay in the monsoon, that a big deal? It made headlines."

"Yeah, last year the monsoon was extremely poor. Another year like that in a row, river beds will turn bone-dry, and there will be drought and widespread unrest."

"I see. And the rains are seasonal?"

"Yeah."

"There are some new breakthrough desalination techniques being developed. And a college friend of mine has a startup around water wastage monitoring," he said, and went on to describe both the projects with a great deal of enthusiasm. The brothers had the same bewitching baritone voice, though the undertones and inflections were decidedly different. And as she listened to him talk of something he felt passionate about, she could see both the similarities and the differences between them.

After a while, as the conversation trailed, Vidya tuned to a pop channel on the radio as she concentrated on her driving and Josh stared out, taking in all the sights and sounds, humming along under his breath with Coldplay's "A sky full of stars."

He was nice, she thought in a deliberate understatement. Would they stay in touch after he returned? Not that it mattered, she told herself hastily, firmly pushing aside the twinge she felt.

They crossed the River Cooum, and she saw Josh gazing intently at the plastic waste floating on the filthy, murky waters. He did not venture any opinion, derogatory or otherwise.

Her relative called to confirm Ramanathan would speak with them. She was warned, with a great deal of hilarity, that she was on her own though in getting away from him once he got started on his pet project.

A talkative man was good news under the circumstance.

She sped up and concentrated on the road, her thoughts weighed down as much by what Ramanathan would potentially reveal as about the budding attraction.

Chapter 23

It was late morning when they arrived at Ramanathan's office. Josh surveyed the surroundings with an offhand interest, mulling over what he needed to get out of the meeting.

It was a longish, three-story building of an indeterminate cream wash over a plain façade with rows of barred windows. The heat was searing, and the wind was barely strong to rustle the small shrubs and plants in the front. The coconut trees remained still and stoic.

A few employees walked toward what looked like a small cafeteria, while a few others, all men, stood by the pavement smoking. They followed him with their eyes, some even turning to gape with undisguised curiosity. Two women, walking past, loudly and animatedly discussing something, on seeing him seemed to lose train of their conversation.

Josh trailed close to Vidya. Most men sported a moustache, he noticed, and some of them had red or yellow or white stripes or dots on their forehead. The middle-aged women with red dots prominent on their foreheads and braids adorned with flowers mostly wore saris. The casual, and in some cases generous, show of midriff flesh had him pondering about cultural contexts.

He wondered if Vidya wore saris.

"Do young women not wear saris anymore?" he asked. Then deciding they were on terms that allowed for something more direct, he modified it. "Do you?"

"We do, I do," she stuttered slightly, making him smile. "Not for everyday wear though. On occasions, like weddings."

Vidya asked someone for directions, and they were soon ushered into a long hall. Josh dabbed at his forehead, thankful to be indoors.

Men and women sat working at individual desks arranged in rows. There were paper files stacked on almost all the desks, making Josh wonder what they did with their computers. There was a din of muted conversations and the drone of ceiling fans.

"Thanks to you, everyone is staring," she mumbled.

"Don't underestimate yourself," he quipped.

There was a brief smile, but she stared ahead.

"Seriously? Doesn't your boyfriend compliment you?" he pushed on.

"Of course he does. All the time." Not even a slight faltering, he had to hand it to her.

"I bet, especially when you wear a sari," he muttered under his breath.

She bit her lips and strove to suppress the smile.

They arrived at Ramanathan's office on the far end, and after a polite knock, went inside. Ramanathan was tall, of a medium build, with receding hairline, a grey mustache, and wore glasses, which he removed as he stood up. He wore a short-sleeved shirt of a deep purple, untucked over black pants. Most of his forehead was covered with white marks that Josh presumed to have some religious significance, Tom would know what. He extended a hand from behind his large desk.

Vidya introduced herself and him. She didn't state his last name, possibly because Ramanathan could have made the connection between him and Tom.

"Joshua?" Ramanathan questioned as though he wanted to know the last name, but as he continued, Josh realized that was not the case. "Very nice name, biblical, Moses's brother. I had a school mate named Joshua."

"Ah," said Josh, deciding not to correct him, slightly taken aback. He hadn't been in a place ever where the name Josh was not common enough to elicit such a comment.

The office had half-glass walls with promotional materials stuck on them. Through the gaps, he could see a few curious glances as people walked by. On Ramanathan's desk pressed between the tabletop and a glass pane were a single-page calendar, a picture of a bronze Nataraja, and pictures of what Josh presumed were saints and sundry gods. On their side, facing them strategically, were various insurance-related brochures.

Ramanathan's self-important air was unmistakable as he made it clear he was talking to them only out of a sense of responsibility. He didn't entertain visitors during office hours, he explained unsmilingly, but since Josh had come all the way, he had made an exception.

Josh introduced himself as a Chola bronze aficionado, looking to buy an icon, preferably a Nataraja, for his client. Ramanathan wasn't too concerned about Josh's credentials and was more than happy to highlight his.

He began on a broader note about Indian culture and history; his tone acquired shades of lecturing as he talked about India's spiritual greatness as well as ancient military prowess—there were evidences of atomic warfare millennia ago, he informed Josh. From what Josh could gather, the Delhi Sultans and the British had subsequently stripped India of all its glory. Josh was amused to notice Vidya squirm impatiently.

"Alright, anyway ... " his voice trailed after a while and he pressed an old-fashioned buzzer. A man popped in.

"What would you like to have?" he enquired solicitously.

They opted for coffee, and the man left.

"Mr. Ramanathan, we are here ... " started Vidya. Josh tapped her hand under the table. Not having expected that, she almost started, and stammered until she realized his intention.

Josh took over. "I read your articles and your Facebook posts, and I figured you'd be the right person to advise me on how to buy the best bronze."

"Very kind of you." Ramanathan made a gesture as if in dismissal of the compliment, but he was clearly pleased. He talked of his scholarly works most of which seemed to concern the cultural and spiritual angle. That got Josh worrying about the usefulness of the visit.

He gently steered the conversation toward the article.

"Your recent article about the aging process for bronzes was quite illuminating."

Ramanathan responded at length, but it amounted to vague information on a "hot process" that involved immersing the idol in chemical compounds of specific proportions, "ammonium chloride and the like," he said with a clever air. He had not himself seen the process in action, he clarified, only the results.

Josh knew, by her quick glance toward him, Vidya, too, had noted the significance of it.

"I hear the artisans at Sarathy's are really good at it," said Josh, in a voice of cool certainty that brooked no doubts about his knowledge of Sarathy's. "We went there yesterday, but nothing caught my eyes, certainly nothing that demonstrated the technique effectively."

Vidya betrayed a momentary surprise but quickly schooled her expressions back into a gentle curiosity.

"They have some good pieces ready-made, but if you ask me, it is better to get one made to order," said Ramanathan implicitly confirming his association with Sarathy's.

"Yes, I am thinking of an idol with dark patina. The store has a workshop in Swamimalai, I understand?"

"Yes, the price might be high but I can vouch for the finish. A few months ago, I saw a Nataraja idol, about seven feet high with a well settled patina that was spectacular."

Exhilaration seared through him at the confirmation. He saw Vidya stiffen, and if Ramanathan had been an observant man, he would have noticed the strain on her face. She could never play poker, Josh thought with an inward smile.

There was a brief interruption as coffee arrived in ceramic cups, and the attendant placed one in front of each of them. He left after Ramanathan dismissed him with a hand wave, closing the door behind him gently.

"Money is not a problem; my client has a very discerning eye. He wants an idol that's aged beautifully, something one cannot tell from an antique," Josh resumed.

Ramanathan laughed derisively, "An expert can always tell."

"Is that so, sir?" Vidya questioned, with the exact amount of wide-eyed, innocent curiosity that cinched a response. Josh could have kissed her.

Josh took a sip of the coffee and then wincing slightly, placed it firmly back on the table. It was a crime to call that sugary, milky concoction coffee.

"Yes, of course! The artificially aged idol I saw a few months ago at Sarathy's? If any, it seemed, at first glance, like it belonged to the tenth century, of Sembian Madevi School. But we must remember those were early days of bronze casting, and the sculptors were still experimenting, they wouldn't have made such large idols. Besides, I have pretty much seen all the Nataraja shrines and the idols in the museums in Chennai, Thanjavur, and Pondicherry, to name a few. Their fingerprints are in my brain. It wasn't like any of them." Ramanathan paused to take a delicate sip. "There were also other clues. The plinth should have been plain, not as ornate for that period. The sash around his waist, again the knot doesn't fit the period. And, do you know what a Urchava Murthy is?" He turned and quizzed Vidya.

"Yes," she responded stiffly; Josh could tell she wasn't appreciative of his questioning her. "The Moolavar is usually made of stone and remains only in the sanctum, and the Urchavar, typically a panchaloha idol, is taken around during festivals so people can pray from their houses."

"Good," Ramanathan said in a patronizing tone. "These days most youngsters don't know anything about our culture. They are all trying to mimic yours," he derided to Josh.

"And yet here I am," replied Josh with an ironic smile. This delighted the man.

Exploiting the momentary distraction as Ramanathan took another sip of his coffee, Josh winked at her. She smiled and relaxed a little.

Ramanathan cleared his throat and continued ponderously, "The bronzes, typically Urchava Murthy as you said, have holes in the base for shafts to go through. Devotees carry the idol by bearing the shafts on their shoulders. In this idol's base, there were no holes. So all in all, clearly a modern piece."

"Hmm ... " Josh kept his voice mildly curious, furiously trying to recall if Tom ever mentioned any of these inconsistencies.

"Still, you don't find such workmanship nowadays. The *stapati* who made this particular idol, I am told, is an old man who comes from a family of sculptors, generations of sculptors actually."

Josh hesitated, wondering if pushing further would come across as unnatural.

Vidya, thankfully, did not. "So, you were suggesting we get one made to order, would we be able to get it made by the same *stapati*?"

"I am not sure about that, I understand the sculptor is no more, or is blind, or something like that." Ramanathan dismissed the topic, woefully uninterested, or unaware of any further information.

His own interests were on the religious, and spiritual aspects of the idol. Josh did not begrudge the man his stage and half-listened to his words as he quoted generously and unintelligibly from medieval hymns and chants, exhibiting almost an evangelical zeal to share them.

The air conditioner hummed in the background and sheets of milk layers settled on the cooling coffee.

Ramanathan spoke of the idol's representation of the universe's cyclic nature of birth and death. "Dance of bliss, dance of frenzy, they have such soul-moving power," he intoned. The theme sounded sombre, full of references to self-loathing piety and after-life.

Ramanathan's monotonous presentation or even his own deliberate apathy, did not prevent Josh from acknowledging the profound impact it would have on someone like his father. He recognized the sacred significance of the idol, beyond the aesthetic or the scientific views he had encountered thus far.

He uncharacteristically wished he had taken the pains to listen to his father talk of philosophy and spirituality.

At a point when he decided he had been polite enough, Josh shifted gently, stating, "We should be going. We have taken a lot of your time,"

"Yes, I must get back to work too." Despite the words, Ramanathan looked as though he would have liked to continue talking. "If you are around, you could come to my discourse this Sunday," he said and rummaging in his bag, he found a leaflet that he extended to Josh.

They stood up, and Josh thanked and shook hands with Ramanathan who beamed with pleasure.

As though a sudden thought occurred to him, he declared, "You know, I will put in a word to Shivaraj. He owns Sarathy's and is a good friend of mine." He took out his phone and typed as he spoke, "I will tell him, Mr. Joshua, to give you a good price."

Josh watched helplessly, not sure what to make of it, but the man had already sent the text, and there was nothing he could do but thank him again.

Ramanathan walked from behind the table, all the way to the door and he shook hands once more.

They left, retracing their steps back in the hall and after a few moments, realizing she was very quiet, Josh turned toward Vidya to see that she looked visibly distressed, upset.

"Are you okay?" he queried concerned, slowing down.

She nodded, but he saw with shock she was blinking back her tears.

"Those hymns, they were my mom's favorite," she responded, her voice hollow.

Josh stopped walking, but within a moment, she had recovered enough to motion him to proceed with a brisk, "Let's go, then."

That turned out to be for the best because Josh was stunned to realize he was about to put his arms around her, without a care or cognizance of the surrounding.

Chapter 24

He remained silent as they exited the building, a little rattled about that unusual surge of feelings. There weren't as many people outside now, and the traffic was lighter. The sun was high in the sky, a white ball of super energy that one could not gaze upon, and wisps of clouds passed on few and far between, barely breaking the monotony of the endless wash of saturated blue. It felt acutely muggy.

I must call Tom, Josh thought, but he hesitated, chewing over the conversation, trying to get to a coherent view of what he needed to tell Tom.

"I have to have black coffee to get over this sugary taste in my mouth," he declared, grimacing. "Is this what you drink when you claim to drink Madras coffee?"

Vidya gave him a somewhat watery smile. "I have it strong. Let's go to a coffee shop. We need a place to sit and talk anyway. I saw one nearby when we came in."

After driving a small distance, she parked the car under a shady tree by a quiet lane. They got out and walked toward the café. The coffee shop was in a corner next to a gym that had a billboard of a surprisingly young Schwarzenegger flexing his muscles. The gym was on the second floor of a dusty old concrete building stairs of peeling plaster, but the café right next door was all gleaming glass and steel. The coexistence of opposites in every aspect of life was jarring.

The café was empty and quiet. It was almost time for lunch, so after a survey of the unappetizing display of cupcakes and pastries, they settled on croissants and wraps with a latte for her and an espresso for him. They took their order and sat by the window, away from the counter.

"So what do you make of Ramanathan and his involvement?" she asked.

"There is something odd there, I will give you that! He firmly believes it is a contemporary piece and not an antique."

It was possible, remote but possible, that Tom had made a mistake, he thought. He had to take into account Tom's emotional attachment to the idol. He had seen it in his expressions and heard it in his voice.

"It's time to wake up Tom." He sighed.

Earlier, despite it being 3 in the morning for him, Tom had acknowledged Josh's suggestion to talk at eight through a curt Fine. It was now getting on eight in London.

The phone rang for some time, and when Tom finally answered, his voice had the gruffness of someone who had just awoken.

"Hi. Is it eight already?" he asked sleepily.

"Just about."

"Hm. Okay. Where were you yesterday?"

"Tom, sorry to drop it on you like this, but I'm afraid I have bad news."

There was a beat of silence.

"I expected it after the drama last night," said Tom in a quiet tone, clearly bracing for it, his voice fully alert. Josh couldn't hear any background noise, but he could imagine Tom straightening up on his bed.

Josh told him quickly about the journal and about the ASI certificate.

The momentary silence was telling.

"I see."

Despite his brother's obvious best efforts to be nonchalant, Josh detected the catch in his voice.

Tom cleared his throat. "I see," he repeated. "The ASI cleared it as a modern piece, huh? What a shame!"

"Tom, that is just it," Josh said hurriedly, in some vague attempt to soften the blow. "It could very well *be* a modern piece."

"Don't be ridiculous." Tom's words were immediate, dismissive. "Obviously that's what they would have listed it as; otherwise, they couldn't have shipped it."

"Tom, listen," started Josh and saw Vidya watching him closely, trying to follow the conversation.

Josh quickly scanned the area; they were in a corner, and the lady at the counter was on the phone speaking in a low voice, lost in her own world.

"I am putting you on speaker. Vidya is with me."

Josh put Tom on speaker with low volume, and they both leaned in as Vidya took over explaining the newspaper article and the meeting with Ramanathan.

Josh couldn't help but study her face as she stared at the phone intently and explained what they had learnt that morning. He knew he was staring and that was not the moment, but he couldn't stop—the light frown of concentration, the curl of hair brushing her cheek, the well-manicured hand and the gentle motion of her breath.

"That's nonsense, guys." Tom's brush-off snapped him out of it. "It's not a fake. I have seen the idol with my very own eyes, just yesterday."

Vidya relayed Ramanathan's views.

Tom made a derisive noise. "Lack of holes for the pole was likely intentional, in those proportions, they must have set out to make a main idol. He is wrong about the knot, there are other idols, granted only a few, from that period with similar knots. He is right about the plinth, but wrong in his conclusion. It is a later addition that is all, I peg it at twelfth century. The idol itself, along with its small base, is tenth century. I know what I am talking about."

Josh met Vidya's eyes silently. It was unlike Tom to refuse to see the possibility, to be obstinate, and Josh could not tell if Tom was supremely confident or was in extreme agitation. He suspected Vidya thought the same, but neither voiced their opinion.

Josh sighed. "What do you want me to do, Tom?"

Tom grew silent. "I will have to think some more about this. Let me first get up and get ready before I plan my next steps. Call you later, okay?" he said somewhat abruptly. "Just don't do anything until you hear from me."

Josh wondered if Tom was finally regretting the ill-advised trip. Tom must realize it was too late for him to feign ignorance; he had to stop the press release, yet he was dithering.

They hung up, and Josh picked up his croissant. Vidya too started eating quietly in an unspoken understanding of his need to not rehash the conversation just then.

She still looked subdued, sad.

"You okay?" he asked after a few minutes of silence.

"Yes, I am fine. I just ... miss her ... in the most unexpected moments," she said in a quiet voice, understanding his question. "That particular hymn, it's over a millennia old, it's grand, it's subtle, it's poetic ... He didn't do justice to it in his recital. When my mom chanted the *Thiruvasagam*, it was ... it was something else."

She quoted it in her mother tongue, words still unintelligible but the rhythm and repetitions resonant and rich this time.

"What does it mean?"

"I don't think I can do justice to it, but a very loose translation would be, 'Victory to my lord, Victory to His feet, Victory to Him who remains in my heart every instant ... 'and so on."

Wanting to lighten the mood, feeling unduly bad about seeing her unhappy, he joked, "Didn't you say your dad is a godless commie? How did that work out for your mom?"

She smiled a little, but not with the mirth he had expected. He might have put his foot on it.

"Hey, I am sorry," he said gently, extending his hand to cover hers resting on the table. Tears welled in her eyes again but she swallowed and nodded.

The attendant brought their coffee, her latte with a heart in the milk foam and he slowly, reluctantly removed his hand from hers.

"What if it is an antique?" Vidya asked as they sipped their coffee.

"All right. Let's assume someone stole it or found it somewhere and brought it to whatshisname, that owner of the store. Any small-time operator would have needed someone like him who had the setup and the network to make the sale."

"Yes, apparently he is a bigwig."

"Who?"

"Shivaraj, the owner." She then related what the officer from the Port Authority had told her. "Didn't I text you about it?"

Josh had a vague memory of a text that he had not paid attention to the previous night. The warning brought home the potential danger, and troubled him. Was he being irresponsible bringing Vidya into the mess?

"How did Ramanathan get in the picture then?" she questioned.

"I was just thinking about it. Assume Shivaraj didn't mastermind the theft and that someone brought the idol to him. He'd have needed a second opinion, someone like Ramanathan to authenticate."

Vidya stared at him and then raised her brows. "But Ramanathan didn't."

"I suspect Shivaraj got the confirmation he wanted from Ramanathan's initial reaction. He must have then confused him with hot distress processes, blind sculptors, and all that. Anyone in Ramanathan's position, because of the improbability of the idol being an antique, would have presumed the explanations true."

Vidya chewed her lips in thought.

Josh leaned back, silently staring out the French window. Buses and two-wheelers ran smoothly, and a few pedestrians walked the roads unbelievably without any protection to their heads. Traffic noises filtered occasionally inside.

"I can see the logic, but what do we do with it?" she said after a while.

What can they do next? Except for the ASI certificate, there was not a whiff of information about the idol; the stolen data was a dead end. He wondered if he could leverage Ramanathan's message to the owner of the store and meet him in person. Perhaps something would come of it?

He suggested that to her and Vidya agreed that was better than nothing, and she started to put through a call to the salesman. With a quelling look, he gave her his phone. "I don't want him to have your number."

She shrugged, but did take his phone to make the call.

After a short conversation, she hung up. "He says he will talk to his boss and call back."

About five minutes later, as they finished their coffee, they got a confirmation back.

"Shivaraj will be at the store in an hour but can apparently give us only a few minutes. Let's go. Hopefully, the traffic will not screw us," she said, already getting up.

Josh followed suit, and they walked with a sense of urgency toward the door, both reaching for it at the same time. His hands brushed hers on the door handle and he felt the distinct sizzle of a static shock, and could see from her reaction, so did she.

He touched her arm briefly but firmly and at her enquiring look, said with exaggerated relief. "Just checking, don't want that to happen every time I touch you."

She gave him a look of mock exasperation and punched his arm. "That's the last of the touching, mister."

Josh was delighted to see the smile back on her face.

He tapped into his phone and keyed in the address as they settled into the little car and buckled up. "Both Google and Waze are predicting heavy traffic on the way and a journey time of one hour."

"What do they know?" she said dismissively.

"It's just information, not a challenge," he muttered, clinging for dear life, as she started the engine and roared off.

Chapter 25

The roads got wider and the pavements well-made indicating they were already in the affluent neighborhood where Sarathy's was. They had arrived within an hour, owing no doubt to her crazy driving through narrow lanes, whizzing past construction-laden roads, consistently making every signal at the last moment, and blithely squeezing through impossibly small spaces between pavements and big buses.

Feeling the adrenaline rush, forcing his mind to focus, Josh tried to formulate a plan. They were going to come face to face with the man who was possibly the mastermind of a major art theft. But worry for her safety interfered with his concentration, worry and guilt and an unfamiliar feeling of inevitability.

He bodily turned toward Vidya in the small cramped space.

"Listen, I don't want you to ... I don't think you should be part of this meeting. You drop me there and stay away until I call you back."

"What are you talking about?"

"I don't want him to know you're involved. Ramanathan just mentioned my name in the text. Let's not do something stupid," he said with feeling.

"Define stupid," she giggled.

"Vidya!"

"Come on, all that Shivaraj knows is that you are interested in buying a bronze. Why shouldn't I come?"

"Why? Because you live here! You told me he has a lot of reach. It's risky. I don't care how offended you are, I don't want to put you in danger."

His tense words failed to make an impression and were thwarted unceremoniously. Worry-ridden thoughts echoed in his head. Should he call off his meeting? What other options did he have? As they drove, he

161

made a few more attempts to reason with her but she looked completely unconvinced.

"Why don't you wait in the car?" he tried again, feeling his own agitation in his loud voice, as the store came in sight.

Much to his irritation, as though she was bent upon aggravating him, in response, she simply parked the car and merrily greeted the attendant, who unfortunately seemed to remember them from the last two days.

"See, I am involved anyway. Even the attendant remembers me," she responded, her voice reasonable, at the least acknowledging his concerns.

But that was not enough. Josh grunted in frustration. "Listen to me now, that is different—" he started, but before he could continue, she shushed him, her expression suddenly watchful as she noticed something in the mirror.

Josh turned to see an Audi stop by the curb, unmindful of the traffic being blocked and forced to drive around. A middle-aged man, tall and muscular, wearing a long-sleeved shirt and pants that were of expensive material and likely custom tailored, got out and strode purposefully toward the store. His matching tan shoes and sunglasses were certainly designer items that pronounced his wealth. His gaze, not missing the car parked, paused on Vidya, then skidded past her to assess Josh before he turned and walked in.

The attendant stood up hastily, his hand raised in a half salute of deference, and opened the door into which he vanished.

"That must be Shivaraj. He has seen me now, so I might as well come in."

She got down. Josh followed, glaring at her. She bit back a smile, irritating him further.

They went in and were asked to wait for a couple of minutes, and then the salesman informed them "sir" was ready to meet with them.

Deciding to take one last chance, he turned and told her in a stern, formal voice that was more for the salesman's benefit than for real, "If you'd please wait here?"

She looked at him, her eyes narrowed, her lips clamped thin. He held his breath. Their eyes met and her expression softened.

"Yes, I will wait here," she said calmly as he suppressed a sigh of relief.

Josh walked through a small foyer into a medium-sized room. It was furnished luxuriously with an L-shaped couch upholstered in a rich maroon and gold cotton and a hefty wooden coffee table. Translucent curtains were drawn on the large windows creating a sense of privacy, if not secrecy. Two Indian paintings, in moss green and brick red, adorned the wall, the scenes and their significance he failed to recognize; on one corner was a mini-bar and on another stood a stone sculpture of a naked couple locked in a passionate embrace, startling him with its explicit detail.

"A Khajuraho reproduction," said Shivaraj following his gaze. He got up and shook hands with Josh and waved toward the couch, inviting him to sit. He snapped his fingers at the salesman who stood by the door.

"Send two cans of Coke. You will have some Coke?" he turned and asked Josh.

"Sure."

Clearly, Josh was not important enough to be offered anything from the bar.

Shivaraj sat, flinging his hands across the backrest, his legs slightly apart, occupying considerable space, firmly establishing a sense of ownership and power. He had a suave look about him, his accent reminiscent of British posh. His rimless designer glasses and smart phone that lay discarded on the table, and his platinum ring and Rolex watch, showcased his wealth as well as a taste for ostentation.

The air of invincibility and prosperity that surrounded the man, his every expression and gesture, felt undeserved, and made Josh profoundly and immediately dislike him.

Josh opened the conversation with the Audi's performance in Indian traffic conditions and a comparison of notes on a few other luxury cars, before explaining he was there on behalf of a client who had superior tastes, sticking to the same script that he had followed with Ramanathan.

"At this time, I'd not like to go into the details of my client. I'm sure you understand," he said.

Shivaraj said that it didn't matter to him and that he'd be happy to help. He checked an incoming message on his smart phone, and Josh seized the opportunity to express his interest for that latest model. The man proudly showcased it and handed it to Josh. Josh balanced it in his hand and inspected the look and feel, while they exchanged their opinions on smart watches and smart phone models next.

After a mild knock, the salesman returned, bringing with him a tray with glasses and chilled cans of Coke. He opened the cans and poured. Shivaraj spoke to him in his native tongue, clearly berating the man, before picking up his glass. Out of the corner of his eyes, Josh saw the salesman leave after a series of miserable nods.

He placed the phone down carefully. "You have a connoisseur's taste."

The man shrugged, but Josh could spot the gleam of pride in his eyes. "My client does too, and he has a keen eye. I'm interested in a bronze that would look elegant and impressive in a multi-million-dollar home."

Shivaraj's response was leisurely. "There are quite a few in our showroom. Did you get a chance to see them?"

"They are alright, but I need something classy, that looks real, like an antique," Josh said.

"Yes, well, you can't get an antique from India. Government policies are very clear, and there are laws that prohibit such exports," Shivaraj replied. The voice was neutral, but he rolled his eyes, indicating a disagreement with the policy. "My salesman tells me you are interested in commissioning one; it takes a lot of time and money to make one to order. Are you sure you want to go that route?" he asked.

"I believe Mr. Ramanathan reached out to you. He talked of this remarkable piece he saw in your gallery," Josh said.

"Yes, he texted me about your interest," said Shivaraj, his tone still smooth, but there was a change in his expression, a slight tightening of the jaw, a narrowing of his eyes that gave away his displeasure. He was not happy Josh had come to know of that particular idol, Josh could tell.

"If you insist, we can make what you need; our sculptors are the best you'd find anywhere," he said.

They haggled over the price a bit. Josh had a feeling Shivaraj was as much playing the game to gauge him as Josh was, and so far neither of them was giving anything away.

"How about that Nataraja that Ramanathan told me about?" Josh asked, making a bold move.

Shivaraj didn't bat an eyelid this time; he was certainly expecting the question and was fully prepared with the answer.

"Unfortunately, that one is already sold."

"Will the buyer resell for a profit? Can I meet him to make an offer?"

"No, the buyer is not here," said Shivaraj, surprising him with the casual admission. "You'd have guessed?"

Was that statement as innocuous as it sounded or was he sending Josh a message that he knew about him poking around the Port Authority of India data? Shivaraj took a measured sip of his coke, eyeing him closely from above the rim of the glass. There was something scheming about his eyes that repelled Josh and the way he had lorded over his employee did not sit well with his egalitarian outlook.

Josh kept his face impassive, reminding himself to keep his head.

He ignored the question. "How much would it cost to make another one like that?"

There were more than a few moments of hesitation before Shivaraj spoke, causing Josh to suspect he was not sure how to play it. Josh could be a genuine buyer after all. "I'll have to check, it depends on many factors."

"I am sure you can swing another one of same quality," Josh repeated, allowing a slight inflection to his tone.

Shivaraj's smile was feral. "Each bronze is unique, but of course the quality of our products is always first rate."

Josh asked for details on the price and delivery timeline. Shivaraj in a very un-businessman like fashion, turned somewhat evasive.

"I'll be in touch once I get more details."

After that, he brought the conversation to a quick end. Josh was not entirely sure what opinions Shivaraj had formed of him and had a feeling he had made up his mind about what to do next.

Josh took his leave and Shivaraj stood up and shook hands.

"You have someone with you?" Shivaraj asked as he walked out with him, his eyes resting on Vidya standing in a far corner, a bored expression in her face.

Josh thought quickly, and carefully putting on a trivializing tone, said, "Just a part-time assistant I got through an online agency." He shrugged for good measure. Nothing in their behavior during the past two visits could contradict his statement.

His heart quickened as she turned toward them. He sincerely hoped she would not choose to walk over and attempt to talk to him.

Shivaraj's glance swept over her in an utterly blatant and obnoxious appraisal bringing about a sudden and very strong need in Josh to punch his face. He thought he was feeling horribly like a boyfriend, his feelings seemingly graduating from protective to possessive.

He bid a quick goodbye and walked toward the door signaling to her haughtily, and was immensely relieved when she played along. She was wonderful, he thought.

She must have caught on to something, or she perhaps suspected, as he did, that Shivaraj was likely watching them, for she, too, remained aloof all the way until they got into the car and drove out.

She turned toward him precariously the moment they pulled away from the street though. "What happened?"

"Eyes on the road, ma'am," he said, motioning toward the street.

"Josh!" she exclaimed, giving vent to her frustration of not knowing what had gone on. "What did you learn? Come on, where do we go from here?"

"To my hotel," he responded, purposefully misunderstanding.

"Figurative question, Josh." Her lips pursed into a downward droopy line which he had begun to recognize as equivalent to an eye roll.

Josh smiled, but not wanting to test her patience further, quickly recounted the conversation almost word for word.

"So, that's it? A dead end?" She sounded thoroughly dejected. "And you thought he was going to beat us up."

Josh shrugged and looked outside and there was a brief silence. A small kid from the pillion of a bike stared at him, his face literally inches away.

"What else can we do?" she asked, frowning thoughtfully.

That question showed her implicit faith in him, as well as made him realize he reciprocated her sentiments. It was one thing to lust after her but completely another to like and trust her. He shook his head to clear that thought. In a different world may be something would have come out of it. Right now, he needed to concentrate on the problem at hand.

His decision made about the next step, he turned toward her.

"Would you be compelled to report me if I do something illegal?"

"I can't believe I am saying this, but it'd depend on what you do."

"If I were to hack into someone's phone?"

"You can hack into his phone?"

Josh grinned with a quick sidelong glance.

"You already have?" She turned toward him, with wide-eyed excitement.

"Yes, well, let me just say he shouldn't have bothered about his drink and the temperature when I had his unlocked phone in my hand. I have some spyware running on it now."

"What does it do?"

"What do you need?"

"You are a dangerous man!" she exclaimed. "Enough with the suspense, what did you find?"

"No, I don't know yet. How about we head to the hotel? I will need to setup some stuff."

"Yes, let's go. Right away!"

After surveying the traffic up ahead, she swung into a short narrow road that he'd have sworn was not a car path. They came out the other end unscathed and merged into a wider road.

After a few silent moments, she turned toward him, her eyes wide. "Hey, have you put your spyware in my phone?"

"No." He laughed. "Why? You got something to hide, some interesting selfies, perhaps?"

"Absolutely! Nude pictures—," she waited for a fraction and then, "—of my boyfriend. You are welcome to look."

Before he could think of an answer to that, she quickly added in a serious voice, clearly in an attempt to change the subject. "I am glad we do have something to go on with. I can't wait for you to set your spyware up."

"It won't take too long."

"I wonder what we'll get from Shivaraj's phone."

"Let's hope not his nude pictures," he stated drily.

Chapter 26

By the time they reached the hotel, the sun was finally on its way west, and the few clouds low over the horizon were lined with an orange tint. The lobby was almost deserted, and the lounge was occupied by businessmen having coffee, deep in discussion. Josh considered the scene before him and then decided it was not private enough. He invited her up and noted, with interest, the momentary hesitation in her eyes. She then nodded regally, clearly overdoing her charade to keep a business distance between them.

The young man near the lift smiled at him and wished them a good evening. As he swiped his keycard for his floor, Josh had a sneaky suspicion he had made a fool of himself the previous evening. They walked through the cool, shady corridor toward his room.

Vidya looked distinctly uncomfortable walking up to his room with him. There was something intimate about it, he supposed.

"Is there a problem?" he asked.

She started shaking her head as if to deny it but then thought better. "My boyfriend is of a jealous nature."

"The one that keeps popping up in our conversation from time to time?"

"Yes, the one and only. Don't mock, he could beat you to a pulp."

"Ooh, I am quaking in my boots."

"Poor Josh, not really James Bond material huh?"

"I am the son of two hippies, okay? I am all for 'make love, not war'."

He ushered her in as she laughed.

The room was at a bearable temperature, and the hum of the AC that came on assured him it'd become cool enough soon. The room had been fully made up by room service and had a pleasant smell. His bags were out of sight, so were his clothes, presumably hanging inside the closet.

She walked in hesitantly and sat on the edge of a chair by the round table.

"It's a nice place. Tom chose this hotel," he said, and setting his backpack up on the table. He sat on the chair opposite to her.

The table that separated them was just a couple of feet in diameter, and he found himself staring at her face up close. The late afternoon sunbeams lit up her dark brown eyes, turning them to a rich amber, and brought out the auburn highlights of her hair.

The close quarters gave a sense of further proximity, though she wasn't necessarily any closer to him than usual. There was something charged in the atmosphere, but he wasn't sure whether it was only in his head or happening to both of them.

She couldn't possibly have a boyfriend, he told himself again. He mentally shook himself and opened his laptop and set to work.

Vidya sat at the edge of the chair, waiting, chewing her lips. She looked at the door dubiously a couple of times.

"Relax. I'm not gonna bite you."

She pursed her lips and gave him a look. "Not that! I am wondering if the cops are going to burst in," she said, waving at his laptop.

"The more realistic scenario is that of Shivaraj's henchman bursting through the door," he said amusedly.

She looked apprehensive, that he hastened to reassure, "I am very careful of the footprint. I am connected through a VPN, hopping over servers in Europe, he cannot prove it's me."

"He didn't come across as someone who would wait for proof."

"It won't be easy for him to spot the spyware; he will need to know exactly what to look for. Key logging and uploads are done in appropriate intervals, battery drain would be minimal."

Josh continued to speak as he took a look at the data the spyware had collected for him so far.

"We met him at about 2:30 and left around 3:15. Let's see who he's been calling since then. He has received two calls and dialed three numbers in the last hour. The first call he made within five minutes of our departure was to someone named Prabhu. Then to Home, and after some time to someone named Karthik."

"Karthik was the name of the salesman. Maybe Shivaraj had left by then and called him from outside."

Josh quickly cross-verified the number he had saved two days ago and confirmed it was the same person. "Okay, that means Shivaraj left shortly afterwards too."

"Let's try finding out more about this first number then."

Vidya moved her chair closer as he pulled up as many details as he could about the number.

"Tamil Nadu region number. The zone is Tan ... ja ... Thanja ... vur?" He knew for sure he was butchering the word.

"Don't ever say it like that in Tom's hearing." She leaned in, her face thoroughly animated. "That person could be in Swamimalai, where most of these stores have their workshops. The town, very close to Thanjavur, which was the Chola capital by the way, would be in that region."

Josh felt her excitement, which was infectious. He was very familiar with the perils of jumping to conclusions based on small clues like that, but he also knew, equally, that sometimes the small hunches were the ones that broke the case.

"Okay, so he called someone named Prabhu, possibly in Swamimalai. There are a lot of things I can potentially do now. But the chance of him finding out about the hack proportionally increases as to how drastic I act."

"Let us not do something unless we have to," she said, calmly disabusing him of any notions of adventure.

"Aw, come on. The damage is done anyway." He grinned. "Let me look up his mail. Maybe his bank details and then maybe reset all his passwords."

She leaned in and, picking up a magazine from the table, playfully hit him on his shoulder. "You look like a kid in a candy store."

"Okay, okay, spoilsport, what would you suggest?"

"What if we just call this Prabhu guy?"

Josh looked thoughtfully at her, considering the idea. "Yes, but have you thought about what you'd say?"

"I will ask if he wants a personal loan and try to glean as much information as possible."

Josh stared at her, bemused for a moment, and then handed his phone. It was actually a pretty good idea.

"Let's use VOIP on my phone. If he bites, ask as many details as you can."

She dialed Prabhu's number, putting it on speaker. When a male voice answered the phone, she greeted him in a chirpy voice, wishing him a good afternoon. Josh could hear a lot of background traffic noises, and the man spoke in Tamil. Vidya switched languages and spoke rapidly, sounding quite professional. Josh caught "fifteen percent interest" from the firehose of words and gathered she was now making the pitch for a loan. He heard the word "car loan" and chuckled, getting the drift of the conversation; she gave him a quelling look.

The conversation continued for some time, with Vidya putting on her best saleswoman tone. The word "address" popped up, and Josh listened intently, curious if she could pull it off.

Vidya showed a thumbs-up sign to Josh and scribbled a bunch of things in the hotel notepad. When she hung up, he could see the excitement in her eyes and in her smile. He had a sudden desire to pull her close and kiss her.

Oblivious of his line of thoughts, she waved the notebook at him.

"I don't know about the other information he gave me, but he is in Swamimalai, and he is connected to the sculptors there."

"Did you hear clanging sounds in the background?" he teased.

"He pretty much told me that he is working in a foundry; even gave me a street name. He said he is willing to meet the bank officers tomorrow for a loan."

"What's the street name?" asked Josh, pulling up the address on the ASI certificate to cross verify. He whooped triumphantly when they matched.

"Very clever social engineering," he said, raising his hand for a high-five.

"What's that?" she asked, hitting his hand gently.

"Um ... I guess it's cheating without a computer?"

Vidya plopped down on the chair, still clearly feeling exhilarated, and they stared at each other. She quieted down a little, and a thoughtful look came into her eyes.

"So Prabhu works for Shivaraj. What can we do next?"

"He is in Swamimalai, and Shivaraj had called him within five minutes of our departure. Prabhu, I bet, is the link to the old blind sculptor, if one exists that is. If not, he is likely the henchman on the ground, possibly the thief."

"Yes, I agree."

"To get to the bottom of this, we got to find him. All roads point to Swamimalai."

"Yes," she echoed, nodding in a thoughtful frown.

During the short silence that followed, Josh stared out the window at Jupiter, or was it Venus, bright outside on the blue sky gently turning grey, and contemplated on the developments from the last few days.

"You know, when Tom suggested I go to India, I thought it was completely insane. I was utterly convinced it would be a useless exercise. That I won't find anything that I couldn't find with my laptop," he observed reflectively.

"Now you think it best to go to Swamimalai," she said softly, finishing his thought.

He stared at her blankly for a moment and then shrugged. "Who would have thought? Yes, I think I should go there."

"You or we?" She didn't sound offended, merely curious.

Josh hesitated. "Are you sure you don't mind coming with me?"

"I think I must. I owe it to Tom to protect you." Her eyes twinkled.

"What about the jealous boyfriend?"

"I am sure jealousy is good for him," she retorted, undeterred.

"When do we start?"

"Shall we plan to leave around eight tomorrow? I am not too comfortable driving in the night, and besides, I have to break it to my dad."

He nodded. He wanted to poke around Shivaraj's phone as unobtrusively as possible and prepare as well. He needed a good night's sleep after the long day, and he needed Tom's blessings. The next morning sounded about right.

Tom had been surprisingly silent after the morning call. Josh wondered what to make of that.

She stood up, getting ready to leave.

"Weekend trip already? Our relationship is progressing fast, miss," he quipped.

She smiled, but he could see she was not completely unruffled. There was slightly heightened color, but she recovered quickly.

Josh very much wanted to not let her go. He wanted to grab her and kiss her thoroughly. "Do you want to get a drink, maybe grab a bite?" he asked benignly instead.

The disappointment he felt at her refusal, though it was delivered with obvious reluctance, was acute and the regret in her eyes did nothing to soothe it.

Usually, he was the one leaving, wanting to go home. It was odd he wanted to spend time with her, despite having spent all day in her company. He told himself it was because he was in a strange country with no one to call a friend.

Then he smiled a little. He wasn't thinking about the world and all his friends at his fingertips. Or perhaps Tom was right. The digital dimension did have some unshakable boundaries.

He walked her down, lingering on making small talk, like the previous day. They stood by the hotel lobby, talking some more, and then he said he would walk with her to the parking lot. They stood by the car for even more time, their conversation meandering on various topics. Finally, she had to leave.

He walked back trying to convince himself he'd get over the attraction soon. Definitely as soon as he left India, if not before. In the meanwhile, who knew how things would progress. It wasn't a crime to have a good time.

Josh tried calling Tom who cut the call with a curt text that said, *'Hang on! Will call you in a bit.'*

He did the thirty laps in the pool, which was almost getting to be a regular thing now, and went for dinner in one of the restaurants instead of ordering in.

Accepting the waiter's recommendation he settled for a fish curry with rice. His attempt to catch up on the news and tweets and email was willingly paused while he exchanged silly flirtatious texts with Vidya throughout dinner. About her so-called boyfriend, his so-called hot date—he hadn't even thought of the woman he had talked to the previous day—their upcoming weekend trip, and then pushing the envelope with a message about the replica he had seen in Shivaraj's office.

Dinner was divine; he had not tasted anything like it in the Indian restaurants he had occasionally patronized in the US. The snapper was fresh, the flavors novel and sharp and the kick from the ginger and chilies and the creamy coconut had him truly enjoying a meal after a long time.

Through the large windows that opened to a corridor, he could see the queue to the dance bar next door was long. It was a Friday evening, after all. The young Indian from the previous evening, walking in with his set of cronies like a punk rock star, waved at him. Josh raised the glass of Sauvignon Blanc that he was holding, in response.

He felt an odd disorientation as he saw the young man, the well-dressed folks around him in the restaurant, and the rich food. Yuppie bubbles were more widespread than he'd have thought.

Chapter 27

As she drove out of the hotel, Vidya decided to buy some groceries; she wanted to make sure the fridge was stocked and there was enough food for her father.

She found her car to be a handicap; if she had been in her Scooty, she could have cut through the smaller lanes and got parking spots more easily. As it were, she weaved through the ebbing traffic of the *mada* streets, and after some wasted minutes, slipped twenty rupees to the attendant and double-parked a short distance from the corner store she patronized. Josh would get dizzy at the scene, she thought with a smile. He would never make it scrambling to the store like she did, weaving through the traffic, elbowing through the crowd. The cacophony of honking and people talking, and devotional music blaring from one of the temples would have left him feeling faint.

Rushing through, she bought some *thokku* and *podi* and pickles and *appalam*, and then dashed to the street market to buy some vegetables, all the while wondering how she could convince RST. She recalled their morning conversation a bit worriedly.

She was in no mood to cook. She considered picking up a *parotta* from RST's favorite hotel, but then ruing the fact she would have had to walk quite a distance, she decided on one of the home-style restaurants instead. Besides, he would see through the ploy if she willingly brought him the very unhealthy dish.

She got into the car and called ahead, but still had to wait for the food to be packed once she reached there. The plump woman who greeted her was a longtime acquaintance and as always happily took her time to share neighborhood gossip.

She was finally on her way home. The evening was still warm, but there was a good breeze bringing some relief.

She had been exchanging texts with Josh throughout in the intervening two hours. She had deliberately taken a few minutes to respond everytime, and she noticed so did he. It was as though neither of them wanted to escalate but, at the same time, felt it was too good to let fizzle. The last one was testing the boundary and she was in a dilemma whether to ignore or engage.

The traffic was heavy with commuters clogging the main arterial road. Lost in thought, Vidya drove almost on reflex, inching every now and then.

She was mulling over the upcoming conversation with her father again when she checked her rearview mirror and saw a man in a two-wheeler behind her. Considering there was enough space for him to snake through between her and the curb, it was odd he patiently waited behind her. He was wearing a helmet too.

The idea of going to Swamimalai with Josh felt exciting, but for all the wrong reasons. It was the excitement of spending another day, all day, with him.

Did he have a girlfriend? Was he a romantic, a passionate lover?

She wanted to talk about Josh to someone. Just talk. She had many cousins, acquaintances, and friends, but of late, Tom was the one she spoke to about such matters. Under less urgent circumstances, she might have considered broaching the subject with Tom.

She had texted Tom earlier asking to call when he could but hadn't heard from him except for a simple, *"In the middle of something. Will do."* Come to think of it, it was odd that Tom hadn't spoken to them since morning. She texted RST that she was getting delayed.

She saw the motorist again at the next traffic signal, causing her some unease. This time, he was by her side, but when the signal turned green, he didn't drive out first, as all the motorists usually did. He settled behind her. After three turns and a narrow running of a red light, he had stayed behind her, and she knew she was being followed.

He must have been on her tail since the time they'd left the store. Vidya's heartbeat quickened with dread.

She took a deep breath, trying to figure out what to do. She dialed Josh's number and put him on speaker.

He picked up the phone on the second ring and greeted her with a "So, you want to discuss the sculpture?"

She paused at this teasing greeting, but, not having the luxury to respond to that, said without preamble, "Josh, I think I am being followed."

He went silent for a moment and then uttered a forceful expletive.

"What do you mean you're being followed? Where are you? You left more than two hours ago!"

Vidya was taken aback at the tension and utter panic in his voice. He must have realized the tone of his questions as well, for he audibly exhaled and said clearly struggling to rein in his emotions, "I'm sorry. Are you sure?" He still sounded shaken.

"Yes, it's a man on a two-wheeler. I don't think he means any harm. He is just following me," she said. He made a noise of derision at her optimistic statement.

"Give me a minute but don't hang up." She could hear him talking to someone on another phone.

He came back after half a minute while she continued to drive at a snail's pace. Another ten minutes, and she would be home.

"I called the reception desk to check if anyone had enquired about me. There was a call for me while I was at the restaurant."

"From who?"

"He didn't give a name. Shivaraj is doing some checking on his own, must have had us followed from the store."

"Why would he?"

"What have I gotten you into?" The fear in his voice was so palpable, she felt warmed by it. "I should have never listened to Tom. It was a stupid, stupid thing to do, getting you involved. What the hell was I thinking?" He swore some more and then went silent again. Vidya had an uncanny vision of him running his hands over his hair and pursing his lips.

"You know, Josh, if the idol was a modern piece, Shivaraj had no reason to get us tailed. I think—"

He interrupted, but in a calmer voice. "Listen, never mind all that. Just go home—it's a good thing you don't stay alone. He is just trying to gauge the level of your involvement, so just stay put tonight and go about your normal routine tomorrow."

"And you?" she asked mostly out of curiosity to see what his answer was going to be. Was he going to head back to London that very night?

"I'll take it from here. It's best you don't know my next steps." The grim determination in his voice, which told her he was going to see it through, was quite sexy.

Realizing now was not the time to argue with him, she meekly agreed to what he said. He lingered on the line, clearly upset, asking her every few seconds if the man was still following, how safe her street was, how safe her home was, did she park on the street or inside the garage ...

She smiled to herself, despite the situation. If allowed, he would have likely stayed on until she reached home, driving her crazy in the process. Over his vociferous protests, she rang off, mollifying him with an assurance that she'd call as soon as she reached home.

She took a deep breath, and thought through the situation calmly. All she needed to do was shake the motorist off the trail for the time being. She could still leave for Swamimalai with Josh as planned. If she managed to lose her tail in an unsuspicious manner, Shivaraj might be lulled into thinking he could pick up her trail the next morning at the hotel. He could always get her address through her car registration, by greasing some palms at the transport office, but might not feel compelled to do it overnight.

She kept driving, getting closer to her house, an idea slowly forming in her head.

Deciding on a plan of action, Vidya took a minor detour and drove to a small temple near her house and parked on the street in a no parking zone. It was late evening, and the temple was bustling with activity. She got out, picked up her purse and the keys and just the bag of dinner. After thinking for a moment, she left her sandals in the car and walked barefoot toward the entrance.

She wished her car be towed, but she knew she couldn't depend on it. It was twilight and soon it would grow dark. The headlights in some vehicles had just started coming on.

The man parked his bike a little farther away and removed his helmet. She caught a glimpse of him, registering he was youngish, and had a moustache. She quickly turned. Inadvertently, she had already established a pattern by going to the grocery store and the restaurant, and she hoped he wouldn't follow her inside.

Vidya set forth on her next course of action. She headed toward the flower vendor sitting near the entrance. She knew Murugan from when she was in high school. He was as old as her dad, but following her mother, she, too, called him "Anna," big brother.

The plantain leaf set on top of an old wooden box in front of him had fresh flowers, jasmines, and marigolds strung and set in a ringed heap. He was stringing a new garland of roses, his hands moving in a rhythmic pattern. He greeted her with a smile.

"I haven't seen you for a long time. From a distance, I felt like I was seeing your mother, only she wore cotton sarees unlike you in your modern attire. She used to come every Friday to the temple. I cannot believe she is gone. How's your father?"

Unasked, he picked up the jasmine string and cut a yard from the pile and handed it to her. Her mother's usual.

She replied that her father was well, asked after his family. He talked of his new grandson and showed her a picture of him on his mobile.

She turned slightly and, out of the corner of her eye, saw her pursuer was heading to a tea shop.

"*Anna*," she continued in Tamil, keeping her voice mildly concerned, "my car has stopped."

"*Adada*! Do you want me to call a mechanic?"

"No, it's alright. I'll ask Ramesh-annan to bring someone. Can you keep the key with you for now? I'll catch an auto home."

Her cousin Ramesh, was heavily involved in the temple activities and was a familiar figure to the vendors there. He came every evening to the temple, usually a little later. After he agreed, she passed on the key along with the money, hoping her shadow was not paying attention. The distance and the gathering dusk gave her confidence.

Walking inside, she went through the motions of prayer, jostling through the heavy crowd. Men, women, and children thronged, brushing and bumping past, trying to get a glimpse of the deity in the inner sanctum. Chants and temple bells filled her ears. The smell of flowers and perfumes and sweat was cloying. Almost mechanically, she put her hand out to be warmed by the *deepam* fire and then received the Tulsi leaves and the holy water. She bit into the Tulsi, its astringent and pungent taste still on her tongue as she walked around the shrine.

She couldn't see the man who had trailed her anywhere near or even outside. The walls and the crowd and the growing darkness provided a strong cover for her.

Utilizing the opportunity, she quickly slipped through the small opening in the side wall to a pathway to the next road and eased out. She walked fast, unmindful of the sting in her bare feet, euphoric she had lost him, and afraid he might find her at any moment. An empty auto rickshaw drove past, and she hailed it and literally pounced in. Her breathing slowed as it puttered along on its way.

She called her cousin and made arrangements for the car, stuttering slightly at the lies she was concocting.

As soon as they came to a stop, after paying the auto driver, she rushed into her house, thankful there was no one else on the road except the mongrel that was busy inspecting a pile of trash.

RST opened the door, his face a mask of controlled displeasure.

"I got delayed but have already brought dinner. I will be right back," she said and, dropping her bags on the table, headed straight to her room.

She called Josh right away and he picked up the phone before the first ring completed.

"Where are you?" The worry in his voice was intense.

"I am home all safe and sound, and I managed to lose him," she said with a triumphant note in her voice.

"How did you do that?" he exclaimed. "Even with your maniacal driving, I'd have thought it'd be difficult to escape a motorist."

She giggled and explained her ploy. Switching on the fan, she sat on the bed, relaxing finally after the tense moments of the previous half hour.

"Good work! Vidya, still be careful, will you? Act normal tomorrow. Go to work and stay there."

She rolled up her hair into a bun and wiped the sweat off her neck. She had to take a quick shower and then set up dinner. It was getting late, but she wanted to make sure Josh didn't leave for Swamimalai without her.

RST stuck his head in and saw she was on the phone. He gave her a look of suppressed impatience, bordering on exasperation. He thought better of saying anything and walked away.

"I have to go now, I'll call you a little later. But I am not going to go to work, I am going with you to Swamimalai tomorrow."

"No, listen—"

"No, you listen. Do not dare leave without me."

"It's dangerous. If something happens to you—"

"I am going to Swamimalai with or without you, okay? The former is the better option all around."

"Let's think some more about this," he responded, sounding uncertain.

"Josh, I mean it. There is nothing to think more about."

After a beat he muttered, "And here I was moping around that I'd never see you again."

She smiled, and as though he sensed her pleasure, he added, "I mean, I can't get rid of you that easily, can I?"

"No. And our weekend trip is on, mister," she said, chuckling. Her heart was singing. He really had sounded forlorn just then.

He didn't say anything but simply grunted. "Yeah, well, just tell the nudist he is forewarned."

She drew a blank. "What?"

"The jealous nudist?" There was laughter in his voice now. "You have forgotten your boyfriend?"

She bit her lips and then giggled. "I sure will tell him."

She was still smiling, even after she cut the call, as she rushed to shower and change.

Chapter 28

Dinner proceeded in stony silence except for the occasional clinking of the bowls. RST was clearly upset with her. She could feel the tension emanating from him. She tried to think of an easy way to start the conversation about her trip, but as the minutes stretched in silence, she realized she was only making it more difficult for herself.

They had reached the final course of curd rice when he abruptly asked, not looking directly at her, "Are you going to elope with the American?" It was delivered with enough provocation and sarcasm to not be taken literally.

She had expected it to be easy to talk to him because he was normally a patient listener who didn't interrupt or erupt at the slightest excuse. But for once, she was seeing a different side of him.

She inhaled and then said, "Of course not!"

RST met her eyes with a strained smile and said, "I was afraid of that."

"I said I was not, Appa!" she exclaimed.

"I heard! So it's something worse! What's going on?"

Vidya decided it was best to come clean. She started recounting the events of the last two days. He was perfectly still and remarkably calm until she started on the events of that afternoon. His face took on a stunned expression when she described the meeting with Shivaraj.

"What were you both thinking going there?" he asked in an explosive tone she had never heard him use, way higher in heat and volume than normal. It was unfortunate Ramesh chose to call at that precise moment. She picked up the phone, biting her lips in predicament. She had not yet told her father about the car or the tail.

"Vidya, the car started. I don't see any problem. I just came, so after I finish the prayer, I will bring it over," he offered.

"No, no it's okay, it's late. Why don't you drive it home, I'll get it tomorrow," she mumbled, facing RST's frowning countenance across the table.

She disconnected the call as soon as she politely could. Ramesh must have been puzzled at her tone, after all under normal circumstances she would have been happy to invite him home.

"Who was it?"

"Um … Ramesh."

"Ramesh? What did he want?"

She mumbled it was nothing.

"Was there a problem with the car? I thought I heard an auto."

Her phone rang again and she saw Josh's number flashing on the screen. She cut the call and messaged him that she'd call in a bit and that her car had been picked up. It was not the best moment to talk to Josh, she knew, as she saw RST's impatient face.

Bracing herself, she quickly narrated what had happened that evening.

He looked thoroughly shaken and after a full minute of silence he observed, "Ramesh called to confirm picking up the car then."

"Yes."

Having finished his dinner, he stood up without any further words, and walked over to the living room. His gait was slow, and for a moment, he looked his age and more.

She had glossed over the trip to Swamimalai, speaking in passive voice, not outright saying she intended to go. She suspected, though, he knew what she had in mind.

Thinking of all the groceries that were stuck in the car, she cleared the table and the kitchen. She spoke to Ramesh again and found, much to her relief, that he had taken the pains to open the bonnet to check the engine. It was reasonable for her tail to assume something was wrong with the car. He was on his way home, he told her. Vidya wished she could ask him if he was being followed but of course she couldn't, so she thanked him and ended the call.

After quickly finishing her chores, she came into the living room and saw her father deep in conversation with someone on the phone.

"I cannot possibly allow her to do that, Jagdish," he was saying.

Jagdish uncle! He called Jagdish uncle! She thought frantically. He was not really her uncle but her father's friend, but more importantly he was also a superintendent in the police department. She stood with her heart pounding, glad that due to some instinct she had not told her father about the spyware in Shivaraj's phone. The superintendent wouldn't have taken that lightly.

She glowered at RST in helpless anger while he deliberately ignored her and calmly finished the conversation.

"Appa, you called Jagdish uncle without my permission!" she exclaimed in outrage.

"Yes, I did. Why shouldn't I? Someone has to behave like an adult."

"Because, because ... " she sputtered. "If the police get involved, Shivaraj will ... I don't know what all he could do."

"All the more reason for you to not be involved, and let the police handle, I'd think."

She took some deep breaths, trying to calm down. What was done was done, but she needed to first understand what he planned to do.

"What does uncle suggest?"

RST pursed his lips and shook his head. "Unfortunately, he is in Mumbai for some conference and will not return until Wednesday. He said he would make some calls."

Looking immensely tired, RST sat staring out the window blankly. He was just recovering from his surgery and she knew she ought not to stress him, but she could not let it go.

"The more people know about it the less chances we have of uncovering the truth."

"Ah I see. And when did you pass the IPS?"

She pursed her lips and stared at him in consternation. He was being difficult.

"Appa, I have to go to Swamimalai," she reiterated.

"Why? What exactly do you plan to do there?"

She chewed her lips, frowning; their vague plans would only invite derision.

"If Shivaraj suspects something, he will cover his trail very quickly. He might already be doing just that after finding I am nowhere to be seen. If he hears the police are on his trail—"

"You know Jagdish is clever, as well as a man of integrity. He is not going to tip off anyone, nor would he be indiscreet. The right thing to do is to tell him what you know and back off."

"But someone else in the department might. You know that."

"Look, you both are not going to uncover anything that cannot be uncovered by the police, all right? Do you even know which direction Thanjavur is? You have never set foot outside of Chennai by yourself."

"You know that's not true. You are just saying random things." She registered in passing she had never heard him speak so loudly or so scornfully. Neither had she defied him like this before.

"It is true enough! Don't push it," he said, his voice rough.

"I know what your problem is—you don't trust your daughter going off with some man on a trip. All this pretensions of forward thinking is bogus," she lashed.

He visibly struggled to regain control as he drew a calming breath. In a quiet but stern voice, he said, "Don't you dare try that injured tone with me. I wasn't born yesterday; I can tell, you are pushing for this foolish expedition because there is a part of you that does want to spend time with that chap. I am trying to look past all that. This is a completely ill-conceived trip, even ignoring that. I'd like to meet this young man who is so callously putting you in such danger."

She bit her lips and glared at him. She tried to match his tone and inflection.

"It isn't his idea, you keep him out of this. I am going to go whether you agree or not," she declared, before moving away.

She did resist the urge to run to her bedroom, but could not help banging the door shut after.

***

Feeling edgy, Josh paced. He had finished his dinner and had just returned to the room when Vidya had called. The last hour or so had been nerve wracking.

He checked Shivaraj's activities and was dismayed to see an email from Shivaraj to Banner asking him if he'd had good luck with the last shipment. But soon the dismay turned to relief. That email meant Shivaraj didn't know yet where the Nataraja was, and Banner was highly unlikely to incriminate himself in an email. There was a good chance Shivaraj was just toying between caution and greed. Still, it was a ticking time bomb.

He moved toward the mini bar and then stopped with his hand holding the refrigerator door as his phone rang.

It was Tom.

"Where have you been?" Josh asked, his voice weary.

"What happened?" asked Tom immediately, sensing something in his voice.

Standing by the window, staring blankly at the bright moon high up in the eastern sky, its golden glow almost washing out the constellations, Josh quickly briefed him.

"What the hell were you thinking?" Tom erupted. Josh held the phone an inch away flinching as Tom raged and rebuked him, completely out of character, for his irresponsibility in putting Vidya in possible danger. After a full minute, during which Josh took it all in silence, Tom finally pulled himself together. "I guess, whatever I say will not make you feel worse than you already do."

"Yes," he admitted starkly.

Tom exhaled audibly. "This morning when we spoke, I decided it was time to talk to the authorities. After stopping the press release, it took me all day, I finally got a chance to meet this detective in the Art and Antiques Unit of the New Scotland Yard. They are woefully underfunded. Anyway, Detective Willis seemed very competent. Apparently Banner is a person of interest in a few other cases too. He said he will look into the case. Couldn't you have waited? I told you to stay put!"

"You went to the cops?" he asked more for the sake of asking something.

Tom wouldn't have wanted to bury the trail. Josh was ashamed he had even thought for a moment Tom would do anything that was unethical, that he had doubted his integrity. He had gone to the cops the minute he knew the idol did not belong to Eichendorf like he had always said.

"Of course. The provenance is clearly fabricated!"

"You are sure it is an antique?" Josh asked.

"Yes, absolutely." Tom's answer was categorical. He sighed. "I'm feeling terrible; this is all my fault. I shouldn't have pushed you both. But when I see a great piece of art, I feel a connection to humanity—the artist, his times, his space, all the viewers, the impact it's had on them, I don't know, Josh. It felt like it was worth giving my life."

"All right now, take it easy."

Tom grimaced. "Okay, maybe that is taking it too far. And I must admit it's not worth Vidya's life. It was a stupid thing to get her involved."

"Only Vidya's?"

"I'd give you up for a twenty-first century bronze."

"Yeah, yeah! Has Eichendorf been notified?"

"Not yet. Detective Willis advised me to wait until Monday, he said he needed to prep, talk to Interpol and all that."

Josh moved away from the window and sat on the bed.

"Tom," he said slowly, thinking through his options," I think we have a very small window before the trail gets buried."

"What are you saying?"

Josh took a deep breath.

"I want to get to the bottom of it, try what I can for the next two days."

There was a short silence after which Tom's voice came on, softly querying, "Why?"

"I saw Shivaraj! He sure did it! We cannot have him get away with it. Where's the justice in that?"

There was a silence on the line that felt heavy to Josh. He said in a voice that was almost belligerent, "Guess you think I am being hypocritical, and that there is no difference between him and me and that it was just four days ago that I said—"

"Josh!" Tom interrupted, his voice gentle. "Stop."

There was a pause and then Tom said simply, "You are nothing like him."

"Yeah, okay," he mumbled.

"What does Vidya think of all this?"

"She is a complete pain in the ass! She is insisting on going to Swamimalai. In my defense, I did try to dissuade her from meeting Shivaraj, but did she even consider my suggestion? No!" Josh grumbled.

"Yeah, she is spirited." Tom's tone was lovingly indulgent.

"Yeah right! You should see her driving. She is maniacal!" *And smart and funny and beautiful.*

After a small silence, Tom said, in a soft voice, "Josh? I don't want Vidya hurt."

"Of course not, if she gets hurt it will be over my dead body."

"No, I don't mean that. I meant ... she is not ... Um, you sound like you like her and I am just worried."

Josh hesitated, inadvertently causing a telling silence.

"You like her that much?" Tom queried softly.

"Shut up Tom." Josh reclined on his bed, hand behind his head, phone held to his ear, not wanting to examine that question too closely.

There was a pause, but thankfully Tom decided to let it go.

"So you are off to Swamimalai, huh? It's very close to Thanjavur." Tom's voice sounded forlorn. "You're going to Thanjavur!" he repeated wonderingly.

"Yes," Josh started and then stopped, as awareness stuck. Here he was, a thorough philistine, who had no respect for culture and history, getting to go to the place that Tom had studied, imagined, adored. Tom had never been to India. Thanjavur, a place he was an expert on, a place whose history he probably knew even better than most people living there, existed only as pictures for him. He must be feeling the impact of his handicap more than ever.

For the first time, Josh felt inadequate as a brother. They always chose places in Western Europe for their vacation. Wheelchair-friendly places where Josh simply left Tom to his devices and went on his outdoor pursuits. Tom liked it that way, too, and wouldn't have wanted Josh to fuss over him. But, had he used Tom's independence to his advantage? Couldn't he have been a little more sensitive, a little more helpful? His self-congratulatory notion of being a good brother mocked him.

The silence on the line was indicative of the poignant moment. Josh cleared his throat. "Tom, when all this is over, this November, I am bringing you here. We will celebrate Thanksgiving here, okay? I won't take no for an answer." If money was not a problem, he figured, he could get anything done in India.

Tom laughed lightly. Perhaps he, too, was suppressing some tears. It was a good thing they were talking on the phone, Josh thought dryly. He felt his throat clutch. "Hey, Tom, I'm so sorry, man."

"It's all right, Josh. I am glad you are getting to go there, really. Just don't get killed."

After hanging up, Josh tried calling Vidya, and was greeted with the tone of someone abruptly cutting the call. A message that she would call back soon and that her cousin had picked up the car followed suit.

After texting a brief reply to her about Tom going to the cops, he went online, and as expected, found Shivaraj had received a call around the same time as when the car had been picked up. The call had lasted for only a few moments. Josh noted down the number.

He took a deep breath and went online to plan his next move.

Chapter 29

Vidya sat on the bed, seething helplessly at her father's precipitous actions. Recalling Josh had tried to reach her, she walked to the dining room to get her phone, studiously ignoring RST, who was again on a call, presumably with his superintendent friend. She read the message from Josh with growing concern and called Tom first.

"You went to the police too!" she exclaimed as soon as he finished enquiring after her. "If they make any enquiries, Banner would go underground. If Shivaraj hears about it, he would destroy the trail."

"First, what do you mean 'too'?" Tom's voice was calm and curious.

She told him what her father had done just then.

"That's great! I am so glad he did that. I'll ask Detective Willis to get in touch with your father's friend if possible; get me his number and email please!" Tom unlike her was obviously relieved, even happy about her father's actions.

Vidya let out a frustrated breath. "Tom, we cannot just let it all go, not at this point."

"This is not child's play, Vidya. Shivaraj—"

"I am not asking your permission. I am going to go to Swamimalai whether you like it or not," she ground out. She did not think twice about the sharpness of her tone, she was used to being herself with Tom and was secure in her knowledge of his understanding.

Tom groaned. "Are you sure?"

"Yes."

He sighed deeply and then asked in a soft voice, "Are you okay with him?"

The "him" she knew meant Josh and the question was loaded. Vidya faltered for a few moments and then said, "Yes, yes, he is okay." She sounded breathless and breezy, even to her own ears.

"So … you like him?"

"Why would I not like your brother?"

"I see … you like him that much?"

She bit her lips, wrestling with the question, worried about what she'd find as an answer.

Tom waited for a beat, and then sighed volubly. "This is worse than I thought," he remarked enigmatically.

He let the topic go with that and gave her a hundred instructions on checking in, on listening to the police, on not taking any risks, all of which she agreed to without a murmur, happy at Tom's tacit approval.

After a while, with a soft good night and wishes for a safe journey, he ended the call.

Vidya sat biting her lips, reflecting on Tom's concerns, catching the irony. She had been more sympathetic to Tom's fears than her own father's, had been more forgiving of him to have gone to the police than of her father. Her reaction to RST's actions was unkind, unjust. She sighed deeply, she will have to talk to him and convince him, calmly. She could not embark on the crazy journey without his acceptance.

But she must. For the question of the origin and what history the Nataraja idol hid, loomed large, depriving her of the ability to even consider returning to her normal life without a resolution.

***

Josh collapsed his bag, making it smaller, and packed it with a subset of clothes. He could not possibly leave anything from his backpack; who knows when he will need one of the ten different USB adapters he packed. He called room service and ordered a nightcap just to make sure someone saw him retiring for the night.

He checked Shivaraj's call log again. There was another call between him and the shadow that had lasted for a good five minutes. Shivaraj must have quizzed him about the evening in detail before signing off for the night.

His hotel phone rang, breaking the silence. Josh picked up with a curt "hello," but the line remained silent and then, after a moment, went dead.

Josh slowly replaced the handset, smiling mirthlessly to himself. He spent the next few minutes rigging the hotel extension to automatically forward calls to his temporary number.

He waited until about half past nine, and then dressed in his shorts and hoodie, his bag slung over his shoulder, he walked casually out. The lobby was full of well-dressed people, and he could slip out unobtrusively as the doorman and the other bellhops were busy managing the cars coming in. It was Friday night, and the bar was a happening place.

Thanks to his morning walks, he had some bearing and was able to walk purposefully through the exit gate. No one followed him, not even a stray dog.

The night was still quite warm, and Josh remembered Vidya's words about the delayed monsoon. The sky was cloudless and the breeze too gentle.

He walked briskly toward a different hotel, where he had already booked a room for the night. Turning a corner, he followed the directions he had downloaded, thankful the evening traffic had thinned out. The road was dark and poorly lit except for the glare from the passing vehicles, causing him to hesitate for a second. Then with a shrug he proceeded.

Small shacks of shops and eateries were open and people were standing on the road talking or walking about, despite the lateness of the hour. The traffic noise had given way to loud conversations, TV noises, barking dogs, and rhythmic sounds coming from the eateries. The excuse for a pavement was in an appalling condition, and Josh gingerly hopped and jumped over broken slabs and walked precariously on the road from time to time. He narrowly escaped a cow, a wildly weaving auto, and a bicycle with no headlight, but not a mosquito going by the sting he felt on his arm. The foul odor from piled up garbage, of rotting food, possibly a dead rat and human excrement choked him.

He didn't notice them at first, not until he was upon them. The homeless woman settling for the night in a makeshift blanket on the pavement by an electric pole and her two small children, half naked, half draped in rag clothes, one on her lap and one crawling about on the filthy path.

The crawler looked up at Josh, smiled, and gurgled. Her hands in her mouth, she was drooling and babbling, her dark eyes sparkling in the poor light. She reached and caught hold of his leg, a butterfly touch of her soft hand on his bare calf.

Josh stumbled to a halt, his stride faltering as all his senses absorbed the moment. The profound shock he felt from the experience left him momentarily paralyzed.

The mother reached and grabbed the child out of his way and deposited her firmly back on the pavement, her angry words needing no translation for him. The opulent hotel with its Italian food and hundred-dollar bottles of wine was visible from where the little children and their tired mother sat. The dissonance was unbearable up close, without the barrier of a car window that had unbelievably, deceptively muted it until then. Emotions swelled in his heart.

He walked on, jumbled thoughts of pity and sadness and even a sense of futility and most of all anger, thrashing about in his head. Anger at himself and the world, in general. His conviction in a future world of pristine, metallic cleanliness and digital orderliness shuddered and shook.

He walked on.

After about a hundred yards, abandoning his plans to walk, he caught the next auto-rickshaw and asked to be taken to the hotel. The man quoted an exorbitant twenty dollars, but Josh was too tired mentally to even think about that, let alone argue.

Later, he lay down on his bed in that air-conditioned room, where outside noise didn't reach, and he thought of Tom and he thought of the little child, of bubbles and blinkers. He thought with a concentrated deliberation, but not just to solve a problem, to also study, himself and the web around him.

***

Six months ago ...

As always, he got the packing job. He was one of the oldest employees, working for over seven years now for the store. He packed, loaded, unloaded, and delivered, over and over. He drove a small van that he kept clean, and on the days when there wasn't any work in the store, he did personal drops for the boss or for his family members.

He knew how to pack handicrafts made of wood and metal and papier-mâché, massive, small, with protrusions and planes to be shipped to the far-flung corners of the earth. He never wasted material, space, or time, working with quick and precise movements.

That had been a particularly hard day with a lot of small baubles to pack and deliver all around the town. He had been having a late lunch when he was called into the boss's beachfront property.

It was a shock to behold the seven-foot Nataraja, unlike anything he had seen before, for the first time. His family deity was Vishnu, the one presiding over Tirumala. He was a pious man who undertook pilgrimages and tonsured his head and gave offerings for every happy occasion. He thought of Vishnu as the supreme protector, but this particular Nataraja overwhelmed him for some reason. Was it the direct gaze looking down on him as he stood? Was it the playful smile? He did not know. But he knew he would never forget the idol.

He packed it up more reverently than ever. He put more than enough of the foam padding and nailed the wooden crate safely and securely. He had been told this was going to be shipped to some foreign land, to London or New York perhaps.

His son didn't do well in exams and was of late roaming around with bad company. The Nataraja had reminded him of his overdue pilgrimage to the abode of his deity. For a second, he paused, his hand on the crate, and wished his son would be successful in life, better than a packer, maybe a doctor or an engineer.

Chapter 30

It was early morning, just touching on seven and Chennai was waking up to the weekend as busy as ever.

As soon as she drove in through the hotel gates, Vidya spotted Josh. Clad in a cream T-shirt and jeans, he stood by a pillar, arms folded, and one leg at an angle resting on the wall, sundry bags by his side. He spotted her right away and came over, his long strides quickly getting him to the car. She anxiously scanned around and noticed nothing out of ordinary. He threw the bigger bags on the back seat and settled comfortably, clearly thankful for the extra legroom.

"Ah, the sunglasses. Clever disguise and you perfectly blend in," she joked as soon as she greeted him.

"Yeah, so much so I feel I have a bull's-eye drawn on my chest."

"How was the room?" she asked him as she pulled away from the hotel.

"This is a good hotel too, big, clean room with good service."

"You didn't check out from your other room yet, right?"

"Right. I still have some of my clothes there, and I left the sheets rumpled as though I had slept in, so housekeeping won't notice anything suspicious immediately."

Vidya drove through the street looking into the mirrors nervously for anyone following them. Thankfully, she found no vehicle even remotely interested in them.

"So, is this your other car?"

"Oh no, this is one of my uncle's. My father spoke to him and got him to lend it to me for the weekend; he felt it best not to go get my car from my cousin's house. He was very anxious this morning, came with me to my uncle's place to make sure no one was following me. I hope he hasn't caught a bus heading for Thanjavur." She sighed.

"Seriously? He would do that?"

"I wouldn't put it past him. He was quite upset. Until the very last minute, he was trying to stop me. He forbade me from going, and when that didn't work, he pleaded, which I have never seen him do. That didn't work either, so who knows what he will do next."

"I get it," he said with feeling. She had to smile.

After several rounds of discussion with Jagdish that had lasted well into the night, RST had reluctantly reconciled to the idea of her going to Swamimalai. Jagdish, he had shared, had reassured him of police support in case matters worsened and had gone so far to add his opinion that the two of them going to Swamimalai might not be a bad idea.

After the initial alarm, she was now convinced the situation was not dire. She ought to have been concerned, worried about what the day held for them, but all she felt was a warm glow of pleasure at spending the day with Josh. She could not discern any nervous energy or apprehension about him either.

The heat wasn't yet prickly, the warmth still bearable, and there was a pleasant wind moving the branches. She drove through city roads with traffic that was just beginning to pick up.

"It feels like it's going to be a beautiful day," he remarked, looking outside.

"Yes," she agreed.

"The sort of day to go out on a weekend trip with your girlfriend in a convertible," he said his eyes twinkling.

"Yes," she agreed and added with a smile, "the sort of day when you'd have no doubt of coming back in one piece with the said girlfriend."

"Who am I afraid of again? Shivaraj or your boyfriend?"

She chuckled. "So what's all that?" she asked, pointing to the plastic bag that he had kept on his lap.

"Right." He pulled out a flask and a couple of small paper cups.

"You brought coffee?" she exclaimed.

He laughed. "They didn't have proper cups to go so they lent me this thermos." She thought of all the goodies she had bought the previous evening, the excitement and anticipation she had felt, of sharing them with him and watched with resigned amusement as he poured the coffee into the cups and arranged hers carefully in the holder.

He rubbed his arm as she noticed the mosquito bite marks.

Sipping their coffee, they spoke a little about the previous day, but were mostly amicably, comfortably, silent.

After the confines of city traffic, they picked up speed as she got onto the national highway toward Thanjavur.

"Our Nataraja might have travelled the same road in the opposite direction," Josh observed.

"Possibly," she agreed. They talked about the logistics of moving an idol and of the other heists from the past.

"How is it that the Pathur Nataraja was found buried? I thought these idols were holy. Why would someone bury it in the first place?"

Vidya tried to recall her history lessons from high school.

"It has to do with the invasions from the Delhi Sultanate, and then later from the European powers."

"I take it they were not good for bronze idols?"

Vidya smiled. "Any idols. There is this huge stone Shivalingam in Madurai temple broken in half, a massive stone, cut deeply in the middle. Said to be the handiwork of Khusro Khan. It must have required a lot of religious frenzy to split it. There was also the looting, these temples were prosperous."

Josh looked up information for the Delhi Sultanate of Madurai and was soon reading out accounts of dramatic battles and sieges in the harsh summer of 1311, the first of such invasions. He pieced together the timeline for her—the decline of the Chola Empire, and the rise and fall of the Pandya kings.

Over the dull roar of the highway, Josh read of Malik Kafur, a eunuch slave turned general in the army of Alauddin Khilji, and of the tragic tales of the Pandya brothers who went to war against him. The looting and the pillage of the temples in the marauding army's path and the negotiations to protect the Madurai temple felt intense even after hundreds of years. He read of more wars through the years, as late as the eighteenth century that brought further dangers to the idols.

Finally he clicked off the phone and said, "That's enough to go on."

Stretching within the confines of the car he asked, "There's ... still tension between the two religions, isn't there?"

Vidya turned to look at him briefly and shrugged. "Yes, for that matter between every religion and every other, I suppose. Fueled by historic insults and memories of superiority and fear of the future."

"Tom often quotes, 'Those who forget history are condemned to repeat it.' You know what I think? Those who wallow in history are also condemned to repeat it."

She appreciated that comment. In her mind, Josh was now Josh, his own man, not just Tom's brother, and if she wanted to make a detour to Mamallapuram, it was not because it was a first century seaport, but because she thought Josh, like her, would have liked to go for a run along the sandy beach as the waves surged and flowed, furrowing the sand around his feet.

"Doesn't it capture your imagination though, what these artisans built centuries ago?" she asked wanting to know him better.

"No, what captures my imagination is that it is not too long before you could 3-D print a personal bronze idol just like that," he responded snapping his fingers. "Imagine that!"

"Tom would be horrified at the thought!"

"For sure!"

They laughed together.

As the car swallowed the miles, they talked of her aspirations, she really wanted to be an economist not a banker, his impressions of India, "haphazard" was the word that came to his mind, of music, "Do you like jazz?" and "Have you ever heard Indian music?" and periodically about the idol, "What will we find?"

When it was just getting on nine in the morning, her phone rang.

"It's my dad," she told him before picking up the call.

"Is everything alright?" RST's voice was laden with worry.

"I am fine. We are driving down without any incidents, and you?" she asked.

"I am alright. Thought you would be interested to know Ramesh just drove the car back."

"Oh that's great. There are some groceries in the back. Will you pick them up and put them away please?"

"If that's the first thing that came to your mind, then I should be the one going to Thanjavur," he replied with dry humor.

"What do you mean?"

"As soon as Ramesh told me he was coming, I waited by the window and spotted the man who followed him."

"Oh!" How did she forget that?

"I noted down his bike number and have given it to Jagdish, not that I expect any major revelations."

They talked a bit about the drive and then he ended the call after a few minutes, repeating himself uncharacteristically, begging her multiple times to be safe.

She relayed the news to Josh.

"Wait a second! That gives me an idea."

He released his belt and leaned over. Extending a hand toward the back seat, almost brushing past her shoulder, close enough she could smell the aftershave, he picked up his backpack. A pulsating awareness prickled her.

Struggling with connectivity, he worked on his laptop for a while, finally seeming to have got what he wanted.

"Yes! Just as I thought! Your shadow called Shivaraj just a few minutes ago, and then right away, Shivaraj called another number, very likely someone out to tail me. Ask your father to give these two phone numbers to his police contact," he said.

"I'd have to explain the spyware," she pointed out worriedly, reminding him he was exposing himself.

"It's alright," he said and smiled reassuringly, tenderly too, in response to her anxious glance. Their eyes met for a brief second and Vidya felt an unspoken understanding of their mutual trust pass between them.

She called RST back and relayed the phone numbers of the two men set to trail them. A man of limitless curiosity, her father asked her a hundred questions about the hack before he hung up noting down the number.

Right when she finished her call, his phone rang.

"It's a call forward from the hotel," he motioned her to be quiet and picked it up with a curt "Hello." Vidya waited with bated breath, thankful there was no honking and the highway sound was almost white noise.

He lowered the phone, "Whoever it was cut the call as soon as they heard my voice. That should keep things at bay for a while."

The sun climbed steadily up, traffic moved smoothly except around tollgates, where drivers seemed to exhibit extra aggressiveness, and the highway grew monotonous as they drove on.

They were past Madurantakam, crossing the vast lake, which was low on water, making good time. They should have stopped for breakfast earlier, but they had both been caught up talking and now she was not sure how far away the next good hotel was.

"Game for some tea?" she asked him.

"Thought you'd never ask. My belly's grumbling."

Laughing, she got off the main road to stop at a small shop, just an enclosure really of naked bricks and wood with a counter top and a tin roof. There were large cauldrons of hot water and milk already boiling, and on the counter were glass jars with sweetmeats.

Josh took a few pictures and a short video of the man making tea. "For Tom," he said, catching her eyes on him.

A little later, they stood quietly sipping the tea and munching the sweet bun. He raised his head and stared unseeingly at the high wisps of vaporous clouds streaking through the monotonous blue skies. There was a strange expression on his face.

He then turned to look at her and smiled.

"My mom ran a small bakery out of our house. This reminds me of a cake she used to make for us for after school," he said, waving at the roll. Then biting on to it, with the tea glass in one hand, he fiddled with his phone on the other and pulled up pictures of his parents for her.

In one vivid shot, his mom sat on a bench at a bus stop, wearing a frock patterned with flowers, with a bandanna on her forehead. His father, leaning on a pole by her side, sported a thick mustache and a kurta with an Indian print. They had a guitar by the side.

"They look like hippies," she remarked. "Your mom looks so sweet."

"They were hippies. Though by the time I was born, they looked less so." Josh looked at the picture somewhat wistfully.

"Tom told me they were in a commune when he was born."

"Yeah, I believe he was to be called Dharma." He smiled as she laughed. "By the time I was born though, they had settled down to a more mundane life, from that of free love and dope, to that of Reagan and Madonna."

"Were you close to your mom?" She thought of how close she had been to her own mom.

"Not really, she was close to Tom. She would read us big books, would talk of history, obscure philosophy, drag us to museums, you know, the works."

"And you weren't interested in that I take it?"

"Of course not! I was interested in getting on the Internet, mostly to get free porn."

"I hope you are more refined now?" She teased.

"Yeah, Tom's been working on me. I might pay for it after all."

She laughed catching the joke. She knew Tom insisted on paying for content, for art and music and books.

He took her empty glass and handed it over with his own, continuing to speak, "My parents were quite old when I was born. I'm pretty sure I was an accident, you know? I gave them such a hard time. I think I was somewhat of a disappointment to them."

"I am sure that's a bit of an overstatement. Tom has talked about how proud they were of your academic achievements."

Josh shrugged, smiled a little, and paid for the tea.

Vidya instinctively knew he was a private person and was unlikely to impart such intimate feelings easily. But it did not seem strange he had chosen to share it with her, she knew she would too, and she also knew it had nothing to do with her friendship with Tom.

The blue sky was vivid, and the morning heat almost balming. She would remember that and the gravelly dirt road with no greenery, the crooked end of the roof, and the toothy smile of the shopkeeper who made the tea for a really long time. And Josh, nostalgic, with a little-boy-lost look, raking his hands through his hair, would forever be seared in her memory. She felt deeply unsettled.

"Shall we?" he asked.

They got back to the car and over the next few miles, agreed, argued, bantered, and had such a good time that Vidya perversely wished they hadn't. She was constantly troubled about getting way in over her head with him.

Soon her phone rang and it was RST again asking her where she was, if she was alright. She reassured him and disconnected with a promise to call him every two hours.

"I'd be worried too. I can understand," he said sounding sympathetic. Biting into an apple that he picked up from his bag, he extended another one to her.

"He is usually lost in his own world; our mom was the one who talked to us, and kept a check on us. They are very different, my parents. It was an arranged marriage, between two people who were polar opposites."

"Do you think they were unhappy?" He asked the question tentatively, hesitantly, sweetly mindful of not offending her.

"Not unhappy, I don't know. They had some similarities I suppose, both scrupulously honest, not easily ruffled. But I sometimes think my mother would have been happier with someone else, someone who appreciated her better. He never gave her jewelry or flowers or chocolates. Never said any words of love."

"You mean, not in your hearing," he corrected gently. She cast a quick glance away from the road toward him, at his comment, somewhat taken aback. He continued eating the apple with a studied nonchalance.

"I suppose so," she said frowning at his words. "You know the only gift he has ever given her, all through the years? Rocks! Pebbles, I should say, from every riverbed he visited. We have a collection of them at home, glass bowls full of them, from the Ganga, the Yamuna, from rivers of the communist bloc—Volga and Danube and the Yangtze! It's his idea of an elaborate joke or ... or a statement I suppose against gifts and such."

"Is that what he says?" he asked curiously.

"No, he doesn't stoop to explain, but ... " she paused, at a loss for words. She knew her father, it was hard to describe; he was not given to the finer sensibilities, he was prosaic.

"Your mom saved it."

She felt Josh's eyes on her, and she could sense he wanted to say something more, but thought better. He didn't have to explicitly say it; he had seeded that thought in her head already. Was it her own childish projections of what happily ever after should look like that was making her reluctant to see the real state of their marriage? Was it she that had somehow amplified their differences? The question echoed in her head, troubling, challenging. She swallowed.

"My mom used to collect small pieces of cloth," he shared, breaking the silence, possibly in an effort to make the conversation casual.

"Hmm?" She raised a brow.

"Textiles fascinated her. We had a small box full of scarves and handkerchiefs and hand towels at home. Silk and cotton and rayon and wool. We didn't have much money, but that hobby was her indulgence. The pleasure she got from it!" He smiled and then said, "What hobbies do you have?"

Smooth, she thought smilingly to herself, at the way he had changed the topic in a different direction, and played along.

Underneath all that was said and unsaid, ran a thread of not just comfort, but also intimacy. She knew the confined space and the close proximity over long hours were bringing it to head. She had to brace herself for the eventual heartbreak when he left. The days ahead suddenly felt bleak.

She pulled back from the dreary ruminations and the conversation meandered over many topics as the road stretched long and hot ahead of them.

Chapter 31

The traffic was controlled on the four-lane highway, and Josh was willing to concede she drove steady and well. Drivers routinely straddled lane markers setting his teeth on edge, but thankfully she remained within bounds.

The silence between them was comfortable, both talking at levels and intervals that were soothing. They compared notes on cricket and baseball, and Josh expressed his perplexity about Bollywood songs he had caught on TV while Vidya hers on the American sitcoms.

They had spoken of deeply personal things, meandering into unchartered territories. It was clear to him she had some unresolved issues with regards to her parents, but it wasn't like he had it all figured out. He could see his words had provoked some strong feelings in her, but she had recovered quickly, like he would have. Despite their differences, they were discovering similarities too and that bothered him. It felt unfair that he only had a few days with her. He did recognize had it been a different circumstance, he would have described his feelings as progressing toward or perhaps already head over heels in love with her. He was resisting, he knew that too.

The sun climbed high, the air-conditioner inside fought valiantly against the heat outside. She switched on the radio to lively music, something that was clearly modern and popular. He could tap to the beat. There weren't any channel that played English music, reminding him he was going into the heartland.

They passed a truck full of people, some standing, some sitting, with brightly colored clothes, all cheerful, chewing tobacco, laughing and chatting. Josh was astounded as they drove behind them for a while. The sun beat on their brown faces, glowing, with sparkling eyes and gleaming white teeth. They were fully packed together in the small space, and the drive couldn't possibly be comfortable, yet they seemed gloriously alive.

"They must be coming from a wedding or some happy function," she told him, seeing him staring at them with his mouth agape.

A few minutes later, they passed another truck packed with cows, which Vidya dryly informed him were being taken up for slaughter.

Josh checked Shivaraj's activities, thrilled with a steady stretch of 3G connection. He had spoken once more to the two shadows, but not to Prabhu. He must be contemplating his next move still. A call to her father informed them the cyber division police were now tracking the two men who were very much in Chennai, one near the hotel and the other near her house. The superintendent was planning to return to Chennai the next day, cutting short his trip, she shared.

After they sped through a few more miles, in a blur of dreary flatlands with a rare grove or two, Josh said, "You know, it's funny. In my imagination, the terrain was rocky and we'd go through forests and ruins."

"And some tribal men and women would come and get you, maybe put you in a rotisserie to slowly cook?" she retorted. He had to laugh at her indignation and his own cluelessness.

They spoke to Tom for a few minutes, waking him up early, updating him of their journey.

It was about half past eleven and a little too early for lunch, but the tea and roll and apple hadn't been enough. There were no proper rest stops, and he was not too sure if he was adventurous enough for the roadside hotels. The next big town, Perambalur, seemed a good twenty minutes away. He still had a bag of goodies. Spotting a small service road, lined with large fig trees and small houses, he suggested they take a break. She pulled off of the highway and stopped by an unassuming building with shady trees, their many branches peeping over the barbed wire fence. Faded words announced it to be the local library.

They got out, and Josh immediately felt the sun on his forehead, and nose, and arms. He took out his bag, and as they were trying to figure out if they should sit in the car with the door open or on the hood like he wanted, a man walked out from the building and said something to her.

"He is inviting us to use the bench inside," she said, and soon they were seated on a wooden bench with a simple backrest beneath a tree thick with foliage.

A crow cawed somewhere, a sparrow flew in ready to peck, and almost inevitably, a stray dog appeared, wagging its tail.

It felt like a picnic, a simple picnic. She spread out an old newspaper, which she borrowed from the man inside, on the bench, by his side. He took out small tubs of jam and butter softened by the heat, and muffins and croissants and two large bananas.

"Where did you get all this?" she asked, clearly impressed.

"I told the guy I was packing some stuff from the complimentary breakfast. Guess they took pity on me and decided to let me."

He took pictures of the food and Vidya and sent them to Tom. Tom came back with a *Bread and Jelly in India? Tsk, tsk …*

They snacked on the meager food slowly, sitting side by side beneath the tree, laughing about this and that, throwing some food for the dog and a little for the sparrow, in between. His body, after the long hours of artificial cooling, was warming up, but thanks to the shade, not yet to alarming levels. Occasionally, the breeze was strong enough to be felt and brought with it the perfume of tropical vegetation that he couldn't name.

He felt he was striving hard for cool amicability when inside he was feeling heady. The highway lay a little afar, shimmering under the hot sun, and but for the vehicles driving past noisily, there was hardly any other sound. Once the food was done, the dog wandered away and the sparrow flew on.

He stretched his legs and threw his arm against the backrest. "So what's that?" he asked with a butterfly touch on her arm. The round mark was clear on her caramel skin, revealed by her short sleeve.

"An inoculation mark. You guys don't have that?" She asked smiling, and a stray breeze lifted her hair that danced around her face as she turned toward him, her eyes bright. He ached to kiss her and it must have shown in his face, for her laughter slowly receded and the mirth was replaced by something intense and muddled.

"People don't kiss in public here, do they?" he asked.

"No, not at all!" She shook her head, swallowed, and then looked away. After a few moments, she turned to him with a smile, "Hey, my boyfriend doesn't take lightly to this kind of flirting, okay?"

"Seriously?" he said, as he caressed her inoculation mark with his thumb. "I am trembling."

"We should get going," she stood up, stammering. Josh reached and caught her warm hand. Their eyes met for a still moment. Then biting her lips, she wiggled, not wrenched, her hand out of his gentle grip, and he let go and got up too. They cleared the table, stuffing all the trash in the same plastic bag. After she thanked the man inside, they walked back to the car, their hands and shoulders brushing together as they bumped into each other a few times.

He did not regret the question, but perhaps he should have kept it more playful. Asking it in a serious tone had resulted in the awareness that sizzled between them.

There was a charged atmosphere in the car, and as though to break it, she bemoaned that she hadn't brought any good music. "I wish you could hear some Indian music," she said.

"Ah, you are not thinking in the digital dimension," he returned and, after braving a slow connection, got some singles downloaded.

They swallowed the miles with Carnatic vocals in the company of Sanjay and Krishna and Nityasree. He doubted he would have made such an effort to pronounce the artists name let alone appreciate the music, even for Tom. *I am in love,* he thought wryly and then somewhat uneasily. He felt wound up, brimming with potent feelings.

It was late afternoon by the time they reached Thanjavur, and Josh, in some desperate madness, wished the hotel had sold out of all rooms and they would be forced to share one.

"I am sorry, sir, there is a convention in town. We have only one room, we cannot honor your reservation." *Say it, say it,* he thought as the man tapped his keyboard and stared at the screen.

No such luck. The hotel was almost deserted, and they got their individual rooms on the same floor. They rode the elevator in silence. It was just two floors, and after they got out, Vidya's room came up first.

The corridor was silent, and he paused in front of her room as she fiddled with the key. He dropped his bag by his side in the narrow corridor and stood crowding her against the door. She looked up at him wide-eyed. There was something electric, something dazzling about that moment—a heightened state.

He was sure they were going to kiss, and stagger inside the room, clinging passionately at each other, but then she stammered something about meeting him back in the lobby in fifteen minutes and vanished inside, closing the door in a hurry.

He stood there for a few moments, unable to sort out the frustration and disappointment, before finding his own room. Throwing his bag on the table, he looked around. The room was nice but not in the same class as that of the posh, five-star hotel in Chennai. The walls did not have wood paneling, the television was smaller, and there was no mini bar. Josh walked into the bathroom, which was clean but wasn't fancy, and stared at his reflection in the mirror.

From what he had observed, he had a notion that Indian culture was somewhere in between, neither overtly permissive nor terribly repressive, but that vague understanding did not give him the answers he was looking for in terms of his next move.

Did she not want him too? How could she not?

The sound of the exhaust fan provided the white noise for him to think.

"What the hell are you doing?" he asked his reflection.

He was in India to help Tom, to find the origins of an important idol, not to chase after the first hot woman he saw. He needed to get some perspective. He needed to get his head together. He needed to stop staring at his reflection.

After taking a few minutes to freshen up, he went down, determined to play it cool.

Chapter 32

Josh was already waiting for her in the reception area by the time she got down. He stood up and smiled briefly. In his untucked, button-down shirt that he had layered over the white tee, he looked casually elegant and self-assured.

Afternoon sunbeams slanted into the lounge that was pleasant, with low seating, and a nook with a small garden that brought the outdoors in. The natural light played on the leaves and reflected on the water noiselessly cascading down a stone fountain. A large framed Thanjavur painting of butter-thief Krishna, made of gleaming golden foil studded with gems, adorned the wall.

The middle-aged man in a suit manning the reception smiled at them, but Vidya also caught a speculative glance.

Small towns, she thought to herself, but as they walked toward each other and then together, she noticed the space between Josh and her was not as far as it had been in Chennai, and there was also a subtle familiarity in their body language. She moved away a notch from him. He did too, as though he was thinking the same thing.

Deciding to grab something to eat, they walked into the deserted hotel restaurant. It was way past lunch time, but she knew tiffin would be available. A middle-aged waiter, with a broad smile, invited them in with an old world hospitality and charm.

She ordered herself a dosai, but Josh settled for Chicken 65, his face serious, oddly reminding her of the first day she met him.

The food was soon served and the waiter refilled their glasses of water. Reacting to his infectious smile, Vidya engaged him in a conversation, commenting about the weather.

He too rued the heat, "This is Thanjavur, and you see the canal outside madam, bone dry! I really hope we get good rains soon."

She agreed and enquired about the business. "The hotel looks deserted."

He smiled. "Most guests have gone out. Of course, this is not the peak season, schools have reopened and it's still a few more months to go for tourists from abroad," he shared. "There is one big tourist group staying. They just left for a demonstration in Swamimalai."

Vidya's attention snapped and Josh too looked up with curiosity.

"What sort of a demonstration?"

"It's a demonstration of bronze idol making; it's a must watch," he recommended, beaming proudly. "You might be able join them if you leave soon, it takes about an hour to get there."

Josh nodded his agreement at her questioning glance, albeit with a shrug. There was something decidedly cool about him now, almost standoffish, that she forbore from enquiring about.

They ate quickly and mostly without any words and after getting the logistics sorted out, were soon walking toward the car on their way to Swamimalai.

"Hmm ... " Josh frowned at the paper where the receptionist had written down the address for them, half way typing it into the maps app for directions.

"What?"

"It's in the same street as Sarathy's foundry."

"Good, maybe we could do a recon," she replied keeping her voice equally even.

They drove, going past small towns with clusters of shack shops and small hovel like dwellings that lined their path. Between the towns were empty fields with small patches of greenery. The state highway was an undivided road, busy with two-wheelers and buses. Schools were closing for the day, and young girls and boys distinct in their uniforms, walked or cycled home carrying their bags, clutching long notebooks, talking merrily.

Vidya had never been to Thanjavur, but knew of the significance of the area in culture and history and as the granary of the region, of agriculture being the primary occupation. But mostly she saw brown, dry, tilled lands without much greenery. *They are waiting for the rains,* she thought, vaguely recalling the crop season that started in June. Some farmland, she recognized from the colorful flags and painted stone borders, were being converted to plots for housing. She had seen ads for it on TV before, but mostly indifferently.

Josh spoke to Tom and told him of their safe arrival and spent the time fiddling with his laptop. She could tell something was bothering him, but she let him be.

They reached Swamimalai, and she parked the car on a street littered with small shacks selling filter coffee or prayer things. Newspaper sheets strung on jute ropes announced the headlines in 36-point fonts. Sachet garlands of soaps and shampoos hung too. Streamers with little flags of a political party ran from poles to poles.

The evening sun beamed molten gold on the temple façade that stood majestically against the blue sky.

A throng of women stood by a tap that was dispensing a weak stream of drinking water, their plastic pots in fluorescent green and bright yellow and blood red snaking around in a long queue. She really ought to pay attention to her father's columns, Vidya thought frowning to herself.

She asked a man on the street for directions to the foundry, not trusting the one that Josh was relaying from his app. They walked for a couple of minutes, and she had had to check with two more people before they found it.

They joined a set of tourists a few young, most middle aged, who were milling about, waiting for the demo to begin, all armed with their tablets and phones. Some were fanning with their hats, ruing the sweltering heat.

"Supposed to have started at 4," a man said in a mocking tone, looking her up and down.

Vidya bristled with annoyance at the implied inefficiency but then decidedly ignored the comment.

After the initial greetings, Josh for some inexplicable reason became intent on making friends with a young woman who after a few curious glances toward Vidya, possibly summing her up as a guide, became progressively more interested in him. They joked and laughed. Vidya studiously avoided turning in his direction and thought uncharitably their laughter was jarring and incongruous. The other man tried to strike up a conversation, but not particularly liking the way he leered at her, she moved away as politely as possible and turned her attention firmly to the ancient craft about to unfold in front of her.

The dusty hall had a tall tiled roof, and deep red flooring and sculpting paraphernalia was laid out on gunny sacks. The place in her imagination easily transformed to a medieval foundry, perhaps not much different from what it was now, with thatched roof of dry coconut fronds and bamboo poles, with men shirtless, wearing their *vetti*, speaking the same language but without the English adulterations, using implements that were only little different. She took a few pictures for Tom, desperate to share the moment with someone she loved.

Soon the stapati, a middle-aged man clad in white shirt and white vetti, his forehead covered with *vibhuti* stripes, arrived. He gave a brief introduction to the lost-wax casting process in a thick accent that was perhaps difficult for them, but fired her imagination nevertheless. He showed them a stunning mold of a goddess, delicate and beautiful, made out of a mix of bees-wax and dammar and ground-nut oil. The wax mold in itself, Vidya thought, was worthy of being called high art. The stapati's assistants applied handfuls of *vandal*-clay fully covering the mold, thick as a mask, hiding away all the beautiful details. More clay was pasted and the mold was secured with wires.

The onlookers sauntered behind the stapati, sweating and fidgety, as he moved outside and crowded into a small open space. A different, already dried up clay covered mold was now placed atop a coal stove from which thick flames burnt steadily, heating it and melting the wax within. The wax dripped from a small opening, washing the image out with it.

The wax was declared all melted away by the stapati based on the amount of the now gooey paste that had collected, and it was time for them to see the next step.

The assistant brought forth a crucible, which in itself was almost white-hot, giving the impression of him holding a flame with a pincer. The hot alloy within, of molten metals, of copper and tin and zinc leaped and crackled, searing her vision in orange and yellow and a rare streak of blue. To soft exclamations in alien tongues, he swiftly poured the liquid bronze into an opening in the clay mold until a small rivulet of metal spilled over.

They picked up a mold that had already cooled off and slowly, laboriously, painstakingly, they washed and chipped the clay, and layers of it fell away, dark and clumpy.

A bronze idol of Ganesha, with wide ears and an infectious smile, emerged shimmering in the late evening light. Vidya felt a shiver run through her body.

She looked inevitably at Josh, and for a moment, he, too, was looking at her over his phone, silent, his expression gentle. He held her eyes for a timeless moment but then returned his gaze to his phone.

The stapati chiselled and filled in the details, and soon the idol was finished except for the eyes. Installation and the opening of eyes would be done at an auspicious time, they were told.

The demonstration done, the party broke up, and it was time to leave. They walked out into the late evening in groups, Vidya by herself. They talked of programs for the next day, of their visits elsewhere, and Vidya stood apart unable to summon the energy to participate. Elsa, the young woman, was inviting Josh to join them for dinner, and he was agreeing to it with alacrity.

Two children came by and begged for money as they all stood outside waiting for the driver to bring their van. They touched the sleeves of the foreigners, who looked besieged and badgered, likely worried about all sorts of super diseases. An assistant from the foundry shouted at them, threatening them with a thrashing and they ran away having only gained the packet of biscuits that Vidya gave them.

She waited until the group got into the van, standing by herself, since Josh was still hanging around Elsa. Finally, after the van moved, after waving them bye, he turned.

They stared at each other awkwardly for a second.

"Do you want to go look for Prabhu now?" he asked.

Vidya felt drained and was not sure of the virtues of looking for him so late in the evening. As though he realized what she was thinking, or perhaps he was keen to keep his dinner appointment, he asked if they should pick it up in the morning.

She agreed, feeling lonely and upset that she had made a mistake embarking on what she felt now was a futile trip.

They trudged toward their car past the group of women still waiting for the water.

Chapter 33

The early June sun, after a mighty showing, had just set, and Josh could spot the big dipper—bright on the sky along with other stars that were beginning to show up.

The drive back was one of an uncomfortable silence. Josh recognized the demonstration had captured Vidya's imagination and she would have liked to have shared it with him. Honestly, he had been caught up in it too and had felt like holding her hand, but had strove to stay away.

He watched idly at the passing scene outside the open window, pondering over the occupations of the modern world. 3-D printing that idol would be equally magical, he was sure. He reassured himself of the old argument of creative destruction. Yet he felt uneasy as he thought of those artisans, wondering if perhaps his predilection for technology prevented him from deeper reflection, or worse, compassion.

A call came in shaking him out of his reverie. It was a call forwarded from his hotel number and Josh hesitated and decided to let it ring. After the call died away, he checked Shivaraj's call log. There were calls to both the shadows but none to Prabhu, which Josh decided was good news.

Josh checked to see if there had been a response from Banner. There was one, but it was benign, assuring Shivaraj of good tidings soon to come.

He tried to guess Shivaraj's state of mind, and predict his next moves. Until the afternoon, he must have been cautious but not necessarily concerned. It was now evening and their continued absence must begin to grate on his nerves.

Josh shared his conjectures with Vidya.

"He would have by now easily checked up on my father and our family."

"There is a good chance he would assume you are an innocent person caught in this," he remarked hopefully.

"What do you think he suspects you of?"

"Either I am a disreputable buyer or I am with some sort of law enforcement. He is trying to figure out which."

He pondered over what else he could do to buy some time.

Deciding on a plan, he called the salesman he had met at the store. The man recognized who he was as soon as Josh said his name.

"Mr. Shivaraj said he would reach out to me, but he hasn't. May I get his number?" he asked politely.

The salesman, as he had hoped for, said he would check with the boss and call him back.

Josh monitored the phone activity and saw there was indeed a short call between the salesman and Shivaraj. It was the salesman who called him back to ask if Josh was free for a drink that evening with "Sir".

Josh scrambled for an appropriate response. The salesman was on the speaker and as though she read his mind, Vidya hit mute and said "Mahabalipuram", enunciating slowly.

"I am in Mahabalipuram and won't be able to make it tonight, how about tomorrow?" he asked.

The salesman said that he would be in touch and ended the call.

Josh monitored the log with bated breath. First came the call from the salesman to Shivaraj. "Come on now," he muttered. Then came two more to the two shadows.

"Shivaraj likely bought the story and just called off the shadows. Your policeman uncle would be able to confirm in a short while."

He cracked an awkward smile at her. They had been in complete sync when he had answered the phone. So much for cooling off, he thought with a grimace.

"Watching those sculptors make the idols today, clearly, the technique is still alive," he remarked neutrally.

"Yeah, the idol could be newly made and artificially antiquated, or it could be an original. Both are possible." Her voice was academic, as though she couldn't care less about his flirting with Elsa.

Had she? He shouldn't want to know, but he did.

"Why stop with one? Wouldn't the sculptor have made more?"

"I thought about that," she said after carefully negotiating a road full of people getting off from a bus. "Making a large idol would require a lot of effort and capital, and I don't think the market exists for modern idols of that size. Also, it may be true what they said about the stapati going blind."

"Yeah, but the odds of that are really less, don't you think? An old man, who knows the technique so well, making one idol and then unable to do more? That seems quite fantastic."

"Or deeply moving. What a last hurrah!"

They spoke in brief bursts breaking the silences from time to time, about the lost wax method, the proportions of metals, and the artisans.

The easy camaraderie had been replaced by a discomposure that felt like a first fight between new lovers. And worse, one where he knew he was in the wrong. He shook his head and smiled wryly at his own state.

The traffic slowed to a crawl bringing Josh's attention to a procession coming from the opposite direction. The road was narrow, and the vehicles pushed further to the left to accommodate.

On a wide pedestal, borne by shirtless men, with poles weighing down on their shoulders, stood an idol. The bearers were moving forward in rhythm, stopping intermittently for the pious to offer their prayers.

Draped in a white glossy cloth, framed with garlands of pristine white jasmines and yellow marigolds, adorned with sparkling jewelry, the idol gleamed under the bright artificial light. Pipe music filtered above the noise of the traffic. The priest lit a small flame on a plate and raised it high, showcasing the idol.

He was wrong, even in the museum in Chennai, it had been incomplete; the idol was to be experienced thus. With the lingering warmth and a barely discernable breeze against his skin, the ring of the bells, the chants, the plate of fire going round and round, the glint of the metal, the half-naked priest, and the faithful pausing on their way.

When was that idol cast, how many generations of priests had decorated it, how many faithful devotees had prayed to it over and over? What was the cultural, economic or even political impact of such a tradition? Josh felt like he finally understood Tom's vocation.

He noticed Vidya closing her eyes for a moment, her fingers tapping her chin in what he could see was an almost reflexive reaction. Another man stopped his motorbike, brought his palms together in a gesture of prayer, his lips moving in some soundless chant.

Josh thought of smart glasses and holograms, of augmented reality and virtual reality. He pondered over a need for context sensitivity and then of an uber museum that'd allow for such sensitivity to be implanted temporarily.

He smiled catching the irony of his own instinctive reaction. Would he ever be willing to examine the notion that technology perhaps diminished such experiences?

The chants and the pipes grew louder and he could smell the perfume of the flowers as the procession went past. The smile on the handsome face of the idol turned mysterious and its benevolent gaze was almost directly upon him before the men bore it away.

They reached the hotel soon after and headed for their rooms in silence. Her bye was quick, her body language closed, fully turned away from him, as she fidgeted with the keys.

"I'll meet you downstairs for dinner," he said and, with long strides, he too walked away to his room without a moment's pause.

***

Vidya watched him walk away with a frown on his face. She could tell he was troubled, but was not entirely sure why. She sat on the bed quietly brooding for a few moments.

She was there for a nobler, grander purpose, she chided herself; she ought to snap out of such maudlin feelings.

She called her father to tell him she was back in the hotel and was safe, and felt happy to hear his voice, reassuring in its composure.

"Jagdish will be landing shortly, he said he will call me. They are tracking all three cell phones, of Shivaraj and his two thugs."

Vidya gave him Prabhu's number too to be relayed to Jagdish uncle, now that everyone knew about the spyware Josh had planted.

"All these modern cell phone tracking! One look at the idol and Stierlitz would have solved the mystery of its origins," RST claimed tongue in cheek. Vidya laughed at the reference to the fictional Russian spy. Growing up, for every American spy movie they saw, they had had to read through a Soviet equivalent.

"Did that man who was following me turn up again?"

"I saw him once, driving past our house, around noon, but he didn't stop. He may have hung around, I didn't keep a strict watch."

They speculated a bit about whether her tail could have asked someone about her whereabouts, perhaps the man who owned the mobile ironing service, or perhaps the security guard at the nearby apartment complex, but decided it wouldn't matter much even if he had. No one else knew where she was after all.

"Appa, you be safe, okay? Don't open the door without checking," she said worried.

RST laughed out loud in response.

"Appa, I am serious."

After making sure he had ordered dinner, she ended the call soon as it was getting late for dinner.

Vidya went down to find no one at the lobby. She walked over to the restaurant and saw Josh had already joined the group and was seated next to Elsa, nursing a beer, deep in conversation. A few from the party waved her over to join them, and she didn't care too much for what seemed like a half-hearted hand rise from him.

Perhaps it was for good, she thought philosophically, seeing him behaving like a jerk was perhaps the fastest way to get over her feelings.

The last thing she wanted to do was join them, but good manners prevented her from walking away. She found herself seated at the farthest end next to an elderly woman who didn't speak English and across the man whom she hadn't liked. The man ogled at her and made remarks that bordered on being racist and was definitely boorish. The woman smiled kindly from time to time, but had no conversation.

They all talked of Indian food and green chilies and the elegance of the sari that she found unreasonably exhausting. Elsa, from across the other end of the table, made it a point to say she loved her *kurti*. Vidya was irritated, but she was sensible enough to know she was being unjust.

Once, Josh met her eyes before immediately turning, no, jerking his glance away. The action was so quick and deliberate, and his subsequent indifference too studied to be natural.

She pecked at her food listlessly as she engaged in desultory conversation. When her phone rang, and Tom's number flashed on the screen, she was more than relieved to have a legitimate excuse to leave. Apologizing generally to the group, she walked out of the restaurant.

"Hey, Josh didn't pick up my call. Where are you guys?" queried Tom.

Vidya walked over to the pool side and sat in one of the plastic lounge chairs, thankful for the breeze, hoping the hotel did some fogging against mosquitos. The night was clammy and gauzy clouds raced on the dark skies, but the wind had picked up. There was a slight rustle, and the coconut trees swayed gently, comforting her.

"Having dinner. Josh is busy flirting with Elsa," she replied and then bit her lips at her unwarranted disclosure. Hearing Tom's soothing voice brought a sudden lump in her throat.

"Is he now? And who is Elsa?" asked Tom in measured tones.

"Never mind that." She forced a laugh. "Oh, Tom, did you see the pictures I shared? You should have been here. It was amazing. I missed you."

Tom was silent for a few moments. "Yeah, I did. I wish I was there too. Hey, kiddo, don't be upset, all right?"

"What do you mean?" she asked, somewhat dreading his answer.

"I don't know what I mean. But I hate to hear that forlorn note in your voice," he replied, his voice gentle.

"Why would I be forlorn when there are friends such as you?"

"Why would you be? I'm being silly."

They talked of Swamimalai and the artisans and her mood gradually improved with Tom's cheerful, understanding company.

After the conversation with Tom, not having the heart to rejoin the party, Vidya went up to the restaurant and quickly took her leave after settling her bill. She sat in her room, blindly watching some evening news, all the time wondering about Josh and Elsa.

The conversation with Tom had restored some balance in her, and she felt calm enough to question the odd way Josh was suddenly ignoring her. They hadn't particularly had any altercation that warranted such a cold treatment. In fact, the day had been heady; that moment after the check-in had been positively sensual.

His actions were more perplexing than offensive. Then instinctively, with sudden insight, she understood he was trying, ineptly, to push her away. Was he affected too then?

Wasn't it too soon to acknowledge even to herself that she was falling in love with him? That, the jealousy and the sadness was all stemming from that fundamental, basic emotion?

Whatever the reason was, she felt this was a good respite. It was something to hold on to in the middle of a heady rush down, to pause, and to climb back to sanity perhaps.

She felt calmer as she reclined on her bed and selected a set of Rahman melodies from her playlist.

Chapter 34

Waving bye to Elsa, Josh firmly stepped out of the elevator. He'd noticed Vidya leave and had, out of sheer spite and obstinacy, stayed for an hour longer lingering over dinner. He was frustrated that his mind had wandered over and over to what Vidya might be doing. He had, with his clumsy behavior, made things worse. All he had found out was despite being next to a really pretty, interesting girl, he had been most aware of Vidya's every single move.

It was about ten, and things were quiet. As he walked back, he saw the light under the door of Vidya's room. He hesitated briefly but eventually continued walking over to his room.

Noticing he had missed a call from Tom, he called him back, and they spoke of the day. Tom wasn't very confident about tracking the origin of the idol and seemed resigned to the possibility they might never know. Eichendorf would be notified on Monday and all hell would break loose. He said Detective Willis had heard back from his Indian counterparts in the country's Central Bureau of Investigation and was going to have a meeting on Monday with the officials of the white-collar division.

"I had lunch with him," he said in such a studied, casual tone that Josh had a sudden suspicion Willis was gay and that Tom liked him. His protective instincts were up, but he bit back any questions he might have asked.

They talked a little about the demonstration. Lying on the bed, Josh shared his observations about the many facets of the country, that of the urban rich, the urban poor, and the rural artisans. Tom didn't say much but Josh had a feeling he was being deliberately restrained, letting him draw his own conclusions.

"I am moved and touched by what I am seeing, but you know Tom, oddly I keep going back to thinking about home."

"Yeah?"

"Yeah. I mean this is so obviously a more populous, developing country with less resources. But there are multiple facets to our country too and income gap and poverty."

"Of course. And poor artisans and teachers and farmers."

There was a pause when Josh lay frowning at the ceiling.

"Yes, that's the thing. I kept thinking about a homeless family that I saw on the way yesterday. How could people just ignore that little baby and go about their own way? Then I thought of this homeless shelter by the street corner back home that I drive by every day without a care. You know what I realized? The world is rigged in favor of apathy."

"Excuse me, whoever you are, it's nice talking to you, but can I get Josh back on the line please?"

Josh laughed.

After their laughter died down, in a soft voice, Tom asked, "None of my business, but did you have a good time with Elsa?"

Josh started. "What did she say?"

"Why would Elsa say anything to me?"

"Not Elsa, you know who."

"She just said that you were having a good time with a delightful girl named Elsa."

"Did she sound upset?" he couldn't stop himself from asking.

"Why would she?" asked Tom, a little too innocently.

"Tom, please. Was she upset?" Josh didn't try to hide his interest in the answer. Interest? Who was he kidding? It was angst.

"How old are you, thirteen?" asked Tom, his tone more severe than the last time he had asked the question.

"Come on, Tom, I want to know."

"Why? What are you playing at?"

"I am not playing at anything. I just—we are both adults, she—"

"Josh, it is not—" Tom's voice grew stern. "You know what? You are my brother and I love you. But you hurt her, I will break your leg." With that dire pronouncement, Tom ended the call.

Sighing deeply, Josh tossed the phone on the bed and stood up. He paced a little and then with an exasperated grunt, took out his laptop and forced himself to concentrate on his mail and news. The world of software security seemed so very distant for the first time. He felt restless.

It will be all over in two days and she was Tom's friend. The right thing to do was to maintain a polite, courteous, pleasant—hell, he wasn't fooling anyone, least of all himself.

He felt an aching need to be with her. Then and forever. Deciding to take care of the then and worry about the forever later, he took his key and went to knock on her door.

He could hear the faint music stop and see the light shift behind the keyhole, and then she opened the door, just a little, and stood filling the opening. He leaned on the doorframe at her serious, questioning look. She pushed back a little, but still not giving way.

"Josh?"

"I couldn't sleep," he said.

She swallowed and looked at him, her eyes wide open. He took in her appearance as quickly and completely as his desire demanded, and what he saw only fueled it further. She wore a cream-colored nightdress, the neckline of which was at the lowest he had seen on her and offered a tantalizing view of luscious brown skin.

He rambled on. "I came back from dinner and spoke to Tom, caught up on my mail. Have nothing else to do. I can't seem to be able to sleep."

He saw the uncertain expression in her eyes. She cleared her throat. "You could ask housekeeping for a sleeping tablet," she said.

She looked adorable, smiling that little smile of hers.

He leaned in, still standing on the threshold, and kissed her, keeping it feather light and quick.

"Josh!" His name sounded half like a reprimand, half like an invitation. He kissed her again, this time fully aware of the aggressive nature of it. She smelt of something woody and floral that he couldn't place, tasted of toothpaste, and her butterfly touch on his arms was thoroughly arousing.

He was still standing outside of the room, in the corridor, but his hands had pushed the door farther ajar as he took her in his arms. When he raised his head, he could see a dazed look in her eyes right in sync with what he was feeling.

"May I come in?" he asked.

"No," she said. It was not an abrupt no, but a sort of tentative, and contradictory, no, a no wrenched out of her.

He attempted to push past her but stopped, as she didn't give way. "Josh," she repeated, and this time there was a desperate quality in her voice.

"Let me in, Vidya," he said.

"Josh, you spent the whole evening flirting with ... "

With Elsa, he knew. He sighed and ran his hands over his hair.

"You're going to throw that in my face now and punish me? You know it was—"

"Why did you do it?" The question was not accusatory, not even curious, but gentle.

Josh groaned in helpless frustration, which mostly sounded like a growl to his own ears. "I did it because ... " He paused, not knowing how to finish the sentence.

"Exactly," she said.

He looked at her in surprise and realized she had, in a bizarre way, understood and was simply reminding him of his own good sense to put some distance between them. That she understood him, even that stupid act of his, pushed him beyond the brink and he wanted her like he had not wanted anyone else. He took her in his arms again.

She closed her eyes for a moment and then said, "I can't. Please. Ask me again, and I will probably say yes. But I will bitterly regret it."

For a moment, he was torn. To hell with her regret. "Bitterly? Even after that kiss you say bitterly regret?" he asked sardonically.

She laughed shakily.

"Listen, I feel like this is scripted," she said, trying to make him understand. "Like I am getting carried away by the moment."

"Oh, come on, this isn't scripted," he said.

"No?"

"No. Now if all other rooms had been sold out, then ... "

She laughed.

Holding her a little away, he looked at her face searchingly. He curled a strand of her loose hair on his finger and then tucked it behind her ears.

"Getting carried away is good."

"Not if the price is heartbreak, surely? I can't ... Do you want to reduce this, us to a one-night stand?"

Tom's words about not hurting her echoed in his head. He had not thought it possible, but he wanted to do the right thing, despite himself.

Once more he pulled her to him, planted a hard bruising kiss on her lips and took a step back, removing his hands from her arms.

"Cold shower it is," he said, unable to contain the sarcasm and annoyance in his voice. "For the record, if you come knocking, I will let you in and would absolutely have no regret."

She grinned.

"All right, close the door and lock it already," he said with a sigh.

She inhaled deeply, moved closer to him, and put her hand on his chest gently. Smiling, with a look in her eyes that made him feel like he was a hero, she pushed him out of the doorframe and slowly closed the door.

Josh stood there for a moment. He could turn and knock on the door again. He could tell her this meant more and that he had changed his mind.

"Go to your room, Josh," she said from the other side of the door. There wasn't much chance now to get her to open the door. Oddly, he felt like smiling as he walked back to his room.

***

12 months before ...

They called him the cleaner. He was in his early teens, though he couldn't have told exactly how old he was. He was an assistant to the long-distance truck driver, doing odd jobs that ranged from cleaning the truck to getting the man his bottle of whiskey every night to massaging his legs. They hauled heavy loads like granite stones across the country.

The driver was an older man, more benevolent than most other drivers. On bad days, he slapped him hard or rapped his knuckles, but he never did any of those unbearable things the other driver had done. On good days, he gave him his magazines so he could learn to read. The boy could read Hindi a little and loved reading about his favorite actor Salman Khan. During those long journeys in the south, he had only the milestones and road signs to read in Hindi.

He called the driver "uncle" as he was a distant relative of his. He had been born somewhere way north, closer to the towering mountain ranges. They spoke a different language there and ate different things. He thought longingly of the parathas his mom made for him, thick and warm. He was looking forward to the journey home. This was his first trip to a distance so far. He hadn't known his country, India, was this big. There were no snow-peaked mountains here like in his part of the country, just endless plains.

That evening, they took a detour from the highway. Driver uncle told him they were going to do a private job and that he was not to talk about it ever. Soon they stopped by a small road. The boy saw a tractor by the roadside and a couple of men by its side.

Driver uncle lowered the ramp, and they hoisted the load up. It was a heavy object, with sharp edges of a metallic nature, but he didn't know what it was as it was rolled up in thick sheets. He wondered if they'd got the job since they had the implements to hoist it up easily. It must have been something important since that man called Prabhu got into the truck with them and accompanied it all the way.

The older man stood by the roadside, looking tired, blinking and peering. The younger man waved a curt bye, and they got in the truck, the boy sitting by the window, squished up. In the rearview mirror, he saw the old man wipe his eyes and bring his hands together above his head in what was the unmistakable gesture of prayer throughout his country. Did he hear the words "Om Namah Shivaya" whispered in the wind?

They reached Chennai as dawn broke over the eastern sky to stop for a warm cup of tea. The boy had his first brief glimpse of the sea, with its barely discernable line in the distant horizon that separated the water from the sky, the wild frothy waves crashing about over and over and the miles of powdery sands stretching far.

It was soon time to drop the object off, and they stopped at a large house that looked like something he had seen in the movies. The boy stood, trying hard not to gawk, afraid he would be reprimanded. As they finally placed the package down, the young boy wished he could also read well, well enough that one day he would become a rich man and own a house like that.

Chapter 35

The bright light crept in through the sheer curtains on the ground glass windowpanes waking Vidya up after a good night's sleep. Having no chores to do, she got ready unhurriedly, before checking in on her father. After the initial greeting, she asked if he had made any plans for breakfast.

"I walked down to have a nice masala dosai," he admitted, naming one of the nearby restaurants.

"Appa!" she chided as she straightened her belongings and packed her bags. "They douse it with oil, and you chose masala dosai? All that potato!"

"You shouldn't have left me alone," he returned and she could hear the teasing tone in his voice. "Good news is I didn't see anyone hanging about or following me."

RST asked her about Josh, in a tone of studied indifference that she found half amusing, half endearing, and her answer that she hadn't got out of the room yet seemed to cheer him.

"It was a long drive, you must have been tired yesterday," he said as though he wanted to know how they spent it.

"We talked of this and that. It didn't feel long," she answered mischievously.

"Oh?"

She waited a moment before explaining some more, "He talked of his parents and his brother."

"And you talked of your grouch of a father?"

Vidya was surprised at the comment. It was a thinly veiled reference to some of her own accusing words, delivered seemingly lightly, but she discerned a mild dejection to it.

Josh's words from the previous day came back to her. She hesitated for a moment. "No, just about how you fell in love with amma at first sight," she said instead.

The story was that he had been adamant about not wanting to marry and as soon as he had seen her mother had said yes. She felt like she was testing him, as though she was giving him an opening to describe his feelings when he first met her mother. She half expected him to change the subject.

There was a beat of silence. He cleared his throat, "Not at first sight." There was a slight inflection that didn't escape her.

"What do you mean?"

"I didn't say yes then, not when I first saw her. I went to meet her the next day at the bank, to tell her that I was sorry, but life would be miserable for her if she married me."

Vidya almost held her breath as she sat down heavily on a chair. "And?"

"And ... " he hesitated.

"Appa? What?" she exclaimed, impatient.

"I said my piece and was about to leave when she," he cleared his throat again, "she said that she liked me, my integrity, my principles, that she had read my columns in the newspapers. She said she knew we valued the same things fundamentally. She acknowledged we'd have our differences, but thought our marriage would be the most enriching experience of our lives."

"And?"

"And nothing." He laughed, clearly shy now.

Vidya sat, shell shocked at the disclosure, her breath caught in her throat and she could only manage a simple, "Mmhm ... "

"Vidya, listen, I ... um ... I have come to realize of late, you think I didn't appreciate your mother enough. I did. I do. She was the love of my life. I honestly don't know how you could have not known."

She found tears well and stream down her eyes.

He asked if she was alright, worried at the silence, repeating her name. And she managed to tell him in a voice that was steady that she was still annoyed with his choice of breakfast. He hung up after joking about the big fat meal he was going to have for lunch, his voice carrying with it the happiness that comes out of relief.

She washed her tear-stained face and stowed her bags neatly in a corner, all the while thinking of the small glass jars full of pebbles that sat on her mother's dresser, on the dining table, on the side table in the living room, by her bed side.

After locking up, Vidya emerged into the corridor and stood waiting for the elevator, recalling Josh's surprisingly insightful comment the previous day.

She heard light strides and knew it was him before she turned. Her mind stumbled over her unsorted feelings for him. It could have been an illusion brought on by the shared adventure, but her heart told her it was more than that.

Josh, dressed in a dark emerald green T-shirt and jeans, his backpack strung across his shoulder, holding his sunglasses, was heading her way. She wished him a bright good morning as they both got into the elevator.

"Morning. Sleep well?" he asked, somewhat grumpily, as she hit the button for the lobby.

Vidya laughed and in a surge of emotions, impulsively hugged him and going on tiptoes bestowed a light kiss on his mouth. He looked at her, caught in surprise, and before he could react, the elevator door opened on the first floor and she had to move away as a large family joined them.

Pushed to the back of the small elevator, they stood in close proximity. He must have sensed her reticence due to the people who'd joined them, for he remained silent, grinning at the roof, the grumpiness gone.

As they got out and the family moved away, talking loudly about something, he said, his gaze staying on her face, "That was certainly not according to a script."

"Today is a new day," she responded with a twinkle.

"So it is."

The restaurant was almost deserted.

"Apparently our friends left early," she told Josh.

"Saves me some embarrassment," he said sheepishly.

Vidya couldn't help but guffaw, and he rolled his eyes. "Oh stop," he said, but he, too, was smiling.

"You look very Indian today," he commented as soon as they sat down.

She looked down at herself, somewhat self-consciously, unsure if he thought she looked good or not. Since they were in the heartland, she had chosen to wear a churidhar with a dark brown dupatta draped over her top, which likely prompted that comment from him. She adjusted the dupatta on her shoulders and then tried to give him a nonchalant look.

Looking lazily up and down at her, he related an earlier conversation he had had with Tom about her being hot. He finished it by saying, amusement dancing in his eyes, "Now you look hotter. I'd so right swipe you."

He was a charming rogue, she thought, at the onslaught of his wolfish grin.

"What do you want for breakfast?" she asked, taking a business-like tone.

"Chocolate, I could eat you up," he persisted. And then grinning, he sighed. "Since I'm also interested in finding Prabhu before we explore the possibilities of the new day, I'll have to come up with a suitably benign choice."

The cheery waiter from the previous afternoon came by greeting them, and she ordered a proper South Indian breakfast, insisting Josh must taste the idlis and the dosai. He shrugged, indicating he was game.

"So, to what do I owe the pleasure of this new day?"

"Your own behavior."

"Really? You liked my flirting with Elsa that much?"

She chuckled.

"So, what's our plan for the day? We go up to the foundry and chat up Prabhu?" he asked settling comfortably, throwing an arm over the back of the chair.

"I suppose so. I am out of ideas."

They both acknowledged the difficulty of tracking the idol from then on. She shrugged off a certain unease that she was feeling, as though they were overlooking or even endangering something; it must be a natural fear of the unknown.

The idlis, white and fluffy and piping hot, and the dosai, crisp and paper-thin with multi-colored condiments, were placed on their table. Josh forked a small bite of the idli into his mouth as she waited expectantly.

"Hmm ... it's bland. It's like a cake in which someone forgot to put sugar or any flavor."

"You have to dip it into the chutney!" she exclaimed in indignation.

"Okay, okay." Dunking another piece of the idly into the coconut chutney and sambhar, he went back to the meeting with Prabhu. They talked a little of possible approaches to getting information but mostly fell back to bantering, if not flirting heavily. Despite his lukewarm reaction to the dishes, he managed to wolf down the lot, down to the last vestiges of the tomato chutney, along with a big banana, a glass of orange juice, and some toasts.

They finally walked out to her car, half an hour later, talking agreeably about the hotel and their stay. It was a warm day as was to be expected, but there were more cotton candy clouds on the sky and a pleasant westerly wind that she could feel against her skin. She wound the windows half down as they drove back to Swamimalai with the wind against their skin.

***

By the time they reached the street leading up to the temple, it was mid-morning, getting on ten. Bicycles and motorcycles lined the poorly paved road, and the hawkers were moderately busy. She parked the car under a shady tree and got out.

It was dusty and warm, with distant strains of pipes and jarring noises from automobile horns. They walked peering at the few boards displaying the door number, arriving finally at Sarathy's. Only to find the surprisingly small foundry locked. Vidya realized with dismay it being a Sunday, many of the shops and foundries would be closed.

"Perhaps the universe is telling us to give up and go back," she said dejectedly.

"Let's tell the universe we won't," he grinned. It was infectious and she smiled too.

"Come on, let's walk a bit. There has to be someone who will talk to us."

They walked up the length of the street until they came upon a little shop of thatched roof and a small rickety door that was open. After a wordless nod of concurrence, Vidya walked into the hall inside, asking permission to enter, with Josh trailing her close.

A middle-aged man of stocky build, likely pegging them to be curious tourists, invited them in. The floor was of an indeterminate dark color, covered with dirt. Seeing her dubious look, he motioned them toward a battered wooden bench. Dressed in a white inner vest and vetti, he sat squatting on gunnysacks, his tools by his side, chiseling a bronze idol of Saraswathi, intricate and delicate, just under a foot.

He chatted amiably as he worked, answering their questions about his trade and the artisans with sensitivity and a good deal of pragmatism. The same young man who had shouted at the poor children the previous day, possibly an errand boy, brought tea in a glass, and the artisan in habitual hospitality sent him away to bring them tea as well.

Josh surprised her by asking him if he could buy the idol. The sculptor hesitated at first; it was a commissioned work for a gallery in Delhi he explained. But after a look at Josh's face agreed to sell it to him. He'll make another one for them, he clarified with a smile.

They sat sipping the tea that arrived, milky and sweet in small glasses, while the man continued working.

"Is there someone named Prabhu who works around here, I believe at the foundry down the road?" she asked him casually.

"The one by that neem tree?"

"I suppose so," she answered, not having noticed the tree.

"Yes, isn't he that short fellow with that crooked nose?" he asked the assistant who was hovering about.

"He is such a cheat, a cutthroat," the sculptor said, which she quickly translated to an impatient and curious looking Josh. At her cautionary look, Josh schooled his excited expression into indifference, or at least tried to.

"Oh, that's too bad! Someone in Chennai recommended him to help buy good pieces. This man," she pointed to Josh, "is thinking of ordering a few idols, and we thought of going through Prabhu."

"Prabhu just sits around and drinks all day. Makes his money selling mediocre pieces at a high price to unsuspecting tourists. Gives us all a bad name," the sculptor said, shaking his head in indignation. "He works with some art gallery in Chennai, I believe. He doesn't have the appropriate reverence for the profession. He is not himself a sculptor, just a middleman after money." Finished with the chiseling, using a soft cloth and oil, he went about polishing the idol to bring forth the sheen.

He gave her some contacts who he thought would help them find good idols at reasonable price and offered to show her the idols he could make as well.

Vidya felt guilty about the false hope for business she was setting, but continued on. "This is bad news; we heard Prabhu sold an idol of a Nataraja to a friend of this man. That's why we sought him. Do you know that idol—supposedly quite tall?" she said, gambling a little.

She could see Josh had caught on to her gestures and the odd word enough to know the drift of the conversation. He looked intently at the sculptor. The assistant who sat nearby making himself useful, handing out the things the artisan asked for, had an odd look on his face. He shifted uneasily at the mention of the Nataraja.

"The one made by Sundaram stapati? I know him, not well though," said the sculptor. "I heard about this idol too, didn't know it was a Nataraja. The stapati, I heard, needed money urgently for a complex eye operation and Prabhu exploited the situation." He shook his head in disgust.

Vidya translated it all to Josh, who whistled softly. The story about the old, blind, stapati just got credence, they realized.

"Is that Sundaram stapati from this town?"

"No, I haven't seen him in a while," said the man. "He visits us occasionally with some small idol or other to sell. Isn't he from Gandharvakottai?" he asked the assistant.

"No, I think he is from Paruthikudi?"

"Wasn't that double death from his village? That farmer suicide?"

They speculated on a few village names between the two of them, but couldn't agree on one.

"He hasn't been making anything big for many years as far as I know." The artisan mentioned the name of a popular eye hospital with branches throughout the state. "When I saw him last, it was just before Deepavali I believe, in October, he mentioned he was going to go there, but I never saw him again."

The conversation trailed when it became clear he didn't know anything more about Sundaram.

The Saraswathi, the goddess of wisdom, all done, was ready to be sold, and the sculptor set the assistant to bring the packing material.

Josh paid up and they talked of other things, careful not to ignite any suspicion, until the idol was boxed and taped, and handed over. They took leave with some vague assurances about coming back.

As they got back into the street, Vidya smiled a little at the way Josh was clutching the box. "So you did get a bronze idol for Tom, huh?" she asked.

"It's not for Tom," he admitted, almost reluctantly. "It's for me." He turned to meet her eyes, and she knew he had recalled her name meant wisdom. Nothing further was said, but the intensity of feeling along with mild embarrassment that she could discern in that momentary gaze was incredibly romantic.

As they walked toward the car, Vidya noticed the assistant was trailing them, and she remarked something inane about the weather to draw him into a conversation. He told her he would be happy to get her to other shops, seemingly wanting a piece of the action for himself. He too reiterated that she shouldn't work with Prabhu. In fact, he added conspiratorially, he heard from someone the idol that Sundaram stapati is said to have made was actually found in a ditch. He just wanted to caution her, he said. He could find out about the stapati if she would like, he offered.

Vidya tried hard not to show any emotions except suitable outrage. "Of course I won't deal with someone like that. You should take it to the police," she said vehemently. He hemmed and hawed and she thanked him for the warning and dismissed him as casually as she could.

They got into the car, she executed a quick turn, pulling away from the spot and the assistant who she could still see in the rear-view mirror, as she informed Josh of what he had told her. "Should we get him to help us? He might know the name of the village, I think he wanted money."

Josh frowned thoughtfully. "That man seemed like a mischief-maker but it does prove others have speculated about this idol too! I don't trust him. I don't like the idea of asking for his help. He could lead us into a wild goose chase."

"It's not like we have a lot of other options," she observed. "I can only think of calling Prabhu."

Having got on to the state highway, unsure where to go next, she parked by another large tree by the road. She switched on the AC and the cool breeze swept the car, as they both sat quietly mulling over what they had heard.

"Sundaram stapati is the key to all this." Josh observed sighing. "This place is so steeped in history, but then there are also so many modern foundries that it is possible Sundaram made the idol, and it is also equally possible he found it in a ditch. Damn!"

Motorcycles and bicycles passed by, a bus rattled past. They sat both staring unseeingly, furiously thinking of their options.

"There must be hundreds of Sundarams in hundreds of villages nearby. We know he is old, but that is a very common name from ancient times, like your John or David."

"Asking around is risky and am also not sure how useful that'd be."

"Yes." She drummed her knuckles on the steering wheel. "You certainly can't look up his Facebook page or expect him to have sent an email ever. We are at the end of your digital dimension."

He sat still for a second. "That's funny. You know until you said so, I never thought of the digital dimension. Thank you."

"What for?"

He took out his laptop tucked under his seat, as she watched him uncomprehending, a frown on her face.

"Our Sundaram stapati had a vision problem," he said softly.

"The eye hospital!" she exclaimed.

Josh booted up his laptop. "What's the name of the hospital again?"

Vidya told him and eyeing with much curiosity, asked him, "Are you going to hack into their system?"

"Why bother with all that when I have you?" he said and handed her his phone with a mock salute.

"What do I say?" asked Vidya, her brows arching.

Vidya watched in fascination at his bent head and pleated brows. He looked up within a few minutes, after browsing through a site, coming up with the nearest branch that was thankfully open on Sundays.

"You are calling from the Chennai head office, you need to get the details of a patient who has come therefor a follow-up. The top doc there, Dr. Neeraj, is personally interested because of the case history," he said, giving her quick instructions.

Vidya dialed the number and when it was answered, relayed her query in as professional a voice as she could muster.

"Tell me the ID number, madam," said the receptionist in a respectful, yet tired voice, half distracted by an impatient voice asking her how long the wait was.

"The patient has forgotten that. He doesn't have his card with him," Vidya responded, injecting some exasperation into her words. "Are there many Sundarams?"

"Yes, madam," the lady said after a few moments, "Fifty or so."

"Just a second." Putting the phone on mute, she quickly relayed the response to Josh.

"We need to narrow it down further, ask her if she could sort based on age maybe," he suggested.

"What's his phone number, madam?" the lady asked as they were discussing furiously, thinking through options.

"Phone number," he repeated snapping his fingers, catching the question. "Give her Prabhu's phone number."

They waited for a few tense moments, and then the lady was back online, confirming that, yes, a Sundareswaran, aged sixty-five, had indeed come to test his eyes months ago. "Glaucoma case, seventy percent loss in left eye. We did a cataract in both eyes. We don't have a full address on the file, he has just filled it out as Keelainallur. Is that him?" she asked. Hard pressed to suppress the excitement, Vidya confirmed that indeed they had the right man.

The receptionist asked if she should she send the copy of the file to the Chennai office. Staying consistent, Vidya asked to send a scanned copy of just the report and gave the plausible sounding email address that Josh came up with based on the contact information in the website.

"Keelainallur," she tried the name of the village tentatively, after ending the call.

"Do you know the place??"

"Never heard of it."

Josh tried searching for the village name in the map, while she supplied him with different spelling options, but came up empty. There was a Keelamathur, a Keelapalur, but no Keelainallur.

"We have to find this Keel-ai-nallur and more importantly Sundaram," he said softly. "Would there be like temple registers or something we can check?"

"Unfortunately not. We don't keep records like that."

As they drove back toward their hotel, she called RST who, relieved that they didn't have to encounter Prabhu, was more than happy to help find the village.

"Did he say a double death?"

"Yes."

"I think I know. There was a farmer who committed suicide in Pudukottai district last summer. On the same day another family man died of a liver failure thanks to alcoholism. It was in the papers because it touched on two burning topics."

He hung up muttering something about looking up his notes and reaching out to his contacts, now caught up in finding the place.

"We could ask Tom too, but it's too early for him."

"Let's call him. I will finally get my revenge."

"What do you mean?"

"You know what his idea of a well-spent Sunday is? Go to the park and read a book all morning, have a warm, healthy home-cooked lunch, read New York Times and Guardian and Washington Post Sunday editions, and then—wait for the highlight—harass Josh. First thing my morning!"

"How sweet, he calls you every Sunday."

"Sweet? Yeah, right!" He rolled his eyes.

The phone rang a few times until they heard Tom's sleepy greeting on the speaker.

"Good morning, Tom," Josh crooned at the top of his voice, grinning ear to ear. She winced, feeling sorry for Tom.

After sleepily mumbling for a moment or two, Tom became wide awake as they recounted the day so far.

"Found it in a ditch!" he exclaimed excitedly.

"That's what he latches on to!" Josh muttered to Vidya. "Short of hearing from the horse's mouth, you aren't going to believe that he might have made it, are you?"

"I'm a hundred percent sure that no horse or for that matter, no man alive will claim to be the sculptor. You know you can deduce these kind of artificial aging through microscopic examination."

"But you haven't, have you?"

"There is no need to!"

"Okay, either way, we have to find this place ... Keelai-na-lur ... "

"God! No Josh, don't ever try that again. Have mercy." Vidya laughed at Tom's pained tones.

"Fine, do you know the place or are you going to continue mocking me?"

"I have encountered the name before, I am pretty sure it's within Chola territory, gone to the Pandyas after the Chola decline. I suspect there is a Shiva temple in that village." There was palpable excitement in Tom's voice. "Let me freshen up, look through my papers, and then call you."

Soon after the calls, they arrived in the hotel, and sitting on the deserted lounge tried different map applications and government data and newspaper accounts. Wikipedia had the village name listed in its voluminous texts as an abode of Shiva.

"The ditch digging story might have some merits after all," said Josh, his face grim.

Except for some vague descriptors that put the village in the nearby Pudukottai district, they had no concrete directions to go on. The newspapers just mentioned the name of the village but no coordinates. After some enquiries, the chatty waiter, clearly an authority on all tourist matters, was called for consultation. He could only suggest they go to Gandarvakottai and ask around.

As they debated the merits of the approach, a call came in to Josh's cell from the Sarathy's salesman.

"Are you back, sir?" he asked deferentially. "Would you be able to meet, sir, this afternoon?"

"I am on my way, should be there," he looked at Vidya signaling with two raised fingers, "in the next couple of hours. I can certainly meet him."

"I will check with sir," he said before hanging up.

"You just sped up the clock didn't you?" she said frowning.

"He wouldn't have believed anything else I said. I would have checked out of the hotel, if I were going away for more than two days."

Vidya agreed to that, but again was seized by a strange foreboding. She saw in her mind a stop watch running down very fast.

After a light lunch, not talking about the next steps explicitly, but feeling the excitement, they set off again in the direction of Gandarvakottai that everyone seemed to suggest.

Vidya shrugged off the fear and unease that came back to her as only natural. As though he knew what she was thinking, he covered her hand on the stick with his and pressed it reassuringly. "We will get to the bottom of it," he declared.

Vidya started the car and drove out.

Chapter 36

Josh was sure they were lost.

It was almost one, an hour since they had left the hotel.

They had driven through small towns, sometimes just circling thanks to poor directions, past small brick dwellings with tiled roofs that stood on either side of winding roads. Sometimes they crossed bridges over mostly dry beds of fine sand that on happier times would have been streams, now only with rare puddles of brown muddy water.

Finally, Vidya's father had come up with the brilliant idea of going to the nearest post office and an enquiry there had directed them away from the highway into the hinterland. They had also been given the correct name of the village, which was a purer Keelainallam. Map apps found the village but gave them a double dotted line that seemed to suggest there were no roads.

True enough, the condition of the road had deteriorated further and further, and the last leg had simply been over a really narrow unpaved road that could barely accommodate the car, through acres of empty agricultural land.

The mid-day sun blazed hot and bright on the majestic expanse of the tropical sky with puffy clouds. There was nothing but barren, dry brown beds that gave a feeling of desolation, or the occasional coconut groves, with hardly any signs of modern civilization. Many patches were tilled and seemed ready for planting, but clearly there hadn't been any rain. There was no traffic noise and no birds cooed. The maps didn't know a thing about the area.

A goatherd, shirtless, slowly drove his thin herd around the car, staring curiously at them, as they waited for the traffic to pass. Vidya stuck out her head and presumably asked for directions to which the man seemed to wave them on.

"I feel like I am travelling back in time," said Josh. "Except for my cell. I still seem to be getting patchy network connectivity."

They continued on for a few more minutes, picking up a lot of dirt, and there seemed nothing all around except the hazy horizon, distant violet hillocks, stray trees, a grove and the ever present scorching sun.

Which was probably why, when they came upon the temple complex, it was as if it had materialized out of thin air. They had just come off a small slope, past a grove of coconut trees that had hidden its view from them.

Vidya slammed her foot down on the brake, and they stared at each other. Josh frowned.

"Josh," she said quietly. "There is a case of someone stealing the idol from a—"

"Let us not jump to conclusions," he cautioned calmly, but couldn't help being intrigued.

They got down and stared at the dilapidated looking outer walls in a state of impending ruin with dislodged stones. A large wooden gate, which looked old and flimsy, was shut, but the wicket gate hung loose. The dusty wedge of a tower, colors seeped off, the sculptures almost undistinguishable from the short distance, rose behind the wall and shimmered under the sunlight.

There was a smattering of grass where a couple of emaciated goats grazed. A cloth cradle hung down from a tree, and a woman gathering dry sticks stared at them. A little kid, half-naked but for a small shirt, his mass of dark hair covering his forehead, was walking about, chewing on some grass. As soon as the boy saw them, he went running to hide behind his mother.

Vidya greeted the young woman, a teenager really, and started talking in Tamil, translating the conversation for him from time to time.

"Have you come to pray?" asked the girl. "But the temple is closed, there's hardly anyone. We don't even have a regular priest anymore," she shared.

"What temple is this?" Vidya asked.

"It's a Sivan temple," responded the young woman, staring at them curiously.

Josh surveyed the surroundings. There were a few large tropical trees that he could not name, and a small cluster of little mud dwellings at a distance with thatched and tiled roofs, presumably constituting the village of Keelainallam. The boy peeped from behind his mom and stared at Josh. Josh waved at him, and he promptly hid again.

A middle-aged man on a bicycle, coming from the village, stopped at the sight of the car and them. "Journalists?" he asked.

After a momentary hesitation Vidya claimed she was a research student. He talked more volubly, willingly about the temple in response.

"He says the temple is cursed," Vidya translated. Standing under the shade provided by the large tree, the man listed in all seriousness stories about the misfortunes that had befallen the various patrons over the years. The superstition could easily be the cause for the ruinous state of the temple, Josh guessed.

Vidya asked him about the village.

"Most of the people have moved out to Thanjavur, to Pudukottai, and other places, only old people live here in the village. With the rains failing, there are no jobs here. I just came to visit my mother who is unwell," he added with a gesture of helplessness. After talking a bit about their hardships in a resigned tone, he got back on to his bicycle, ready to leave.

"Can we go inside the temple?" Josh wanted to know.

"You can, but the inner sanctum is closed. The temple was locked up for close to two or three decades due to a legal dispute. The litigators are dead and no one cares," he replied and with a wave he left. The feeling of understated despair that emanated from him, touched Josh, and he could not completely shrug it off as he followed Vidya to the temple. The girl walked along with them, chattering amiably, as they headed toward the wicket gate.

When Vidya asked her about the stapati, Josh noted her animation and realized she knew and liked the old man even before Vidya translated her words for him.

"Yes, I know him. But he doesn't stay in the village. He stays over there," she said, pointing to a small, lone dwelling of ochre mud walls on the edge of the grove about five hundred yards away from the temple. A gravelly path sloped toward the hut and then beyond, vanishing into nowhere. Josh watched closely as Vidya continued translating.

"He is a very nice man, very helpful, sometimes he minds the boy when I go for work. He made a clay rattle for the little one last week," she added with a happy smile that lit up her face.

The sun beat down on their faces, and Josh could feel the sticky sweat forming on his back and arms and forehead. He looked dubiously at their footwear and then at the sunbaked stone pathway. Thankfully, he noted Vidya had decided to keep her sandals on.

They walked in, and the goats trudged along with them. The girl followed them with the baby now in her arms and the older kid ran ahead to patches of shade. She continued talking, apparently making some comments about the weather, asking if they were going to take photographs.

The outer walls that hadn't seen any fresh paint for decades looked dry and dusty and was quite broken.

"The sanctum," Vidya pointed to the structure inside the large space that was shut up. A simple pagoda stood atop the rectangular structure. It was of modest proportions, not particularly imposing, nothing noteworthy, quite dull in reality. The open corridor around, gravelly with broken stone slabs and weeds that had shriveled and shrunk, shimmered in the heat.

There were a few other smaller appendix in various corners, but all locked up.

"The lady says it's a Shiva temple, so there must be a lingam idol inside, not a Nataraja," Vidya remarked as though she was reassuring herself.

"What about that other thing, the one that's taken out for procession?" asked Josh.

"Well, our whole premise was that it couldn't be a *urchavamurthy*. There were no pole holes, remember?" she said.

"Still, can you ask her?"

"Do they celebrate special days, do they do processions?" she asked carefully, making the question neutral.

"No, nothing like that," said the lady, dampening his spirits. "I have never seen a festival in this temple."

They trudged around the sanctum, staring at the intricate arches and pillars carved on the length of its walls.

"We are going around the *praharam*," Vidya remarked with a smile. He guessed it must be a ritual.

On the back, the outer walls were in a better shape, but the path way was full of rubbles. In the inner walls, the arches formed niches for various stone sculptures all pathetically eroded or damaged. The pavilion must have been of glorious beauty at one point, but sadly, now it was only a shadow of its previous grandeur. The sculptures looked miserable out of years of neglect and exposure to elements, with missing limbs and broken noses. Tom would have shed tears at the state of the temple, he thought.

"Oh my God!" Josh was riveted at the sight in front of him.

"I know, Tom would be heart broken," Vidya said misunderstanding the reason for his exclamation.

"No, yes, but that's not what I meant," he said. Something in his voice must have alerted her. She followed his gaze to a prominent stone sculpture of a Nataraja smack in the middle of the wall.

Josh quickly took out his tablet and clicked open a photo of the bronze in Tom's possession.

"Look at the proportions," he said unable to curtail the excitement in his voice. "Look at the oval frame, look at his expression, at that demon's expression under his feet! Yes, the cobra's head is missing and so are his fingers but—"

"The bronze is a copy of the stone sculpture," she said, finishing his sentence. They spoke at the same time, in a rush, in disjointed bursts.

"The sculptor must have copied this ... "

"He must have seen this—all his life ... "

"That's why the visual markers are misleading Tom ... "

The girl was looking curiously at their animation, so they tried hard to keep their voices neutral, to keep their expression just mildly curious. Vidya took some pictures and made some small talk to her, while thoughts tumbled around in his head in a frenzy.

"Let us go see if the stapati is there," he urged impatiently.

Waving goodbye, leaving the young family by the temple, they walked down, in quick energetic strides, through the winding path sloping toward the little hut. Within a few minutes, they reached the small dwelling situated pleasantly in the shade of a large tree that he could not identify, forming a canopy with sun shining through small crevices.

A small rope cot leaned against the mud wall, a tin sheet masqueraded as the door, and black tarp sheets were drawn on top of the broken tiles and the thatched roof.

Vidya called out.

Josh could hear a crow caw somewhere, but otherwise, it was very quiet except for the rustle of the wind. As he scanned the surrounding, he spotted a ditch about thirty feet away on a downward slope that he could barely make out its contours.

"Un-fucking-believable! To the very last moment," he muttered.

Vidya frowned as she followed his gaze.

An old man came out with sure steps. He was bare-chested and bare-foot with just the traditional white cloth wound around his waist. His greying hair and wrinkles pronounced his age but his physique looked hardened by years of labor. A square strong jaw and steady hands cancelled any impression of frailty that came from age. He wore no glasses, and he peered at them.

Vidya spoke to him, presumably introducing themselves.

He tilted the cot down easily, gesturing toward it, asking them to be seated. He went inside and brought them two glasses of water. Josh gulped the surprisingly cool water lustily.

He could see the house was just a single room, bare except for a small door-less cupboard in a corner. A few oddly shaped jars filled one of the shelves, and a small bundle of clothes lay on another. An old-fashioned camp stove sat in a corner.

"Students?" the man asked, surveying them. He turned slightly as though he preferred to see through his right eye more than the left.

Vidya seemed to give him a vague answer about doing some research on old temples. The old man talked in general of the temple and the Chola dynasty in answer to their opening questions that Vidya dutifully translated.

"We heard it is an unlucky temple."

The old man smiled; it was a gentle, almost sad smile. He squatted down on the floor.

"This was a thriving, prosperous temple. There are verses sung by the great saints about it. As the Chola dynasty declined, so did its importance and somewhere along the line, such stories took root."

"The temple is almost in ruins now."

"There was a dispute over the patronage of the temple that effectively locked it up. Whatever minor pujas were being conducted stopped too. I suppose the superstitions have grown stronger over the years, as a result of the unfortunate circumstances."

"Have you been here for long?" Josh was curious to know.

"I have lived in the village off and on since I was born. I moved out a few years ago to this piece of no-man's land." The stapati's answer sounded vague.

The conversation tapered to a halt, they sat silent on the rope cot, and a gentle wind rustled the big tree and played with Vidya's hair. Josh ran his hands through his hair.

He took a deep breath and made a decision. He unlocked his tablet and brought forth the picture of the idol as he handed it to the old man. Vidya nodded her understanding.

She asked, her voice gentle, "Do you recognize this idol?"

Sundaram stapati took the gadget hesitantly, squinting at the picture. Josh thought the old man's hands shook a little and he detected a spark of recognition in his ancient eyes as he touched it almost lovingly. The touch screen reacted, sliding to another picture, and with a startled apology, he hastened to give it back to them.

Josh reassured him everything was all right and brought the picture back.

The old man held their gaze with a thoughtful look. "Where are you from again?" he asked, frowning slightly.

They ignored the question.

"Can you tell us who made it?" It was odd that he felt compelled to pose his question in a non-accusatory, non-interrogatory tone and Vidya accepted it too as is and translated, her voice gentle.

Closely watching his face, Josh could easily detect the surprise, caution, and gravity that flickered in the old man's eyes. He remained silent for a few moments, clearly troubled, carefully considering the answer, scrutinizing them warily. Was it a natural caution and confusion due to the unusual meeting or was there an undercurrent of something sinister?

"I did," he admitted to making the idol, in a tone that was merely matter of fact.

He could be lying, Josh knew that, but there was something about him, a quiet dignity that ultimately did not brook any further suspicions.

It was painfully obvious that he was poor, but that aside, he did not come across as someone who would have sold a sacred idol for profiteering, even for an eye operation. It was a Sivan temple after all.

Josh leaned back, his arms behind him, weighing down on the rope cot, and stared at the vast blue sky.

He then picked up his phone. *Guess what, Tom? The horse is alive*, he muttered as he typed.

Chapter 37

They drove back to Thanjavur soon after, mostly in distracted and distressed silence. As it was often the case in such matters, the return journey seeming quicker to Vidya than the onward one.

They had chatted with the old man for some more time. He had taken them on a tour of sorts of a small make-shift foundry behind the hut where he made his bronze artifacts, where they could see scraps of metal bits, clay mounds, and wax.

Vidya had noticed two lovely lamps, of an intricate design that just needed polishing, but he had declared the pieces inferior. He had stopped making icons, he had shared. His field of vision on the left eye was very narrow, almost negligible, and his right was alright after the cataract but wasn't good enough for making bronzes, he had lamented.

"What is that ditch for?" Josh had asked at one point, as though he had wanted even that last bit of information squared away.

"It's to harvest rain water for the village," the man had replied and had bemoaned the failure of the monsoon the previous year and hoped for the benevolence of the rain gods that year.

He had asked a few times where the Nataraja was, and in an impulse, Vidya had told him it was in London.

"Is it really in London?" he had asked in wonder and pride. "London," he had repeated.

They had returned, driving past the temple, just pausing to wave goodbye to the woman sitting by the shade feeding her baby and at the boy who had grown brave enough to venture a few feet out to wave back at them enthusiastically, his eyes sparkling, his teeth gleaming against the dark brown skin.

Josh tried calling Tom, the ringtone on the speaker dissolving the silence. It rang over and over, with no answer. So did RST's.

"So that was it!" she observed.

Josh shifted as though he was waking from a daydream, took a deep breath, and nodded. "Yep, that was it."

"What happens now?"

"I am not entirely sure. Eichendorf will probably be used as leverage by the police to get to Banner. I doubt they would be able to make it stick, though. Banner and Shivaraj could simply say selling it as an antique was all Eichendorf's idea." He sounded gloomy and disappointed, like how she felt.

Their part was over. Negotiations and agreements and charges will be forged elsewhere now by other people, while they went back to their normal routines. It made her painfully aware of the fact that Josh could be gone as early as the next day and she might never see him again. She swallowed the lump in her throat.

They arrived at Thanjavur, the journey mostly lost in thought. Vidya was unsure of her own unsettled feelings, which she attributed to the end of the adventure and Josh's imminent departure.

After she parked, they got out and started walking toward the lobby. She didn't notice him until he was almost upon them. His purposeful approach and the crooked nose alerted Vidya to his possible identity barely a moment before he spoke.

Prabhu was thin, and a good two inches shorter, hardly her image of a tall, muscular henchman. His clothes were commonplace; he wore several rings with religious symbols, and images of the gods, and sandalwood paste and vermilion streaks adorned his forehead. The cunning, shifty eyes made up for more than the shortcomings of his build and negated any impressions of piety.

He must have been lying in wait for them, for what she could not guess. She looked at Josh who had not yet realized who the man was, but before she could alert him, Prabhu started speaking.

He eyed Josh with a confrontational curiosity, and her with suspicion and more open hostility. "Who are you people? Why were you asking around about me?" he asked.

Vidya feigned ignorance, asking him in a polite tone who he was.

"I am Prabhu, I work in the foundry," he said frowning, his eyes once more going over Josh.

"Oh, you are Prabhu," she responded, trying to keep her tone calm as Josh stiffened by her side. Her mind raced at the possible reasons he could be there.

Seemingly taken aback and unsettled by her casual demeanor, Prabhu persisted, although there was a slight hesitation now. "Yes, I heard you asked for me?"

"Someone said you have good bronze pieces, and this man wanted to buy some idols." She deliberately kept her explanation vague and peppered with a lot of English words. She could tell by Josh's grim expression he had caught on.

"Who? Who suggested my name?"

"Someone in Chennai, anyway we are now talking to other people and we don't need your services," she made her dismissal sound apologetic.

Josh was intently following their conversation and gestures but thankfully remained silent and watchful. He moved unobtrusively between Prabhu and her as though he was preparing for an escalation of the situation. That protective gesture was heartwarming even under the circumstance.

"I am not here to sell you anything. That man had no business telling you I am a cheat," Prabhu was getting loud again, full of bluster.

The hotel security turned with a frown, and Vidya started walking toward the lobby, not engaging with Prabhu, keeping her expression indifferent. "I don't know about all that. You go complain to him," she responded.

"I am trying to make a living, and I don't know why that man would say I am a cheat. He is no saint." Prabhu continued to walk with them.

Josh had now firmly put himself between Prabhu and herself and was walking slowly but surely toward the lounge, subtly directing her as well. Vidya continued dismissing Prabhu with few words of disinterest and impatient nods. Josh picking up the stray word or two, now told Prabhu in the mildly tired and exasperated voice of a tourist, "Don't want to buy, no buy, no buy."

Prabhu seemed muddled, and undecided on his next steps. He surveyed the lobby, and saw the receptionist and the security guard watching him carefully. Vidya could read his mind considering the utility of following them. They left him standing in the lobby, frowning after them, apparently having decided to not come after them.

"The assistant from the shop must have told him about us enquiring," she said as soon as they were out of his earshot.

"Yeah, must have shared our hotel and car details too from that demo! That two-faced bastard," Josh responded with feeling.

"There is nothing Prabhu could do now," she observed, thinking through the situation. "We know what we need to know."

Josh frowned, his lips pursed in a lopsided line, jaw set. "The assistant would have told him we were looking for the stapati."

They got out of the elevator and walked slowly toward her room.

"True, but has no way of knowing we have already been to see him."

"If Prabhu enquires around … he would come to know we were trying to find Keelainallur." They stood by her door trying to anticipate what would happen next.

Josh took a deep breath, "Either way he would be calling Shivaraj in a matter of minutes."

"I suppose so. There's nothing we can do. The police will have to decide on the next steps."

"Shivaraj is going to act innocent. He is going to get away with it, isn't he?" Josh asked in mild frustration, standing with his hands locked behind his head.

"Not really, no one has paid the money yet. We won." she pointed out. "You know, in a con movie, we might have even rooted for him to succeed. Fooling a British museum into paying a lot of money for a modern idol. What sweet revenge for all those artifacts they looted."

He made a noise that was somewhere between a groan and a guffaw. And then he shrugged and exhaled deeply as though what was done was done and it didn't matter anymore.

After a small pause, she queried, "See you downstairs in ten minutes?"

There was but a brief hesitation, a look, an almost imperceptible sigh, then he nodded and walked past to his room, running his hands through his hair. It was ironic that they both were so attuned to recognize that was not a moment for amorous overtures.

They met ten minutes later in the lobby that was thankfully empty, and after checking out were ready to leave.

After a short stop at the gas station, trying to get to the highway to Chennai, perhaps because her mind was crowded with a million thoughts,

Vidya lost her way. Josh's map app wasn't taking into consideration the one-way streets, and after some muddled circling, she turned randomly into a street toward a bridge.

They came upon the Thanjavur big temple unexpectedly.

She braked hard on an upward slope heading and parked the car to a side. They both stared at the temple in stunned silence.

There it stood, the pinnacle of Chola architecture, awash with the golden beams of the late afternoon sun against the blue expanse of the tropical sky where clouds floated lazily. Something tugged at her heart, but she couldn't bring herself to get down. Neither did Josh express any intent to do so. He did not even take a picture but sat staring at it. Perhaps he was thinking of Tom.

A pervasive feeling of incomprehensible melancholy filled her as they stared at the centuries-old temple.

"Why does it feel like a tragedy?" he asked after a few moments, echoing her thoughts.

"Well, no death, no spectacular soliloquies, not much of a tragedy really," she tried to joke.

"I didn't know you had such a grasp of tragedies," he said dryly.

She stared carefully ahead and considered her words.

"Last few days we were in such a constant state of … of animation, exhilaration that the end of the chase now feels like a letdown, perhaps."

"Yeah, that's a good way to fool ourselves," he observed with a pensive frown, staring into the distance. It was best she didn't answer that.

"You know, this is the best possible ending; all in all, it's a win for everyone," she said instead. It was in a way. No antique had left the country, the con didn't work and Tom …

"Not entirely true for Tom, but I suppose it could've been worse," said Josh reading her mind.

And what sort of an end was it for them?

As though he heard the question, he held out a hand and closed it around hers in gentle pressure and warmth. They sat there in silence, hand in hand. He turned and looked down at her, a raw expression in his face, about to say something. But he checked himself, looked away and after a couple of moments said in a voice that held studied indifference. "I had planned to bring Tom here for Thanksgiving. Shall the three of us visit the temple then?"

That cautious understatement of a question still managed to convey to her he too was not ready for it to be the end. There was sunshine and bird song and her spirits uplifted, it must have shown too on her face as she nodded. It echoed on his in the form of a mischievous smile as he turned to gaze at her. "On one condition."

"What?"

"Lose the boyfriend by then?"

She laughed, "I'll consider it."

With a smile and a deep breath, she started driving again. After a few miles spent in comfortable silence, Josh swore forcefully, shattering the peace.

"I forgot about the metal analysis," he said swearing some more. "Turn around, we have to go back. I am such an idiot. When we first spoke about this, Tom told me that the metal content, the ... the proportions in the alloy were consistent with what it was in the tenth century, not that of the modern idols. The old man didn't make it."

"He looked us in the eye and said he made it!"

"I know! And we just believed him. But, no! He couldn't have."

She frowned trying to follow his agitated torrent of words. Slowing down to a halt by the side of the road, she asked, "Couldn't he have used the older proportions?"

"Possible, but extremely unlikely. Shivaraj? He would have engineered something deliberate like that. That old man? No way." He paused, frowning. "Do you see him making an idol with that level of premeditation to cheat? No, despite his lie, I don't think so. Something is off."

"Could he have reused an older bronze or something?" she asked half-heartedly, playing the devil's advocate, looking to turn the car nevertheless.

"Of that size?" Josh shook his head, as she made the U-turn and set off toward the little village. "No, we got taken in. It is a goddamn antique."

Josh pulled out his laptop and cursing the slow connection checked Shivaraj's phone records.

"Prabhu called him, fifteen minutes ago."

She turned to see a deep frown creasing Josh's forehead, his eyes immensely troubled.

"So Shivaraj knows we are here."

"Yes, but that's not it. It could be worse," he spoke with a grim urgency.

"What do you mean?"

"God, I am so stupid. We lost a good half hour because I am a first rate idiot."

"You have said that already, I get it. Can you get past that?"

"Listen, let's say you were Shivaraj and you got caught with the idol a few months ago. What would you say in your defense?"

Vidya thought for a moment.

"I'd say that it was a modern piece and that the old man made it. If questioned further, I'd insist I never knew it was an antique and that I trusted the stapati."

"Exactly, so it was no harm to let the old man live as an insurance."

She was beginning to understand the reason for Josh's anxiety.

Josh continued, "Now, the idol is out of the country and the stakes are higher. Shivaraj doesn't know what all we know, but he just found out we are asking around for the old stapati."

"—and Prabhu."

"Prabhu is a cutthroat, he would run, but the old man? He just became a threat to Shivaraj."

Vidya saw the terrifying logic of his words. The old man was the only way they could link Tom's idol to Shivaraj. If not for him, Shivaraj could easily produce yet another seven feet modern idol to fit their story.

He might decide to silence the old man in an attempt to quickly bury the trail. Even if he didn't, she had no doubts Prabhu would.

"Call your dad," he said just as Vidya picked up her phone. She dialed her father, her heart quickening in dread.

RST's calm voice answering the phone was reassuring and she felt her momentary panic subsiding.

"Appa, where are you?"

"I am with Jagdish, we just had lunch together and am about to go home. Sorry I didn't realize you had called me earlier."

"He is with Jagdish uncle," she relayed to Josh, feeling relieved.

"Good, have him stay there." Josh groaned as though another unpalatable thought occurred to him. "And can you ask him to get some protection to poor Ramanthan too? We can't risk it yet."

"Josh, you are frightening me," she said in a low voice away from the mic.

"Vidya, what's going on?" RST asked, sounding worried, obviously having heard some words. Putting him on the speaker, she started recounting the events leading up to the call, her words tumbling one after the other in great speed.

"Vidya, listen carefully," interrupted Jagdish uncle's voice. RST must have pulled him in to overhear the conversation. "Remember we are tracking Prabhu's phone? I just checked in, it looks like he *is* on his way to the village. Your friend may be right. Is there a way to warn the old man?"

"Oh God! No."

"I am going try and send a policeman there. Okay? Prabhu is not too far ahead. You go to the hotel and wait for my call."

Josh shook his head in protest, as she did too. "Uncle, we are going there now. The policeman will never make it on time."

"Vidya, no, listen—" RST interrupted, his voice distressed.

"No, appa, I must ... "

Over their vehement protests, she simply ended the call promising to call back shortly.

Josh's phone rang. Tom's voice greeted them, incongruously cheery on the speaker.

"Hey, you guys, I got it. I was in the library and had my phone on silent earlier. But I have great news."

"Yeah?" said Josh his voice tight and rumbling as they sped on the bumpy road.

"Yeah! I found my reference, two of them really, one likely from the eleventh century and another from the twelfth, and it's brilliant. 'Keelai nallam aadum amuthe.' Vidya, are you listening? Dancing manna! Clear reference to Nataraja. The next one even better, 'Keelnallatharase, Gnana natesa!' Do you hear? What else do we need? Absolutely, positively there was a Nataraja idol in Keelainallam—I am pretty sure that's the old name of the village. I don't know who your horse is Josh, but he is definitely lying," Tom declared with triumph.

Vidya and Josh exchanged a grim look.

Tom continued blithely unaware of the developments. "The place, I can infer is south-east of Thirukattupalli, so in the thirteenth century or so, would have been close enough to the path of Mallik Kafur."

Josh inhaled sharply, recognizing the name. "Kafur?"

"He was a general—"

"I know."

Tom seemed taken aback. "Yes well, quite a few temples were plundered during that period. There are some difficulties in identifying the path the invading army took to Madurai. It is more than plausible the idol was buried to escape destruction. Do you know why I think that? Because I am not able to find any later references to Thirunallam temple or its Nataraja. Nothing after the thirteenth century. It's like the temple was abandoned, wiped out almost. I—"

"Tom?" Josh interrupted in a taut voice.

"What's wrong?"

Josh ran through the sequence of events as Tom listened in silence. Shocked and worried, but focused and pragmatic, with crisp words of advice, Tom ended the call so they could keep the line free for any calls from the superintendent.

Vidya took the busy road in dangerous speed, concentrating on her driving, forcing her mind not to think of what they might discover if they reached late. She felt her hands tremble as she stepped on the accelerator. *Please, God, please let the old man be not harmed,* she prayed. She could now spot the minor road she had taken that morning, branching off of the highway.

"Please may I drive?" asked Josh unexpectedly. At her surprised look, he said, "I will go mad sitting here, please, allow me."

He may have noticed her hands trembling on the wheel, or he may have sorely wanted control. The road was deserted, and Vidya decided it was safe enough to hand over the steering wheel to him. They exchanged seats in haste. She kept the car running and moved over as he ran around.

She called RST and informed him of where they were and also gave precise instructions on how to get to the village. There was a policeman being dispatched, she was told, but she knew in her heart he was unlikely to reach on time.

Prabhu's cell phone signal went off a few minutes ago, RST imparted reluctantly.

Josh sped through, a look of fierce determination on his face, utterly focused on the road. She sat, one hand gripping the handle, another a tight fist by her side, her mother's favorite chants on her trembling lips, her heart pounding.

Chapter 38

As the temple came into her view, Vidya saw, with a jumbled feeling of fear and relief and anger, the motorcycle with Prabhu on it. Josh slammed hard on the accelerator sending the car teetering dangerously across the narrow, unpaved, bumpy road almost skidding into the coconut grove.

Prabhu, having just parked the motorcycle by the hut, getting off of it, turned toward them, alerted by the noise of the approaching vehicle.

She struggled with the door as they drew near, and unmindful of Josh's warning shouts as he braked hard, she stumbled out of the car before it was fully stopped. She knew if Prabhu chose to, he could still harm the old man and perhaps them as well. But he was by himself and was unlikely to have any guns; besides she was too furious to calmly consider all that.

The stapati stepped out of his hut and gazed anxiously at the scene unfolding in front of him.

Prabhu stood paralyzed for a moment, with an alarmed look on his face at the sight of her. He then turned toward the sculptor, his body language aggressive, and his words loud. "Old man, I told you not to speak to anyone," he yelled as he strode forward and shoved him hard.

Vidya flung herself between them before he could cause further harm. The old man steadied himself against the cot, staggering, but still remaining upright.

When Prabhu made a threatening move to grab her, with a strength brought on by fierce resolve, she shoved him back. He stumbled but was quick to recover, coming back at her, his hand up, his face a mask of ugly fury.

She saw Josh rush in and pull Prabhu off, side stepping from the swipe that was now heading his way. Josh and Prabhu went at each other, a blurred mass of arms and legs kicking and pummeling for a few moments. Josh swung his fist landing a hard punch on the side of his face, before he bodily slammed against Prabhu, sending him doubling down onto the ground.

"Couldn't you have waited just a second?" Josh asked, shaking his hand, throwing his knee on Prabhu's back, pinning him down.

He cast an irritated look at her. "Are you okay?" he didn't miss to ask as his eyes raked her up and down.

She nodded she was fine, her breath still shallow and uneven.

"Fetch a rope or a piece of cloth or something to tie him up."

Vidya first got him the stapati's *vetti* and then after quick consultation with the old man, removed the jute rope that was the clothesline. Josh bound Prabhu up, checked his pockets and took away his cell phone and switched it on, but let him keep his wallet. He didn't have a weapon but Vidya had no doubt of his intentions.

The stapati did not ask any questions. He ushered them to the shade and simply waved toward the rope cot. There was a small cut in Josh's left arm, no doubt from one of Prabhu's many rings, but other than that there had been no harm done.

Josh sat on the cot and pulled her gently down beside him. She too sat, still holding his hand, as her breath levelled, and the sense of panic subsided while Prabhu hurled abuses at them, from his prone position.

"Aren't you going to translate that?" Josh asked with a twinkle.

"I don't understand the half of it myself!" They both laughed.

The relief was heady, and they were impatient to be alone with the old man. They called Tom and her father just to convey all was well, but refrained from revealing anything else in front of Prabhu. The policeman was expected soon, but they were not to talk about the idol yet to him, the Superintendent had warned.

They sat waiting under the shade, as the day's heat began to recede and the shadows grew longer and a mellow breeze soothed them. The mynah bird and the garden lizard hardly showed any interest in them.

They waited impatiently, sitting side by side.

The stapati oddly did not ask any questions, but sat down quietly and methodically cut open some palm fruits. She had a feeling he was resigned to what was coming. He handed out the jelly seeds one by one to them that provided some diversion as she taught Josh how to deftly eat it along with the delicious and soothing water inside.

After half an hour that seemed like an interminably long time, they spotted a police jeep that stuttered by the temple. Then it turned, gingerly negotiated the narrow path and stopped ahead. Two policemen got out and ambled down. The inspector introduced himself, informed her that the superintendent had already briefed him and assured her Prabhu wouldn't bother them again.

He asked her a few questions that she answered in neutral terms—they were tourists, Prabhu was following them and was troubling them, she said as instructed. Prabhu himself who had started to moan and complain at the sight of the policemen, now remained quiet, possibly having decided feigning ignorance was the better option for him as well. After another fifteen minutes, the policemen left with Prabhu who was now utterly silent. Vidya knew he was confused and as soon as he got a hold of a phone, he would call Shivaraj for instructions, but she hoped not in the next five minutes.

They finally had the privacy they needed to take their quest past the final breach.

The stapati squatting down on the floor, remained quiet. Josh sat motionless, staring at the temple in the distance. Vidya knew she must ask the question, get that last admission that tied it all together.

"You lied, didn't you? You didn't make the idol." She could still bring no accusation to her voice, only inquiry. She wondered what was making her predisposed to sympathy, was it his obvious poverty or his old age? Was either one a valid justification for what he had done?

"Why do you say so?" The old man faced the question calmly without a protest and seemed merely curious to know her reasons for suspecting him.

Vidya explained to him about the metal analysis, feeling compelled to justify her doubt at the face of his calm gaze.

"What is the proportion?" he asked, his eyes alight with curiosity. When she said she didn't know the details, he recited the proportions he used, his tone implying a disassociation with that of the idol, presumably because he was beyond caring. "Prabhu is a thorough crook, isn't he? He must have come to kill me, to stage an accidental fall into the pit perhaps," the old man observed in a voice devoid of any emotions, his head jerking toward the ditch.

"Why do you think he came to kill you?" she asked.

"He must have let me live only as insurance or may be out of greed." The old man laughed in some inner mirth, his shoulders shaking uncontrollably. "He was very helpful in expanding my rain water ditch way back in December. You see, I never told him where I got the idol from."

Josh rubbed his eyes wearily as she translated. They exchanged a glance.

"But now, perhaps he decided I am a liability, perhaps I have outlived my purpose. He must have known you were enquiring, must have got worried."

The old man said it matter of fact, but the underlying implication that their actions had almost cost his life, wasn't lost upon either of them. Vidya shuddered as Josh reached out to squeeze her hand.

"Did Prabhu pay for your operation?" Vidya asked.

"Not really, it was a free camp. He just hung around for a while acting helpful. I sold the idol for five lakh rupees cash, not for the surgery. A good bargain, considering." He grinned, his good set of teeth gleaming against his sun tanned face, hinting tacitly at the antiquity of the idol for the first time.

"Was it buried?" Josh asked, his tone abrupt, as though he had had enough of the conversation.

The stapati stood up slowly. His eyes sparkled in mischief and inner delight. "I might as well show you where I took it from. It'd have been such a shame if I had died without sharing that secret. *Sivaperuman's* wish is for you to know, I suppose."

The curious glint in the old man's eyes set off alarm bells in Vidya's head. Took it from? They stood up, ready to follow him.

The sun was descending and the evening light played through the clump of trees that rustled gently. The air was filled with the chorus of the birds that were returning home.

Instead of walking toward the ditch though, he walked them back toward the temple, entering it through the same wicket gate.

"Oh god, no! Not from the sanctum?" she asked, her voice strangled.

The old man just chuckled in response, continuing inside, along the length until they came to the back *praharam*.

For a moment Vidya thought the old man was stumbling against a rubble in the corner as he went down on his knees. But then he cleared the rubble and with an innocent looking wedge heaved something. Vidya felt a chill run down her spine.

A creaking noise followed the movement as a stone piece gave way, and a gaping hole appeared on the floor and the old man, without a word, stepped inside and went down vanishing into the darkness.

After a moment of stillness, Josh followed the old man and Vidya did too stepping into the darkness behind him. She bumped into Josh's back as he stopped, steadied herself and straightened. Her eyes slowly adjusted to the little light that was seeping through the opening.

In a disembodied voice, the stapati said, "Here is where I found him." There was a rustling sound and the old man struck a match and a flame flickered. It moved to light up a bronze lamp that seemed to have appeared from nowhere.

Josh paused mid-way fumbling with his phone light.

The stapati had already gone down the few steps and was now walking ahead on a level floor, on what was a corridor running parallel to the *praharam* underneath the ground, lighting up a row of lamps one by one, his movements sure as though he knew their positions by heart.

They took the steps down, and at first, they didn't see. Then, as the flame steadied and a warm glow spread, they saw. Vidya was not sure if the audible gasp was from her or Josh. Her hand fluttered toward Josh, who clutched it tightly, as her heart beat a crazy staccato.

The row of bronze idols, seemingly materializing out of thin air, tall, serene, shimmering, towered over them in sacred silence. The flames remained steady casting shadows and sparkles, illuminating their benevolent gazes.

The old man intoned, "Chathura thandava, Ardhanareeswara, Somaskanda, Rishaba deva, Sivakami, Bikshadana … " and on with the rest of the pantheon.

They walked the length step by step, squeezing through the small space, in the meager light, sideways, wordless, hand in hand, gazing at each and every one of them in stunned silence.

Vidya walked on, her mind too muddled, her heart too full, to even fully comprehend the marvelous, spiritual, magical moment.

Only when they finally stumbled out did she feel the tears that had streamed down her cheek and noticed for the first time her body was quaking. Josh put his arm around her briefly squeezing her to him, and she soon composed herself.

They sat there perched on dusty stones, staring at the silhouette of the gopuram against the dark grey sky with emergent stars, and the stone sculptures on the niches that were mere protrusions in the fading light.

After a while Josh went back to take pictures, possibly having been too dazed to do so the first time. The stapati sat next to her on the ground, quiet, except for an occasional cough that echoed in the still night.

She imagined the old times, an evening a thousand year ago, the corridor with blazing torches, with men and women walking where she sat, and the idols in all their glory, the aarathi flame going round and round. She could almost hear the drums and the pipes and the chants. Her lips trembled once more as she recited her mother's favorite chant to herself.

Josh came out and closed the stone carefully. Wiping her tear stained face with her dupatta, Vidya stood up, Josh threaded his fingers through hers, pressing her hand in a reassuring grip and they trooped back to the old man's house.

Chapter 39

The twilight gave quickly away to darkness and Josh could see the golden glow of the gibbous moon on the eastern sky. The two of them sat down wearily on the rope cot, side by side, thighs and arms touching. Josh waited, as Vidya pulled herself together. He could understand how momentous it would have been for her. Even as someone sorely lacking in the spiritual side, as Tom had put it, Josh had been profoundly shaken by the weight of that moment, and still felt the gaze of those idols seared in his retina.

The sculptor put a small vessel of water on the old-fashioned stove to boil and started making tea as he told them his story, waiting for Vidya to translate his every word.

"They must have created the *nilavarai* to save the idols from an invading army. Other temples recovered from such attacks, this one didn't. We could speculate, perhaps those in the know died ... "

He spooned loose tea into the boiling water

"How did you discover it?" Josh was curious.

The old man fetched two glasses and squatted by the stove. "My family is of a long line of sculptors. And my grandfather always used to tell stories of the beautiful bronzes, stories handed down through the generations, of family pride about how our ancestors were favorites of the great Rajaraja himself, of the best bronzes in the kingdom. The idols were thought to have been moved to various temples around the country to escape destruction, but he said that was not true, that they were somewhere buried in this area. A number of them, rare ... "

They sat engrossed as he continued the story in simple words, talking gently about himself.

"I didn't earn much money making idols. I went out to the city to work in a restaurant. Married, had children, lost my wife, don't know where my son is. My daughter died some years ago; killed herself over some man. Fifteen years ago, I decided enough was enough and returned home. I made some bronze knickknacks for a living and spent the rest of the time wandering in the temple, it gave me solace. A priest came once a week and, in the last twenty years, not even that." The stapati paused, to hand over the glasses to them.

"And you found the entrance?" Vidya shivered a little, despite the hot tea and the warm evening.

"Yes, was it an accident or providence, I don't know. I literally stumbled over it. There was something different about the stone. It wasn't as easy to open it as it is now, but I was determined and I found the opening."

"Why didn't you tell anyone?"

He nodded acknowledging the question as though he had considered the same over and over.

"I should have. Somehow I couldn't, I dithered, and I told myself that I should wait to know who owned the temple. For a few days I was torn, but then ... the first month passed and then a year, and nothing happened. I made regular visits, cleaned the place, lit some lamps once in a while. And that's how it has been for the last ten years."

"Ten years?" Vidya whispered. "They have been in the dark all this time?"

"They have been there in the dark for ten centuries," said Josh dryly. The old man smiled as though he understood.

She shuddered a little and Josh impulsively put his arms around her and kissed the top of her head, unmindful of the audience. The old man certainly caught the action but to Josh's relief, he ignored it.

"What was the final trigger that got you to sell the idol?"

"Money."

"Not for you?" It was not a question, but a statement of belief.

"You would have read all about the double deaths in the newspapers. Everyone talked of it over and over for a few days, they said there would be relief, that someone would take care of the family, but time passed and no one cared. Comparatively we are a reasonably well developed state, with plenty of opportunities if you are strong and willing to migrate. Still ... ours is an eternal hand to mouth existence, one illness, one draught is all that is needed to bring everything crashing around.

What could they do at the onset of such great tragedy? One of the dead man's wife had passed away couple of years ago and the other's drank a bottle of pesticide two months later. And three teen aged girls remain."

"You sold the idol and gave away the money." Vidya voice was a mere whisper.

The old man smiled. "Wouldn't you have? They are now in a boarding school near Trichy; the money will last them until two of them finish high school. Hopefully, they will do well and get a job, stand on their own legs and help the younger one. I have seen them grow up, pick firewood from here, help their family. I couldn't let them die. Or worse."

Vidya translated, a sound of desperate concurrence emerging from behind her throat.

"In the grand scheme of things, I suppose just helping three girls doesn't mean much, but that evening when I went in to clean the idol, I knew the mocking smile in His face was for me. He was taunting my inaction, questioning my piety."

Josh winced a little as the words smote him in a fitting culmination of the last few days.

The stapati spoke in a soft voice, of the villagers, of jobs in the new world, of artisans, of history, of ancient wars and soon the conversation trailed as it grew dark.

With a deep sigh, Josh finally stood up and pulled out his phone. He looked at Vidya, pausing for a moment, and she nodded her agreement. It was no longer to be a secret, his, theirs.

And the next pair of eyes that deserved to see the idols after hundreds of years was Tom's.

He dialed Tom's number.

For a moment he couldn't speak and then, "Tom, it is unbelievable, you must come here, right away! You must see them as is before anyone else, you must ... "

He could hear his own voice growing into an urgent whisper, fading into a sigh, narrating the events. Tom for once, was rendered speechless. Finally, when he hung up, he had left Tom galvanized into action. The connection was spotty and Josh couldn't upload the video, but he knew Tom had more than enough imagination to understand.

They made calls to her father too setting in motion events that he knew in the next few days would rock the news feeds. They sat there, with the unspoken agreement to spend the night in that little hut, too drained to even think of driving back anywhere.

There wasn't anything to eat except two small bananas, the old man said apologetically. He offered to walk down to the village but neither Vidya nor Josh wanted him to go anywhere yet. Vidya shared the packet of chips and cookies and the bottles of water that she had bought back in Thanjavur for the journey to Chennai.

It even seemed fitting to him they went to bed a little hungry.

Josh went to the car and changed to his shorts and tee. Borrowing a straw mat from the old man, he setup his simple bed, giving up the rope cot for her. She offered to sleep on the floor.

"Don't be silly!" he responded roughly, and lay down on the mat, with his hands behind his head, staring at the sky.

The stapati settled inside the hut on another straw mat.

The torturous heat was subsiding and the branches rustled, bringing welcome breeze. A lone bird cooed somewhere. The moon, a near full disc shone behind coconut fronds, coating a faint sheen of silver on the tops of the trees and the thatched roof, giving the night a magical quality that he knew he would remember for a long time, forever perhaps.

The night was sleepy and still, and Josh felt incredibly alive, yet at peace with himself. He thought of his parents and Tom. He thought of art and farming. Life outside of his yuppie bubble. Of people, different yet alike. He thought finally of Vidya whose silhouette, he didn't have to turn to see, was already etched in his mind. He wanted to have his arm around her, hold her close, but not out of lust, rather not just out of lust, he corrected himself wryly.

After a while there were no thoughts, just her soft breathing and that woodsy perfume of hers, and they lulled him to sleep.

***

Six months before ...

The sculptor rolled up a new white vetti that he had bought specially, around the Nataraja. He had borrowed two cows, which were tethered right inside the annexure. He needed to get the heavy idol out without anyone being the wiser. He opened two of the slabs to create space. With great difficulty, with the block of pulleys he had fashioned, using the cows and his own muscles, he hauled the idol up, covered in white cloth, and tied up in ropes. It was the middle of the afternoon and the goatherd was farther out and the young mother from the village was too pregnant to be picking up firewood. He was all alone.

He brought it slowly out, pushing and prodding, gasping for breath and the late afternoon sunlight lit up the cloth causing the sculptor's hands to shake. He was afraid to open the cloth, that he might be fully blinded by gazing upon the Lord in all His glory. He slowly got the cows to walk toward his hut, dragging along the rustic platform on wheels he had fashioned upon which his Lord lay.

After getting the cows back to the village, he returned, tense and anxious. He sat paralyzed for some time before daring to open the cloth. His Lord's face up close under the bright day light, blurred yet brilliant, smiled at him. The feeling of liberation was immense, wonderful and devastating all at once.

He pushed the platform behind the little shelf, draping the idol that was too large for his little hut with the new vetti and with old sheets. He would go to Swamimalai and find that fellow, Prabhu, in the morning. He wished with all his heart the idol would find a new place that was worthy of it. Where only a loving hand would touch it and a loving gaze would behold it and a loving heart would worship it.

Chapter 40

It was a sound of bells that filtered in through her deep slumber that pushed her to wakefulness. Orange and yellow and white patches shifted inside her heavy eyelids and she opened them sleepily to the unfamiliar canopy of the trees filtering the morning sunlight. Vidya sat up slowly to realize she was alone and the only noise she heard now was that of the birds.

Bells rang again, and this time, she recognized the sound. She saw Josh riding an ancient bicycle and the stapati pillion-riding perilously. He stopped a few feet away and grinned at her. His hair was tousled and windblown, and he looked bright and full of energy. The stapati got off, clutching a plastic bag, out of which peeped a loaf of bread.

"Ah, the sleeping beauty wakes up," Josh remarked.

"While the prince charming seems to have gone foraging for food," she retorted grinning.

He got off the bicycle and bowed. "Milady. We brought you water too," he pointed at the two buckets of water that stood by the wall. They must have already made a couple of trips while she had slept on.

Vidya got up a little embarrassed, tied her hair, and went looking for a place to wash up. There was no bathroom, and she had to drag a bucket toward a cluster of trees farther away for privacy.

When she came back wiping the water from her face and neck, the stapati handed her a glass of sweet milky tea and some toast. Josh sat polishing off an omelet hot off the skillet. He proceeded to top it off with some toast and a banana, clearly ravenous. The old man seemed to have taken a liking to him.

"We went to the nearby village shop and got some stuff." Josh enthusiastically showed her sundry pictures of chicken and thatched roof huts, talking excitedly of his adventure, his blue eyes sparkling like marbles.

After breakfast, they went once more to the temple, careful no one noticed, and made a simple catalogue of the idols, before sealing it back.

Despite his claim that he could die peacefully now, they decided the old man ought not to stay there just in case Shivaraj got any ideas. He reluctantly agreed to go to Trichy and stay with a distant cousin since they categorically refused to leave without him.

They set off to Trichy and arrived in the bustling town by mid-morning.

After buying him a phone in the town, and teaching him how to use it, they dropped him, with worried instructions to be safe, to not to go out by himself, to be wary of strangers ... He smiled and reassured her that everything will be alright, that it was now destined to be.

They began their return journey to Chennai, well before noon, stocked up with bottled water and eatables. The temperature was finally moderate and there was a good wind. Josh fiddled with the radio and asked questions about the food, the language, everything but the bronze.

They called Tom who they suspected hadn't slept at all and, drowned them with updates.

"Where are you?"

"On our way back to Chennai, man," Josh responded.

"What? Are you sure? What if someone traced you both? What if something happened to the idols?" Tom's agitation and worry was palpable in his voice and in the squeaking of the wheelchair.

"Relax, Tom. It's destined to be alright now," Josh joked.

Tom grumbled a bit before letting go of the topic. "A whole lot of people are now involved, but, I haven't given them the details of the location or the find. Things are moving at a fast pace, they are waking up judges to issue warrants and all that. There will be a meeting tomorrow afternoon in Chennai. God knows how many stopovers I am going to have, but I will be in Chennai by then. I'm going to need your help Vidya."

"Would love to Tom," she responded, thrilled about the idea she would get to meet Tom finally. Josh wouldn't be there, of course; she knew he had tickets for early morning the next day. Now that Tom was going to be in India, she wondered about Josh's earlier promise to visit them for Thanksgiving. Would she ever see him again?

As she drove, Josh researched on the Internet to setup various things that'd make the journey easy for Tom. A spare light weight wheel chair that he could stow, a car that he could rent where his regular wheel chair can be fitted, hotels in Chennai and Thanjavur with proper handicap access ... Vidya reassured him she would make sure Tom was comfortable.

She called RST and briefed him. Jagdish was mobilizing a set of important people too and they were tracking the two men, he told her.

"What about Shivaraj?"

"His mobile phone is at home, but Jagdish thinks he isn't."

"They let him escape?"

Josh frowned, logged in, and confirmed the phone was still at the residence. But he soon found a ticket to Singapore, via Bengaluru the previous night. Vidya relayed that to RST. Shivaraj must have heard of Prabhu's arrest and must have driven out to Bengaluru even before they had mobilized a policeman to shadow him, shrewdly leaving his phone behind.

Still, this was too big to be buried. Law would move, albeit slowly, and there would be extraditions and jail terms, and ultimately justice would be served, she was sure.

They stopped by the highway and quickly ate the unimaginative roti and curry that she had packed from an eatery. They continued on, talking again to RST, Jagdish uncle, Tom, reading up on the history, and speculating events of the past.

As they drove on, wind picked up and clouds gathered, eclipsing the late afternoon sun.

Exactly at the same moment when she thought it would be wonderful to stop by at a small teashop, Josh asked if they could do so. They both got out of the car and ran into a small shop covered by a tin sheet roof just as it started raining. The vendor smiled at her and started preparing the tea that Josh declared he had begun to like.

Perhaps it was a freak storm, summer showers, or perhaps it was indeed the much-expected monsoon arriving early. It poured down in fat drops, making a great deal of noise battering against the tin sheet of roof.

The vendor proceeded to make bhajis. The oil was hot, and he sieved out the deep fried brown bhajis dripping with fat, dropping them into vessels covered with plantain leaves.

They drank tea and ate the hot snack, squeezing out the excess oil onto old newspaper sheets standing in for tissue. Vidya was worried about the oil and the spice, but Josh bit into them with child-like enthusiasm. When she raised her brows, he grinned. "I think I'm fully acclimatized," he declared.

"Look at the smile on his face," he said with wonder, jerking his head toward the vendor.

"Yes, he says he is happy that it's finally raining."

Two women ran in to take refuge in the shack, both laughing. They put their baskets, covered with towels, down. As they took out the already wet towel to wipe themselves of the rain, Vidya noticed the fresh flowers tied into long strings, wound and wound, heaped on the basket. Marigolds, and jasmines strands and a few loose flowers too and among them some red roses.

Inevitably Josh noticed it too and with a sardonic smile, bought her some. The flowers did not have a long enough stalk to make a bouquet, so Vidya wore a couple on her hair, Indian style, and held the rest in her hand.

"They are saying they are soaked, but they are happy it is raining." Vidya felt compelled to translate their cheerful words.

"I can see that. I haven't seen such unadulterated happiness up close in a long time. Rain has always been a minor inconvenience for me. Problems of drought and flooding were all distant, academic stuff that I read about in newsfeeds. It brook no particular emotions," he said, looking fascinatedly at the two women.

They looked back at him with equal fascination. The way he was standing close to her made them curious, Vidya realized, as did the universally recognizable gesture of a man buying flowers for a woman.

She turned to gaze at him. He was clad in a lumberjack plaid shirt that withstood the stray drops of rain, with the stubble that added to his outdoorsy look, but beyond that, it was his expression of wonder that made him exceedingly attractive.

"Rain will never be the same again," he said. Then his hand stole toward hers and held it as they watched the rain quietly together.

The women chattered away. The shopkeeper made more bhajis that Vidya bought for the women, and the rain continued to pound, making little rivulets in the mud.

Vidya felt contentment, even joy seep through her. Josh's hand tightened, and he smiled without looking at her, as though he understood.

Soon the rain receded, and the women left, chattering away with their baskets on their hips.

Vidya and Josh started back on their way to Chennai talking of this and that, listening to music. His return trip joined the list of items that was being studiously avoided.

Chapter 41

By the time they reached Chennai, it was evening and it was annoying to be stuck in Monday commuter traffic. The noises, the heat and the ways of the concrete jungle were more jarring than ever.

As they got closer to their destination, Vidya considered saying something about his imminent departure, but wasn't sure what. "Would you be sorry to go back?" was absurd, "Would you remember me?" pathetically needy.

"Would you like to come home for dinner?" she asked instead, as she came to a fork in the road that'd either take them home or to his hotel, fully expecting him to refuse with a litany of excuses—"I'm sorry, I'm tired, early flight to catch ... "

He accepted with alacrity, even seemed to brighten at the prospect of having dinner at her place. Soon she was parking her little car by the compound wall and they were getting down.

The mongrel bounded up to her, wagging its tail, while barking suspiciously at him. The ongoing game of cricket was suspended as the players pitched questions at her noisily, while curiously eyeing Josh. Where had she been? Would she be joining the game? Josh for his part seemed to be thoroughly charmed by the lively scene.

Her father, who had just returned home along with Jagdish uncle, opened the door and welcomed them in. He hugged her in a rare demonstration of emotion and then shook hands with Josh.

Naturally she knew that behind his placid smile, RST was assessing Josh, but oddly she was also aware that Josh was uncharacteristically self-conscious.

RST and the superintendent were full of questions and over coffee— "I made decoction," RST had proudly declared—they discussed the next steps. There was going to be a meeting with legal experts the very next day and they would open the subterranean corridor the day after though police were already in the village, Jagdish informed them. No one else knew of the exact entrance yet. Josh thanked him for the gracious gesture of a day's delay which they knew was to accommodate for Tom's arrival.

"He is the hero after all," acknowledged Jagdish with a smile. "In the meanwhile we got plenty of work to do, we will make sure we get a proper confession from the stapati and get whatever warrants we need."

He wondered if Ramanathan was an accomplice which Vidya vehemently disagreed. "If not for him we wouldn't have cracked the case."

"We would have. It'd have taken a little longer," Josh retorted.

"The poor man! As it is, he is going to feel terrible about his part. We should try and keep his name out of the papers," she said.

The three men looked at her indulgently as though she was some sentimental fool, causing her considerable irritation. They did agree Ramanathan was likely a pawn.

They talked a bit about the potential aftermath.

"At the current levels of religiosity in no time there is going to be a huge, glitzy temple there and it will become big business," RST remarked sarcastically.

"More jobs, sir!" returned Josh dryly.

They all laughed. Soon Jagdish took leave, reassuring her of police protection for a while for them.

Despite RST's suggestion to order in some dinner, Vidya decided to cook. Josh had to taste the wonderful flavors of a proper South Indian home cooked meal. As they talked, she labored over a fiery *vathakolambu*, and a delicate spinach *kootu*. Then in a fit of anxiety that it might all be too exotic and thus unpalatable for him, she roasted potatoes and made tomato *rasam* that she served like a soup.

She set up the table with care.

Josh ate everything in large proportions with evident gusto, insisting on using his fingers. Granted his skill in picking up a mouthful of rice with his fingers was that of a four-year-old, but still, it was sweet. Even RST was amused.

Josh talked about his parents, and RST was suitably impressed. More than their interest in the *Upanishads*, he was enthusiastic to know about the anti-draft protests.

She served sliced mangoes for dessert, which they ate sitting in the living room. She sincerely hoped Josh was well acclimatized, concerned about the rate with which the mangoes were disappearing into his mouth.

At one point, Josh asked to go to the restroom. She stood up to show him the way, and as soon as they walked away from her father's eyes, he crushed her into his arms and kissed her hard. When he lifted his face, his eyes were full of frustration and remorse. He let her go, and she made a good deal of noise stepping inside the kitchen.

Soon it was time for him to get back to the hotel.

Vidya presented Josh with a cotton scarf that she had picked up in Thanjavur, just before vacating the room. When he raised a brow, she told him with a smile, "For your mom's collection." He said nothing but gravely took it. Either he was too moved or thought it was silly.

Despite her offer to drive him, he insisted on calling a cab and before she knew it, was inside the taxi ready to leave. She nervously jabbered she'd text him about all the exciting stuff that'd happen in the upcoming days. He grew progressively silent as she blabbered on.

The taxi left, and the two of them trudged back home.

"Interesting chap," said her father.

"You mean for a capitalist?" she tried to joke.

RST smiled, but as his eyes took in her face, to her horror, she felt tears welling. RSTsimply stroked her head.

She moved away hastily, mumbling about cleaning up.She quickly cleared the table, put away things, cleaned the counters vigorously, and, having nothing much else to do, went slowly to her room.

***

Fourteenth century ...

The priest tasted blood as he staggered at the hard blow to the back of his head. The frenzy in the eyes of the soldier standing in front of him was terrifying.

It was mid-morning and the sun shone bright as always but the street, lined with single-story dwellings of tiled roofs and thinnais, was devoid of any normalcy. The sounds of his children chanting the vedas, and a vision of his wife busy in the kitchen working along the other womenfolk of their large family surrounded him for a moment. He cherished the satisfaction of knowing they were all safe, carted away a few days ago farther east.

"Where did you send the idols?" someone shouted a translation of the enemy soldier's words, as another blow landed cutting across his legs. The priest stumbled down on his knees this time and his vision became blurred as a ringing filled his ears.

He shook his head in refusal as he coughed up some blood.

He could still see the temple gopuram, though just barely. Tears streamed down mingling with sweat and blood. It was the first day in over a few hundred years when the morning puja had not happened, and the first day in over twenty years when he himself had failed to perform it.

"Your last chance," the man thundered, as the soldier brandished his sword. "Where did you move them? Answer!"

There must have been a problem with the alignment of the stars when the idols were cast; why else would they have such a destiny, consigned to the dark underground.

They were idols of his gods, idols worshipped by his ancestors, but beyond the piety brought on by being a deeply religious man, he thought of their elegant beauty too. He wondered if the stapatis' families were safe. The Perunthatchan and he had concocted the plan. They had taken into confidence only three other men, a mason and his assistants. They had closed the temple, making a big show of moving the idols elsewhere, planting that rumor in the hope the Kafur army would spare them. And secretly, painstakingly they had built the nilavarai and placed the idols there.

He could never give them up.

"To Vira Dhavalam," the priest responded in a last stance of defiance, naming the town that had already been ransacked, enraging the soldier. He kicked him on his stomach, sending him sprawling on the dusty road.

He felt the sharp edge of a sword on his throat. He could hardly see anything now, except for the beautiful face of the Nataraja, his favorite of all the bronzes. He knew his time had come. He began chanting the Thiruvasagam, his enunciation clear and resonant as always, "Not a slithering snake, not a mighty javelin, not a tiger, I fear not any of these. For I have known my dancer lord—"

As he heard the whoosh of the sword sweeping in on a final rush down toward his throat, he hoped that one day, not too far long, the idols would see the light of day.

Chapter 42

After a relaxing shower in sun-warmed water, wearing her nightdress of comfortable cotton, full of bright red floral patterns, Vidya retired to bed, but stayed awake.

She thought of her mother, of Tom, of the old man, and the temple. She knew something had irrevocably changed in her, though right then it was all an unsorted jumble of emotions brimming within. Later, she would rethink her career. But for now, she knew she would pursue those ideas on developmental economics that were forming, still nebulous and nascent in her head. She knew she would read her father's articles too.

She tried not to think of Josh.

It had been more than a couple of hours since Josh had left, and there had been no message from him, not even a formal goodbye note. She couldn't bring herself to send one either. She would have loved to talk to Tom about her state of mind, but he was already on a flight, racing toward her. She rejected, with a self-mocking smile, a vision of her weeping into Tom's shoulders as soon as he landed.

The clock's hands moved fast, and she tossed and turned, and it was soon four thirty in the morning, and Vidya thought Josh would have got up. She got up, too, and freshened up. It was five, he would have got ready and possibly be having a large cup of black coffee. She made herself a Madras coffee and sat sipping it in the dining room, staring at the chair where he had sat the previous night. Five fifteen, he must have packed his bags, gone downstairs, and checked out. Half past five, he must have caught a cab to the airport.

She heard the mongrel barking into the dawn. Her phone beeped. *Hi.* The text from Josh was innocuous.

She texted back. *Hi.*

Her phone rang and she picked it up at the first ring.

"Hey, good morning, did I wake you?" Josh's voice was soft, almost caressing.

"No, I couldn't sleep at all," she said honestly.

"Good," he said, sounding relieved.

"Good?"

"Yeah, it's a good sign you couldn't sleep. I couldn't either." The mongrel barked some more, and for a moment, she thought confusedly she could hear it on the phone too.

"Are you on your way?"

"Hey, is your boyfriend for real?" he asked instead of answering her question.

"No, Josh." Vidya sighed. "Listen, I—"

"Wait, in that case, could you come outside? I'd like to see your face for the rest of the conversation."

"What? Outside?" She was already scrambling out of the chair, running on light foot to the door. She fumbled on the bolts, opening them as swiftly as her excited fingers would allow, and stepped outside the house.

He ended the call and grinned as soon as he saw her. He was standing outside in the pre-dawn light with a big smile and sleep-deprived eyes.

A taxicab stood a little farther and the mongrel awoken from its slumber seemed more interested in it than in him.

"What are you doing here?" she asked as he stepped into the little foyer and gently closed the door behind him. She smoothed her hair, likely mussed-up because she had braided it into a thick plait for the night. Unconsciously, she crunched up the shapeless, comfortable, and dowdy cotton nightdress she was wearing.

"You know about testosterone, dopamine, serotonin, adrenalin, especially adrenalin, stuff that gets secreted when you feel high, when you think you like someone? As time passes, as the intense situation wears off, when you have to face the person first thing in the morning, day after day, reality strikes, and you're sort of left with no help from the hormones." He had evidently put a lot of thought into that little speech.

"Okay?" said Vidya, not quite comprehending where he was going with it.

"That's what I've been telling myself the last few days."

"Okay?"

"Now, see, that must all be true, but ... "

He moved closer and took her hands in his.

"What?" she asked.

He reached out and tucked her stray curls behind her ears.

"You do look beautiful just out of bed first thing in the morning, two days in a row. So there is hope of the said hormones being active for a long time."

"Josh!" she said, half impatient, half laughing. She was also terribly conscious of her unglamorous, well-worn nightdress, and coffee breath.

"So what I'm trying to say very badly is, what if this is the real thing? What if you are my ... er ... umm ... God, this is embarrassing ... my soul mate, for want of a better word? What if this whole thing is the universe conspiring for us to meet?"

"Such hubris! So, what are you proposing?"

"Interesting choice of words," he said, grinning.

She bit her lips.

He took a deep breath. "Look, there isn't a manual for this, and even if there was, I usually don't read manuals. So?"

"So?"

"I don't know! Can we at least talk about it?"

"Talk about what?"

He gave her a telling look at her pretend nonchalance.

"Talk about us! About endless possibilities. Who knows what we'd arrive at?" he said.

"All right," she agreed, knowing full well she was grinning and possibly looking at him adoringly.

"Seriously? 'All right'? That's all you're going to say?" he asked, rolling his eyes.

"It's not like you have declared eternal love," she pointed out.

"There's time for that." He smiled.

"And hope." She smiled in return.

He rummaged in his pockets and held out his hand and she saw on his upturned palm a pebble, smooth, shiny, of a pale ochre with grey streaks. "I picked it up at the temple," he explained. She took it, her fingers closing lovingly on its cool surface.

Leaning on the doorframe, arms folded, he gave her a look that sent her heart skittering.

"So what now? American coffee in the airport or Madras coffee at your home?" he asked.

"Coffee can wait. First this," she said and, leaning across, pulled him by his collar toward her and kissed him, not so lightly.

The morning sun creeping through the windows announced it would be another bright day.

About the Author

Radhika Nathan believes in the miracle of words and the rain. Her favorite pastimes include reading, listening to podcasts, and gazing at monsoon clouds. Writing forces her to think and re-examine a point of view or a preconceived notion. Post her debut novel *The Mute Anklet*, a historical romance with a dash of mystery, Radhika examines the intersection of art, romance, and mystery in *A Time To Burnish*.